Stepping on Fingers

Doug McPheters

Stepping on Fingers
Copyright ©2023 by Doug McPheters

ISBNs
9781648733970 (Hardcover)
9781648733963(Paperback)
9781648733987 (eBook)

Other Books by Doug McPheters

My Dream or Yours?

Goshawk

Scholarly Works

Co- Author: "Die Tagkeit deutscher Banken in USA,"
Recht der Internationen Wirtschaft

"Ulkomaisten Pankkien Perustamis – Ja Toimintaedellytykset Ydysvalloisa," Taloudellinen Katsaus

DEDICATION

"Stepping on Fingers" is dedicated to Ashli Babbitt, an Air Force veteran, killed by Capitol policeman Michael Byrd, on January 6, 2021, for no reason, while merely exercising her Constitutional Right of Free Speech at our Nation's Capitol

"We have put together, I think, the most extensive and inclusive voter fraud organization in the history of American politics" Joseph R. Biden

PROLOGUE

Nearly horizontal sleet hissed against wet tree trunks close in front of me. For just a moment, the hissing stopped and I could barely make out a slim tower at the bottom of three very long steps leading down an overgrown hill on my right. The last feeble rays of a scarlet sun blinked in the shards of a circular windowpane in the third story of a wooden building.

I pulled myself over a mossy granite ledge. Then I dropped into the corpses of rotten pine logs on the other side and sank nearly up to my hips in granular snow and frozen, wet leaves underneath. I stumbled down what may have once been a path toward the building and the roaring water behind it. I saw that each of what looked like long stairs was actually a row of massive granite blocks with a dark chasm behind them. The wind died down again, but for only a heartbeat. My eyes traced the rows of granite blocks from the dilapidated wooden building along each of the long stone steps until the top step disappeared into the tangled underbrush.

There was another, parallel row of rugged granite blocks many feet away on the other side of the chasm. The chasm was a long trough of granite filled with dark water, tree trunks and branches bleached nearly white by many summer suns.

At the bottom of what looked like abandoned canal locks were the rusting remains of an Audi gas-powered car and a tiny, white and black kitten mewing piteously on the lower limb of one of the dead trees, just inches above the water swirling through the trough. Down the hill, the granite trough continued in giant steps down toward a still pool in the curve of the river, before the trough s water hurried downstream. Waiting forlornly at the bottom of the three giant stones steps, the tower now looked more like an abandoned house, the river's dark waters plainly visible through the empty sockets of what might have been its first and second story windows. A single crow pecked at the crevices of a warped windowsill, ignoring a broken front door that swung wildly in the wind and thump, thumped on its sagging frame.

And then it came to me: I was looking at the remains of locks on the canal that once carried barges along the banks of the Black River, just south of Carthage, New York, laden with industrial goods and supplies. Those supplies from New York City and Albany were carried along the Erie Canal, up the Black River Canal, destined for the port cities of the Great Lakes beyond, when America was young and still growing west. Decades before the terror grew in America.

I watched the Black River surging north, downstream toward Lake Ontario. Its raging waters smashing intricate panes of shell ice crowding its sodden banks. I didn t know why, but I was drawn toward the thundering cascade, every step of mine crunching through the delicate canopy of ice left suspended on stalks of dried marsh grass when the flood congealed during last night s hard freeze. Although I couldn t see very far ahead in the dim light, I knew the river was there. I could smell it, taste its earthy moisture.

Needles of driving sleet stung my chest, nipples and thighs; all as naked as the day I was born. My heart thump, thump, thumped at the top of my throat, trying to escape my heaving chest. I couldn t go on much longer! My throat was so dry I couldn t even swallow – I put shards of ice in my mouth to at least gain some water. Every time I tried to move, my feet sank down, down into cold, oozing slime under the crackling icy surface. Gulping in the damp air, I fell to my knees, looking around me for something, anything to drink, somewhere to rest but spurts of my own frozen breath mocked me in the mirror of shell ice. The hair between my legs was frozen and white - I d grown old before my time!

Balancing easily on the cylindrical brown top of a dried cattail nearby, a brilliant yellow and black Evening Grosbeak ground his ivory bill thoughtfully:

Help me! My wing is broken. Help me!"

How can I help you, little bird? I ll probably freeze to death here, alone in this wretched place, or these slivers of ice will drain whatever is left of my precious blood, drop by drop, into the roots of those dead swamp plants you find so comfortable."

Something was tearing into the base of my skull, a silent, ripping power drill. Sticky fingerprints of the last nightmare clouded my eyes. I desperately wanted to scour away their crusty residue from my eyelids, but my hands wouldn t move. My knees felt like I was running in a vat of cold molasses. I tried to get away but nothing happened.

I couldn t escape this awful place! Why were they doing this to me?

A blue glare was metastasizing in the sleet swirling around me, its light diffused by the cloud of tiny, sharp grains.

Ahead of me, through the haze, I could just make out a slim young woman lying face down on a long metal table. A pair of heavy, brown leather bracelets bolted to the dull surface strained both arms taut above her crudely shorn dark, red curls. A wide-mesh net of synthetic fabric held down her mid-section, only partly concealing her nudity. Both of her bare feet were chained to the table. As I looked more closely, I could see goosebumps standing out all along the unbroken expanse of her creamy skin, from her ankles to slender forearms. Except for some coarse new stitches at the base of her skull, her statuesque body was unmarked. Just briefly, her emerald eyes fluttered open.

HERE A NIQAB, THERE A NIQAB

David Garvey, a Manhattan corporate lawyer, was moderately tall with blue eyes with blond hair that had started out as nearly invisible but was now light brown. Thin from running and other exercise, David had slowed in recent years from gaining a titanium knee replacement a few years ago to bypass an old hockey injury. As a former goaltender, this corporate lawyer sported a noticeable scar from letting his ancient mask slip and catching a sharp slap shot with his nose. His law practice specialized in business and civil matters, mostly international mergers and acquisitions.

David had achieved additional notoriety for his very successful and legal loan-sharking operation in the remains of the Soviet Union. That business became so successful and noticeable that Saddam Hussein, aided by his nephew, Tariq al-Tikriti, tried to make it theirs. Tariq was assigned to steal David's fund in order to help Iraq get out from under biting international financial sanctions long before Saddam dangled from the end of a rope. Along the way, the Iraqis tried to kill David, killed his Finnish lover, and kidnapped his two sons.

At the same time, the woman in charge of the day-to-day operations of David's loan-sharking operation betrayed him. The Iraqis 'attempts to steal David's business ended up in Federal court in New York. David beat back the German bank that Saddam Hussein had co-opted in order to destroy David's company's credit arrangements with that institution. That victory involved David's going against his lover, Margaret, who led the lawyers representing the German bank and was kidnapped during that case. David moved on to other very interesting legal disputes even though his loan-sharking business continued to generate enormous amounts of cash. Although David and his colleagues had rescued Margaret near the end of that adventure, she had drifted away from David, afraid that danger would always follow David and those around him. As much as David missed her, he couldn't disagree with her concerns. As if to validate those concerns, Tariq al-Tikriti continued to be a major thorn in David's side.

Frank Gillespie, David's former law partner, was ethically challenged. He didn't mind using the firm's credit cards to take his family on expensive vacations but then pretended to come up short when the bills arrived. Gillespie's more nasty practice was to go to his clients and have them pay the firm's bills directly to him personally instead of to the firm. That damaged David personally during his divorce from the mother of his two sons. His soon-to-be ex-wife benefited from her accountant's audit of the firm's books because it showed substantial receivables still on the firm's books, which Gillespie had already collected personally. Under NY law, a spouse was entitled to grab part of the value of any incorporated business owned by the other spouse, such as David's law firm. But since she was only a highly paid employee of a publicly traded business, the value of her job was beyond David's reach. The damage was compounded by the fact that the amount of those receivables never reached the coffers of David Garvey and Frank Gillespie's law firm.

That morning on the IRT subway platform under Grand Central Station, David watched through nearly opaque dark glasses and the featherweight, black niqab's narrow horizontal eye slit. He hoped to be indistinguishable from the crowd of subway riders and other people around him. But David could clearly see Frank Gillespie's dribbling powdered sugar from his cinnamon doughnut onto his courtroom suit jacket. Gillespie was juggling his COVID-19 mask so that the platform minders would not interfere with his trip to court in lower Manhattan. Gillespie and other passengers were jostling back and forth over the nubbly, yellow safety strip on the edge of the subway platform beside the downtown express track. They were trying to end up in the right position to push into the next open doors of the downtown Lexington Avenue subway. Everyone waiting on the platform wore a cloth facemask of the sort which first became required during the CCP virus plandemic but never went away and now appeared in numerous colors and designs even though it was well known that fabric masks offered no protection of any sort against any virus transmission. The fabric weave of these masks was simply much broader than tiny viruses, like trying to stop mosquitos with a barbed-wire fence. The expectant crowd watched silently as an empty work train thundered by on the express track.

David remembered when prison trains filled with political dissidents rolled south toward the Staten Island Ferry, landing on the way to its ultimate destination on the Fresh Kills Landfill on Staten Island, a huge garbage dump. That incarceration site selection was designed to maximize health damage to dissidents. Straphangers could see through the window bars that all prisoners wore leather masks as well as more permanent ear coverings designed to make normal conversation almost impossible, effectively silencing the dissidents during their malignant trip.

Just like in the old days, Gillespie occasionally worried

about his now greying mustache as if trying to make it go away. He was probably on his way to New York State Court at 100 Centre Street in Manhattan. Pages of several colored document files peeked from what looked like a U.S. Luggage Catalogue Case on wheels, loaded with a laptop and cables for courtroom electronics connections. The pudgy lawyer was having trouble moving his luggage case from side to side while trying to keep his balance and move his court cart at the same time.

As if invisible in his long chador, David Garvey floated quietly behind Gillespie, hoping no one would notice his black leather Chelsea boots. David had never forgotten the huge amounts Gillespie had stolen from their law firm during David's divorce, which ended up costing David twice - less cash for the business and false amounts for the benefit of the mother of his two sons because of the false amount of receivables her accountant's audit reported. Ever since Gillespie had escaped accountability by arranging to get a judge willing to let him put a finger on the scales of justice. David had seethed for years and years, but now the pot was boiling over. David Garvey did not believe in always turning the other cheek.

"Gimme you wallet, whitey. I be oppressed" boomed from behind David along with sounds of someone's being hit and pushed. That made him quickly turn to see the speaker fall to the concrete platform after the snick of rounds being jacked into a weapon and a sharp crack, probably a pistol - two quick shots and a loud scream, followed by low groans. Most in the crowd rushed away from the jerking body, with eyes averted, pretending to not notice but still aiming for the next open subway door. Then, David heard a calm voice with a Brooklyn accent mutter," he came to a battle of wits unarmed." David reached reflexively for his own loaded 9mm Beretta in the right shoulder holster under his chador (David was left-handed).

David was worried the professionally dressed woman still jammed against Gillespie's right shoulder might remember him as the platform under him began to vibrate with the throaty rumble of the coming train's arrival, its headlight flashing. David yelled," Do you remember me?" in his best rendition of an elderly Saudi woman, making sure to roll the "r," as is done in colloquial Arabic.

David gave Gillespie a sharp hip-check. Gillespie lost his grip on his litigation bag and tumbled onto the train tracks, landing in a puddle of used condoms, cigarette butts, and yesterday's third page of the New York Post. Gillespie looked around, dazed, and acted like he couldn't imagine what had just happened. He looked down at his cell phone in the fetid pool, soaking his loafers, then turned to see glaring headlights of the rapidly approaching downtown #6 train. The lurching subway train's motorman looked horrified behind his windshield. He slammed on its brakes and repeatedly honked its horn, like the very hammers of hell, as the train's nearly locked wheels screeched against shiny, steel tracks. The elderly motorman tried in vain to stop the on-rushing subway train.

Gillespie grabbed for the concrete platform's edge, trying desperately to pull himself out of the path of the oncoming train. For just an instant, time seemed to stop for David. The irate lawyer leaned just close enough to Gillespie's terrified face to hiss through the narrow slit of his niqab, "Payback for stealing from me, you self-righteous prick!" David Garvey briefly saw a reflection of his blue eyes in Gillespie's delicately manicured fingernails just before he stomped viciously on Gillespie's clawing fingers and rubbed them over and over against the hard metal edge of the subway platform,

Angrily squealing brakes and a meaty thump mesmerized everyone else on the subway platform. David Garvey slid sideways behind a nearby staircase to smoothly slip out of his flimsy chador while everyone's attention was on the subway train that had passed over Gillespie's corpse and opened its doors. He folded the black fabric and his niqab into a neat square, then slowly walked north on the subway platform, up another staircase filled with a torrent of people rushing down onto the subway platform, probably hoping to catch the downtown train that had just squealed to a stop. Against the flow of pushy commuters, the New York lawyer struggled to climb a flight of dirty stairs, nearly tripping over the remains of a sandwich, to finally reach the next level, cross toward a regularly slamming exit gate and up still another flight of stairs. He held the dirty railing with his right hand to keep from being knocked backward. Once at the main station level, David walked slowly along polished marble corridors, past expensive shops and into Grand Central's cavernous main hall. Then he turned left to reach another set of banging doors to arrive at the north side of 42nd Street, looking across at the brightly lighted Pershing Square bistro under the grimy Park Avenue overpass that winds around Grand Central Station and ultimately to Park Avenue South. David crossed 42nd Street at the crosswalk as the walk light blinked in his favor, walked along the sidewalk to his right, and cut through traffic blockades onto Park Avenue South at a deliberately slow saunter before taking a right on the first side street to head toward Madison Avenue. As he noticed a construction site for a new condo building under busy construction just around the corner, David looked behind him to see if anyone was following and then deftly tossed the fold of black fabric, dark plastic glasses, and powderless plastic gloves into long, rectangular, wooden, concrete forms at sidewalk level of the construction site. Liquid concrete cascading from the slide of a rumbling cement mixer rapidly buried them all.

Soon, David Garvey was sitting down to a cappuccino with cinnamon under the umbrella of a sidewalk deli in the sunshine, where he promptly fell asleep as the tension of recent events began to seep away. But then, David was jarred awake by the hum of his mobile phone when the NY1 app on his cell blinked:" Muslim woman pushes prominent NY lawyer to his death in subway mishap, apparently unrelated to a shooting on the same subway platform," followed by "stay tuned for the next disastrous storm." *"Prominent NY lawyer, my ass,"* David thought *"his idea of a complicated transaction was where you had to change planes with the bag of cash."* As the stress of eliminating Frank Gillespie and escaping without apparently being noticed continued to subside, David drifted off into what he had recently learned from his most interesting client, Lea Holderness, and what she had shared with him about her turbulent life after getting pregnant and being left behind by the famous father.

North Country Justice

I was standing completely still and straight in a suffocating, windowless room under the Bare Hill Correctional Facility in Malone, New York, not far from the frontier with la République du Québec, both hands manacled tightly behind me. Lighted only by an intermittently buzzing fluorescent fixture, the dilapidated chamber felt and smelled like an abandoned storehouse. A large iron cross dominated the front wall - its three o'clock arm bent up in the middle at a right angle. A strong winter wind outside shook the few windows in the chamber.

As visions of what might be in store for me ricocheted through my mind like so many loose marbles, a lanky rumpled, black three-piece suit, smaller, tarnished bent cross on his left lapel, stumbled past me. He made his way slowly toward the only chair on the floor of the courtroom, to my right, behind a scratched institutional gray metal desk. A thick, syrupy smell trailed behind him - sour mash whiskey. Just before reaching his seat, he paused for a split second, and mechanically dipped his cleanly shaven head in the direction of the raised bench and the broken cross above it. Then he looked at me dismissively and dropped into the squeaky chair with a very bored sigh.

A nasal voice blared from a hidden speaker somewhere high in the front of the courtroom:

"All rise! The Court of Public Order for the County of Franklin is now in session! The prisoner will approach the bench!"

I looked anxiously around to see whom the auto-clerk could possibly be talking about. But I was alone in front of the high, wooden bench except for the young man slouched in the chair beside me, and a humming lens pointed in my direction from under the lip of that elevated place for the presiding official. Suddenly, a door in the outer wall opened a crack but was promptly sucked shut by the icy wind outside. A diminutive, black-robed figure struggled mightily with the shrilly whistling door and then, momentarily gaining the upper hand, pushed it toward the wall with a grunt. Breathing heavily, what I thought might be the judge jumped inside and let the wind have the heavy door. Crash! The woman scampered up several creaky wooden stairs to the raised bench looming above me. Low, black heels showed briefly beneath the jurist's black flowing robes before she settled into a high-backed wooden chair. I thought she might be looking down at me but I could not see her face.

"Rap! Rap!" she thumped a thick, wooden disk on the bench in front of her with a sturdy oak gavel. Even that sharp sound couldn't distract me from the impenetrable black veil that completely obscured her head and face, a broken metal cross swinging from a fine, mesh chain around her covered neck. Entirely opaque, her hood concealed all evidence of the judge's humanity. Only her long, slender fingers and carefully polished red nails gripping the gavel revealed anything at all about her.

"Put your mask over your mouth and nose – it is mandated. Besides ignoring the mask mandate and thereby jeopardizing the health of others, you have been found guilty by this Court without hearing or jury of offending the people by openly challenging the No Hate Speech Act. Do you have anything at all to say in your defense before the Court passes sentence? Make it short!" the judge rasped in the androgynous mechanical tones of her voice distorter.

Trying to slip the dirty, paper mask over my nose and mouth, I bit my lip nervously, until the taste of iron filled my mouth. Then, I looked down at the young man sitting beside me in his creaky wooden chair, hoping he might help me out of my predicament. Avoiding my anxious look, he casually reached into his jacket pocket, produced a withered, green apple and began to chew it noisily.

"What am I supposed to do?" I whispered impatiently to the bored black suit. He didn't even look up from his apple.

"Er, like, whaddaya mean?" he mumbled through chunks of soggy apple, spraying tiny bits of apple pulp and peeling on the hip of my prison jumper.

"You gonna help me? If you're not, who is?"

"Can't rightly say. Like, don't know if it's even my job to help ya. Just here as a court-appointed witness. Me, I'm, like, ya know, just supposed to make sure ya get on that there prison train outside before it leaves. Ya unnerstan what I'm saying? Maybe ya otta ask the judge...No..... on second thought, she already seems angry enough, if ya take my meanin'."

"Isn't anyone going to help me?"

Looking off into the distance, he wrapped the apple core in a piece of scrap paper from under the desk and stuffed the tiny bundle into the same jacket pocket that the apple core had come from. The young man swallowed, coughed lightly and reached inside his mouth to dislodge pieces of his snack from between two molars with a yellowed fingernail. On the way by, he pushed his upper dentures firmly against the roof of his mouth and his upper jawbone, then clamped his teeth shut to make sure the lower set was properly seated. He wiped his mouth with the back of his left hand and tried to sneak his tobacco-stained mask back over his mouth with his head lowered, probably hoping the judge wouldn't notice he hadn't been strictly observing the mask mandate.

"Like, why on't ya ask a yudge rather an keep talkin' about it?"

Overwhelmed by fear and disgust, Lea turned toward the bench.

"But I didn't do anything wrong! We have the God-given freedom of speech. I was supposed to teach my students the truth and..."

"You are unrepentant!" the judge interrupted, silencing her with the rap, rap, rapping of her gavel. "You have shown no remorse for stirring up the still pool of the closely-held beliefs of the Government. You also have contempt for the Government's health mandates. You have plainly not asked God to absolve you of your sins or to take these heresies from you. In face of the utter lack of any mitigating factors, pursuant to the powers delegated to this Court by the provisions of the No Hate Speech Act, I hereby sentence you to immediate transportation to Penal Colony 627 without possibility of pardon, parole or redemption. Courtroom deacon, push your mask up over your nose and deliver the prisoner to the custody of the Guardians, for transportation to the transit prison and thence to Penal Colony 627 without further delay!"

After what seemed like ages, the wooden chair beside me creaked and scraped on the floor. The young man yanked my shackled wrists and dragged me toward the shrilly whistling door. Giving me an annoyed glance, he shook his head. The vacuum in the corridor outside seemed to be gently pulling me out of that stifling courtroom, toward whatever lay ahead for me.

"Let's go, Miss! Like, ya got an appointment in a place that'll, like, ya know, make this here North Country seem like, ya know, Ft. Laudeedale. Like, I mean, lucky one of them there Mooslim courts didn't get their teeth into ya. I mean, like, them there Mooslims take particler offense at uppity bitches such as yerself."

The judge stood up from her seat behind the bench, clattered down the steps toward the whistling door and tried with all her might to pull it open.

"Wait! What about my little girl? Who'll take care of my Clara if I'm sent away?"

Pausing in the middle of her tussle with the heavy door, the judge looked back at me over her shoulder and croaked:

"You should have thought about your family and your other civic responsibilities before taking it upon yourself to offend the No Hate Speech Act by attacking it. Think of your daughter while you serve out your sentence!"

"How could I not think of Clara every minute?" Much later and thousands of miles east of that stuffy courtroom, Lea blinked away warm tears as she stared blankly into the growing murkiness outside the makeshift operating room, looking south over the frozen, snow-covered grounds of Penal Colony 627 and toward the wave-lashed Chukchi Sea beyond. She'd learned in college that, long ago, the British Crown in *24 Geo. III, c. 56 1786*, had established the punishment of transportation, sending convicts as well as other miscreants and undesirables to far-away places such as Gibraltar, New South Wales in what is now Australia and Tasmania to serve out their sentences. Lacking sufficient prison space in its domestic lands and wishing to hide its population of political dissidents, the so-called progressive government of America had revived that practice in the 21st Century by leasing space in particularly undesirable parts of the world such as the frozen, northern coast of Russia, Denmark's icy Greenland or the steaming jungles of Guyana.

Lea and her minder paused respectfully in the drafty outside passageway to let the judge pass. Lea held back, perhaps in the unrealistic hope that the judge might change her mind. Then they both watched the woman who had sentenced Lea to finish out her life on a frozen island near the Arctic Circle clatter into the darkness at the top of a long flight of industrial metal stairs to the right. The judge lost her grasp on the metal railing, tripped fell down the last few icy steps and tumbled to the dirty floor covered with rock-salt below. To Lea's left, a narrow corridor wound back toward the serpentine cellblocks. Lea could taste the beginnings of breakfast in the winter air but had no hope of getting something to eat anytime soon.

"Whassup?" the minder mumbled into a tiny microphone at the corner of his mouth that Lea hadn't noticed before. "Like, I, like, ya know, thought I tole ya never to, like, call me at work, Jolene. Not never!"

What sounded like a bee buzzing in the minder's earpiece was all Lea could make out of the other side of the conversation.

"Yes, Jolene, ya know, like I'm putting the harlot on the train. Juss like I tole ya I would. Now you make damn sure you, like, tend to your needlepoint. Like, I mean, I don't want no grief at meeting tonight. An 'like don't never call me at work again."

Then Lea's keeper tripped quickly down the short flight of stairs leading outdoors, two steps at a time, clutching his flat-brimmed black hat in one hand and dragging her close behind him with the other. The arrogant young man stopped at the bottom of the stairs before a partly open sliding door and, letting go of Lea's cuffs for an instant, jerked the door open with both hands. Then he yanked Lea out of the back door of the Franklin County Courthouse, onto an uneven concrete platform.

As she struggled to keep her balance on the icy floor outside, sub-zero air instantly froze the hairs in Lea's nostrils. The young home-spun pushed Lea toward a hulking pair of guards stationed on either side of the single-entry port of an armored train car, assault weapons swinging at their waists from leather straps around their necks. A single line of ragged prisoners moved slowly between the two guards, each prisoner surrendering some sort of document on the way into the waiting train.

Wearing black home-spun trousers and matching frock jackets, heavy, dark leather work boots and flat-brimmed dusty black cloth hats, both guards were dressed almost identically. Each guard's mouth and chin were covered by a black fabric mask, a long, scraggly beard sprouting beneath it. Tiny flakes of fine, new snow drifted through the gap between the dilapidated canvas awning over the edge of the platform and the waiting coach's nearly flat roof. Through the train's dirt-streaked windows, Lea could see a crowd of prisoners pounding furiously on the compartment's far-side walls and windows, trying desperately to attract the attention of loved ones in the clot of steaming parkas milling around the grumbling string of train cars.

"Where's this Jezebel bound, Hezekiah? Lemme have 'er papers!"

The lankier of the two guards held out a gnarled hand toward Lea and her escort, a single golden stripe on his otherwise plain black sleeve denoting his superior rank. Lea's minder surrendered a single, thick sheet of paper covered with large letters to the transit guard, who looked puzzled but fed the document clumsily into the waiting slot of a computer terminal at his elbow. Another androgynous voice began to slowly read Lea's deportation order aloud, as all three men raptly watched the tinny speaker:

"...to be transported by convoy to Penal Colony 627."

"627. Ya know, that'll sure fix up her sacrilegious soul for permanent, Hezekiah," the gold-striped guard observed.

"Praise be!" Lea's keeper muttered.

Without another word, the other guard clamped a ham-like fist over Lea's manacles and jerked them up over a high rail extending out of the open entry port of the waiting train, forcing her to pirouette unsteadily on the tips of her heavy boots. Fondling Lea's taut buttocks, he launched her restrained body forward, sliding her along the rail into the waiting car, where she swung along in fits and starts, like a carcass of beef on the killing line of a slaughterhouse.

"All aboard, honey," he leered after Lea's jerking body. "Like, I know you're just gonna love 627. Someone told me just last week it's only 43 below over there right now. With that tight ass, you're just what that collection of deviates is looking for. Have a nice God-fearin 'life!"

Dangling helplessly from the overhead rail, Lea looked back to see the minder smirking at her, as he bit into yet another withered green apple.

Inside the crowded compartment, a robotic arm dragged Lea's jerking body along the rail then dumped her onto a wooden bench beside a vertical window-slit. Corroded stirrups reached out from under the bench in front of her and firmly clamped Lea's feet to the gritty, aluminum floorboards.

Several paces in front of Lea's smudged window-slit, a

pair of padded dark blue arms showing the forest-green sleeve chevrons of the Lost Sheep League held a frightened child above the angry crowd, her yellow snowsuit standing out over the dowdy crowd. A sudden gust of wind blew a tattered false-fur hood back from the youngster's face. It was not Clara but that child's beautiful corn-blue eyes (like Clara's) were red from crying. Lea was horrified! Her only child, older than the youngster she could see, in the hands of the League? It dawned on Lea that the government bureaucracy must now officially consider Clara's mother to be dead! According to the "authorities," Clara no longer had a mother! An orphan! Even in this time of great emotional turmoil, it didn't escape Lea's understanding that her fate had been decided long before her hearing before the female judge with the voice distorter.

The little girl Lea could see kicked and flailed with her chubby arms, trying with all her might to get away from the gloved hands lifting her over the mumbling sea of anxious faces. The distraught little girl looked frantically up and down the long row of nearly identical train cars. Lea hoped against hope that her own daughter was trying to catch at least one final glimpse of her mother. But did she did know if Clara was even outside the train? She pressed both palms hard against the thick, darkened glass, trying to let Clara know where she was. Suddenly, Lea felt a hot flash of embarrassment as she noticed that almost all the other prisoners were doing the same thing, also to no avail. Through the soles of her feet, she could feel the uneven growl of the train's Fairbanks-Morse diesel engines, their tempo increasing. Wildly casting about to escape her keeper, the little girl Lea could see showed no sign at all of having seen her mother. The little girl's lonely terror burned itself into Lea's desperate brain, to be replayed in almost endless loops of sleepless days and nights to come.

The long train shuddered as its couplings picked up slack, then screeched against the rusty tracks as it began to pick up speed, breaking free of the brittle crust of shell ice coating its heavy, steel wheels from the prior night's hard freeze. An angry, red sun glowered just above the southeastern horizon, barely visible through the engines' pungent exhaust fumes spilling over the crowded railroad siding. The string of dimly-lit railroad cars was surrounded by the milling crowd of onlookers, stamping their feet and clapping their gloved hands against the fierce cold. But the roar of the babbling crowd rose over even the growling diesels.

"Free the Spirit of Nokomis!" a beefy warrior shouted, shaking his jet-black topknot in frustration.

"OUTTA MY YARD! OUTTA MY YARD!" three elderly women banged in unison on the side of Lea's car with wooden shovels.

"Free Jenny Jones! Free the press!" still another agitated onlooker screamed, her voice a jagged addition to the frigid morning air.

Jarred from her state of half-awake by the train's lurching and the commotion outside, Lea finally understood she was being taken away from her child forever! Forever! Did Clara even know her mother was being sent away today? Had Clara seen her departing train? Perhaps Lea only wished the young girl had caught a glimpse of her, fading away into a cloud of acrid diesel fumes.

As the trainload of prisoners rolled ever faster away out of the siding, the crowd seemed to slip away and then flutter, flutter by, finally disappearing into a receding cloud of snowflakes and diesel exhaust behind the long column of cars. The speeding double, diesel-electric engines and their unwilling cargo of religious and political prisoners plunged into what seemed like an endless tunnel of dense evergreen forests, farther and farther from home, whistle moaning. "Whooooooooo, whooooooooooo!" Far, far away from everything that mattered to Lea or other passengers on this prison train.

Alternately frantic with fear and numb with despair, Lea soon lost track of what was going on around her during the convoy's circuitous trip east through the wilderness that occupies the northeastern Adirondacks, then south through the Lake George region and later down the west side of the Hudson River in fits and starts on the way to the transit prison on the outskirts of Newark Airport. Day and night she remained clamped into her hard seat beside the window slit, as the train rattled through ramshackle small towns, over rickety trestles. Then, near the end of the journey, past vacant factory buildings and polluted swamps in the jumble of New Jersey's Meadowlands. Once locked into a massive concrete and noisy transit prison beside Newark Airport, Lea spent more than two days stuck in overcrowded holding pens, where even conversation was regularly drowned out by the throaty whine of large aircraft passing close overhead. Later, Lea and several trainloads of other convicts, all clumsily bound together in leg irons, struggled into the cavernous belly of a waiting cargo plane for the night flight to the Baltic port city of St. Petersburg, arranged so any potential observers would have trouble keeping track of departures of the crowd of prisoners.

Three separate trains from St. Peterburg east toward the dawn across several time zones for many days, then two different convoys of diesel trucks ultimately carried Lea and other prisoners over the creaking, blue, ice-roads of the Russian Arctic. Next in unheated trucks due north over the frozen tundra to a ramshackle collection of wooden huts on the southern shore of the Chukchi sea. Finally, a heaving hovercraft carried Lea far from Peter the Great's window to the West on the Neva to a barren island in the Chukchi Sea known only vaguely in America as Penal Colony 627. All along the way, even when the sweet blessing of sleep seemed about to creep over her, Lea couldn't put aside the fever pitch of Clara's heart-wrenching sobs as she must have tried to understand why her mother had to go away forever.

In her shadowy half-awakes, one memory of the seemingly endless train trip kept coming back to Lea, over and over again, long after her feet had forgotten the grumbling of the train's enormous steel wheels through its aluminum floorboards. Especially in the grim, gray surroundings of her Arctic confinement. Along the way, the convoy had been standing during the night on a lonely siding above the western banks of the Hudson River, outside a small town just north of the border between New York and New Jersey. The throaty rhythm of its diesels was strangely absent. Although every light in Lea's car had been extinguished and all the other prisoners were asleep, for some unknown reason she awoke with a jolt. A faint, silvery ring circled the half-moon peeking through gray clouds above, a sure sign of rain or snow to come. In the dim light, Lea could barely make out four roughly clad figures watching the train from a tangled hillock at the side of the tracks. As she watched, two of them crept slowly through the knee-high remains of last year's weeds, choking the hillside. Lea could hear the desiccated plant skeletons whisper and crack as the shadowy figures inched toward the raised set of double train tracks, the crumbled stone ballast beneath the railroad ties crunching noisily under their heavy boots. Brandishing wooden cudgels, they came closer and closer until the tallest of the two slowly raised his tousled head above the lower edge of Lea's window slit. His breath made puffs of condensation around the edges of moist lips pressed against the dirty plate glass - his one opaque eye easy to see. His eyes cast wildly about, like a starving animal searching for its next victim. The emblem of a silver raised fist stood out prominently over his heart. Without anyone's telling her, Lea knew in her heart those ruffians were hunting for her, tracking her down. She tried to scream but no sound would come out of her mouth. Lea looked frantically about the sleeping train car for help, but everyone else might as well have been dead. The two men began to beat on the outside of the train with their wooden clubs. BANG, BANG, BANG! BANG...BANG....

"OUTTA MY YARD...OUTTA MY YARD...OUTTA MY YARD"

Suddenly, a searchlight pierced the pool of shadows surrounding the convoy of trains, scanning up and down the rows of narrow window slits. A low, warbling whistle from the solitary wraith on the nearby hillock called the three others toward him, tightly gripping their weapons as they filed slowly away from the train. Then all four disappeared into the jumbled foliage, leaving Lea to wonder who they were and why they were leering at her through the dirty train window, during this brief stop along her journey to frozen death. Lea had the uneasy sense that she might encounter them again.

Early Retirement

Not even his UV-blocking smoked shades could entirely blot out the glare of late afternoon sun enveloping the lower snowfields of Blackcomb Glacier. Looking up toward those faraway slopes, former Governor Buddy Lassiter imagined the Glacier's upper snow fields where Canadian ski teams practiced even during summer months. The sinking sun made evergreens in the foreground seem to dance and weave. He looked away, toward Whistler Village in the smog-shrouded valley far below, a pleasant 30-minute run down wide, roving meadows of deep, new powder that even Buddy could comfortably enjoy without breaking anything. Screened from the occasional early spring breeze by an almost impenetrable stand of Fraser firs at the edge of the rough plank deck where Buddy reclined, he absently caressed his ample bare paunch, pasty white in the crisp air, his thoughts far away. Apparently deep within himself, this angry bear of a man took a final sip of long-cold double latte and worried his thick, gray hair thoughtfully before sticking a pudgy finger into the blinking magenta holographic letters floating in the mountain air in front of him: C-Post.

"What y'all want," he grumbled in a flat, husky voice of the middle South to no one in particular, taking in craggy peaks in the distance at the same time.

"Lemme bring you up to date," his earpiece responded.

"Better some good news!"

"Well, Gov..."

"Y'all goddamn well better never EVER call me that again! Y'all been with me long enough to know better'n that afta that there impeachment nonsense after that vote where more ballots was counted then was registered voters. Don't never let that happen again!" he yelled in the general direction of the pulsating magenta letters, the bright sunlight and crisp air around him now forgotten. He banged the large, mostly empty porcelain mug imprinted with bold red and black letters proudly announcing "Go Dawgs! on the heavy, rustic table in step with his harsh words: "JUST... GIMME... THEM COLLECTIONS!" Buddy Lassiter kept pounding the mug on the table until it cracked, leaving gooey dregs of his double latte oozing onto the wooden surface

"OK, calm down, Buddy. You want 'em by denomination or region?"

"Tell me how much the great Republic of Texas came up with for those poor, poor orphans," the big man demanded, his sudden flash of anger melting away in the sunny air. A faint smile even flickered across his ruddy face as a red tree squirrel peered over the edge of his table, looking for something to eat, his glistening black nose twitching nervously. He thought about the program they were discussing, what was organized as a charity but almost all of its "charitable" collections to help poor orphans were actually used elsewhere, following the Black Lives Matter model of pushing everyone for donations but spending the proceeds on the organizers and their yawning real estate acquisitions. Nothing from Buddy's "program" went into his personal accounts or pockets but rather the coffers of his foreign "colleagues," albeit without BLM style intimidation and violence. But at least he didn't encounter anything like the BLM result: families of black people killed in riots or their businesses destroyed coming to BLM for financial help only to find out BLM wasn't really interested in that use of its "donations."

"Texas generated over $6 million last week. 67% of that from churches, a big chunk of that from them their Covenant folks..."

"True Believers, you mean!" Buddy bristled.

"Somin 'eating you, Buddy?" his earpiece queried, audible to no one but this tired-looking giant, bags under his eyes a shade darker than last month.

"I most certainly am tarred. Can't ever seem to sleep very soundly. Mebbe it's all the coffee. Mebbe it's the altitude here. How 'bout the northern Adirondack region, the one only partly under central control, ya know, up near that there St. Lawrence Seaway above New York State?"

"Gimme a second, Buddy. That'll take breakin 'down them Northern New York Alliance totals. Let's see.... here's the Oswego Shoreline Constituency, the Tribal Alliance of Reconstituted Mohawks and Tuscaroras, the Tug Hill Plateau Combine... 'Course, here it is - the Frigid Fringe. Someone in that neck of the woods sure must have a sense of humor! Footnote here says it's made up of most of what used to be Jefferson, St. Lawrence, Franklin and Essex Counties before the State of New York lost its firm grip over the wilderness along the Canadian and Québec borders. Lessee, just one more command, now. There it is - two weeks ago, the take for the entire Fringe was $6,320? Even allowing for the sparse population, must be something wrong there! According the historical figures, we took in more than 8 times that for a comparable period last year.

"Ain't nobody gonna be pleased with that! Them folks pay me well to keep all sorts of local and regional alliances growin 'and hummin 'along like so many metastasizing cancer cells, sapping the strength of the central body politic until its hold on the population becomes weaker and weaker. Ya 'know, with them True Believers grabbin 'up local government positions, and pushin 'them religious courts, the bureaucrats in Albany and Washington can't hardly keep up. And what's left of Federally administered territory is swamped with all sorts of nonsense, from child full employment demands to clean sound initiatives. All makin ' it practically impossible for any regular government to pay attention to any of the normal day-to-day business of running its territory. Which makes our clients in Iran just delighted. Keeps the spotlight off 'em. So we gotta find out why collections are down in the Frozen Frontier or whatever they're calling it this week. Might even want to drop in to see some of our folks up there, once the ice goes out during the three days of summer." He slapped his knee, guffawing loudly at his own tired joke before jiggling a pudgy finger in the floating magenta letters to cut the connection with his central office.

While he'd been rattling the cages of the boys back at headquarters, the afternoon sun had slipped behind a cloud. Faint, purple shadows were beginning to fill the nooks and crannies of the valley far below although the craggy peaks still shone like burnished gold in the setting sun. Wrestling his bushy gray head and meaty arms into a coarse British woolen, submarine sweater scooped up from a nearby bench, the lanky Georgian sprawled against the creaky cedar railing to watch slate fingers of dusk creep slowly up from the lowlands toward snow-covered mountaintops. But Buddy Lassiter was already far away, yearning for the only woman who had ever really captured his soul. Not just another willing cavity to slake his frequent and often uncontrollable urges; this one had been markedly different. A strong woman, more than his intellectual equal. And he'd let her slip away!

"Here I am," he thought to himself, *"alone, in this magnificent mountain hideaway, and all I can think about is the business and Lea, the two of them competing for space in my aging brain like a couple of jealous young kids. Damn political expediency! But, Buddy boy, that s no longer a problemo. What do you suppose would happen if I just looked Lea up and see if she d still have me? Shouldn t matter to anyone now, ceptin maybe me and her. Far as I know, the father of her rug rat is no longer in the picture. Didn t treat Lea very well back then. Let my advisers convince me being seen with a rural schoolmarm wouldn t be good for my public approval rating. Well, fuck all that now!"*

Suddenly aware that the mountaintops had faded to a distant gray, Buddy leaned over to pull at his telescope nearer to see if he could spot Jupiter's rising near sunset in the navy sky just above the eastern horizon. There it was, not far from the waning Gibbous moon. Calming though that might be, the Governor stabbed again at the glowing magenta letters floating in the air at his elbow.

"Yeah, Boss?"

"Want you to locate Lea Holderness. You know, my school teacher friend from up in that their Frigid Frontier."

"Sure thing...pluggin 'even as we speak. You'd be pleased, Buddy, at how often we use this here new skip trace program called 'Gotcha!' I can probably tell you whether her car's in the garage or yard, maybe even whether she's having her period. Sorry, Buddy, no disrespect intended. That's odd...."

"Don't fuck with me, Billy Bob! Just gimme what I asked you for."

"No address in the regular file.... Lemme check the job file under history teachers.... Nothing there either."

"You try her federal passport number?"

"Just doin 'that Buddy, but don't forget how many people been tearing them up lately. Besides, opposite her number in the normal file, it just says 'Transported.'"

"And what the fuck does that mean?" Buddy bellowed into the growing darkness in the general direction of the glowing purple letters.

Apparently, she was sent by one of them religious courts you was bellowin 'about a while ago to a prison colony in northern Russia around them gulags. But I just hacked into relevant Covenant files to see that your lady escaped some time ago. You may know better than me but I'm willin ' to bet she's finding her way back to America. No idee how that might work but, if she escaped, she must be on the high end of determined.

"Tell ya what, Billy Bob. How 'bout you arrange connections to get me up to where she used to live on the first available plane outta Vancouver in the morning? Something into Syracuse with as few stops as possible. Have a hover pick me up at the airport there, so we can cover lots a ground on the way up north before bedtime. And while you're at it, tap into those video surveillance systems to see where she's been lately – you got pictures of her from several angles. We don't know when she was sent to that there penal colony or when she got out of there. If she escaped from her prison in northern Russia, she probably got out of there through Finland so make sure you check footage from surveillance systems there, where I understand Chinese systems are in place as well as the US systems the central American government has set up along the coasts and spreading everywhere, perhaps even where Lea used to live. Can't imagine she'd try to come out of Russia another way because so many of those border countries are in one type of turmoil or another. You make those plane reservations and have Tariq meet you at the Syracuse airport."

An Unplanned Procedure

As light and dark began to drift apart, I felt something very heavy holding my wrists tight against a frigid, waxy metal surface. Except for patches of warmth between my legs and under the soft hollow of my chin, the table's greasy coldness pressed tightly against every inch of my bare body - breasts, stomach, legs and arms - sucking away all that was left of my body heat. Only by straining against my shackles could I raise my head, trying to make sense of my cluttered surroundings beyond the intense halo of blinding, blue light around me. Through a narrow, triple window to blowing grayness outside, I saw a bony finger of ice drip, drip, dripping dirty water from a low roof to somewhere I couldn't see under the windowsill. Is that where I'll end up? Each glistening drop was momentarily caught in the gathering gloom by the harsh glare hurting my eyes.

Where am I? Why am I here? Where are my friends when I need them most? Am I sick? This place looks like a hospital. But I don t remember getting hurt. Is someone helping me?

What I took to be a doctor looked up from another

woman strapped to a nearby metal table under similar cone of sharp, blue light. Ochre, dried blood and small patches of fresh, red blood spotted his green scrub shirt and trousers showing through an open, knee-length lab coat that might once have been white and clean. The old man in spattered greens wiped his nose with the back of his hand then tossed a scalpel into a waiting aluminum instrument tray with a clank. Paused beside his third charge, he thrust a bare hand under the man's nose to check his shallow breathing and fumbled for the carotid artery, looking for a pulse before turning toward me. Maybe he'd heard my chains rattle against the operating table as I tried to turn over.

As I kept trying to focus, his long, narrow face, beady eyes and a well-trimmed dash of a mustache floated into view. Not a mean or kind face. Just a face, a very tired and wrinkled face.

"Awake already, Lea? You'll be glad to know there weren't any serious complications. If there'll be no trouble, I can release your restraints."

How could there be any more trouble I wondered as bits and pieces of what had happened to me snapped through my mind like bursts of static on a cheap electric radio? My tongue still felt so thick from whatever had knocked me out that I could only nod weakly.

The green-robed physician pointed a slightly deformed left hand in my direction and squeezed a tiny, black disk he had picked out of a metal bin under the lip of my table. It silently blinked red. My hand and leg cuffs clicked open. Rubbing my chafed wrists, I gingerly turned over, slowly raising myself off the icy metal surface. As soon as the doctor looked away, I quickly slid my feet to the rough wooden floor, away from that awful table. Cautiously at first, I felt the back of my throbbing neck. Nervously combing through what was left of my auburn hair, I discovered a snarl of uneven stitches at the base of my skull. It hadn't been just a nightmare! In a blinding flash, I suddenly remembered where I was. And why they'd sent me to this God-forsaken place.

A wave of despair swallowed me up, like a riptide, an unstoppable current, knocking my feet out from under me, tumbling me over and over as the shore receded in the distance, and I began to sink deeper and deeper into the cold waters. Oh, God! I d sacrificed my only child s happiness and well-being for my own obstinate beliefs. I d completely failed Clara as a mother! What would happen to her? Where, where could her father be? God in Heaven, I ve never asked you for very much. PLEASE, PLEASE HELP ME NOW!

Right then and there, in that dirty operating room, I

Lea surveyed her new home, looking out over the broad expanse of dull, gray snow and wet black boulders between the compound and the sullen Chukchi Sea. Her heart was numb with despair. "*What could I have possibly done to make these people do this to me?*" she wondered. The slowly dripping finger of ice pointing toward the ground outside reminded Lea again of her ultimate resting place in this barren wasteland. The heavy sutures laced into the back of her neck burned and itched, like tiny red ants burrowing under her skin. Try as she might, Lea couldn't keep from worrying them.

Probing gingerly, she could feel a metal ovoid buried under the skin of her crudely shaved neck, roughly at the base of her skull. Unless the matrons at the Newark Transit Prison had lied to her, that pellet was loosely attached to her spinal column, to discourage any clumsy attempts to remove it. Supposedly the device contained a high explosive charge as well as a compact computer mechanism designed to accurately determine its own location. What became known to Lea as the Execution Box received signals from one of the eyes in the sky hanging in high stationary orbit over the Northern Hemisphere not unlike many variations of mapping software.

Lea vaguely understood how the bomb in her head was supposed to work. As long as she didn't stray too far from her place of confinement, the device would remain in hibernation. But if she crossed imaginary boundaries located some 5 kilometers beyond the shores of Penal Colony 627, it would hum loudly for about twenty seconds, then detonate sharply.

Lea was still hazy from whatever drug the doctor had given her before the operation. But she remembered lecturing to her history students about how the English kings had populated an entirely new country by sending convicted felons to what later became Australia. It was a common law remedy known as transportation that removed felons and other undesirables from society. Since the US Confederation and its several autonomous ethnic and religious regions were drowning in a swelling population of political prisoners while illegal immigrants were welcomed and provided many benefits, leasing confinement space from bankrupt shards of the former Soviet Union became the preferred option for incarceration. It was cheaper and no problems with the neighbors such as the ever-present "Not in My Backyard" objectors. Rather than keep Lea and others like her in expensive new prisons in North America as the penalty for challenging the creed of the Hate Speech Act, corrupt Confederation authorities allowed the Covenant to permanently exile them to a previously uninhabited island in the frozen Chukchi Sea. It was devoid of all human life except its American convicts and a small cadre of their keepers, supplemented by Russian employees living on the nearby mainland as well as releasees from gulags in the vicinity. The metallic pill concealed under her skin was designed to keep Lea imprisoned on this windswept crag in the distant ocean with a minimum of supervision and very little expense. She would be expected to feed and clothe herself once her meager food packet was either exhausted or stolen. Or she could indenture herself indefinitely to the Covenant's sweatshop on the grounds of Penal Colony 627. There Lea would spend the rest of her life assembling rudimentary lighting fixtures by hand, for installation along God's Way throughout North America. Punishing hours, little rest and even less food, until her body simply gave out.

As Lea's fogginess subsided and her surroundings came more clearly into focus, she ventured timidly toward the workbench nearest her own metal table. Unlike others in the makeshift operating room, this aluminum table held someone old, a wizened man with stringy white locks, his frail body held down by a broad canvas belt stretched tightly across his thin waist. Lea bent to pick up a broken tongue depressor from the gritty floor as she moved closer. The old man appeared to be sleeping, his eyelids slightly open. His mouth was a round, black hole, entirely devoid of teeth. As Lea crept nearer, the old man looked more and more familiar to her.

A poster announcing a church meeting, what seemed like ages ago, popped into Lea's confused mind.

COME ONE! COME ALL!

HEAR THE WORD OF OUR LORD,

WHO LOVES YOU, WHETHER YOU ARE

JEW, CATHOLIC, MUSLIM, CHRISTIAN OR GOD-FEARER

SUNDAY, JUNE 11 6:00 P.M.

SECOND PRESBYTERIAN CHURCH

CHAMPLAIN AVENUE

PLATTSBURGH, NEW YORK

HOARY GOVETT, M. DIV., PREACHING

Just as clearly, Lea remembered two home-spuns

tearing down that placard from a young oak tree, ripping it to shreds, and hurrying off to find other announcements of the meeting to destroy. Despite her parents 'warnings, she'd taken Clara to hear the famous orator. A restive crowd waited and waited under the watchful eyes of nine home-spuns, but six o'clock came and went, and no Pastor Govett. As the early summer afternoon began to fade into dusk, Lea, Clara, and the others drifted away, muttering among themselves about what could have become of Hoary Govett. Now she knew.

Lea noticed a bloodstained towel crumpled up on the floor, against one aluminum leg of Hoary Govett's bier. She added it to the other trash in her hand and looked around the room for a wastebasket.

Suddenly the old preacher's eyelids snapped open. The depth of his brilliant, blue eyes transfixed Lea. But then she noticed his vacant stare. He turned toward Lea, as if sensing her presence but unable to see her.

"Black wings!" he barked.

"What does that mean?" Lea asked.

"Black wings! Black wings!" Hoary Govett exclaimed, fighting his restraints. "And thus, it came to pass," he croaked before falling silent.

Lea jumped as the doctor touched her bare elbow. He looked furtively toward the door and whispered quietly into her waiting ear:

"You know, I'm only doing my job. Just following orders. Once we put that pellet under your skin and make sure there's no infection, you're free to go anywhere on the island you wish. You can join the others in hunting, fishing or building shelters. What you do with the rest of your life is entirely up to you. Of course, you're one of only twelve women on this island. Many of the other prisoners aren't here for intellectual offenses, if you get my meaning. You're very pretty. It may be very, very difficult for you here. Even dangerous! But I can't do anything about the device under your skin. They make sure I don't have the tools needed to separate it from your spinal cord. But I hate to think of what might happen to you at the hands of those murderers and rapists out there. Perhaps there's another way I could help," the doctor continued conspiratorially, his voice trailing off into silence as he looked nervously about the cluttered operating room and its sedated prisoners.

"What do you mean?" Lea asked softly, looking suspiciously at the liver-spotted hand resting heavily on her naked thigh. "How could you possibly help me?"

The gaunt and graying doctor sighed and touched a

holographic image floating in the air beside the operating table. Instantly, Lea's entire file spilled onto the virtual computer screen hovering beside the low metal table she was leaning against. A detailed description of Lea's offenses and her personal history blinked into bright letters suspended in the air in front of them. Lea gasped at the wealth of detail about her life and personal habits spewing across the virtual screen, things she couldn't imagine ever having told anyone. She chanced a look at her potential benefactor out of the corner of her right eye. Hunched over against a corner of the table, he seemed like a frail man. Lea guessed from the distant look on his face that he'd either already read her file or wasn't very interested in its contents. She returned her attention to the floating images and resolved to let the doctor make the next move.

"You see," he began quietly, "I once had a bustling family medical practice in a little town outside Rome, New York, actually not all that far from where you used to teach. For quite a while after the curtain of political correctness descended over America, my medical practice continued pretty much unchanged. I never performed abortions but later in the face of Federal legislation requiring all doctors to perform them, my office was repeatedly defaced and picketed because I refused to perform abortions. One morning, as I was leaving for work, my wife was blown apart by a car bomb meant for me. She was talking to me through the driver's side window when she started the car. It also blew off part of my left hand at the same time," the doctor observed ruefully, holding up his left hand to let Lea inspect the stumps of his left thumb and index finger.

"Finally, I was arrested and charged for not performing an abortion on a transgendered woman, even though that was medical nonsense. I was also tried in one of the religious courts condoned by the Confederation to appease the Covenant. The court sentenced me to perform these operations and look after the emergency medical needs of you prisoners on this island." "As long as you shall live" is the way the judge put it."

The old man sighed: "As you can perhaps guess, I'm carrying the same kind of explosive device you now have, albeit a more primitive, earlier model."

"I still don't understand how you can help me if you can't remove the hideous bomb you just sewed into the back of my neck," Lea growled through clenched teeth, trying without much success to conceal her growing exasperation. "And that 'I'm just following orders 'was thoroughly discredited at the Nuremberg trials."

"Good question!" the doctor brightened somewhat, ignoring Lea's comment. He reached over to a nearby console and turned on some loud military music with blaring trumpets and thumping drums before continuing his explanation. "I'm required to implant an explosive pellet in the neck of every arriving convict. It's much too complicated to explain, but I would be caught and probably executed on the spot if I didn't do that every time. I know it violates my 'Hippocratic Oath 'to do no harm."

"However," he continued, "the Movement's technicians have apparently developed an electronic device to mimic the global positioning signals that mark out this penal colony. Reduced to the shape of a small necklace, the Movement's amulet fools the explosive pellet at the base of your skull into thinking it's always on this island, no matter where you happen to be at the time. I suspect it broadcasts false GPS signals of the sort the pellet expects to receive, or something like that, but then electronics really have never been my strongest suit. We conducted an experiment - tried out the Movement's device on one of our most disagreeable resident serial killers. We paid a couple of the locals from the mainland to take him on a boat ride, well past the five-kilometer limit, to see how well the Movement's invention would work. Not a bad guinea pig! Life on this barren rock pile would have been ever so much more pleasant for all of us if the Movement's countermeasure didn't work for that particular prisoner. The good news: the Movement's technology fooled his explosive pellet even though he was taken more than 15 kilometers beyond what is supposed to be the boundary line. Unfortunately, or fortunately, depending on your point of view, the new equipment didn't seem to help the convict swim very well in the long, cold Arctic swells. He never returned to our happy home here. For myself though, I'm not confident the Movement's new device would fool my pellet - it's probably the only one of its type here on the island. At least for now, I'm not willing to run the risk of trying to escape. So, I'm pretty much resigned to being here for a while. Besides, I'll bet the Movement would rather I stay here. Someone they can depend on, you know."

"I still don't see how that'll help me!" Lea shrieked, hoping in the next second that her annoyance would be lost in the heavy drumbeats and blaring brass music bouncing off the walls of the makeshift operating room.

"Just getting to that part of the story," the doctor replied calmly, patting Lea on the shoulder. "This piece of rock was leased from the Russian government for the sole purpose of housing American political and religious prisoners. All the convicts are supposedly confined here by the same sort of explosive pellet you and I have - no one worries very much about who comes and goes from this island. People from the mainland, if they can get here, buy things from the prisoners, sell supplies or whatever. As a sop to the Russians, some of the prison administrators were hired from the local population on the mainland, just over the southern horizon. The Russians can leave whenever they like as well. One of my assistants here in the clinic was planted by the Movement. He's supposed to help certain selected intellectual prisoners get back to America. Whenever you're ready, I'll bring him in to meet you because you're on the Movement's short list!"

By now suspicious of everyone, Lea was paralyzed by confusion and indecision. Though still bewildered by her lingering death sentence and the long, debilitating trip from her homeland, at some level Lea had just begun to face the enormity of her situation. But now, after being dragged from her home into the winter night and separated from what little remained of her family, she didn't trust anyone. Dumped into this icebox far beyond the distant fringe of civilization, she couldn't even allow herself to hope there might be some way out of her private nightmare. Lea was mentally and physically overloaded to the point of collapse. And yet, she couldn't give up entirely and succumb to this gray death.

The young prisoner puzzled aloud over the separate pieces of what she had just been told: "If I stay, I'll have to survive the weather, the other prisoners and somehow find food and shelter. If I try to escape, this pellet you just installed will blow my head off. But if your technician from this Movement thing lets me use one of those electronic necklaces, I can just walk out of here? What's this Movement anyway? And what do they want from me?"

"Why don't just I let Egon tell you about that?" the physician answered. Pushing on his left knee to get it started, he stood up with some difficulty and fumbled for a hidden button under the far rim of the operating table. Lea heard a door open at the far end of the room. She turned in that direction to see a short, strapping young man striding toward them through shadows surrounding several large pieces of medical equipment shrouded in dustcovers made of dark canvas and plastic sheets. Although the newcomer was still some distance away, Lea suddenly became conscious of her own nakedness. She snatched a grimy, green, paper gown from a nearby pine counter to cover herself. Feeling afraid and off balance, Lea looked away from the intense scrutiny she felt boring into her from behind Egon's opaque wrap-around glasses. The doctor also tensed noticeably as the muscular young man burst into the bright circle of turquoise light bathing him and his patient. The newcomer jabbed a black, leather-gloved right hand in her direction, his left hand perched defiantly on his hip.

"I've already read your whole file. Know more than anyone could possibly imagine about you, your history or your skills. You got an especially raw deal from the so-called North Country Covenant court. Even the religious offenders usually don't get a sentence as harsh as yours," the powerfully-built specimen declared. Only when he motioned for Lea to sit down in front of him did she understand just how much his arrival had intimidated her. Without realizing it, Lea had stood up as soon as Egon entered the far corner of the space where she had awakened on that cold, greasy metal operating table. Now she looked questioningly at the doctor and then back at the gruff intruder, wondering what to do.

"She wants to know about the Movement, Egon," the doctor said, clearing his throat. "What can you tell her? I don't know very much about what's going on out in the real world anymore."

"Just what I don t need," Lea thought angrily to herself, *"another stiff dick trying to get into my pants!"* But she wilted under the heat of Egon's gaze and looked down at the floor

submissively. Addressing no one in particular, the Movement's messenger appeared to take a bead on the main doorframe of the operating room through the hinge of his folded glasses.

"Most people don't know very much about the Movement," he observed. "Probably better that way. I only know what I'm told to do. And I do what I'm told."

He turned to stare directly into Lea's emerald eyes.

"Your file says you were in excellent physical condition before getting corralled by the Covenant - long distance running, karate and weights. How have you kept incarceration from wearing you down?" Egon inquired, nonchalantly extracting a short, shiny steel rod from the zippered pocket of his leather flight jacket. Carefully watching Lea to gauge her reaction, he bent each end of the rod around the bulging knuckles of his right fist with only moderate exertion and then flicked it into the air, catching it in his left hand.

Without an instant's hesitation, Lea snatched the bent metal rod from Egon's open palm, before he even became aware of her motion.

"That answer your question?" she smirked, feeling at once proud and frightened. "Sure, I don't get to run outdoors anymore, but I have infinitely more time to spend on conditioning now than I ever had before. But what's that got to do with this mess I'm in? Tell me how I can get out of here!"

"These gadgets that can fool the detonator inside your head, they're extremely expensive to build. The Movement doesn't care to waste them on anyone who can't weather the arduous trip back home," Egon countered.

"Why would the Movement want to help me?" Lea insisted. "Why does anyone but my family care whether or not I rot in this icy prison? My only child's kept by the Lost League and I'm not sure her father even knows what's happened to me, much less gives a shit."

Egon shrugged dismissively.

"My job is just to help you escape from this island and put you in touch with people who can get you back to the Confederation. I'm no theoretician. All I know is that the Movement opposes many of the things that are going on right now in the States." He looked at his watch pointedly. "Look, we really don't have a lot of time. Do you want to come with me or not? Make up your mind!"

In what seemed like the endless pause that followed, Lea's options fluttered through her tortured brain. She wasn't really ready to face this kind of tough decision. She just wanted to wake up in a warm bed down the hall from Clara's room, and know for sure this had all been a bad dream. But Lea's more practical side wouldn't let her ignore the possibility of something better, the chance of turning an apparent obstacle into an opportunity. On one hand, she could resign herself to staying on this frozen graveyard in the northern seas, most likely for the rest of her life. Her remaining days would probably be hard, degrading and most likely short in this twilight land of almost perpetual winter. Lea shuddered as she imagined how her remaining hopes and dreams would gradually seep away into the permafrost, leaving behind only the desiccated shell of a tired old woman.

Or she could go take her chances with Egon. What awaited her next was far from clear. *"Maybe my implant will explode while we're crossing the 25 kilometers of open ocean separating this island from the northern coast of Russia,"* she thought to herself. *Would that be better or worse than eking out a miserable existence in one of the colony's work gangs? If the Movement's device works as advertised, I'll get to the other side. Then what?"* Lea tried desperately to compare staying where she was awaiting, a slow death, or risking sudden death and going back to America with whoever Egon would turn her over to.

"Make up your mind!" Egon demanded, moving toward the door.

"I'll go," Lea whispered quietly, without much conviction.

The doctor leaned close and put his arm around Lea's shoulders. "Your things are under the table over there," he said with a wan smile, pointing toward a tattered gray nylon bag. "Could you call my son when you get home and let him know I'm still alive?"

"Sure, of course," Lea replied curtly, her mind already somewhere else. "Just write his number on a piece of paper and stuff it inside my bag." For the first time, she looked the doctor over carefully. On closer inspection, he seemed drawn and tired, as if his battery had suddenly run down. Lea could see the envy in his long, wrinkled face. Maybe she could go home but he knew there was no chance for him.

But as sad as the doctor's predicament made her feel, Lea couldn't muster any real sympathy or understanding for this supposed healer who had torn open the base of her skull to do the bidding of the people who had sent her here to die.

Turning toward Egon, who was already edging toward the nearest door, she asked nervously: "what do we have to do?"

"Just hurry up and follow me. Hopefully we can still make it to the last hovercraft. It's scheduled to leave in less than five minutes," Egon answered tersely.

Without even a look around the cluttered operating room, Lea snatched all her earthly possessions from the dirty floor and followed Egon out into a long, dimly lit corridor.

"Wait," the doctor yelled, "put on this parka and these lined pants! In this weather, you'll surely need 'em outside. Take these boots too!" He tossed a bulky bundle in Lea's direction. She wriggled into the clothing and leaped into an oversized pair of thick, felt-lined boots.

In the darkness outside the compound's triple-layer shell, a string of sparkling arc lights led the way across a stone-strewn field to the nearly empty boat basin, and the dark, choppy sea beyond. As the pair raced along the narrow exit hall, Egon pushed a handful of stainless-steel links against her taut abdomen, like a wobbly baton in one of her Iron Man races back in the upper Adirondacks. Lea grabbed the coiled chain and held it up toward a light fixture passing overhead as the two ran toward the exit. A dull metal heart the size of a small plum hung in the middle of the chain.

"Put it around your neck!" Egon barked as they careened through the compound's double, outer doors.

Lea put her head through the loop of dimly shining links and tucked it deep inside her parka. Its pendant felt cold between her bare breasts.

Ahead of the messenger and the convict, a hovercraft's engines were revving up, and suddenly they were inside and scurrying for seats as close to the hovercraft's closing doors as possible.

Suddenly Egon's impatient tug at her arm aroused Lea from a dreamless slumber induced by the hovercraft's whirring turbines and the oppressive warmth of its crowded cabin. She yawned and pushed back the artificial fur collar of her parka to watch the vessel crawl clumsily onto a ramp of battered barnacle-covered pilings anchored against a dark outcropping of tall, ice-encrusted black boulders. Even before the high-pitched whine of the hovercraft's turbines had entirely faded away, Egon was rushing Lea through a clot of passengers crowding around the nearest open hatch. Outside, the frigid sea air wiped away any lingering thought of warm sleep. Still groggy from her nap, Lea tripped over a large bollard at the edge of the pier's coarse planks but quickly regained her balance by grabbing the sleeve of Egon's thick parka. The motley collection of other passengers trudged silently away down a corduroy road hugging the boulder-strewn shore, toward the small seaside settlement of dingy shacks.

But Egon pointed up a winding rocky path ahead to the left. Following the line of the narrow footpath up the nearest of several low hills, Lea saw two hooded figures standing near the crest of the first summit. Reconciled to Egon's iron grip, Lea stumbled along behind him, up and up, toward the distant pair. As Egon and Lea clambered over the cascade of loose, broken stones near the top of the first hill, he suddenly pushed his charge toward the two waiting men, then turned and ran headlong back down the hill to the idling hovercraft. As he approached, the whine of its turbines increased sharply. Egon ducked into the closing portal and the hovercraft lumbered back out onto the leaden sea. As it began to pitch and yaw in the heavier waves outside the small breakwater, the bulky craft accelerated noisily, wallowing in the inky swells, leaving Lea standing alone in front of the two tall strangers.

She felt alone and very frightened.

Faint starlight illuminated gray wisps of breath curling from under the furry hoods of two men towering over her. Lea waited. *Why am I holding my breath,*" she wondered.

"Do you know who we are?" the booming voice of the taller figure shattered the imposing silence. He was well over six foot four in height with a large nose peeking from beneath the hood of his stained leather parka.

"Well, ah, Egon told me you were from the Movement. He said you'd help me get back to my home in northern New York," Lea answered, feeling trapped even in the vast openness of the desolate hillsides and the dark sea stretching west to the faint remainder of a smudged horizon.

"Before we leave this place, we must have an understanding!" the speaker said loudly. He removed a small ebony box from the outer pocket of his parka and held it out for Lea to see. Smirking at his companion knowingly, he ceremoniously pushed a large button recessed into the top surface of the box. Instantly a throaty hum swelled inside Lea's upper body, radiating from the back of her neck through her chest and arms, to the tips of her fingers and toes. Her frantically searching fingers felt the same sound coursing through the ugly stitches at the base of her skull. Lea looked at the two men in horror and disbelief. She lunged for the box. Her tormentor quickly jumped aside to avoid Lea's grasp but then released the button. Lea's knees sagged as the humming abruptly ceased. He pushed back the hood of his parka so Lea could clearly see his pitted face with a deep scar in the center of his forehead in the dim light. Lea was aghast to see the blind eye that had peered at her through the dirty window of her transport train parked on that distant siding on the western side of the Hudson River.

"That was only a small demonstration," the Movement's courier snarled, turning his head slightly to look Lea over with his one good eye. "If I hold the button down too long... well, you know what happens when you hit a ripe melon with a sledgehammer? Just so you understand who you're dealing with, I've spent many very long years in the camps. Wouldn't even think twice about holding the button down, for a lonnnnnngg time. Like Egon told you, you're going back home, but to help our buddies in the Movement overthrow the bunch of sissies that pretends to be the government in America. You'll do whatever the Movement needs done. Right now, that mostly includes assassinating selected "government" officials and their toadies and fellow travelers. You understand?"

Lea stared blankly at the frozen ground, wondering what she possibly could have done to deserve this fate.

Her countryman leaned over and screamed into Lea's down-turned face, so close she could smell his rotting teeth. "DO YOU UNDERSTAND? I could just hold down this button and leave your remains here to be eaten by wild animals."

Lea understood, but not in the way this vile man

expected. She nodded very slowly and submissively. Her face never betrayed, not even for a fleeting instant, the intense strain she felt from straightening the shiny steel rod hidden deep in a warm pocket of her parka with just two fingers. Something to count on later!

For the time being, these couriers of the Movement might be her only ticket out of this frozen land of the yet-to-die. She resolved to use them as best she could. Winter would be melting into springtime now in northern New York. Maybe Clara would be playing outside in the warm sun in the new day soon to dawn there, many time zones past the faint, orange smudge finally slipping below the western horizon to her right.

Lea continued to look at the ground as the trio trudged further away from the boat basin, over the first, second and then the third and fourth hills, all the while doing her very best to look frightened and submissive.

Lea was still very frightened. But, more than anything else, she was angry, very angry. She wondered how long it would take for the bearer of the Execution Box to turn his back or fall asleep. Lea Holderness yearned for her 9mm Beretta APX Carry semi-automatic pistol with its multi-round magazine that she had learned to use so skillfully even during the Empire State's onslaught against the Second

Amendment, not terribly effective in the frozen North Country.

Vainkala

A drab but well-kept little Finnish town languishes on the Karelian border of southeastern Finland with Russia. Lacking the usual highway frontier border crossing, the stamp of its name, Vainkala, appears only in the passports of train travelers between St. Petersburg, Russia and Helsinki, Finland. After leaving St. Petersburg, Lea's train, the "Allegro," passed through Viborg before reaching the Russian border with Finland. That trip, however comfortable the seats or pleasant the steaming tea in antique glasses, the sound of Russian border police strutting along on the metal rooves of the train's cars before passing into Finland was unnerving and hard to forget. Because experienced travelers know that the surly guards will shortly swagger through passageways between crowded compartments, hoping to seize upon some real or perceived irregularity that would allow them to demand some hard currency as a condition of being allowed to stay on the train to the somewhat more civilized West. Coolly correct European Union passport officials coming through the same train cars after that frontier has been crossed are extremely pleasant by comparison.

Still expecting the worst, Lea kept her head down and concentrated on willing her heartbeat lower, a moment of extreme calm before whatever storm that might erupt next. On either side of her, the Movement's two couriers leaned heavily against her shoulders, one actually asleep, the other just pretending. She could feel the waiting one coiled like a steel spring, waiting to pounce. Since her captors had turned out to be somewhat more clever than first impressions had suggested to her, Lea hadn't yet been able to figure out how the two men dealt with the Execution Box or where they always kept it. While she wasn't positive there was only one box, Lea surmised they passed it back and forth, so she would be kept off balance and might think twice before trying anything. What did they think was the likelihood she would try to grab it? What would she do with it if she grabbed it anyway? Hard to tell. She'd been doing her very best to act intimidated, to play to the Hell's Angels mentality of her two guards. But she couldn't be sure enough to act just yet. The taller one with the rotten teeth, who called himself "Thrasher," almost never uttered a word. When he did it was in clipped, low tones, so low Lea had to strain to hear him. As the train rumbled toward its stop at the border between Finland and Russia, Lea knew Thrasher was wide-awake, even if his good left eye was tightly shut and he was breathing slowly.

On her other side, the younger thug, Willy, had even smiled shyly at Lea several times since Egon abandoned her on the windswept hill beside the Chukchi Sea, when he must have thought Thrasher's attention was elsewhere. Willy, only a couple of inches over 5 feet with curly, blonde hair, fair-skinned and with a pleasant demeanor seemed much less threatening than Thrasher.

As Lea listened intently to the Russian border guards clomping slowly toward them through the next carriage, Willy snuggled against her in an almost friendly way, both hands clasping her left arm. By design, to limit her ability to strike out, or simply seeking some warmth and human contact? Lea couldn't be sure. Then the curly-haired young man mumbled faintly in his sleep. His right hand dropped onto Lea's upper thigh, caressing it lovingly. A carefully contrived grope or an innocent accident? She couldn't be sure. But she gently pushed it aside anyway, trying to focus all of her attention on what might lie just on the other side of the compartment door.

Clumsy fumbling at the train car's forward door latch interrupted Lea's feverish review of her options.

"Documents" a beetle-browed Mongolian bellowed in

stilted Russian from deep beneath his high-peaked, brown officer's cap, leathery palm outstretched as he slid open the door of Lea and her captors 'compartment.

As he leaned over the British family across the aisle, Lea retrieved a counterfeit Canadian passport from an inside pocket of her parka and let it drop unopened into her lap. Thrasher's good eye opened just a crack as his vise grip on Lea's right elbow tightened, fueling her fear of being caught with forged papers. The Asian turned toward her, as if suspecting something was amiss, his hand now under her very nose.

"Canadian, eh? Poorer than Americans!" he sniffed, perhaps reconciling himself to a certain loss of monetary opportunity.

"Wake up! Passport control!" he shouted, kicking Willy sharply under the arch of his worn, soft felt boots. Rudely jarred from his slumber, the young man looked about sleepily, rubbing his bloodshot eyes while fumbling in a concealed vest pocket for something to show. Although the border guard's attention was focused on Willy, Lea could feel Thrasher tensely coiled beside her, waiting to strike. She seized the passport between the thumb and index finger of her right hand and began flipping it absently, like a playing card.

Lea felt the guard staring at her and looked quickly toward him. Without saying anything, he seemed to be asking her a question. She paused for a second and then quietly extended her left hand forward, palm upward. Then Lea touched the center of her open left palm in smooth movement with her right index finger and watched for the border guard's reaction.

He smiled politely and grabbed his comrade roughly by the elbow, pulling him toward to next half-open door leading into the next compartment.

"We're done in here. Come along!"

Once the compartment door had slammed shut, Thrasher cleared his throat and whispered in Lea's ear: "what was that all about?"

"What do you mean?"

"How did you make him go away without looking at our papers?"

"You mean when I touched my palm?"

"Exactly."

"Oh, that's the deaf-mute sign for our Savior, Jesus Christ. Some believers use it as a sign of recognition in difficult situations, like the ancient Christians used to draw a picture of a fish in the sand."

"Whatever. It made him leave us alone..."

Later, while stopped in the border town of Vainkala, after EU border control officers had finished their cursory review of travelers 'documents, Lea's own deep sighs of relief had already calmed and comforted her. She no longer felt the same amount of turmoil around her and even relaxed a bit. Outside the grimy windows, rows and rows of evergreens marched by ever faster as the train picked up speed toward Helsinki. The modern train passed through intermediate stops of Kouvola, Lahti, Tikkurila and Pasila before gliding through modern sidings into Helsinki's central station, Rautatieasema. Dusty Vainkala remained quietly behind, astride the frontier with Russia. Lea brightened – her two keepers from the Movement were becoming more and more expendable. Which one had the Execution Box and how quickly could she get it? She now knew that the trio would be boarding a Liberian freighter in Helsinki's harbor to find its way to the east coast of Maine and deliver them to a boat waiting for them beyond the breakwater there.

Lea and her two minders followed the departing crowd along a clean and uncluttered platform into the station's cavernous marble hall, Willy playfully circled around the other two, looking at flower and food shops and currency exchange booths. All the while, Lea kept her head down while paying close attention to what she thought were surveillance cameras near the eaves of the platform as well as inside the grand central hall. What Lea didn't know was that the Chinese company called Tiandy, one of the world's largest video surveillance companies, working with Huawei's face recognition technology, had leased its equipment to the Finnish Transport Infrastructure Agency. This system was installed in railroad stations and properties throughout Finland, including its central station in Helsinki with recorded information likely made available to Tiandy and its indirect owner, the CCP, and who knows what other customers.

Walking past gates for trains to other parts of Finland, the trio followed signs to taxi stands, in Finnish, Swedish and English. Thrasher walked around the hood of the first cab in line, leaned into the driver's window of the first cab in line and whispered the address of the pier where the Liberian freighter was supposedly docked, as if Lea was not supposed to know. He obviously didn't know Lea could read lips. Lea, Thrasher and Willy climbed into the cab and were on their way to the waiting harbor beyond.

Suffer the Little Children

A flickering candle cast swaying shadows of the stern, black, iron bunk-bed frames over the rough surfaces of the small room's whitewashed walls and the silhouette of a kneeling child, her growing legs bundled in a full, black skirt around her ankles against damp, night air seeping through rattling window-panes. Clara intently followed a tiny stream of clear liquid wax dribbling down the side of her stubby candle, then tried to catch a glistening drop with her index finger before it plipped lightly into the grimy tin pan below. A window-shaking gust outside the dormitory made Clara's glowing candle flutter and hiss even more, driving the roiling pattern of shadows back and forth across the stark walls and two double-decker, iron bunk bed frames. Three of the thin mattresses were rolled up tightly and tied near the head of each frame, with no sheets, blankets or pillows. Only Clara's thin pallet was laid open for sleeping. Looking nervously into the shadowy peak of the darkened room, the little girl shivered and drew a coarse, slate-colored blanket tighter around her shoulders.

A large, iron key rattled in the balky lock! The sturdy

ironwood door squeaked open. Clara jumped to her feet, letting her coverlet fall to the uneven board floor.

"Time for prayers, Daughter," the matron announced crisply, bowing stiffly toward the broken cross on the wall between the two bunk beds. She clutched a smaller version of the same cross hanging from a tarnished silver chain around her wrinkled neck.

"Yes, Ma'am," Clara answered carefully, dipping her head slightly.

"Yes, MOTHER RUTH," the old woman hissed through clenched teeth. From Clara's nine-year-old perspective, her minder presented a long, fleshy hooked nose, bushy, yellow-white eyebrows and a matted lock of dishwater gray hair slipping from under her starched bonnet.

"I AM your MOTHER for as long as you are in the League's care here. You know that. If you ever live elsewhere in the League, you'll be cared for by another, who will also be your mother. Don't ever forget that!"

Clara's beautiful blue eyes, beginning to tear up, examined the angry, deeply creased face and the faint mustache over her minder's primly pursed lips. Coughing softly from the musty odor of mothballs and damp wool exuded by the old woman's ankle-length dress, Clara glanced warily from the matron's gnarled, white-knuckled fists to her laced black block-heel shoes, half expecting a body blow.

"You're not MY Mother!" Clara blurted out petulantly, her lower lip quivering. "Bad people sent my REAL MOTHER far away! Made me cry..."

Whack! A backhand cuff sent Clara careening against her metal bed frame, banging her tousled head on a sharp edge. Horrified at the crimson drops on her fingers from touching the new wound, Clara began to sob softly.

"The heathen who brought you into this world, praise be, no longer exists. The sooner you accept this will of our Lord and Savior and do what you are told, the easier your stay with the League will become. As the Deacon, Mr. Goodnough, told us at meeting time, the Good Book says, 'suffer the little children to come unto me.' Luke 18:16 You know, Clara, the Good Book gives us very clear and specific rules on how to live every aspect of our daily lives. As to you, little lamb, there's one verse our minister read to us that seems particularly appropriate: 'the wrath of God cometh on the children of disobedience.' Colossians 3:6 Well, my wrath at your continued disobedience is considerable, young lady! I intend to make you suffer, suffer and suffer until you repent of your manifold sins and submit to the will of God as embodied by my instructions."

"My father's going to come for me!"

"Oh, really? Your father?" the matron sneered. "You don't even know who your father is. Do you?"

"MY MOTHER says he's an important man!" Clara insisted defiantly. "Said he'd come if I ever needed him," she continued hopefully.

"Kneel for prayers," the matron demanded.

"Not tonight, Mother Ruth," the frightened little girl pleaded.

"You know there are NO EXCEPTIONS my little lamb," the old woman intoned, both hands extended skyward, palms upward, a distant look on her face. "KNEEL! NOW!"

An evening star showed briefly through a break in the overcast sky over the ramshackle Carthage, New York facilities of the Lost League, just up the Black River from Lake Ontario. Only a few faint lights still burned in the individual cells. An uneasy silence had settled over the weary children and their overworked keepers, broken only by the occasional sound of bone striking young flesh and a shrill cry rising behind a bolted, wooden door.

"No, no, no, Mother Ruth! I'll do whatever you want. Please don't hit me again..." disappeared in a choking sob.

In another part of the Western Hemisphere, Clara's father felt a faint twinge, which only briefly interrupted his drunken sleep.

Taking Inventory

Tariq al-Tikriti took a deep breath of the cold, damp early spring breeze, trying to clear his head. He leaned over the aluminum railing of the observation deck atop Syracuse - Hancock International Airport, scanning the airfield apron for his appointment's aircraft and its arriving passengers. The western breeze was probably from ice-locked Lake Ontario in the distance, but Tariq couldn't be sure. He had a very bad case of the flu or a virus, despite two inoculations and one booster against the strains currently being circulated throughout the Confederation including northern New York – all courtesy of the Wuhan Institute of Virology in the People's Republic of China. No matter how hard Chinese germ warfare scientists claim they tried, they couldn't seem to come up with a vaccination serum that wouldn't promptly mutate into another dangerous viral strain once it was released around members of the general public or political and religious prisoners. Or if they didn't simply expire from the inoculations or boosters themselves. Be patient, the Confederation government kept telling the American public – wear your masks, get the vaccinations and boosters and more boosters and stay home from work. And people continued to be paid to not work, generating more dependence on the source of those checks. Because of mushrooming Chinese influence, America's feckless Administrator had outlawed privately produced American vaccines in favor of Chinese versions. But those Chinese scientists didn't have to spend any time in the Confederation even though more powerful government abuse was common in China.

Tariq had formerly been Saddam Hussein's bagman in the brutal dictator's attempt to escape international sanctions by taking over David Garvey's burgeoning Eastern European loan-sharking business. But, owing to the Fearless Leader's unpleasant demise, Tariq had moved on to become an all-purpose advisor with respect to the Covenant for Iran's interests and whatever favors were needed by its ally, the Chinese Communist Party. Of course, Tariq's loyalty depended on a variety of offered pay scales but his principal focus at the moment, in keeping with Buddy Lassiter's own preferences, was distant but turbulent Northern New York.

Northern Air Flight 203 from Vancouver, Winnipeg and Chicago had just rolled up to the Syracuse airport's skyway, only twenty minutes late. The diminutive Iraqi shuddered to think of former Governor Buddy Lassiter's glad-handing the passengers and crew of the Guangzhou-built Boeing 854 as he worked his way toward the airport's passenger lounge, so much like yet another of his seemingly endless political campaigns. Even without presuming to question the Chinese Premier's diligence or foresight (may Allah protect him), Tariq wondered how this boorish cracker could possibly be of any help in the eventual salvation of the American people. True, Buddy Lassiter had been very helpful to the cause while still in office, albeit for some very large payments, originating in China, to several numbered bank accounts in Cyprus and Liechtenstein. But Tariq was trying to run a complicated operation here and the former governor couldn't be bothered with even simple arithmetic. Much less keeping his eye on the ball or his hands off the women who seemed drawn to him. *"Time to stroke yet another insecure Southern male ego,"* Saddam's favorite nephew thought darkly. He paused to take a deep drag on a double-dose Marlboro from a Shanghai factory before pushing his way back inside the crowded terminal.

"Tariq, my man, how's your hammer hangin'?" the big Georgian heartily thumped the neatly-tailored Iraqi on the back and swallowed him up in an unwelcome bear hug.

"I am fine, Governor. Just peachy, except for this miserable flu. And yourself?"

"Can't hardly complain, Tariq. All the plumbing still works. What more could I ask? And I haven't heard from that bitch I used to be married to in over six months. You been gettin 'any? Ya know, really ought to take some pussy for that cold!"

"Er, maybe we should find our driver, Governor. Miles to go before we sleep and all that," the young Iraqi sniffed.

The two presented a strange spectacle. A smartly dressed, younger man, 5'5" tall, wearing a blue, pinstriped suit, dark overcoat and glistening, butter-soft cordovan loafers. Carrying a slim Crouch & Fitzgerald briefcase under one arm, the Warrior of the Faith's nephew moved purposefully toward a trio of elevators leading to the short-term parking level, his dark eyes carefully scanning the crowd around them.

Towering a full 12 inches over the young Iraqi was the hulking Edmund J. "Buddy" Lassiter, former Governor of the great State of Georgia. Buddy's generous paunch was threatening to burst the buttons of a fashionable dark blue silk shirt, even though one shirt-tail was already dangling precipitously over his wide, brown leather belt, his trousers held together with a large ornamental silver buckle celebrating some Hispanic achievement or another. Lassiter lumbered along, one step for every three of Tariq's, eyes, searching the crowd for hands to shake, flesh to press.

Although the terminal was extremely crowded, it was also surprisingly quiet, as if everyone in the bustling crowd were on the way to a family funeral. Many wore more than one paper facemask as protection against the endless "plandemic." Even though the American Center for Disease Control had admitted more than once that paper masks (mostly imported from China by the mendacious central Administration along with an endless variety of "Covid" tests, many of which seemed designed to actually spread the virus) were entirely useless in stopping the flow of any virus, like trying to stop mosquitos with a chain-link fence. Let alone "Covid-19" which had been independently proven to actually be the ordinary and regularly occurring seasonal flu.

A mother, father and four children, all dressed in clean but plain home-spun, probably farmers, trudged silently past the two outsiders, eyes averted as if avoiding some sort of potential affliction. Perhaps because neither Buddy Lassiter nor Tariq were wearing any sort of face covering. Languishing at the edge of the passageway, what probably had been a newsstand years ago showed only rows of empty shelves. The only item for sale being a Covenant-approved Good Book, with an unattended cash box to receive the required donation; as evidence of the rise in petty crimes, the cash box was entirely empty except for a pair of small coins.

Swaddled in a billowing, shapeless, gray smock, a wan young woman, little left of her blonde hair from some recent amateur butchering, worked her way slowly across the corridor floor with a wet mop and a bucket of very dirty water. *Swing left, swing right, wring out the mop, dip it into the pail, swing left....* Tariq realized he was staring at the deep, red "A" burned into her forehead. Perhaps feeling his gaze or noticing how differently he was dressed, she looked up from her work, but Tariq turned away in embarrass-ment.

Just ahead, at a narrow point in the corridor, two gawky lads dressed in gray home-spun blocked their path.

"You are entering the sovereign territory of the Tribal Alliance of Reconstituted Mohawks and Tuscaroras. Declare and surrender your contraband."

"*Wonderful,*" Tariq thought to himself wearily, "*we can t even get out of this fucking, chicken-shit airport without these cretins we bankroll getting in our way.*"

"And by what authority," the young Iraqi sniffled half-heartedly.

"God's orders. Show us your personals!" came back an arrogant reply.

"My what?"

"Your personal carrying place!" the shorter inquisitor enunciated slowly, as if speaking to a dim-witted child. "Your documents, non-believer!"

"Praise be to Allah, I am indeed a believer!" Tariq spluttered.

"Pastor Mr. Heimlich says the Good Book tells us only those who believe our way are God-fearing. Do you profess belief in the Covenant?"

The Leader's man on the spot considered attempting a religious discussion with this lean, angry young man but decided that was likely to be an exercise in futility. Like arguing with one of those quaint Marxists about the definition of democracy or with a young child about the color of unicorns. Instead, he retrieved his folding alligator-skin wallet from an inside jacket pocket and held it out tentatively for inspection.

"You have graven images," his interrogator observed matter-of-factly, rifling through the several pockets of Tariq's wallet. "All are forfeit!"

"What right do you have? That's a picture of my mother and sisters. Give it back!"

"Luther, check his papers," the one holding Tariq's photographs directed his assistant. He took the Cypriot passport and held it under a machine emitting a blinking, blue light.

Tariq al-Tikriti listened with Buddy Lassiter as the text of his passport was read aloud in a nasal computer's monotone. He looked at Buddy in surprise, realizing that neither of the two Covenant people standing in the way of their exit could read.

"This happen often?" he asked Lassiter under his breath.

"All the time, all the time," the former Governor sighed. "Ya need to give 'em somethin 'to show for their trouble, something they can claim they confiscated. If you don't want 'em to keep that picture of your folks…"

"You have a suggestion?"

"Got any foreign money with people or a face on it?

"Actually, I have some Sahawari money. There's an engraving of their head honcho on it."

"Good! Give 'em that. Then they'll let us go. They know me. Only picked you out because you look foreign and probably aren't Christian."

Tariq handed over a maroon banknote. At that point, the two young guards seemed to lose interest and allowed the two travelers continued on toward the nearest elevator to Syracuse International's underground garages.

Like an excited young but bulky Labrador, Lassiter bounced alongside, ready to play "fetch" with whatever his Iraqi controller had in mind. Tariq could almost imagine Buddy's tongue hanging out, dripping saliva on the polished tile floor and vigorously wagging his stubby tail. "*Whatta putz,*" Tariq al-Tikriti muttered to himself, nearly tripping over a wheelchair-borne beggar's outstretched artificial leather boot to the left of the only open elevator door. Both men suddenly noticed they were alone with the shabby panhandler at the end of a long, now-deserted hallway.

"You got something for me, big guy?"

Tariq instinctively turned to the 6'5" senior citizen towering over him, assuming that the mendicant was addressing the famous former Governor.

"Wellll," Lassiter stuttered, "what can I do for you, kind sir? My father used to beat me, was an alcoholic. I had to work my way..."

"Not you ass-munch! I meant Mr. Moneybags here, with his fancy New York, fashionable clothes, recent shoeshine, expensive Cartier watch and all. You here for some do-gooder international project, Mr. Slickness? Maybe you could share some of your Euros with me on the way in, like before they get swallowed up by the Covenant for its own narrow little purposes, while the rest of us in the neighborhood starve to death.”

He pounded on the tile floor for emphasis with a stout, wooden pole. Feeling more than a little uneasy, Tariq noticed that the beggar’s long stick had a heavy metal cap on the end. The beggar’s heavily gloved, right hand gripped the other end of what looked to Tariq like a formidable weapon.

“I certainly have no idea what you’re talking about, kind sir. Although it’s none of your concern, I’m just out of business school, loaded with student loans, without even a regular job. Just because I happen to dress well, that’s no reason to assume anything about my economic status. And what are you doing begging right under that sign? Don’t you even see that sign? It very clearly says: “No begging unless for God-fearing purposes.”

“Well, first I can’t read very well. Second, you and your running mate are part of the problem. I’m going to fix the latter.” he growled, spinning his wheelchair smartly backwards, away from the open elevator, away from the two outsiders. Tariq’s stomach began to churn as he cast wildly about for some means of escape. Lassiter, on the other hand, slowly turned to face the beggar, now cranking the wheelchair furiously toward them, a fiendish look in his bloodshot eyes.

"Jump in the elevator, Tariq!" Lassiter ordered, dropping into a crouch. Launching himself toward the whirring appliance and its red-faced driver, like the linebacker he had once been, he yodeled," Go Dawgggggggssssss!" Lassiter put down his bushy head and galloped over what might have felt for him like a mere five yards toward the opponent's goal line, separating him from the oncoming wheelchair and its now screaming occupant.

Crash! With a surprising head of steam under his belt, Lassiter rammed the beggar's upper torso, head-first. The considerable momentum of Lassiter's unexpected lunge ripped his target out of the chair's nylon-mesh sling seat. The two collapsed in a heap, the former Governor smothering his protesting target like a cheap suit. Its left wheel whirring crazily, the tubular aluminum appliance bounced once on the stone floor and came to rest on its right side.

Except for the slow humming of the wheelchair wheels, Tariq could hear nothing. Wishing to be almost anywhere else, he ran his fingers back and forth through the "Close" holo inside the elevator doors. Even though it looked like

Lassiter needed help, Tariq al-Tikriti was momentarily frozen by the struggle going on almost right under his nose. Too frightened to step out of the elevator cab and give his charge a hand, he didn't know what to do. He watched in horror as the beggar pushed Lassiter aside with little apparent effort and pulled himself to a standing position using the long pole. Its cover tossed aside, Tariq could make out a nasty looking iron spear tip on the beggar's pole, complete with barbs. The beggar began to run toward Tariq, the spear held back, arm straight, the way a javelin thrower prepares to launch his missile. Tariq thought between gasps, *"he isnt even a cripple!"* Feeling a wave of nausea coming over him, Tariq waved his fingers through the "Close" holo of the elevator ever more frantically. He looked around the elevator for some means of escape or protection. Nothing but shiny metal walls and the controls that just would not work!

By now, Buddy Lassiter was scrambling clumsily to his feet, pointing repeatedly to his left ear, the one with the earplug from his phone. It was clear to Tariq in a split second that the former Governor couldn't save this deceased dictator's nephew from Tikrit.

At last, something clicked behind the elevator's control panel. Slowly, more slowly than Tariq might have wanted, the elevator doors began to slide quietly shut. The beggar's unintelligible screaming became even louder, followed by a low grunt, as he released the spear. For a split-second, time seemed to slow down for Tariq.

The spear hurtled through the air, straight toward Tariq's chest. Still looking frantically about, the young Iraqi leapt into the corner of the elevator closest to the thrower, hoping against hope to find some shelter from attack behind the left elevator door, as it edged slowly toward the center of the car. Tariq's glacially moving metal shield was growing larger and larger! With a resounding clank, the spear's iron head slammed into the elevator's back wall, just below where Tariq's belt level would have been, as the doors kept trying to slam shut.

Would the spear keep the doors far enough apart to prevent the elevator from moving? Tariq wheezed a wary sigh as the elevator began to hum, while its doors repeatedly clicked together, as if trying to dislodge some foreign material from its mouth. Looking up at the floor indicator, he was relieved to see "Main Concourse" wink out and "Parking Level 1," then "Parking Level 2" blink on. Trapped by the doors, the spear tip suddenly pointed downward as the elevator started to descend. Tariq heard a loud crack as the heavy elevator severed the spear's oaken shaft. He gritted his teeth and covered both ears to block out the jagged, screeching sound of the spear's broken edges grinding along the concrete wall of the elevator shaft. Then the remains of the spear handle dropped over the upper lip of the entrance to Parking Level 1, squeaked along the inside of the stainless-steel door to Parking Level 1 and then began to screech even louder and deeper on the concrete walls of the elevator shaft below.

As the elevator door finally slid open at the lower parking garage, Tariq held the ear-plug of his phone tightly in his left ear as he ran toward the waiting hover, trying repeatedly to blow his nose into an immaculate silk handkerchief. The hover's gull-winged door automatically opened to receive him.

"Where to boss," the cartoon face of the hover's autopilot grinned.

"Quickest way to Malone, New York, but first the nearest exit out of this mess and directly to Interstate 81," he bristled excitedly. "Wait! Open the door again! Here's my, err, colleague, now."

Lassiter puffed up to the idling hover, his face beet red from the unexpected exertion of running down two flights of stairs.

"How'd you get away from that idiot in the wheelchair?"

"No real...challenge...home-spuns...showed up...right after...you finally got...the elevator closed.   Here," he wheezed, "hang this cross off...the terminal...in front...where the watcher...can...see it."

Tariq hadn't seen one of the Covenant's crosses up close before.   Made of silver or perhaps highly polished chrome, this 6-inch tall cross looked much like any normal version he remembered from before the Covenant and the God Fearers came to power, except for what would be its eastern arm.   Like many other Christian crosses, Catholic, for example, this one was not an actual crucifix - there was no body on it.   But its three o'clock arm was bent up in the middle at a right angle, reminiscent of the Nazi symbol.   The young Muslim wondered what that adaptation was supposed to signify.

"Git that cross up front, Tariq!"

"What's the hurry?"

"We won't get past the watcher if you don't. Here comes the watcher's booth just down the end of this row."

Sure enough, in the darkness between their slowly moving hover and the ramp leading out of the lowest level of the airport, Tariq could just make out a blue glow in the distance, slowly growing in intensity as they drifted toward it on only minimum thrust. He leaned over the low partition in front of them to comply with Buddy's urgent directions, toward the grinning caricature of a driver in this autonomous vehicle. Stretching even further, Tariq swung a small loop of the cross's tiny link chain, trying to catch it on the electronic terminal's corner post. Clunk! Winding the chain up like a miniature bola, the young Iraqi tried to circle the metal post. Once, twice, three times. Each time, he almost lassoed his quarry, but no cigar.

"For Chrissake, Tariq! Give it to me. My arms are longer and you'll drop it."

"I know what I'm doing, Governor, if you please," Tariq shot back defensively.

Undeterred, Lassiter knew best. Like the political pro that he had been since the fourth grade, he effortlessly shouldered the Great Leader's favorite nephew aside and grabbed for the heavy cross with his powerful left hand.

"If you don't mind, Buddy!"

In the tussle, the object of their efforts slipped from Tariq's sweaty fingers and clunked loudly to the floor in front. He could instantly feel the blood rising to his face, scorched with embarrassment.

"So what ya gonna do, Mr. Moneybags?" the annoyed

Southerner taunted his minder.

"Since you're too PORKY to drag your butt over the partition, I'll just leap lightly over there and attach the precious cross right where this famous watcher can clearly see it, in all its distinctive glory," Tariq al-Tikriti retorted adroitly, hopping into the hover's front compartment and snapping the metal chain around the target post. "Now, what's so fucking important about this watcher person seeing that weird looking cross?"

"Ya'll don't get it, do you?"

"What do you mean, Governor?"

"Ah may not be the brightest star in the heavens, but ah know how these here Covenant folks operate. Just like most other bureaucrats. Very mechanical, matter-of-fact and extremely picky. Every question has a black or white answer only they know about. No one we're likely to run inta has even an ounce of discretion. Like them there folks checking documents back at the airport - they get specific instructions and aren't allowed to deviate from them even a bit. Check the box, go on your way. Come up with something one of them needs to think about and the system gets constipated. Could take a lifetime for whatever you want to move through the system. Show this guy up ahead one of his own crosses and he can check the box and let you go on your way. Then he can go back to sleep or recite verses of the Good Book from memory. But whatever he does, it won't involve gettin' in our face any longer. Get it?"

"I'm not sure it's necessary to be quite so insulting."

"Well, my man, you ain't seen nothin 'like you're gonna see if you so much as open your Hamilton-trained mouth once we get to this fellow just ahead standing under that there blue light. Like, just let me do ALL the talking, Tariq. I mean it!"

Tariq couldn't keep his eyes off what lay between them and the fresh air outside this dank parking garage. Like a malignant blue lily, the watcher's booth ahead sprouted squarely in the middle of a flat place at the bottom of a winding ramp leading up into the shadows of what must be the only exit to the outside and the world beyond. There was just room for one lane for traffic on either side of the booth, one for incoming and the other for exiting vehicles. A stout, black-and-white pole blocked the exit lane they would have to pass through. A sturdy black, iron hinge bolted the barrier pole firmly to a massive concrete block on the far, right side of the exit lane. The other end of the pole was attached to a rope that disappeared into the darkness above the guard's station. The other end of that rope hung out of that same cloud of gloom and was wound several times around a polished brass cleat on the near side of the booth in neat seaman's triple hitches, with no loose end visible.

The knot in Tariq's stomach tightened several turns as the booth's occupant came into view. Clearly, the young Iraqi had expected yet another rumpled home-spun. On close inspection, albeit from some distance, he was startled to see a tall, ramrod-straight officer clad in a tightly fitting naval blouse, accented by a neat vertical row of polished gold buttons that directed Tariq's attention, first to the man's gray handlebar mustache and then his piercing blue eyes. From the polished black leather belt, just above the edge of the booth, to the peak of his military officer's hat, set off by well-worn golden braid, everything about this man said, "I mean business!" And, partially hidden from Tariq's line of sight, what looked like a holstered pistol hung from the black leather belt. The dictator's treasured nephew looked nervously toward Buddy Lassiter, who grinned idiotically.

"What next, MR. EXPERT?"

"If you're talking to me, you arrogant little shit," Lassiter replied, "I'm going to just sit here on my oversized ass and see what kind of stuff you're really made of."

"What....?" Tariq gulped, beginning to perspire as the

hover glided closer and closer to the guard booth. "What if we get stopped? You'll get caught too."

"Maybe yes, maybe no. Remember, I spend a lot more time here than you do. You have no idea of the friends I've made."

"Hover, turn around and go back to where you picked us up!" Tariq al-Tikriti directed in his most authoritative tone.

"Don't ya'll do that Hover! That's even dumber than I expected, Tariq. There ain't another car anywhere near the guard booth. Like it or not, we're committed to go through that exit lane. Without a whole lot more fuss or bother."

The whirring of the hover's turbines slowed perceptibly and Tariq imagined he could hear gears grinding somewhere under the hover's hood.

"Now you did it, Buddy! These things freeze up when they get conflicting instructions. By the beard of Allah, you're definitely off the payroll if we get arrested here because of your insubordination."

"You wouldn't!"

"Not only that, but, if I have even one breath left when this whole mess is finished, I'll personally see to it that your bank account in Cyprus is vacuumed clean as a whistle before you can warble "Go Dawgs" even one more time. Now, tell me what to do, and make it snappy!"

"Tariq, y'all sure do know how to hurt a guy! I wouldn't leave you, er us, in the lurch...."

Carefully eyeing the guard station and its solitary occupant, Tariq glanced nervously around the vast dark spaces of the underground garage. As before, there were no other moving vehicles to be seen. Why was that?

"Hover, proceed toward the exit lane, slow speed" Tariq al-Tikriti whispered softly. As the craft began to smoothly accelerate, he fumbled in an inner pocket of his suit coat and handed Buddy a sheaf of important looking documents only partly concealed by a worn red leather case.

The Governor snatched the offering and slid toward the hover's left gull-winged door with no small amount of effort. He didn't notice the pair of light, almost invisible wires trailing noiselessly behind the crimson packet, back to the inner pocket of Tariq's suit jacket.

Pulling up a pace or two short of the guard station, the hovercraft slowed to a stop and automatically opened its left wing. Lassiter leaned through the open space, his best baby-kissing smile plastered on his jowly cheeks.

"Documents! Your papers, please," the guard demanded, his left hand extended, reminding Tariq ever so much like a carefully groomed Stasi border guard on the border checkpoint between West and East Germany before the Wall came down.

"Why how are y'all today, Colonel? Believe everything's here you need," Lassiter babbled, passing his identity card to the guard along with Tariq's documents.

In the hover's back seat, the young Iraqi bent over an oblong black metal box, to which the two wires were now firmly attached. As he slowly turned a small rheostat in the clockwise direction, the black box began to whine, louder and louder, until Tariq covered it with the tail of his suit jacket to muffle the sound.

"Yours I've seen recently, Governor. And, you know very well I'm a Commander, U.S. Navy, retired, or at least I was until the latest reorganization. But what's this mess?" the elder naval officer sniffed, pausing to flick an imaginary bit of lint from the shoulder of his blouse. He began to leaf through the collection of papers in the red leather folder.

"I'm sure as possible everything's in order, your Honor," Lassiter said.

In the shadows of the hover's back seat, Tariq took a

deep breath and pushed a solitary, glowing red button on the top of the oblong black box.

With a sharp crack, followed by the overbearing smell of ozone, the guard grabbed at his chest as if he'd been hit there with a sledgehammer. Buddy Lassiter jumped back, banging his head on the idling hover's raised gull-wing.

"Help me, help me," the guard gurgled from the sheet metal floor of the booth. "I can't breathe, please, please....I'll die if you don't call help," he pleaded more faintly.

Buddy pulled himself up the side of the guard booth and peered cautiously over the edge. His crisp uniform soiled beyond salvation, the retired naval officer lay huddled on the concrete, in a fetal position, gasping weakly for breath.

"Sorry, old man, but I gotta relieve you of that there hog leg," Buddy Lassiter said as he leaned far over the edge of the booth to slip the guard's weapon from its holster and unclip its lanyard. Looking around the deserted underground garage furtively, the Governor checked to make sure the gun's safety was engaged and then slipped it into one of his voluminous jacket pockets. "What the hell was that, Tariq?"

"Just a little portable capacitor I keep in reserve for special occasions. Flip up that barrier, Buddy, and let's get out of here."

"Yesssirrrr!" the big man replied, lustily raising the barrier, swinging it up into the gloom above them, as he collapsed heavily into the hover's back seat beside the smirking, young Iraqi.

"Hover, proceed as previously ordered. Maximum speed."

Spinning up of the hover turbines almost drowned out the crash of the heavy black-and-white pole, first on the forward housing, then smashing through the craft's windshield, showering both men with small bits of safety glass. By now, the hovercraft was already moving slowly away from the silent guard booth. The pole's third bounce cracked the rear window before dropping limply off onto the exit lane's oily pavement. A heavy clicking inside the hover's power compartment warned Tariq that each turbine rotation was now taking little bites out of its housing.

"My God, Buddy! Is there anything else you can do to hurt us?" he exclaimed angrily.

Lassiter quietly inspected the intricate stitching around the soles of his shiny brown loafers in detail as the hovercraft wheezed up the inclined ramp toward the nearby interstate highway, dripping oil and trailing an ever-so-faint cloud of gray smoke.

Where's my Client?

Tiller extender in his left hand, line to the vessel's main sheet in his right, David Garvey leaned far backwards, almost dipping the back of his head into the choppy waters of the Long Island Sound whizzing under his trim Ideal 18. He was on a starboard tack toward the Green's Ledge Light. Although the afternoon was bright and sunny, with only a few fleecy clouds, he couldn't quite escape the pull of his early morning dream.

Jarred awake by the screeching of heavy metal wheels, he'd looked nervously around the darkened train car, wondering where he was. Dirty clothing hanging from the overhead bins swayed with the lurching motion of the rumbling train. Ship of the dead, he remembered thinking to himself - every seat in the compartment filled to overflowing but every other passenger either asleep or worse. He shivered, trying to figure out what was going on. On the adjacent track, another long string of passenger cars, going in the same direction, seemed glued to David's train. But the interior of the other train looked like a cavernous, polished marble railroad station, entirely empty of people except for one young girl walking quickly across

Angrily blasting its steam whistle, a black-and-red McAllister tugboat with a fully loaded garbage barge in tow, towered over the tiny sailboat, dead ahead in the choppy waters. The huge vessel had finally riveted David Garvey's attention. The tug was so close David could feel the thumping of her diesel engines through the cold seawater surrounding his little vessel.

"Port your helm," David Garvey whispered gravely to himself as he looked quickly over his left shoulder before pushing the wooden tiller sharply away from him. As the

Ideal came about almost instantaneously, David slipped behind the tiller, carefully keeping his grip on the main sail, now in his left hand. His open bottle of Dogfish Head 90 IPA fell onto the deck at David's feet, gurgling into the gutter. "Shit," David belched and kicked the dripping bottle out of sight under the gunwale.

After the turn, his sailboat was pointing toward the decaying remains of the long-gone ferry piers near Bayley Beach, once the site of an amusement park at the end of the old trolley line to Rowayton from the center of the City of Norwalk, Connecticut. Leaning back against the starboard gunwale to ponder what to do about his missing client and cousin thrice removed, David let the main out slowly until the bumping of waves against the hull faded away. The bright sun and fresh salt air cleared his head, helping him begin to think creatively about the problem at hand.

Poor cousin Lea - caught up in one of those special religious courts authorized by a pandering Congress, politicians anxious to extend the reach of earmarks and other pork beyond what even the sleaziest, previous hacks in the Deep State could have possibly imagined. The result of decades of agitation by liberals and those further left anxious to impose their narrow views on the rest of North American society: the Hate Speech Act. It evoked distant memories of the Spanish Inquisition, although it did not yet contain provisions for the auto-dé-fa. In effect, the so-called Hate Speech Act allowed church leaders of the "God-fearing" variety to set the agenda of a new court system, to rule on questions related to the contents of the Good Book, which they thought relevant to almost every sort of daily activity. As the result of still another amendment to a weakened Constitution, passed by a thin margin in a non-election year, the Religious Respect Act, at least according to its proponents, covered just about every subject of interest to ordinary citizens. Fortunately, in Lea's case, as the result of sloppy drafting by its sponsors, the jurisdiction of the new courts was concurrent with the Federal courts. In other words, there might be some way to get a second bite at the apple of Lea's transportation to Penal Colony 627.

David wiggled his index finger in the floating holographic image of the scales of justice projected from the Ideal's on-board computer, snug in its watertight case against the nearby main mast. A library menu appeared in the air, faintly eclipsing the rocky Connecticut shoreline in the distance. "*Let s see,*" he thought to himself; "*let s take a look at how the right of habeas corpus plays out in the face of decisions of the new religious courts.*" He entered the search pattern, with instructions to deliver a copy to his home computer, and scanned the horizon once more, his nimble brain rapidly sifting through several open issues at the same time.

A small speck appeared in the center of the floating image his holographic computer screen. As it grew like a rapidly inflating balloon, all of the surrounding text was pushed aside, squeezed into the screen's margins until the words became unreadable. In a split second, a lush, red curtain filled the entire holographic screen. Without warning, a glistening scimitar blade slashed through the red curtain and sliced it into many pieces. All the pieces floated to the bottom of the computer screen, where every letter contained in David's legal research pattern joined them. Watching the shards of fabric fade from crimson into a duller shade of red, David Garvey began to hear sounds of marching feet, terse commands in Arabic and military music heavily laden with at least three different types of brass horns. The fabric remnants melted into a bloody pool. One command rang out, the Arabic word David knew to be "halt!" In the parade-ground hush that followed, the faint sound of laughter was barely audible but grew louder and louder, until it because almost hideous.

"We're watching you, David Garvey," the young Arab cackled from somewhere in the ether. "You won't get away so easily this time!"

David Garvey watched in horror as his computer went dark. Above the sound of waves lapping softly against the Ideal 18's hull, the young lawyer heard his hard drive spinning to a halt. The knot in David's stomach tightened - the voice he had just heard was chillingly familiar.

The Great Writ

As Tariq al-Tikriti's hover finally limped out of the bowels of Parking Level 2 at Syracuse International Airport, David Garvey was ducking under a dripping yellow and orange umbrella crowding the corner where Pearl Street runs west into Foley Square. Just up the street from the newer Federal Courthouse in Manhattan and around the corner from City Hall. Edgie Flens looked up warily at the young lawyer from his game of checkers with five soy dogs and as many soy burgers on the grease-spattered grill.

"Got a case on this morning, Mr. Garvey?" the vendor asked, leaning his corroded spatula against an open tin of Spanish olive oil and rubbing both hands slowly with a badly stained green apron.

"Could be, Edgie. Anybody been asking about me?"

The sidewalk chef nervously scanned the rain-soaked plaza before answering.

"Ya know, I could get in trouble, just talking to you," he said, rubbing his right shoulder thoughtfully and motioning slightly with his chin toward the roof of the newly renovated Supreme Court building at 60 Centre Street behind them.

"Why's that, Edgie?"

"People 'fraid a you since that German bank case. Like, some say you unplugged Judge Garcia's clerk, permanently. And then there's that home-spun hangin 'with the gargoyle on the roof of 60 Centre. Word has it you been steppin 'on Covenant toes, Mr. Garvey."

"Very interesting, Edgie. You know the story on the Covenant? Most people don't. It's portrayed as an organization to protect religious rights and so very prayerful but actually it's a contractor for the government. Manages the government's concentration camps for political and religious dissidents and the intake systems for it while keeping the religious right in line. By the way, heard anything about a fix being in on Judge Chu?"

"Generally or your case in particular?" Flens asked.

"Whatever you've heard. Anything that might lead me to wonder whether someone has a thumb on Judge Chu's scales of justice."

"Well, I know Judge Chu's in Room 4C today, if that's any help. Like, you probably know, Judge Chu gave all the right answers on the Covenant screening test before she got confirmed by the U.S. Senate as a Federal judge. Probably not that hard when ya know all the questions and answers before the test. I know she's supposed to have lifetime tenure, but the last impeachment of one of the Federal judges here because of what the Covenant considered an objectionable Twitter feed has most likely got 'em all worried, not to even mention his prior writings. And at least a couple of Federal judges or nominees were judges in state court before, so there may be opinions to scrutinize. Can't afford to ruffle the feathers of any noisy group, and Covenant's noisier than most. You told me once about the Earl Warren story. Think you said Eisenhower nominated him to be Chief Justice of the Supreme Court based on his conservative record as a three-term Governor of California, then he turned real liberal and wrote the majority opinion in <u>Miranda v. Arizona.</u> That decision guarantees people under arrest the right to lawyers and that he wrote some other very liberal opinions. Given he turned tail on Reagan, his promoter, Reagan might have wished to have him impeached. Lots of folks like the Covenant don't want that to ever happen again, straying from the ideology that got judges confirmed. But no way to impeach little ole me - I just sell dogs and burgers."

"Sure, Edgie. Of course," David replied, making a point of trying to spot the home-spun on the roof of the state court building as he turned down the street toward the modern

Federal courthouse. David Garvey couldn't imagine why he deserved serious Covenant attention, even if he was trying to get one of its political prisoners out of distant foreign incarceration. Funny thing, he thought to himself, I could probably name ten lawyers right here in Manhattan that regularly kick sand in the Covenant's righteous face, and no one's giving them any trouble at all. What's so special about Lea Holderness? Aside from that, what possible interest could I be to the 'God Fearers'"?

A few minutes later, as David Garvey emerged from a burnished chrome elevator on the 4th Floor of the newest Southern District Courthouse, the strong smell of floor polish caught his attention. He looked up and down the gleaming marble corridor, trying to figure out the direction of Judge Chu's assigned courtroom of the day. *Try to remember what you were just told*, the older lawyer thought to himself, *slow down, relax, remember what the security guard said to you downstairs when she handed you the electronic pass. That s better!* It was coming back to him: third door panel on the left, after a right out of the elevator. Just as they whispered shut, David Garvey jumped out of the path of the closing elevator doors. In this courthouse, elevators were programmed to take passengers to only one floor. If David hadn't escaped this elevator at Judge Chu's floor, he would have had to start all over again in the courthouse lobby.

Far down the long, polished corridor, two figures caught his eye. Although the two were walking slowly in his direction, they were still a considerable distance away. Without his glasses, David Garvey could only make out their basic shapes and colors - a hefty gray-clad woman with her arm around the shoulders of a diminutive female dressed in a long, black robe. Their heads were close together. As David watched with increasing interest, the pair stopped in front of the third door panel on his left, the home-spun hanging back slightly as the other figure passed the right sleeve of her ebony robe past the chamber's doorjamb. The panel slid open without a sound. Since David Garvey was drawing closer and closer to the two women, he couldn't miss the home-spun's arm around the shoulder of her companion. Deep in conversation, the two stepped through the opening in the highly polished wall, before the panel slid firmly shut behind them. "*What is going on here?*", the lawyer wondered to himself, a sinking feeling beginning to nibble away at his otherwise confident demeanor.

Pausing to adjust the knot of his navy-blue, silk bow tie in the marble mirror that was the wall of the corridor, David Garvey took a deep breath, slowly exhaled and waved his plastic electronic pass methodically over the holographic field of the chamber's concealed terminal. A section of the stone wall slid noiselessly to one side, revealing a windowless, but well-appointed anteroom carpeted with a thick forest-green pile rug. As soon as he stepped inside, the panel quickly slid shut and clicked faintly behind him.

Two women sat at the far side of the round birch conference table - one wearing flowing, black robes, probably covering some sort of bulletproof vest, the other a simple, gray home-spun floor-length dress. Both of the home-spun's hands covered her companion's right hand. Their heads were bowed. Startled by the newcomer, both women looked up. "Amen," whispered the gray, home-spun dress, whom David took to be his adversary. The black-robed woman jumped up and beckoned David Garvey toward the circular table, directing his attention toward a glowing holographic image of some court papers in the center of the work surface. *"Let me guess, I ll bet the one in the black choir gown is the judge"* passed through his mind, but he was struck with the similarity of the room and the furniture to another case, another time in his life. *"Poor Judge Fischbein, beaten to death in his own courtroom in the same courthouse by an angry sumo wrestler, and I watched it happen!"*

"Judge Chu," he ventured, extending a hand toward the jurist, receiving a limp, dish-rag response. "I'm David

Garvey. My firm, Garvey, Stahl, represents Lea Holderness in this proceeding."

"Please be seated, Mr. Garvey. This is Sister Cynthia, Righteous Counsel at the Covenant's regional headquarters here in Manhattan. This should be very short. Sister Cynthia has already familiarized me with the facts and law of the case."

"Excuse me, Judge Chu. But don't I get a chance to speak?"

"That won't be necessary, Mr. Garvey," the judge ventured, avoiding his glare. "You've got a lot of explaining to do."

"Pardon me, your Honor, but don't I get a chance to tell my side. Wasn't that why you called me down here for this conference."

"Don't get smart with me, Mr. Garvey! The facts are the facts. Doesn't matter where I get them as long as they're correct. Sister Cynthia is very reliable and I have no reason to doubt her word. Do you doubt her word?"

"Your Honor," David Garvey stepped gingerly," my opponent may be quite reliable, but she's an advocate for the Covenant, which is holding my client, hardly an independent source of information. By the way, your Honor, I checked the records downstairs; this person, if her name really is Cynthia Forthright as stated in the papers, is not admitted to practice before this Court."

"Is that true Cynthia?" the judge asked quietly.

"We all have so much of the Lord's work to do, your Honor. We can't be expected to get held up by these minor administrative procedures. I'm admitted to practice in the Eastern District of Missouri. That ought to be enough."

"Your Honor," David jumped in, sensing an opening, "she also failed to complete mandatory pro bono work on behalf of people seeking asylum from persecution for violating China's one child policy. Here's a certificate documenting my own work on that important cause."

Her face darkening, the judge received a tiny disk from the young lawyer, as he tried to suppress a slight grin.

"What's going on here, Sister Cynthia?" she demanded sharply, pushing a lock of straight black hair behind her right ear. "While I'm wholly sympathetic to your point of view, you aren't giving me much to work with!"

"Your Honor," David Garvey interjected, "I really must object to the Court's apparent lack of neutrality! I, for one, would never use the word, but some in this situation might be thinking in terms of bias or prejudice."

As those words slipped from his lips, David knew he had overplayed his hand.

"Mr. Garvey," the jurist intoned, "your disrespect for this Court is exceeded only by the weakness of the claim advanced on behalf of your client. Let's talk about Sister Cynthia's motion to impose sanctions on you for violating Rule 11. Your papers are demonstrably at odds with the truth, and you must pay for wasting the Court's time, and the scarce time and resources of the Covenant and its lawyers."

"I've seen no Rule 11 papers, your Honor. What are you talking about?"

"I understand from Sister Cynthia that your habeas corpus petition is wholly bogus..."

"Excuse me, your Honor, I fully expected the Covenant to argue it is not my client's jailer. The Covenant always claims it doesn't control the administration of Penal Colony 627, but that argument is entirely fictitious..."

"Don't interrupt me, counselor," Judge Chu spat back. "Your habeas corpus claim falls flat on its face if the Covenant does not have custody of your client. Sister Cynthia tells me, whether or not the Covenant should be considered the administrator of Penal Colony 627, that Lea Holderness escaped from that facility more than a few weeks ago. We'll now consider the Covenant's motion for sanctions against you and your firm, for persisting in a habeas corpus proceeding when the prisoner was no longer in, what we assume for purposes of the Rule 11 motion only, the custody of the Covenant. What amount of sanctions did you have in mind, Cynthia?"

David Garvey grabbed the edge of the table for support as he sank weakly into one of the nearby sliding chairs. Was it true? How did Lea get out? Where is she now?

"Your Honor," he ventured faintly, "this is entirely new information to me. My petition was based on secondary information, since the Covenant refuses to publish its penal colony prisoner inventories, in violation of all applicable Federal regulations, I might add. If my client is, in fact, no longer imprisoned at Penal Colony 627, I will, of course, withdraw my habeas corpus petition."

"I'm not sure that fixes the Rule 11 issue," the judge continued. "I'll expect a brief on my holo by close of business today, Mr. Garvey. And don't be late with it!"

With a tentative glance at his opponent, Judge Chu swept from the room, leaving David Garvey alone with a smirking Sister Cynthia. He was steaming.

Once in the silence of her chambers, Judge Chu allowed herself a weary sigh. She carefully extracted a faded and cracked photograph from an inside pocket of the sleeve of her voluminous, black robe. Holding it up to the gray outside light of another storm-filled day in lower Manhattan, the judge could barely make out the features of a man she knew to be her husband. Her nightmare was coming true! It had been so long since she had touched his face with hers, she was beginning to forget what he looked or smelled like. The judge knew she had a job to do, that she must follow orders, but knowing that her own husband was living out his golden years in one of the Covenant's penal colonies pushed her almost beyond the limit. And, she knew David Garvey had not the slightest inkling of how much she sympathized with his cause or how little help she could be to him.

Memorial Day

Lea cautiously stepped out of the narrow shop where Drakulič built creative painting and picture frames for tourists and residents of Camden, Maine and surrounding communities. She looked up and down the crowded sidewalk suspiciously but then basked in the clear blue skies and warm breezes from the Atlantic Ocean. Lea marveled at the excited crowd around her, some wearing masks and many waving little American flags, although she looked unobtrusively for surveillance cameras up and down the street. The happy sight reminded her of home and the many holidays she had enjoyed with both of her parents before Clara was born long ago. She almost cried when a little girl nearby in a red-and-blue striped summer dress asked: "Would you like an American flag?" and offered her one.

Lea took a deep breath, looked around her and then toward the heavens, and said to herself," *Thank you, God, for helping me escape from that awful prison colony, for being with me during the long trip back to America. Please be with me as I head toward Northern New York to free Clara from the Lost League and begin my work for the Movement. But thank you for this beautiful day and weather. In Christ s name, I pray, Amen.*"

Propped up by nearly identical VA-issued aluminum canes, two bent, old men in dark, blue uniforms leaned over to salute a headless gray granite statue of a Union Army rifleman as the mournful sound of "Taps" echoed down the red brick facades of downtown Camden's trendy shops. Ian Drakulič looked suspiciously up and down Camden's main thoroughfare, the noises of the holiday crowd fueling his concern. "*Bad enough,*" the Serb thought to himself, "*the fog had been thick off Ocier Point while I bobbed up and down in the low swells in what could only be described as a medium-sized whaleboat, waiting for the small Liberian freighter in those interminable hours just before dawn when a breeze came up and blew away the mist.*"

Now, Drakulič, Lea, Thrasher, and Willy were distracted by the sounds of the beginnings of a parade in the distance as it moved up High Street toward them. The parade was led by an American Legion Drum and Bugle Corp., a small but impressive unit with three types of bugles (piccolo, tenor, and bass, providing three-part harmony) and the staccato cadence of snare drums, punctuated by thumping of tenor drums, all proceeding at a measured but rapid pace. Lea recognized its tune as "Over the Rainbow," in an energized beat unlike the usual, soft rendition of that tune, recalling Dorothy in the "Wizard of Oz" movie, played by Judy Garland. Perhaps competing themes of hope and yearning intended by the author of "Wizard of Oz," L. Frank Baum, and in his other books. The smartly dressed drum and bugle corps was followed by a troop of Boy Scouts, a den of Cub Scouts and a troop of Girl Scouts, all marching with American and unit flags along with Scout leaders, parents and friends. They were followed by a variety of floats and many different restored antique automobiles including a fully restored 1939 four-door, black Chevrolet plus local politicians lounging in open, expensive convertibles, all slowly on the way toward the cemetery on top of Mt. Batty.

Just then, the giant main mast of the windjammer Claudius French, putting to sea on the morning tide, seemed to pause as it passed behind the statue's rifle barrel at the Conway Memorial across the street from Drakulič's frame shop. For what seemed like a very long moment, the dark blue flag of the State of Maine atop the French's main mast appeared to sprout from the stone barrel of the Civil War breechloader. The mast seemed parallel to the rusted metal rod sticking out of the shards of the Union soldier's granite neck, the result of recent campaigns to hide and rewrite American history and the surging violence of imported and paid BLM and Antifa rioters, even in this quaint seaside village, far from Eastern urban centers. And just as the last note of "Taps" blared from the local school band youngster's battered silver coronet at that! *Could only be a terrible omen,"* Drakulič thought!

Just on a foggy day last week, the young Serbian shopkeeper had taken his lunch break, eating a ham and cheese sandwich while sitting at the base of that statue, relaxing on the soft green grass. "In Memory of Those Who Made the Ultimate Sacrifice During the Great Rebellion of 1861-65," the inscription said. Drakulič wondered to himself: *Could the Union Army rifleman of so long ago have understood the rebellion now underway in the so-called United States he had fought so fiercely to defend? Or how many Mainers had died to topple slavery but whose descendants were being plagued with laws granting reparations to all blacks, even those who had emigrated from Africa in recent years? What about whites who had perished in that war to abolish American slavery while slavery continues around the world today, even in many countries ruled by blacks? And what about the fellow who is half black and half white? Does he have to pay reparations to himself?"*

Even having in mind Drakulič had pretended to be a refugee Kosovar Albanian, in order to enter America illegally and apply for asylum (even if the current administration could be bothered with vetting immigrants, few knew the difference between Serbs and Kosovo Albanians), Ian Drakulič wasn't sure why the trio he'd ferried ashore from the Liberian freighter made him so nervous. Each of his three charges was now dressed like the other sheep in the required, gray home-spun summer wear. Showered and shaved, the two males looked not altogether different from other tourists spending a quiet holiday weekend away from the urban jungles of the Greater Northeast. The woman, on the other hand, was definitely different - well-educated and alert - she had obviously noticed the fingertips missing from the last two fingers of his left hand when they first met, the result of gang violence in his homeland. Drakulič couldn't imagine why it was necessary for her to sneak back into her own country, much less with these two rough-hewn and rude specimens. And yet there was a sharpness about her, as if she just might cut your throat when your back was turned. As Drakulič looked at Lea out of the corner of his eye, his head cleverly inclined slightly in another direction, he could tell she was carefully watching Thrasher, the meaner one of the two males.

"Time to go!" Drakulič announced. "Your bus is leaving in only fifteen minutes."

Each shouldering a nondescript black canvas bag, the

three travelers followed Drakulič wearily toward the shop's front door and padded up its cut slate steps to pick up the sandwiches and drinks he had recently purchased for them from a nearby delicatessen. Then all four stepped back onto the crowded sidewalk, carefully checking up, down and across High Street. Lea tried to hang back as far as she could without arousing suspicion as the group walked down High Street toward Camden National Bank at the center of town, through the teeming crowd of excited parade spectators. Further in front, the younger minder, Willy, dodged parking meters and parked cars as he hurried to keep up with the tall and lanky Drakulič, who was walking in the middle of the sidewalk. Thrasher strode along behind, out of Drakulič's field of vision, but warily scanning the storefronts on both sides of the street. Somewhere behind them, a soothing, brass bell chimed from a high place. Lea looked around to see where that pleasing sound might be coming from. A slender, white church steeple, stark against the cloudless, blue sky, caught her attention. Two, three, four... Willy was also listening to the tolling of the bell. First leaning against the shiny, lime fender of a fully restored Thunderbird convertible then wandering playfully out into the nearly empty street, Willy reveled in the summer sights and sounds of this tidy Maine Mid-Seacoast little town. He was delighted to at last be walking on dry land and breathing clean air. Six, seven, eight...

Its transmission groaning, a bulky Seacoast Refinery heating oil truck, sporting a recent, beige paint job intended to recapture some of its early 50's elegance, lumbered around the corner in front of a bank. The truck turned down High Street toward Drakulič and his three charges and the approaching units of the Memorial Day parade. The oil delivery truck rolled slowly down the street's considerable incline, its engine racing almost uncontrollably, its clutch apparently slipping and its brakes screeching. The truck's driver was hidden deep in the shadows of its high cab. With a noisy grinding of its gears, the vehicle abruptly picked up speed, toward Lea and her fellow travelers. Lea would always remember how the driver's phantom arms seemed to reach out of the cab's dark recesses, ebony gloves tightly gripping the shiny, plastic steering wheel. Nine, ten...

Was it the whine of the truck's screaming transmission, forced beyond its limits, or the squeal of metal as the careening truck ripped off the left fender of a battered, red jeep parked on the west side of High Street that caught poor Willy's attention? Lea would never know. Something made Willy aware of the beige oil truck only at the last second, as it hurtled toward him over the shrinking bit of pavement between them, its overdriven engine protesting even in fifth gear. The truck's high, steel-rail bumper smashed Willy sideways into the highly polished left front fender of the lime Thunderbird an instant before Willy and the sport car became one. The explosive shock rammed the mangled mass of flesh and metal up and over a large, ugly Lexus Mucho Macho sports utility vehicle. In a split second, the screeching carcasses obliterated a bright, red fire hydrant before coming to rest against the base of an antique streetlight. A high-pressure fountain of water leaped from the hydrant's remains. Jarred from its perch halfway up the light post by the sharp impact, a tiny American flag dropped into a growing pool of water, blood and home heating oil in the center of High Street. Eleven, twelve. High noon on Memorial Day in Camden, Maine.

Lea felt a small electric shock at the base of her skull at the exact moment Willy was crushed by the careening oil truck. *Is this my last moment?* she wondered, so frightened no sound would come out of her open mouth. With both hands over her ears, as if to somehow contain the explosion to come, she looked anxiously about for Thrasher, trying to decide whether to try to make her escape.

Thrasher glowered at her from the far edge of the gathering crowd, now focused on what was left of the accident rather than the parade, now stopped and wondering what was happening. As if to taunt her, Thrasher raised the Execution Box high above his head, pointed it in her direction and, laughing insanely, pushed the button. Lea's head screamed! The shock was so severe she could taste the gold and silver in her fillings more strongly than ever before. She collapsed into the fetal position on the sidewalk, holding her throbbing head. As Lea slipped in and out of unconsciousness, a lightly brown-skinned man in gray home-spun clothing leaned over her trembling body. *"At least this won t take very long,"* she thought as his intense black eyes swam in the approaching darkness and then faded away.

A Friend Indeed

As the humming inside Lea's head faded away, she opened her eyes. Drakulič was leaning over her with a warm smile as she lay on the floor of the frame shop. "No sense to bring you here on behalf of Movement and then let you die at the hands of that thug," he said. "I had to hit Thrasher and lock him in the closet in my store before your head exploded," he continued. "Let's get you to one of Movement's good doctors to remove the bomb from the back of your neck – probably should seal it into a block of concrete with a device Thrasher is carrying to control you and dump the entire package in the ocean. I hope he doesn't get out of that closet." The young refugee was interrupted by a loud crash as the closet door shattered, and Thrasher stormed through what had been half of the door into the tiny shop and yelled," *Stay here; I'm going to find what s left of Willy and grab the pool of money he was carrying for me!*" Thrasher quickly lunged out onto the sidewalk in front of the frame shop, dodging agitated and confused spectators milling around the remains of the accident.

"Never was introduced to you," Drakulič said softly to Lea. "You only know me as Ian Drakulič, refugee who met you at edge of ocean and brought you here to my business and let you rest. I'll help you any way I can. Simpler if you call me "Drak" instead of Drakulič if you need to introduce me to other Americans. And, of course, you can also call me "Drak." I'm sure my mother wouldn't mind, if she be still alive."

They both turned as Thrasher burst into the small shop, carrying a bloody money belt. "Forget about the bus. We need a car to get moving toward Lea's assigned area in Northern New York. We're going to look in the lot behind these stores while people are watching whatever is happening out on the street." In the background, the trio could hear the sirens of police cars and ambulances as well as the honking of the fire trucks that always seemed to accompany ambulances.

Lea and Drak followed Thrasher out the back door of the frame shop. It opened onto a lengthy but narrow parking lot which paralleled the back of the row of shops facing High Street, filled with many cars but mostly empty of people. Thrasher immediately walked toward a four-door, black Honda, probably several years old, with Maine license and a University of Maine, Orono sticker on its back bumper along with a Black Lives Matter decal. "*Perfect*," Lea thought. Thrasher had brought a stiff but thin metal ruler with him from the flat, working desk inside the frame shop; the desk looked like it had been acquired from Good Will or a dump. He was about to slip the metal strip into the gap between driver's side window and the door frame of the Honda when he noticed it was unlocked. "Finally, a break," he muttered.

"You two watch for people while I look for another set of plates," he barked, removing a red, Swiss Army knife with its several sets of screwdrivers from his front pants pocket and flipping open one of the screwdrivers. He unscrewed the Honda's front and back license plates then glanced around the parking lot, stopping at a nearby rusty, pickup truck with Maine plates. But then he remembered that many states have different types of plates for small pickup trucks and personal vehicles. Thrasher looked further down the row of parked cars and spotted an elderly, dark green Buick and swapped its plates for those taken from the Honda. As an added precaution, he used the metal ruler to open the Buick's passenger side door and flipped open its glove compartment by merely turning its handle. Thrasher quickly leafed through papers in the Buick's glove compartment and grabbed its vehicle registration, smoothly closed the Buick's glove compartment and its passenger door. He ran to the Honda, added the Buick's plates to its front and back license plate holders and jumped into its driver's seat, sliding the Buick's registration papers into the Honda's glove compartment.

"Unless I can find this car's keys somewhere, I'll have to hot-wire the ignition," he announced. After looking behind the car's visor and feeling under the driver's seat without finding anything, he began prying the ignition from its place on the right side of the vehicle's steering column. Thrasher continued his attempt to hot-wire the Honda's ignition system and finally twisted two of the three ignition wires together, jumping from a slight jolt from the hot wire before dropping it away from his feet like a hot potato. The Honda's engine rolled over and the air conditioning automatically came on. Thrasher loudly announced: "Good news! The gas tank is ¾ full."

He opened the driver's side door to slide out and traded places with Lea, who had been carefully watching how her remaining minder had connected two of the three ignition leads. Then Thrasher climbed into the back seat behind her, pushing several plastic children's toys and a toy bear to the floor on the other side of the back seat.

"Drakulič, you treacherous asshole! Tell Lea how to get out to a major highway toward Boston. And if you ever try anything like locking me in that closet again, I'll do something that will make your voice a lot higher or worse," Thrasher ordered, pointing to Drak's throat with a long, silver knife. Drak quietly slipped into the right passenger seat in the back with his feet in the pile of multi-colored plastic toys while leaning as far away from Thrasher as possible.

"All aboard! Lea, you drive. I'm sitting behind you, and Drakulič will quietly sit on my right. You know what will happen if either of you don't follow my instructions," he promised, leaning forward to wave the Execution Box in front of her face.

Drak leaned forward and pointed toward the north end of the parking lot. "There's an exit on your right. Take left out of parking lot. You then be on High Street where everyone is trying to figure out what to do about oil truck crash. High Street is later Elm Street but they both US Route 1 pointing south toward Boston," Drak advised. "Route 1 take us into center of Rockport, also in Maine. You'll see a Subway sandwich shop on right after a while," Drakulič continued. "Maybe we can get something to eat after these tiny sandwiches run out. It's already a long day and will be longer."

"No," Thrasher spit out. "Too much ground to cover. But stay just below the speed limit."

The Honda rolled through the Maine countryside and small towns until Drak pointed Lea to two lanes on the right to merge onto I-295 south toward Portland and Freeport. Later, at Drak's suggestion, Lea guided the Honda off at Exit 11 to merge onto Falmouth Spur, where she had to slow down further to punch a button on a toll ticket machine with a knuckle of her right hand, thankfully avoiding any interaction with any human attendant or leaving any fingerprints. A little over three miles later, she took a left exit onto I-95 South toward Portland and Kittery, Maine. Miles later, she put her open right hand back over the two front seats toward the Honda's back seat. She said: "I need money for the tolls coming up. The first will be when we take the next exit." Thrasher reluctantly passed her two bloodied ten-dollar bills and several quarters over the top of the driver's seat.

From summer vacations in Kittery, Maine, with her mother and father, Lea knew to take Exit 19 for Maine Route 9, to cut off a corner and take Salmon Falls and Whitehall Roads into Rochester, New Hampshire, the "Live Free or Die" state, a motto coined in 1809 by a Revolutionary War general. She remembered that people were living in the woods beside the highway in huts made of garbage bags alongside the road the trio was traveling – a "benefit" of the freedom residents of New Hampshire were expected to enjoy with its low taxes and meager services. While still in Drak's frame shop, Lea had researched on the Internet places in the Rochester area offering free food and shelter, the most prominent being the Congregational Church in the center of Rochester itself, recognizable by its large, multi-colored LGBTQ+ banners and flags. Lea carefully parked the Honda near the concrete curb across the street from the Congregational Church and disconnected what remained of Thrasher's artistic hot-wiring of its ignition circuitry. The weary trio walked toward the freshly painted white building, bringing with them only their black bags. Along the way, Lea looked at the row of electric poles on the church's side of the street and noticed what appeared to be a pair of cameras pointing up and down the main street. Happy to be getting slightly closer to her home in Northern New York, she resisted the temptation to stick out her tongue at both cameras and looked at the ground to minimize the chance of her images being captured.

Under the Shade of the
New LBTQ+ Banner

After a restless night, the young woman, from her sweat-stained spot on the dingy, fuscia futon, Lea watched faint stars fade from the summer sky as morning crept over the solitary Congregational Church on Rochester's main street with multi-colored banners and a BLM flag flying from its pair of white flagpoles. It seemed like only a few minutes ago that she had stumbled into this plain white church where the travelers had found overnight refuge from the beastly summer heat, long after its many other "clients" had gone to sleep. Jammed between the plaster-board wall of a utility room outside the Church's main meeting hall and the intermittently snoring Thrasher, she watched the new day blossom over central New England through a narrow Plexiglas skylight in the ceiling of her closet. Lea allowed only her eyes to follow a dragon-shaped cloud of fluffy cumulus floating across the gray, then deep, blue sky directly above this "woke" house of God. She absently worried the magic necklace, praying God would grant her fervent wish to be free of its threat.

All around her, the sound of deep breathing and some

restless stirrings as others in the larger room at her feet ascended slowly from the depths of sleep. Sounds of birds chirping outside heralded the new day. For a moment, Lea thought she heard a vireo's call.

Time to collect her thoughts, she reminded herself. Time to plan for the opportunities of another newborn day. A quiet moment to pray for strength and deliverance, before the man beside her, who now called himself her husband, awoke to torment her anew. A thick golden ring, the one Thrasher had jammed over the knuckle of the third finger of her right hand until she wept, was meant to reflect normality and ease their travel west. Lea fantasized, through gritted teeth, about Thrasher's date with destiny which was surely speeding toward him like a runaway train. She shivered, remembering sadly the freedom she'd never appreciated until it had disappeared under that hooded judge's gavel.

"Please, God in Heaven, if you will ever let me savor just one truly free breath, I'll never ever take your grace for granted again. Amen."

But then, reality intruded and Lea shuddered with fear at what might happen next while she still bore the bomb in the back of her neck. She felt the stitches at the base of her skull, now a mass of scar tissue. Lea wasn't sure where Thrasher was taking her but she had no doubt someone from the Movement would be following them. They seemed to be heading in the general direction of New York or maybe toward the newly minted State of Columbia, the old age home of a weakened Federal government, barricaded behind layers upon layers of increasingly impotent bureaucracies and armed troops. She'd have to spring her trap before anyone from Thrasher's pack caught up with them, so they'd have no protection from her wrath.

Double doors bumped open against the flimsy wall of Lea's makeshift bedroom. Her head down, an obese woman with no visible teeth struggled to thread a cantankerous aluminum cart through the swinging doors. One of its gelatinous rubber wheels stuck momentarily in the doorjamb. Steaming amber liquid sloshed over the rim of an industrial-sized metal cauldron, then dribbled onto the floor as she tried angrily to wrestle the balky cart into the quiet room.

"Gawd damn it! Why can't someone fix this fuckin' cracked floah?" broke the silence as Maude Buckland fell hard on her left knee, with a crash that awakened anyone still slumbering. Sprawled awkwardly in the growing pool of slippery soup on the polished, wooden floor outside Lea's door, Maude wiped beads of sweat from her forehead with the back of a latex-gloved hand. "Free food for these free loadahs," she grumbled to herself. "Why do I have to get up at the crack of dawn to fix this slop for these gawd-damn troublemakahs?" Maude looked down, flicked a greasy glob of carrot peels from what used to be a faded nylon stocking covering her knee, and struggled to regain her footing.

"Reveille, you loozahs! Time ta staht the new day! Drop ya cocks and grab ya socks, like my deah old Navy Chief Torpedoman fathah used ta say. Come take a bowl 'cause I only go around once...."

Lea watched as the disheveled crowd in the Church meeting hall crept out of their piles of rags like so many rodents, to swarm around the dripping cauldron of greasy soup, pushing and shoving. As distasteful as the idea seemed, she knew nothing good would happen today if her growling stomach stayed empty.

She looked around the narrow closet where they had spent the night. A dirty mop and pail, a five-gallon drum of floor wax, a heavy-duty floor polisher, three brooms, two industrial grade extension cords, one connecting the polisher to a wall socket and the desiccated remains of two sandwiches, probably left behind by some former tenant of the closet. On the floor outside Lea and Thrasher's abode, Drak slept on. Lea looked over the contents of the closet again, this time more closely, then nervously scanned the milling breakfast crew outside. Maude Buckland had fallen again. Her customers were helping themselves to anything they could grab and run away with as the poor woman struggled to get up.

A sudden calm enveloped Lea. Her attention was drawn back to the large, heavy, circular floor polisher. Its three-pronged plug was fastened securely into what looked like a new quad wall socket. She looked down at her feet disgustedly. "What a pigsty," she grumbled. Thrasher slept on while Drak seemed to be awaking on the nearby floor, several feet from Thrasher. "This has to be cleaned up, at once," she grumbled.

Lea grabbed both handles of the waiting floor polisher and squeezed its power lever very hard. With a noisy whirrrrrrr, the polisher began to buck, slamming from side to side in the narrow closet, scattering dirt, clothing, and remains of long-cold meals in its path. "Have to clean up this mess!" Whummmmmpppp! Denting the closet's bare pine studs. "If I don't clean up this mess, no one will!" Whummmpp! Crushing Thrasher's head against the wall, then ricocheting across the narrow space before bashing Thrasher's head again. Whirrrrrrrr to the wall and back again, this time pounding the man's rib cage. Trying to gain his footing on the slippery floor, Thrasher fumbled in his pocket as he realized Lea was standing over him, powering the floor polisher, just before it crashed into him again. His trembling fingers found the Execution Box. But as the bouncing floor polisher hit him squarely again, the Execution Box escaped his grasp. They both watched it drop to the slippery floor as Thrasher groped for it. Lea prayed his creeping fingers could not reach it.

"You can't throw more junk on the floor! Were you born in a barn?" she yelled, pushing down on the machine's handle, raising its front edge high off the dirty floor to again bounce over the Execution Box. But the floor polisher only squeaked feebly, careening off the nearest five-gallon can of floor wax until it whirred to a stop in the slum-gullion of blood, dirt, sawdust and one crust of a leftover baloney sandwich growing on the floor under Thrasher's broken nose.

"Don't keep making a mess!" Lea screamed at the inert Thrasher. "I'm not here to pick up after you! What do you think this is, your birthday?"

Restarting the floor polisher with one hand, Lea guided its bouncing back and forth, over the gritty floor and the wet, red patch growing around Thrasher's head. She bent to pick up a rusty ten-penny nail in front of her and some pieces of the Execution Box. She looked around for a wastebasket and let go of the floor polisher. The bulky equipment ground to a halt in the corner as Lea carefully inspected the floor of her bedroom, trying to find something to pick up. There was a faraway look in her green eyes. She didn't even notice Thrasher's blind right eye pointed in her direction as she relieved his corpse of the money collection and what was left of the Execution Box.

Suddenly attracted by the smell of food, Lea turned toward the ruckus in the nearby meeting hall. For the first time, she heard the ugly murmuring of the crowd of the unfed, demanding something to eat. Slipping in the spreading pool of soup and vegetables, now dark with grease and grime from the crowd of milling people, she made her way toward the large cauldron on the dripping, metal cart. Lea scooped up a clean ceramic bowl from a nearby counter and helped herself to a large ladleful of the hot liquid. As she began to drink hungrily from her bowl, Drak stumbled sleepily to her side. After Drak took his own bowl, Lea tossed the pieces of the shattered Execution Box and her collection of trash from the closet into the slimy vat of breakfast. Then Lea sauntered lazily with Drak through the hall's large double doors into the coolness of an early summer morning. She slid the ceramic bowl, still dripping with brown soup, under the flap of her black, canvas knapsack. Perhaps something for another time and place!

From what seemed like very far away to Lea, someone shouted: "What the hell yah doin'? Ya think I come down heah foah my health? You come back heah, you loozah!"

Shading her eyes with her right hand, Lea squinted up at the red-orange sun just peering through the top branches of a pair of maple trees next to the Edgerly Funeral Home across Main Street.

"Thank you, God, for the beauty of this new day and my clean room.   Mother will surely give me a cookie after school. Please put all the bad things behind me and help me find Clara. Now, please, God, I need some directions. Where does the sun come up in these parts? Sunset was always in the West when I lived in the North Country - further north in the summer, further south in the winter. Maybe that means the sun comes up in the East here. Let's see, if the sun comes up in the East, then, maybe if I put the sun on my right, then I'll be looking north. Maybe I'll be looking toward home. And maybe if we walk in that direction, I'll get closer to home."

Drak padded quietly beside Lea toward the slumbering Honda, listening to her carefully but wondering if she had finally escaped from reality and thinking about what might come next. "You OK to drive?" he asked her as he held open the driver's side door.

"A little fresh air and getting on the road will help. What'd you think of the tasty breakfast?"

Before climbing into the Honda, Lea asked Drak to help her insert the end of one of her hair ribbons in her coat pocket under the "wedding ring," and grasp both ends of the ribbon. With some careful effort and running her tongue over her upper lip, she was able to guide the gold ring over her third finger's knuckle. "I'm going to keep this in case we need to sell it," she said. Lea then enthusiastically reconnected Thrasher's hot-wire arrangement and, as the Honda's motor purred to life, with Drak at her side, she smoothly executed a U-turn and headed out of Rochester, New Hampshire, toward the cooler White Mountains and what she knew to be the "woke" anarchy of Vermont beyond. Through her inner turmoil, Lea thought she could already see their dense foothills in her mind, shimmering in the waves of heat rising off the asphalt under her ragged feet. Not once did she look back at the white church, the Memorial Day in Camden, Penal Colony 627, her sentencing or any of the alternating terror or the despair in between. At last, she was on her way home!

Lea followed signs to US 202, called Dover Road by some locals, which became US 393, staying on that route into Concord. Continuing on Main Street in Concord, she found a Cumberland Farms roadside market on her left. Lea pulled the Honda up to its gas pump to fill its gas tank. She suffered the inconvenience of having to pay cash to the clerk, in part because Drak's credit cards would not work during the Deep State's repeated interference with the Internet. But they both wanted to visit the restrooms and buy sandwiches and drinks for the coming trip. Lea, who now seemed more balanced to Drak, observed," Isn't it more pleasant when we can make our own decisions." Drak only beamed in return.

Back on Concord's Main Street, which again became US 202, toward Hopkinton, where she picked up US 89, which would lead to Burlington, Vermont. In a quieter and more sensible time, Lea might have considered stopping at the Ben & Jerry's ice cream headquarters just off Interstate 89. But with its new "Black Lives Matter" flavor (did it include a soupçon of burning businesses?) and its decision to suspend doing business in Israel, there was no chance of her wasting time to experience that wokeness when saving her only child, Clara, was infinitely more important.

After what seemed like forever on Interstate 89, Lea took exit 13 onto Interstate 189 toward US 7. That led them to Shelburne Road, tending in the direction of the ferry across Lake Champlain to New York State.

False Gods

Late afternoon shadows continued to lengthen, lancing the day's heat and letting it seep away among the gnarled roots of the dense trees on both sides of the cracked and broken asphalt road. Lea pulled the Honda over to the side of the road so she and Drak could get out of the car for a breather. She bent down to tie the rawhide lace of her torn right boot and hitch up both socks, leaning against Drak for support. Then she noticed the neatly groomed walkway beside the highway with its uniform string of evenly spaced faux-Gothic wrought-iron, knee-height lanterns marching along like a single file of good little soldiers; she hadn't remained at Penal Colony 627 long enough to learn that inmates there made those wrought-iron lanterns for the Covenant. A stone tablet said," God's Way." The tired young woman heard something thrashing about in the nearby underbrush, at least as large as a squirrel; whatever it was stopped as if listening as intently as she was. A large pair of yellow eyes watched her hungrily from the tangled vegetation nearby, so close she could feel its warm breath on her bare left leg. Looking hurriedly both north and south before backing across the tarmac, even though nothing had passed her in either direction recently, Lea stumbled in a pothole and fell sideways. She ended up on her knees, her nose coming to rest just above the nearest edge of God's Way. Up close, its grainy surface made her want to look away - it reminded her of Penal Colony 627, something she wanted to pretend had never happened, and certainly would never happen again. But with night coming on, probably a cloudy night with no moon, Lea knew traveling those mountains and onward toward home would be impossible without some light. After Drak helped Lea to her feet, she tentatively stepped onto the uniform, drab tread of the ubiquitous path called God's Way, toward the nearby town Lea hoped was just around the next bend in the road. Each of her steps slightly depressed the surface of God's Way, causing a small bulb in each of the boxy, wrought-iron lanterns evenly spaced along its border to dimly emit a yellow glow, just enough to show the path and the toes of each of her worn boots. A barely visible glow, pulsing in cadence with each of her steps, emphasized by a faint, tenor male voice in the distance repeating over and over again: "NO FALSE GODS BEFORE YOU."

Got to keep going. Forget about tired. Almost time for supper. One step after another. Left, right, left, right. No false gods before you. Surely not!

"Chingg! Chingg!"

Lea looked up from God's Way. A narrow beam of yellow light up ahead, on the right side of the mechanized path, jiggled in step with each of the metallic sounds. As she drew closer, Lea could make out a bulky, wooden mallet striking something shiny in a headlamp's light beam, at what appeared to be above her own head level.

"Chinngggg"

Chunks of stone were raining into the dry, overgrown weeds under a chisel's attack. Lea scampered toward a solitary home-spun standing atop a wooden extension ladder that was leaning against a statue of what looked like a uniformed man holding two small children. The row of tiny lights beside God's Way at her feet picked up the same pace.

"What are you doing?"

"Chinnggggg"

Granite fragments splattered Lea. She ducked behind the home-spun's gray trousers to avoid the barrage.

"Graven images," he mumbled, spitting bits of stone at the statue, enthusiastically beating a stainless-steel chisel with a two-pound oaken mallet, its business end tearing into the right cheek of the smaller of the two stone children, apparently a boy, Lea guessed from its knee-length trousers.

Lea read a tarnished bronze plaque at the statue's square foundation, now partially covered by falling debris: "In Honor of the Volunteer Firefighters of Belnap County Who Gave their Lives to Save Others."

"Are you deaf? I asked what are you doing," Lea insisted. "When are you gonna 'clean up this mess?"

Looking down at Lea disdainfully, the home-spun dropped the shiny chisel into the hip pocket of his sweat-stained gray trousers, peeled off the headlamp with his hammer hand and wiped his brow with a bare forearm.

"False gods! False gods! The Good Book says no false gods!" he declared.

He put the headlamp back on, aimed the chisel under the nostrils of the boy's statue in the fireman's arms and beat its wooden rounded end sharply with the mallet. The tiny nose and part of its left eye and eyebrow above it dropped into what looked like dry dandelion plants at the foot of the ladder.

From where Lea stood, the wooden ladder looked like suspenders for the fireman's baggy waterproof pants, its two legs straddling what was left of the statue's neck. Only a rusty, vertical steel rod suggested there had once been a head between the firefighter's broad, stone shoulders. What Lea imagined had been the statue of a little girl in the fireman's arms was now missing her forehead, all of her nose and nostrils as well as both ears. The lap of her gray, stone pinafore overflowed with bits and pieces of her face and the fireman's head and helmet. The heads and faces of the stone trio continued to melt away under the home-spun's punishing hammer blows. The shower of debris continued unabated, raining onto the hard-packed ground and what might have been memorial flowers beside the statue's granite foundation. Over the chisel's sharp sound, Lea could hear the home-spun tunelessly humming, over and over, apparently to himself:

"Bringin 'in the sheaves,

Bringin 'in the sheaves,

We'll all be rejoicing,

Bringin 'in the sheaves."

One fierce swing of the home-spun's mallet and more than one-half of the girl's head split off and thumble, thumped into the desiccated remains of the past summer's weeds at the base of the statue. To Lea, the bobbling boulder sounded like something large and hungry chasing its prey through the dense underbrush outside the faint circle of light cast by the home-spun's headlamp. Lea looked nervously over her shoulder, peering into the deepening darkness creeping all around her and up the ladder. She looked up at the dedicated home-spun and she tried to speak, but nothing came out but a faint sob. Lea turned and bounded back toward Drak and the Honda. She reconnected Thrasher's ignition wire arrangement. Then the pair continued along the same highway into the growing darkness.

A Pale Horse

A dust devil danced in the simple, paved path leading toward Charles Lamb IV's front door of sturdy oak planks and black, wrought-iron fittings. He adjusted the scanning camera's focus to carefully inspect each camouflaged electric fence panel on either side of the path. Hidden behind the bleached, gray wooden facade of his grandiose fence, were sensors designed to detect the approach of any warm-blooded creature. Had Father Lamb's security system detected the approach of a traveler?

Had some human steps stirred the path's parched surface or he had witnessed a Divine event, something only he was privileged to see?

Charles Lamb, now in his 70s, had attended all the right schools, starting with Hackley in Westchester County, New York, then the full range of revered Ivies. At Yale in New Haven, Connecticut, after meritorious military service, he completed his double BA in History and English Literature with honors. At the end of his junior year, he was selected for the favored secret society, Skull & Bones, while keeping his commission as a captain in the Army as a chaplain. While living in student housing at Yale, Lamb achieved some notoriety when his wife and high school sweetheart was cooking a Chinese delicacy in a seasoned wok and it caught fire. Ever cautious, Lamb called 911. The operator asked: "are you in a multiple dwelling?" When Lamb answered in the affirmative, the line went dead. Only a few minutes later, there was loud banging on Lamb's apartment door, followed by the door's being broken open and the fire crew's hitting the flaming wok with a huge stream of water from a canvas fire hose; it not only put out the fire but splattered the wok's savory contents all over the tiny kitchen's gray walls.

After what he perceived as most successful time in New Haven, Lamb and his bride proceeded to the University of Virginia Law School, in Charlottesville, Virginia, where he won even more academic honors including Order of the Coif. Nearing graduation from law school, Lamb was faced with the task of sifting through many lucrative offers of legal employment but decided to accept the offer from a large, international law firm in Manhattan, where he'd worked as a summer clerk. There, as a summer clerk, he actually shared a small office with David Garvey, who was then a first-year associate, both learning the ropes of complicated corporate finance transactions. Unlike David Garvey, who left that firm before being considered for partner, Lamb persevered and prevailed, ending up as part of the firm's senior management, at least partially the result of his good works such as opening the firm's first office in Hong Kong.

Much later, there was a minor referral from Lamb and his colleagues to David Garvey's new firm. That referral led to David's helping a Canadian gold mining company amend its credit agreement with a major NY commercial bank. Since David had cut his teeth on doing credit agreements for Citibank, when it as still First National City Bank, and many other New York and foreign banks with offices in Manhattan, that was not even a minor challenge for him. More than satisfied with his efficient and reasonably priced work, management of the Canadian mining company asked David if he could get the Canadian company's voting shares listed on NASDAQ. Although David did not have exhaustive experience in transactions like what the Canadian mining company had in mind, essentially much like a public offering registered with the Securities and Exchange Commission, he was loath to decline such an interesting opportunity and immediately started work. And it felt like a huge plus to David's new practice that the mining company had not gone back to Lamb's larger firm for this more sophisticated transaction. Long after the initial complex filings were lodged with the SEC and the transaction proceeded smoothly, its

Division of Investment Management chimed in at the last minute, claiming, because of the nature of its finances and the large role in its ownership by a wealthy Brazilian investor, that the Canadian mining company was supposedly an unregistered investment company. Being categorized as a company subject to the strictures of the 1940 Investment Company Act is the equivalent of a death sentence for any normal business corporation since it would preclude most ordinary business transactions. Unbeknownst to David, the Canadian mining company did its own research, looking around for "experts" in '40 Act matters and chanced upon a Washington, DC law firm where the resume of one of its partners included a senior position in the SEC's Division of Investment Management. At that time, as well as long before and ever since, people with government experience often use that experience as a way to develop influence and make money in the private sector. In many cases, lawyers people hired for that purported "expertise" are unwilling to actually "pull the trigger," preferring to preserve expertise and influence in order to be hired for the next possible deal, a practice which can continue *ad nauseam.* David understood that mindset and yet worked well with that partner, one Margaret Wilbur. As the transaction unfolded, Margaret and David became lovers and spent as much time together as possible as the pending transaction required travel and meetings in DC, Manhattan and Toronto. Even though Margaret lived and worked in our nation's nominal capital and David's home and business were in Manhattan. But they "worked" together while hiking in Switzerland and skiing in Colorado and Whistler, British Columbia. And, eventually, the SEC's Division of Investment Management was convinced to back off, and the Canadian mining company's listing application was approved, all on the basis of an obscure and probably irrelevant SEC no-action letter named "Tonopah Mining." The irony, of course, was that David had done the pivotal work, although the client, as well as David and Margaret were more than satisfied. Remembering the challenge and joy bred by this transaction always caused David Garvey to never look a gift horse in the mouth, in this case, the initial minor referral from Lamb's large law firm. In the Southwest, Margaret's performance might have been labeled" big hat, no cattle." Despite the successful result David Garvey and Margaret Wilbur achieved, he ultimately lost the Canadian mining company as a client when it was acquired by a larger company. Of course, the new owner had its own legal team.

Nonetheless, David later had to do battle with Margaret and her colleagues in a Federal court in Man-hattan where she was representing the German bank that had financed David's successful yet legal loan-sharking business in the remnants of the Soviet Union from his Königsberg Fund. The Iraqis were doing their best to upset those financing arrangements so they could steal David's fund as a lever to loosen the grip of widespread international financial sanctions. During their joustings in Federal Court in Manhattan, David and his law partner, Frank Gillespie, creatively parried every thrust by the German bank and its lawyers, including Margaret Wilbur.

Lamb later left his management position at the major law firm to take an even more financially advantageous job in a well-known NY investment banking firm. At that point, he traded in his wife in for a newer model and left his two grown daughters behind. Despite substantially growing his influence and wealth, Lamb's new wife left him for someone younger and even more wealthy. As America's politics changed drastically, Lamb recognized how the new "progressive" Federal administration was destroying the value of the US Dollar, so he moved most of his assets into precious metals and himself to what seemed like quiet countryside in New England. There, Lea and Drak chanced upon his mansion on the north side of God's Way. Now outside the American financial community and its political strictures, Lamb had become a practicing Anglican, in part to atone for his many misadventures, and renounced all "here's what's happening now" social religions which now permeated America, often without reference to God or the Bible. More "church" services in "mainline" religious organizations focused on things such as which organizations pandering to illegal immigrants to support or which progressive causes to demonstrate for and how much to support them financially rather than concentrating on actual Christian worship.

As their long day was waning and the sun was sinking toward the western horizon, Lea stopped the Honda in front of the gate in the iron fence surrounding Lamb's mansion. The pair stood within clear sight of his surveillance cameras as Lea pushed what appeared to be an entry bell. An interior screen connected to Lamb's alarm alerted him to check his video feeds. Standing in front of his gate were a supple and trim. A young woman beside a darker-skinned man with tousled black hair, both showing friendly expressions. Lamb was more than interested in young women and had escaped harassment claims of women, both staff and lawyers, at the law firm and later at the investment banking firm. Now, in his country estate away from those strictures, Lamb could devote his entire attention to young women and was particularly attracted to the athletic young woman at his gate. He wished the young man at her side would disappear but recognized that might be only wishful thinking.

"How may I help you?" he asked after putting his right index finger into the floating holographic icon for "conversation" on the frame of his surveillance screen.

"Kind sir," Lea responded with a bright smile, "I'm on my way to New York State to rescue my young daughter from the evil clutches of a 'social service 'agency. I see the sign of the Cross at your front gate. We've been driving all day and hope you might allow us a place to rest for the night. I have a culinary miracle we can use to make our own food, which you and your family might also enjoy." Lea caressed the round, smooth stone in her pocket that she had chanced upon on Camden's Atlantic beach after Drak transported them from the Liberian freighter to shore, her mind focused on the "Stone Soup" fable.

Already entranced by this beautiful young woman at the gate to his lair, Lamb asked," and what is your name?" As soon as Lea identified herself, the gate clicked open, and she and Drak walked inside and up four granite steps to Lamb's front door. Lamb himself opened the heavy oak door and motioned two to enter his home, giving Lea a deep hug while pretending Drak wasn't even there. Lea winced at

Lamb's inappropriate squeeze as his hands wandered over her taut backside. She kept turning over and over the short piece of metal rod and a smooth stone in her left pocket while enthusiastically saying," Thank you for your hospitality." Lea continued with a forced but friendly smile: "If I could use a simple pot of water and a stove in your kitchen, I can make us some really good soup from my special recipe."

Lamb put his left arm around Lea's shoulder and caressed her cheek with his right hand while deeply sniffing her hair – Lea could only imagine Lamb's state of arousal, having in mind she and Drak had been on the road for days in warm weather without the benefit of a shower or any other tidiness. But she let Lamb move her toward his modern kitchen, where Lea directed her attention to his large collection of pots, pans, and utensils, selected a large iron pot, filled it with water, and ignited the gas burner under it to bring it toward a boil. Lea removed the smooth stone from her left pocket and put it in the water-filled pot. She deeply inhaled over the pot and announced," it already smells great. This is going to be a really delicious soup."

Lamb was so focused on Lea that he didn't seem to have noticed that Drak had not followed them into Lamb's cavernous kitchen. Drak stayed behind and was quietly skulking about the first floor of Lamb's mansion, looking for things that might be useful in their quest. He quickly chanced upon Lamb's office through an open door from the mansion's central hall. The office included an ornate mahogany Portuguese partners 'desk and three comfortable leather chairs, a lush, crimson-and-blue Astrakan carpet, a separate seating area with a butler's table, and many framed certificates and pictures of what looked like public gatherings with public officials but no family photos of any sort. Beside Lamb's main desk, there was a wide, open door to a closet. Drak peeked inside the closet to find a large metal safe with its door also open.

"Maybe being in the country with a real security system, this guy doesn t worry about what s going on inside his house – silly," he thought to himself *"or perhaps Lamb was caught off guard when unexpected visitors appeared outside."*

Then Drak caught his breath when he noticed several guns - a rifle, a shotgun, and two pistols, which appeared to be well maintained as well as three trays of ammo inside the open safe.

"Better I go find Lea and Lamb in the kitchen so he doesn t even think about what I found."

On his way toward Lamb's kitchen, he looked toward a grand

staircase leading to the second floor and wondered if they might find a comfortable place to sleep there.

Lea was stirring the pot while Lamb had his hands on her shoulders. She stepped away to look into the closest refrigerator and said: "This soup is going to be great, but it would be even better with some of those fresh carrots." Smitten as he was, Lamb said," Put whatever you like in the soup." Lea asked: "Could you please hand me a cutting board?" With a sturdy, wooden cutting board in hand, Lea grabbed what seemed to be a very sharp knife and began slicing fresh carrots along with onions, celery, asparagus, and parsnips, each landing in the boiling pot quickly. "You're really going to like this soup," she said, offering Lamb a taste. Looking out the kitchen window, Lea could see a large garden and asked Lamb," Can we go out and see what spices you have?" "Of course," he said longingly, and they walked together out into the darkening backyard, where Lea tripped through Lamb's garden and began to pick vegetables and spices. Drak watched them go and thought to himself,

"Lea s doing a great job of playing this guy. Right now, it looks like she has him by crank. One way or another, we need to leave here with some of those guns and ammo that fits and maybe even some food."

The back door banged open against the cream-colored

wall and Lea scampered into the kitchen with an armful of basil, French thyme, bright red, fresh tomatoes, and fresh raspberries. Moving quickly to her cutting board, Lea chopped the basil and thyme and dropped them into the slowly boiling pot while she carefully set the raspberries aside. "Now this soup is spectacular! It would be even better with some beef or chicken. Do you have any?" she asked Lamb. Perhaps having already figured out that Lea might not be an easy conquest, Lamb replied," I have both in the 'fridge" Take what you like," looking somewhat disappointed. Lea sensed that Lamb was almost ready to explode, the pressure of his sexual desire about to outwit more measured interaction.

With Drak and Lamb watching intently, Lea neatly sliced a medium-sized piece of fresh tenderloin, rolled the slices in flour flavored with a bit of cumin and garam masala from Lamb's elaborate spice collection plus salt and pepper, and dropped the pieces into a lightly buttered pan on medium heat along with very thin slices of potato, onion, and essential, finely chopped garlic. She stirred them carefully with a carved, wooden spoon while admiring her version of "Stone Soup" before adding the results of several diced, fresh tomatoes along with a handful of chopped basil and French thyme.

Lea found utensils for the communal table and asked Drak to help her complete place settings on the dining room table and find dessert and soup bowls. Without a word, Lamb pointed Drak toward a cupboard in the kitchen for soup bowls and plates to hold them, as well as dessert bowls.

Lea took a spoonful of soup from the bubbling pot and offered a taste to Lamb, touching his cheek lightly. "How is this for you, Charles, or do you prefer to be called Charlie?" Lamb held her hand to his cheek, blew softly on the steaming spoonful of soup, inhaled a taste, and smiled. "Outstanding!"

"Do WE have any red wine to go with this great soup and the ciabatta bread you seem to have here?" Lea asked coyly, now even more than in tune with how this game should be played. She continued to survey Lamb's kitchen and its cabinets and drawers for other imaginative ingredients for her latest version of "Stone Soup" and for their journey to rescue Clara and return to the North Country. Although the original announcement of her obligations to the Movement had initially repulsed her, she was warming to the tasks, whatever they might be.

"We have an unopened bottle of Alpha Omega, an exceptional cabernet, I believe from a vineyard in California owned by a former Republican member of the House of Representatives from California, one Devin Nunes. It's in the polished wooden wine rack just inside the door to the garden. Why don't WE have a look?"

Lamb put his left hand in the small of Lea's back, maneuvering her toward the garden door. "See," he said, pointing toward three Alpha Omega 2017s as his left hand slid lower.

Lea grabbed the nearest bottle and winked at Drak, who was fully aware of how this meal was unfolding. She applied one of Lamb's expensive corkscrews to the bottle's actual cork and deftly removed it with a faint "pop."

Later, at the table, Lea said," Father Lamb, would you be so kind as to lead us in grace?"

Lamb reached out to hold hands with Lea and Drak, their heads bowed and intoned: *"Dear Lord. Thank you for bringing us together and for enhancing our friendship. May we continue to help each other and come closer together. Please bless this food and bless us to thy service. In the name of Jesus Christ, Amen."* Lea looked at Drak and smiled.

"You know," she said, "this is the first time I've cooked since escaping back to America, and I've really enjoyed getting back to one of my favorite creative things."

"What do you mean, escaping back to America?" Pastor

Lamb asked incredulously. "Were you on a bad vacation?"

"I wouldn't want to spoil this pleasant and warm event, Charles, but I was sent off to a penal colony at the very northern edge of Russia, an island in the Chukchi Sea, by one of those Covenant-run religious courts. Fortunately, I got some help in escaping and coming back to America."

Lea excused herself and got up from the table, picked up all three bowls, and filled everyone's bowl with her creation from the large cauldron of "Stone Soup." Then she set them out on smaller plates beside fresh, cloth napkins at each place. Next, she added several thick slices of fresh ciabatta bread to a large ceramic basket lined with a fresh linen napkin with a smaller nearby plate with fresh, unsalted butter. Nearby was a silver butter knife to match the knives, dinner and dessert forks, plus both types of silver spoons Drak had already arranged at each place. Lea was surprised by Drak's familiarity with the art of place settings. While completing the settings for each diner, Lea added three water glasses and set a pitcher filled with ice water in the center of the tablecloth. Then, Lea carefully placed a ceramic dessert bowl to the right of each placemat. Rinsed, fresh raspberries were already waiting in a ceramic drainer in the kitchen's main sink, awaiting the beating of fresh, heavy cream with a teaspoon of vanilla extract.

Lea asked Lamb "How long have you lived in this delightful home?"

Lamb took a swallow of Alpha Omega and looked at Lea with a warm smile. I very much enjoyed your soup and the way you put this meal together so smoothly – it's a credit to your many skills. I hope the two of you enjoyed it as much as I did. The short answer to your question is that I came here over four years ago and settled in this house to escape the rigors of my prior working life in Manhattan. I live here quietly, practicing my faith, but very much miss the company of others, particularly female companionship. Tell me about your present objectives."

Lea glanced at Drak, signaling that she would tell this tale. "We'll be driving to far western New York to rescue my young daughter from the Lost League in Buffalo, which is quite a trip from here. We hope to be on the road at daybreak."

After the trio had enjoyed the main course and dessert, the meal wound down as the rest of the Alpha Omega was enjoyed. Lea announced: "This has been a wonderful evening, but I'm more than tired and have a splitting headache. Time for me to sleep if that is acceptable to you, Charles. Do you mind if I wash the dishes in the morning, Charles? And where would you prefer that we sleep?"

Lamb looked up from what was left of his bowl of raspberries and whipped cream to the top of his winding staircase. "My suite is at the top of those stairs. There are two guest rooms to the left of my room. Lea, please take the guest room immediately to the left of my suite and Drak the second one to the left of my suite. No, I don't mind if cleanup is tomorrow morning. I hope you have a good night."

Lea and Drak trudged up the winding staircase and entered their assigned rooms. She noted a connecting door to Drak's room and opened it to encounter Drak's smiling face and ventured," if you need anything, I'll be right here" as she bent over to roll back the covers of the double bed in her room."

"Works for me," he said cheerfully, pulling the door shut.

"I'm going to sit in this comfortable chair, looking at the moon outside my window, think about our day and plan for tomorrow, and maybe see what comes up."

It was not long before Lea's door to the second-floor hall crept open. Lea racked the slide of her Beretta, and her outer bedroom door quickly jerked shut. *"One nasty thing eliminated,"* Lea thought as she pushed a large chair firmly against the inside of the door. She undressed, climbed into bed, and pulled up the covers.

As she had nearly drifted off to sleep, Lea heard what sounded like yelling from outside her front door, down the hall toward Drak's room, followed by the sound of someone's hitting the lavishly carpeted floor. She might have been concerned but knew Drak was more than capable of protecting himself. said a prayer, and drifted off to sleep.

It was not yet sunrise when Drak tapped gently on the connecting door. Perhaps part of his brain was still on Kosovo time. He padded over to Lea's bed and sat on the edge of it, and watched as her eyes opened. "What do you have in mind today?" Drak asked, nursing what would become a bruise on his right knuckle.

While still yawning, Lea said," I want to get to the Lost League compound in Carthage, NY, as soon as possible. We have a car and money, so we should leave here as soon as possible, and I don't give a fig about who cleans up Lamb's kitchen." What do you have in mind?"

Drak grinned and filled Lea in on what he had discovered in Lamb's office. "How about we liberate some of his guns and ammo on the way out? Lamb will probably be asleep for a while, and we can get something to eat on the road." "Lamb came to the door of my room last night and

166

yelled at me about whether I had been out picking vegetables in his back garden. He is seriously crazy. So, I had to hit him."

Lea grinned broadly and said," let's get dressed quickly, grab whatever guns and ammo we can carry, and be on our way in the Honda. I can always send him a thank you note later. She snickered and jumped out of bed to put on her clothes and shoes. She pulled a pillowcase off each of the pillows on her bed.

They crept quietly down the winding staircase and stuffed a .45 pistol, a .22 handgun in a shoulder holster as well as several boxes of ammunition into the empty pillowcases. They also took a rifle for good measure. Drak pulled the front door open and then closed it very quietly. The pair tip-toed down the outside stairs, out the gate, and into the Honda, where Lea reconnected Thrasher's hot-wire job. The pair sped on toward Middlebury, leaving the front car doors ajar for a bit in hopes of not waking their host. Then they pulled both doors of the Honda shut and rolled along the country road as the sun came up behind them, then through the small town of Hancock. Lea observed," Even if he had a way to contact us or track whatever his surveillance system recorded about our car, his guns are most certainly illegal in this super"–woke" State of Vermont, even though it was one of the original "open carry" states, so he'll probably keep his mouth shut.

Following signs to the Charlotte/Essex ferry, Lea turned left onto Shelburne Road and, after about six miles, right onto Ferry Road.

Coming down a slight hill toward the ferry landing at the Charlotte, Vermont side of the Lake Champlain crossing to Essex, NY, Lea and Drak could see that the flat white vessel, open on both ends at main deck level, appeared almost ready to depart. Its stern pair of propellers were already kicking up waves against the dock-side pilings. Lea slowed the Honda to carefully roll up the waiting ramp and followed the attendant's direction to park on the vessel's starboard side. She put out her hand to Drak for money to pay the fare. Drak gave her $20. She received $3.75 in change from the attendant – the fare was only $16.25 because the Honda was less than 19 feet long. "That's cheap," Drak noted, "compared with driving around the upper end of Lake Champlain, particularly when we're in a hurry. Let's see if the ferry at least has a snack bar."

Lea noticed what looked like a surveillance camera above the ramp into the ferry as she and Drak walked across the double deck plate toward stairs to the upper level to see whatever food and drink might be available topside. Lea gently turned away from the camera while urging Drak to do the same so they would both be more likely to avoid being identified by that camera.

Across the Empire State

Lea and Drak arrived at the Essex, New York ferry landing on the west side of Lake Champlain just 32 minutes after leaving the Vermont dock, drove down the ferry's ramp, and stopped on the far edge of its parking lot. The pair might have enjoyed the mountain views more if they hadn't been using the ferry's Wi-Fi to access one of the few remaining search sites on Drak's laptop that couldn't track him. They needed directions from where they were to Carthage, New York, where Lea's daughter was being held captive by the Lost League.

Drak looked up from his screen: "You good driver but you no longer have driver's license with you, even if it is State of New York. We have registration papers that match Honda's plates. Maybe you let me drive. As illegal immigrant applied for asylum, I get special privileges and papers plus $3,500 a month, free college, medical and all that other good stuff. And I don't need no voter ID even though I don't vote Democrat without an ID. If we get stopped by cop, I'm in good shape."

Lea climbed into the back seat for a nap and let Drak take the driver's seat and figure out the hot-wire connection.

Drak continued," According to these maps, there are many ways we can get to Carthage. We're only 11 miles from Interstate 87. You know it goes north to Canada and south to New York City. One idea: north to Plattsburgh, then over the top of New York. Or we go south on 87 to what the map calls the Gov. Thomas Dewey Thruway. "Who's this Thomas Dewey?" he asked Lea.

"He was Governor of NY, ran against Harry Truman for President in 1948, and lost even though one major paper reported he won. Unlike Sniffy and his supposed 81,000,000 votes, Dewey never went on to pretend to be 'President.'What else you got?"

"Or we go west on Thomas Dewey to Utica, then north toward Watertown. They are both a long drive. And they're more likely to be patrolled by cops - you know cops have to be concentrated because so many quit after vaccine mandates. Maybe you prefer third choice: through Adirondacks. It means going through lots of woods on smaller roads. Total almost 300 miles to Carthage but probably less chance of some cop playing us."

"Let's do that – head toward 87 South so we can head toward the Adirondacks. It will take a little longer but the last thing we need is to get stopped. Maybe we can find a place to stop in Tupper Lake." Lea looked out at Lake

Champlain and the distant mountains, thinking how much better this was than Penal Colony 627 and Thrasher with his terrible, bad breath, not to even mention her recently diminishing fear of the recently departed thug and his Execution Box. Although she was still wearing the amulet that fooled the bomb sewn into her neck and around her spine, Lea was more than anxious to get rid of it and be past its threat forever because she had no confidence in how long its protection would last.

Drak turned the Honda toward the parking lot exit and followed Station Road, route NY 22, past the famous brick, Octagonal Schoolhouse as the road turned south. Although he was driving just below the speed limit, Drak screeched to a halt as some hairy, little animals Drak had never seen before meandered across the highway in front of the Honda. Lea leaned over the front seat and told Drak they were possums and said they were called a passel of possums, including three little joeys and one larger, more hairy mother possum, called a jill.

After several curves in the road that followed the curling path of the Bouquet River, Drak turned right onto Main Street in Westport, which became NY 9-N, where they continued under the I-87 interchange and left onto its southbound ramp just before the Adirondack Veterinary

Hospital.

Before long, Drak followed Exit 29 toward Newcomb and shortly took a left onto to Blue Ridge Road toward Tupper Lake. That beautiful road wound through Adirondack Park, past Old Forge and to Lowville, the capital of Lewis County. After a couple of missed turns, Drak piloted the Honda onto NY Route 28 then NY 12 and eventually NY 12 into Carthage, where they knew Clara was being held by the Lost League.

Sign Me Up

Lea had originally been repulsed by the idea that her new responsibilities, in repayment for the Movement's help in escaping Penal Colony 627 and bringing her back to America, would include assassinating government officials. But that had worn off as her awful treatment persisted. She began to understand how cavalierly she and others like her were being harmed by most of the new supposedly "progressive" government's policies, as eagerly enforced by the Covenant and put up with by Sheeple in the general population. Ordinary people who had become used to blindly complying with whatever edicts issued from the mouths of local politicians, regional and national bureaucrats, and politicians; many were noticeably lazy or uninterested in whatever was controlling their daily lives. Not to even mention that many of those crooks were profiting from relationships with Big Pharma and China. Almost everywhere she and Drak went, they were told endless stories about "Orange Man Bad" and how that outlook was the undercurrent of 2020 election fraud as the result of the left's schemes. They made Lea wonder why no one had taken Biden seriously during the campaign when he bragged about the great election fraud program the Democrats had created. Many of the things people learned after the 2020 election and what the "progressives" took over in every blue state and nationally would have been considered impossible just a few years earlier.

One of Lea's favorite examples the bumbling Governor Lamont (Lament) of Connecticut, who piously issued volumes of mutually contradictory edicts to residents of the Nutmeg State, such as deeming real estate to be an "essential business (allowed to remain open)." But then prohibiting homeowners from hiring professional photographers to take quality photos for listings (people selling their homes (who followed those edicts were left to rely on amateur pictures taken by agents on their cell phones) as well as closing hair salons to supposedly "fight" the plandemic. But he later clumsily allowed hair salons to reopen as long as they did not use hair dryers, the height of stupidity. All the while, blithely ignoring the lessons of the widely published nursing home deaths on January 25, 2020, in Parkland, Washington on national media, and continuing to push elderly patients with multiple co-morbidities into nursing homes without even a semblance of interest in conditions there or patient health. Of course, when many of those elderly nursing home residents succumbed to various diseases while locked away from their loved ones, their demises were uniformly reported as Covid deaths so that various facilities could collect hugely enhanced taxpayer subsidies. Being a small and quaint state, Connecticut garnered little publicity over these deaths as compared to major disasters in California, Michigan, New Jersey, and Pennsylvania. All the while, Governor Lament blanketed cable channels with self-serving interviews about his wonderful accomplishments as the anger of even liberal residents of the Nutmeg State over unnecessary lockdowns, travel restrictions, and mask mandates metastasized.

Once they arrived in Carthage, it wasn't even mildly difficult to ferret out contacts in the Movement in Jefferson County, New York, just south of the St. Lawrence Seaway. Swaths of people were disgusted with what was going on in local politics even though progressive policies there were decidedly less intrusive than on the national level far away. Even as Governor Andrew Cuomo's successor, Kathy Hochul, began to push many extreme policies such as no cash bail and attacks on the use of natural gas in kitchen stoves and water heaters because of the phony threat of "climate change." Carefully inquiring of customers and staff in a local diner while having ham sandwiches and drinks allowed them to quietly discover leads toward Movement sympathizers in different parts of the Town of Carthage. All made easier with the considerable sum of money added to what Thrasher was carrying before his unfortunate demise and the weapons liberated from Charles Lamb, IV's "heavily guarded" home beside God's Way.

Several furtive conversations at back tables in the diner pointed the pair toward a green, ramshackle house on the next street with a sagging front door and a muscular pit bull staked in the building's unkept front yard with a chain held together with what looked like an electronic lock. Before coming closer, Lea and Drak surveyed the back of the green house and, creeping closer, could see a "Where Go One We Go All" poster on the wall of what looked like a small office under the back roof. Circling the house to stay as far away as possible from the owner's pit bull, Lea racked the slide of her Beretta before gently knocking on the dark green front door. She was surprised by a well-dressed older man peeking around the door frame, a gold monocle in his right eye. He ventured," Whaddaya want?" Lea answered: "Where we go one, we go all." The man smiled slightly and said," tell me more." Lea understood she might be taking a chance but had come too far to back down. She explained," I was transported to a penal colony in the Chukchi Sea for teaching my students ideas opposed by the Covenant. The same female judge who sent me there gave the Lost League my daughter

Clara. She's being held here in Carthage at the Lost Sheep compound – the Movement minders told me that on the way back to America. I need tools to set my young daughter free and to continue my service to the Movement." The man looked carefully around the outside of his house, opened the front door a bit, and said," Please come in. Perhaps I can help. What's your name, and who's this guy?"

Following the man with the shiny, gold monocle, Lea gave him her name and, pointing to her companion, said, "he's Drak, a refugee from Eastern Europe who's been with me since I was brought ashore in Maine, and we found our way here." The man with the golden monocle didn't introduce himself but asked what the pair needed. Lea was long past being bashful and described what they needed: "clothing that will make us look like we're with the Lost League, a poorly written document authorizing us to take Clara, a pistol for Drak, and some ammo." The man with the golden monocle snickered, thought for a moment, and then said," That's a tall order but probably within our resources." He continued," Let me make some visits on foot because we don't use phones anymore in our local area. You folks can get some rest upstairs."

With many miles behind them, Lea and Drak wearily climbed creaky wooden stairs, found two twin beds in what seemed to be a guest room, and quickly fell asleep without giving a second thought to what might be a risk that someone knew who they were and what they had in mind.

Lost Sheep Found

Nervous about their next steps, morning came early for Lea and Drak, but they tried to relax until local business hours arrived in Carthage.

Lea explained that their ultimate destination was Malone, NY. The man with the monocle gave her a paper copy of a detailed road map of available routes and major communities in that part of the North Country as well as the street address in Malone for one of the Movement's operatives. The Movement man called his Malone contact Rodney Herbert (probably not his real name). Rodney Herbert might provide Lea access to important information and access to instructions of the Movement without using her phone. Even though Lea's smartphone was supposedly encrypted, she not only didn't trust the encryption but assumed that Big Tech had provided a way for the government to spy on her calls and text messages. They profusely thanked the man who had helped them in Carthage and their next steps, then stepped out into a warm summer morning.

Lea said: "Let's get started on cleaning up this mess,

first the Lost League and rescuing Clara." Drak climbed into the driver's seat of the surprisingly dependable Honda and busied himself, repeating Thrasher's connection of ignition wires. Their nondescript traveling clothes were neatly folded in the Honda's trunk.

Hidden by a dowdy, black dress, strait-laced low-heeled black shoes, and the requisite Lost League matron's white bonnet atop a grandmotherly dishwater grey wig, Lea looked almost like Sister Ruth. Drak was wearing a complete home-spun outfit of black coat and trousers, including home-spun hat, but with a Ruger Mk. III.22 hand-gun in his right-hand pocket instead of the soggy apple core Lea's minder had kept in his pocket during her "trial" in Malone. Plus, he had two spare .22 magazines in his left coat pocket. Drak's prior life had been replete with various types of weapons, and he also carried a 9mm Beretta in his left hip holster, normally covered by his coat jacket, which he could easily reach by a cross-draw with his right hand. The pair traveled along sunlit streets, mostly empty of other people at this beginning of a normal workday in Carthage, New York. Drak drove the Honda into the parking lot of the United Methodist Church, teeming with cars of parents delivering their young children to what seemed to be a very busy play school and a private elementary school. He parked the car at the far edge of the lot, under two maple trees with sprouting new leaves. Lea and Drak headed toward to door of the church's annex but smoothly detoured to the sidewalk in front of the church, the object being to leave the vehicle where it would not be visible from the Lost League's address. They casually walked around the corner toward their objective.

The Lost League compound was located on the corner of North Clinton and State Streets in what was likely an old rooming house, just around the corner from the United Methodist Church. It had been only a short drive from the green house where they had found the man with the golden monocle.

Lea pushed open its front door and marched up to the Lost League's front desk, a shaky and poorly painted piece of furniture that looked like it had come from Good Will, topped by an open, leather-bound Bible. An elderly woman dressed much the same as Lea sitting behind the desk took off her reading glasses and scrutinized the pair as they stepped inside the creaky front door.

"Sister Tweedy and Brother Wilson, here to complete transfer of Clara Holderness to the Lost League in Alexandria Bay," Lea bellowed, thrusting a sheaf of papers at the old woman. "NOT authorized," the good Sister behind the low desk croaked and tried to stand up. Lea quickly stepped forward on her firmly planted right foot and slammed the minder in the larynx with a sharp left cross. "Where's Clara?" she demanded, pointing her loaded Beretta between the Sister's eyes, touching her forehead. "Don't hurt me," the old woman squealed, fighting back coughs, "I'll show you. But please just put away that gun." "Fat chance," Lea snorted, poking the barrel of her Beretta into flabby wattles under the old woman's chin.

The frightened, old matron cautiously led them up two flights of creaky wooden stairs to a drafty room on the second floor. Clara was sitting by herself on a bare metal bed frame. As the door creaked open, she looked at Lea and yelled "Mommy" even though Lea put her index finger to her lips. Lea gave Clara a soft hug and whispered into her left ear, "we're leaving. You must be quiet while we're getting out of here. Just stay in my arms until we get to our car. We're going to tie this woman up so she can't tell anyone we're leaving." She said to Drak in a louder voice "I'm counting on you to call our contact in Alexandria Bay so he'll be ready with the boat we need to get across Lake Ontario to Canada." Lea looked over her shoulder to see Drak zipping plastic ties onto the old woman's wrists behind her back as she moaned and tried to get away. Then he stuffed a rumpled-up piece of a Lost League flyer into her trembling mouth. "Ready," Drak announced after clipping the zip ties to the underside of the metal bed frame and sliding the old woman under it. The woman was already kicking the wooden floor with her black heels so Drak untied both of her shoes, flipped her over on her stomach and tied her stockinged feet to the edge of the metal bed frame. Then Mommy plus two slipped quietly out the bedroom door and down two flights of nearby squeaky wooden stairs to the compound's lobby.

As they had nearly reached the building's front door, another Lost League staffer, also in uniform of the day, stepped in front of them: "where do you think you're going? I'm Sister Ruth and I'm in charge here." Clara immediately started bawling and wailed "Sister Ruth hits me." Lea motioned with her head toward the latest arrival and Drak slammed her in the face with his right hand that held his pistol, making the crunching sound of breaking small bones. Almost in the same motion, he charged into her with his left shoulder, partly lifting Sister Ruth off her stubby black heels. She landed on her back, with at least a broken and bloody nose and barely conscious. Lea snickered, remembering her favorite Mike Tyson aphorism: "everyone has a plan until someone hits him in the face." She calmed Clara, saying "Sister Ruth will never hit you again. To Drak, she directed "make sure she won't hit anyone else either."

Confident that she had Sister Ruth's complete attention, Lea stood over the dazed matron and bent over to closely look into the terrified woman's rapidly blinking eyes. She said very slowly "I am Clara's mother. You were only given custody of Clara because that disgusting judge sent me to Penal Colony 627 on an island in the frigid Chukchi Sea and you were supposed to take care of her, even if you have no idea about the location of that desolate place. You treated Clara despicably. Hear me well! If you report this to the local authorities and they come after us in Alexandria Bay, where a boat is waiting to take us into Canada, I will find a way to come back here and personally slit your baggy, quivering throat with my razor-sharp blade. DO YOU UNDERSTAND?" Lea swallowed hard as she remembered those were exactly the words Thrasher had spit at her in their first meeting on the desolate hill overlooking the gray Chukchi Sea.

Drak deftly rolled Sister Ruth over onto her stomach. Standing on both of her skinny arms, he repeatedly slammed the back of both of Sister Ruth's hands with the heavy, wooden reception desk. Sister Ruth screamed piteously. Drak zip-tied her bleeding hands at the wrists and ripped a piece from the desk's cloth covering to plug her mouth and poked it in with vigor. "You know", Lea said, "she may suffocate with all that blood and what looks like a broken nose." "So what?" Drak responded as he folded up Sister Ruth's inert and bleeding form and stuffed it into the nearby closet, beside what remained of the Lost League's reception desk, pushing aside a mop and pail and an ancient vacuum cleaner before slamming the closet door. He was delighted to find an actual metal key in the closet's hefty door, which he quickly turned, to make sure Sister Ruth would not cause them any immediate problems. Drak and Lea, with Clara hugging her tightly, scampered down the buildings outside wooden stairs toward the street. After reaching the sidewalk, they walked casually around the corner to the United Methodist Church parking lot to retrieve the Honda, removing their disguises along the way, piece by piece. At the next corner, Drak tossed the antique metal key to the reception area closet into a sidewalk storm drain, followed by a tinkle and a splash.

Once back in the Methodist Church parking lot and having retrieved normal clothing from the Honda's trunk, Drak climbed behind the car's steering wheel while Lea and Clara settled into the back seat. Lea chuckled "On our way to Alexandria Bay" as Drak reconnected the late Thrasher's hot-wiring job. Drak observed "great if either matron remembers that and, if they bother, the authorities look for us in the wrong direction. After your explanation of the facts to Sister Ruth, they may just shut up."

Doing his best to stay just a bit below the posted speed limit, Drak drove carefully through Carthage in the direction of one of the main highways leading them toward Malone, in Franklin County, generally in a north-easterly direction. Lea leaned over Drak's shoulder so they could both consult the paper map to follow what appeared to be the least traveled highway route. They wanted to minimize any chance of encountering police or other officials of any sort and settled into the two-hour plus drive, while listening to Lea telling stories in the back seat of the Honda to Clara. Clara seemed delighted to have escaped the clutches of the Lost League and, after a while, entertained herself, playing with the pile of children's toys in the back foot-well of the Honda. Lea knew they needed to obtain a child's safety seat for Clara at the earliest possible opportunity.

Lea dreamily gazed at the unfolding summer scenery on both sides of the highway and its small towns and farms, savoring the return to her home in the North Country and the early summer smells of new leaves and flowers. Today was vastly different from her barren prison on the island in the Chukchi Sea with its extreme cold, high humidity and dangerous inmate population. For reasons Lea could not fathom, the Willie Nelson words and music her father used to sing kept running through her mind: "I'm your native son, the train they call the City of New Orleans...," made her cry with happiness at this bright new day.

Near the end of their drive, Drak followed Route 30, which became Finney Boulevard, into Malone proper. He slowed down to take a left at the light onto W. Main Street, then, just past Walmart SuperCenter, Drak turned right onto Creighton Road, followed by a right into Valco Road. After a right on North Star Avenue, at Lea's direction, Drak pulled up in front of a dilapidated, yellow double-wide on the side of the street nearest to the Malone-Dufort Airport, where the man with the gold monocle had told Lea was the home of Rodney Herbert. A Piper Cub was revving up its single engine for takeoff upwind at the nearby airport. A wrecked, black Jeep convertible with no tires among beer cans and other trash on a scraggly lawn leaned sideways on three concrete cinder blocks in front of the double-wide. The distressed vehicle had two signs on its cracked windshield: a wrinkled, home-made cardboard sign barely visible from water damage that said "FOR SALE" and another professionally printed plastic sign announced "WE PAY CASH FOR HOUSES" with the name and smiling face of a local, real estate broker. Drak parked in front of the double-wide, leapt out onto the street and opened the rear passenger door for Lea. After Drak climbed into the back seat to continue playing with Clara, Lea carefully picked her way through the rubbish toward the trailer's front door, leaving Clara happily sitting in the Honda's back seat with Drak. Lea touched the warm Beretta in her right coat pocket, just to make sure it was there and reached to knock on the double-wide's metal door.

The door swung open just before Lea knocked, revealing a hefty man well over six and one-half feet tall, dressed in jeans and a "Black Lives Matter" sweatshirt with a raised fist symbol. He sported a luxurious, red beard. Lea said "I'm Lea. Are you Rodney Herbert? Your sweatshirt surprises me. Am I in the right place?"

He looked at her quizzically, thought a moment and responded "umm, right. The guy with the golden monocle. He passed me a message about you – probably best if you continue to call me Rodney Herbert. In the Movement, we use false names to make it harder for government agents to find us or worse. The only name I have for you is Lea, which I'll keep to myself. The BLM sweatshirt is just a bit of camouflage. How can I help you?"

Lea had a long list but started with what she thought might be the easiest requests. "We just rescued my young daughter from the Lost League. We need a dependable place to leave her while I'm out attending to Movement assignments and a nice, young woman we can depend on to be with her when we're not home. My daughter's had a tough time because the witches at the Lost League are really nasty and have abused her. Along with that, I need a place for me, Clara and my helper, Drak, to stay while these events unfold, with at least two bedrooms and a working kitchen. We'll need a house out-of-town but not far. It should have garage space for two because we may need to use at least one additional vehicle. Also, wherever we stay needs more than one road out in case we have to leave in a hurry. Hopefully that's not asking too much on such short notice."

"Shouldn't be a problem although it might take a few hours. A lot of people have left the area because of the lousy economy, lack of jobs and our terrible winters. But the man with the monocle already filled me in on what you might need so we've already gotten started. We've tentatively identified a comfortable house near the intersection of Woodward and Webster Streets, close to the Baptist Church and around the corner from the bowling alley. I don't know about your ammo supply but we could help with that as well."

"You know," Lea continued, "I keep thinking about a science fiction story I read once about a super-natural creature who could put people he didn't like under a nearby cornfield. I can think of at least three people here in Malone who ought to be under a cornfield, starting with the female judge who sentenced me to be transported to Penal Colony 627 on an island in the Chukchi Sea off Russia's northern coast. During my "trial," she was masked and wearing a voice distorter and wore shiny, black heels and displayed well-done fingernails but that's all I know about her. Plus, whoever fingered me in the first place and the local Lost League rep, who I'm guessing is a really arrogant bitch. Can you help me with learning their identities and where they live and work? Photos would also be a real help. While we're getting ready for that, I would also appreciate some buy-in from local leaders of the Movement so that we don't disrupt any of their plans or priorities."

"You've really been planning for this. But that shouldn't take very long. We have several sympathizers who work in what the present administration likes to call the "justice system." The other two present more of a challenge but we'll be working on them as well. I'll leave you a note under the front door mat where we put you up and a penny will be left on the nearest window sill so you'll know when we've been there."

Lea continued "then, there's the question of which public official's elimination would sow the most disruption. I'd appreciate your suggestions."

"Well," Rodney pondered, playing with his beard. "I'm no politician, but it seems to me we have all these little villages and towns in this county - each has a local government but, with all this wilderness and forests and shrinking populations, they don't have much real power or vitality. Plus, there's not much Federal or state authority. If I had to guess, the Franklin County bureaucracy carries more weight than local mayors or committees. Maybe whacking the County Commissioner would cause the most problems for what the progressives want to accomplish here, whatever that is. There's a new County Commissioner, just sent here by the central government and Albany – it's a tranny who hangs out at the Courthouse when not raising money for the progressives. But let's also check that with the local leaders."

"Great," Lea said, "let's talk after we're settled somewhere and blend in my friend, Drak, who's also good with firearms. But first, please put us into a place to stay and connect me with someone to care for Clara while we're working."

"You'll follow me to your first potential hideout. If it works for you, we can get to work on the other things you need."

Lea returned to the Honda, she got into the back seat

with Clara and motioned Drak into the driver's seat. They followed Rodney Herbert's black Valkyrie motorcycle with more gleaming chrome than Lea might have expected, through town and down Finney Boulevard, that became Route 30, the way they'd come into Malone, out into the more rundown countryside. The Movement's messenger turned into the unpaved driveway off a side street, stopped his hummer and lowered its kickstand. He waited until the trio left the Honda, walked to the front door of the house on this moderately kept lot and put a key on a chain into the lock and pushed open the door. The young, bearded man stepped aside to let Lea, Drak and Clara enter. After they completed a quick tour, Lea announced "this will do fine for now."

Your Dream or Mine?

David Garvey leaned over to pick up what he hoped was his final draft of the patent infringement complaint for his client, Lucas Mordoff, against MicroSquash Corporation. Mordoff had invented an electronic device, embodied in app, computer, laptop, or tablet form, which allows the user to select his night's dreams from a vast library of a wide variety of dreams. A customer could download the software from Mordoff's website, knowing he would enjoy his dream of choice whenever sleep came over him, for a modest fee or subscription to Mordoff's library. Mordoff called his product "Dream of Choice."

Perhaps to make David Garvey more enthusiastic about his case, Mordoff tantalized the lawyer by letting him experience "Dream of Choice" by installing the app on David's phone. In this "dream," David would become Tristan Schweintritten, a mounted policeman who lusted after a woman named Laura in an apartment building across the street from his apartment. Tristan had never met Laura in person and could only occasionally see her through a telescope that peeked through his own Venetian blinds. Willing to give it a try, David laid down on his own bed, energized Mordoff's app, and waited for whatever would come next.

Tristan twitched as if startled from the first moments of a very deep sleep. Slowly opening his eyes, one at a time, he found himself striding smoothly down the dusty corridor of a dilapidated apartment building. I know this place, Tristan said to himself. A stark, white door appeared through the gloom at the end of the hall. Without apparent effort, Tristan arrived in front of the door's plain, rectangular surface. The door smelled of fresh paint. He lightly passed his left index finger through glowing holographic images of his PIN from ten numbers suspended in the air to the right of the forest green door frame. At the same time, Tristan leaned into the door to push it open. But the portal's obstinate terminal ignored him, silently refusing to blink from red to green. With a low grunt of rage, Tristan buried a muscular shoulder into the door's center panel, folding it inward in one fierce lunge. Shards of pressed sawdust and a cloud of paint chips sprinkled to the dirty floor around his highly polished military boots. Tristan sneezed loudly. Twice. He reached through the door's gaping hole to spring its catch. His first cautious step through the wreckage landed on an overripe mango, making him skid sideways in its mushy mass before catching his balance on the door's jagged panel. Tristan regained his footing and stepped gingerly over the mess, brushing splinters from his neatly pressed navy, uniform trousers.

Three pair of small, dark eyes looked up at him in terror from the center of a slate, blue Astrakhan carpet. Tristan sneezed wetly again. The smallest child, cowering behind his older sister, was wearing a throbbing crimson Snuggly, one just like Tristan's only son had worn in his first picture. Tristan's overdriven brain suddenly flashed a vivid picture of abandoning everything that mattered to him in this apartment, as his fellow police officers were breaking down the same white door to arrest him. "Please," he whispered to no one in particular, "leave that one alone!"

In a dim corner of the adjoining room, a slim, Asian woman bent over a simmering black wok, slowly stirring its bubbling contents with a long wooden spoon. Cloying odors of tamarind, fresh pungent ginger and tart lemon grass were so strong Tristan could almost taste them. The Thai woman glanced up at the round-eye intruder for a split second but just as quickly returned her attention to the meal in progress, as if he did not exist.

"Score one for Osgood," Tristan said. "Maybe this'll work the way it's supposed to!"

"I meant no harm!" Tristan tried to calm the frightened children in a deliberate tone. "Used to live here. Probably moved out before you were even born. Sorry!" As if to reassure them, he

raised both hands above his head and backed cautiously out through remains of the shattered door, smirking faintly to himself. Easier than he expected, and not a word about Nietzsche this time!

Like flipping shut the cover of a family photo album, leaving the apartment buried his former home and life back in the dim recesses of Tristan's distant memory, where he wanted them. He turned to climb quickly over a pile of wooden boxes and squeezed between two boards blocking a hole that used to be the only window in this long, dingy hall. He hung for a split second from the cracked paint on the window sill outside, then dropped lightly to the ground below.

Tristan landed softly on a mossy hummock beside a pair of Greek columns. He collapsed happily on its springy surface, digging both hands deep into its spongy moisture to savor its life and feel the grainy dirt under his fingernails.

"I DID IT!" Tristan trumpeted into the fragrant morning mist of an early summer forest. He triumphantly threw back his head and tasted a trickle of cool raindrops twinkling through the green leafy canopy far above. A palpable rush of unseen sweetness reminded him of what was supposed to happen next. Rolling nimbly to his feet, Tristan began picking his way across a lush meadow deep with lacy amethyst ferns toward a slice of molten sunrise just beginning to eclipse the purple dawn. He was *almost overcome with the anticipation of Laura's moist warmth. Faintly rancid jasmine overwhelmed scents of all other flowers and fruits near him in this garden paradise. Somewhere, near the far edge of Tristan's awareness, a nightingale began to sweetly sing.*

As if on cue, fair Laura stepped into his path from behind a fragrant cloud of dainty petals adorning a flowering cherry tree!

"Laura, my sweet, you can't know how long I've waited for this moment," Tristan crooned dreamily to himself and to her at once, a duet of adoration.

This time Laura looked different. Instead of flowing gossamer tresses, her exquisite blonde hair was cut close and tightly curled. Laura's taut body was only partly hidden by a lime, linen dress of scant length. But as Tristan turned and gazed affectionately into Laura's bottomless emerald eyes, she touched him with knowing warmth, her long elegant fingers lightly tracing the outline of his shoulders as she looked up at him expectantly, slipping down along his ribs and downward over his black leather belt.

"Where have you been? I couldn't wait for you to get here!" she murmured musically. Her flaming lips caressed the delicate underside of his chin. A pang of delight shivered him to the core!

Tristan was nearly struck dumb! He swept Laura up and bore her away from the wildflower-strewn hillock toward a shimmering sea, as if carrying his beloved over some distant threshold. She was as light as a dream in his arms.

"Come fly with me Laura!" he cried, half begging, half commanding, his fondest hopes unfolding.

Laura's silky touch aroused him. Her caring glance enthralled him. Tristan beamed contentedly. As one, Tristan, the conquering hero, and Laura, the beautiful maiden, soared effortlessly into a glowing, ruby sunrise, beyond all worldly cares.

Suddenly, a curtain of sinister storm clouds raced across the newborn sun! A driving wind scattered its warm glow. Laura's succulent lips, as yet untasted, were moving faintly but Tristan couldn't make out a word she was saying. A barrage of thunder reverberated down empty vaults of towering cumulus surrounding them. And then Laura began to fade until she seemed to slip away through Tristan's helpless fingers, a faint ray of silver light, lost in the growing angry blackness.

"AUTHORIZE FIFTY CREDITS TO CONTINUE," a blaring voice demanded.

"You know I don't have fifty credits," Tristan tried desperately to fend off the cloud of enveloping gloom.

"You know the rules! No credits, no Buck Rogers!" the harsh

voice at the base of his brain stem continued.

"PUHLEEZE! Give me a break? I can transfer the credits on payday," Tristan whined.

"You haven't even reported to your battalion for an entire week," the androgynous voice continued antiseptically. "You may not even have a job left with the Police Department, much less any credits to transfer on payday."

"Is that a no?" Tristan fumbled, trying to buy some time.

"NO CREDITS – DREAM OVER!" the insistent voice bellowed.

 "WAAIITT! Take the lousy credits out of Osgood's account at Second Moravian Bank, number Q990312A64. His balance is more than enough for what you need. And take an extra five for yourself," the despondent policeman gambled.

"You're certainly not Wilbur Osgood! Not even close on the voice scan." the gatekeeper snapped. "If you can't do better than that, the game's over."

"Damn it, I've got personal and specific permission from Wilbur Osgood to take any money I need out of his account!" Tristan spat back, surprising even himself with the vehemence of his rejoinder. "Listen to this," he offered, touching the play button of his beeper, pushing the volume to max against the fury of the raging storm.

"'Dis   be   Wilba   Osgood...BACKOFF...permission

Tristan Schweintritten to...debits my account...Second Morav.."

Tristan gnawed his lower lip, hoping against hope this ploy would work. The recording wasn't the best quality, probably because only that second-hand dot microphone had been available. And there were some pretty obvious gaps in the message. Unfortunately, Tristan hadn't been able to con Wilbur into saying all the necessary words during his several repair trips. But stranded in the middle of his dream, Tristan had no other alternative. Now he at least had to stall.

Fortunately, Tristan had planned for the possibility of this dilemma. He'd planted a trump card in the hidden reaches of the dream's core software. All by himself, Tristan had reprogrammed the dream sequence to carry him and Laura beyond the mere introduction Wilbur Osgood had supposedly been hired to fix, set to kick in just after he and Laura began to fly away. So, Osgood thought he was just another dumb arrogant cop? Just wait! Tristan prayed this gambit with Osgood's bank account would at least confuse the dream machine's toll collector and throw a wrench into the gears of its ability to shut down his dream. Even more better, let him continue the unfolding reverie on his own terms! He couldn't help snickering at how he had used Osgood to disguise illegal alterations to his dream machine while he, the poor dumb cop, rewrote the entire script, far beyond what Osgood could ever hope to imagine.

"So, did you get the money from Osgood's account?" Tristan yelled into the cauldron of swirling black storm clouds.

Someone was shaking him. "Tristan! Wake up! You've been sleeping for a very long time," a husky voice called to him from somewhere beyond his heavy eyelids.

Tristan blinked sleepily and rubbed his eyes. He was lying on his back in the center of an ocher, shag rug, looking slowly around a comfortable but cluttered living room. Who are all those pictures on the wall? Tristan wondered. Let's see, he said to himself, there's a piece of gold-framed embroidery hanging on one near wall, a grandfather clock standing silent guard beside what looks like the front door and a row of three small windows hung with starched curtains. An almost liquid nauseating smell he couldn't quite place seemed to be everywhere.

Tristan squinted through a partly open front door into the late afternoon sun, a weak smudge in the leaden sky. Where could he be? Outside, a brisk wind ruffled neat rows of recently pruned fruit trees lining a babbling brook that coursed gently down through the manicured field toward a paved country lane. In the distance, rows of well-kept thatched houses climbed a gradual hill across the road. A herd of black and white cows grazed peacefully in the distance. Tristan heard someone giggle. He rolled heavily over on his side and tried gamely to raise himself to a sitting position, a process impeded by the large belly hanging over his ample, green uniform trousers.

Partly upright, Tristan faced several people he didn't even recognize, all huddled together on a worn, tan sofa covered with clear but cracked plastic. An obese, blonde woman grinned nervously at Tristan. Her chubby arms protectively encircled the shoulders of two children, one of each sex.

"Laura?" he ventured faintly.

"Yes, Tristan, I'm here." She increased the wattage of her forced smile. "We're all here. We've all been waiting for you to wake up. Haven't we, family?" Laura beamed expectantly, first in Tristan's direction, then at her young daughter and finally toward a sour adolescent who seemed to be glaring at Tristan from behind nearly opaque dark glasses.

"Mother. MOTHER!" Laura sharply nudged a snoring, shapeless, cotton smock slouched beside her. The old woman shook herself and began to rearrange her coiffure, methodically opening and closing several fuchsia, plastic hair curlers in the process, again and again and again. A scratched metal cane rested between her knobby white knees, pointing right between Tristan's eyes.

"DADDDDEEE! Mom told us you're going to be our new

Daddy!" The painfully thin redhead danced around Tristan's rough work boots, a mouthful of glittering braces outshining her embarrassed smile. "Mom says you're going to stay with us forever and ever. Wanna go see the new dress Mom PROMISED you'd get for me?" She pranced anxiously to her mother's side for confirmation and received a meaty hug from Laura in response.

Tristan watched a bloated version of his former self grin broadly and clasp his beloved's daughter to him in a fatherly embrace. He heard himself say, as if from a very great distance: "of course, dear, whatever makes you happy. But first give me a minute to meet the other members of my wonderful, new family." Something seemed to be crawling up Tristan's throat. He turned toward Laura in grim anticipation.

Beloved Laura dragged what appeared to be Pixie's gangly brother out of the sofa's depths toward Tristan, fending off his attempts to dislodge her fingernails sunk deep into a jewel-encrusted earlobe. "Here, spit out that snuff and be nice!" She pushed her teenage son toward Tristan for inspection. "Meet your new father!" "He likes to be called Slash, honey," Laura confided to Tristan.

As if watching a play, Tristan saw himself reach out to shake the young man's hand, pretending not to notice a brace of sharp brass knuckles extended in his direction. The Tristan character smiled wanly and ventured: "I know we're going to get along just fine, son." Tristan tasted stomach acid.

"YUKKKK!" This one even smells like garbage!" Slash covered his long nose, revealing a death's head tattoo on the back of his hand. "At least that loser you brought around last week wasn't such a fat slob! Count me out of this stupid game! I'm goin' out with the gang to bite the heads off some chickens." Laura's firstborn pushed past Tristan and stomped out into the yard. Slash disappeared from sight behind a nearby hedge where Tristan thought he could hear the sound of several motorcycles revving up.

"WAIT A MINUTE! I'm not fat and I don't smell..." Tristan's words trailed away as he tried to look down at his toes. His huge paunch was like a wriggling small child clinging desperately to his ample waist. The stench of long decayed food and his own stale sweat was suddenly overpowering! Puzzled, Tristan reached up to scratch his head. His torn fingernails found only a broad expanse of taut bare skin. "I don't have any hair? What's going on here?" he blubbered.

A spurt of warm liquid trickled down his left ankle into a waiting work boot. Tristan looked down just in time to see a dingy, grey poodle lower its hind leg and turn, trying in vain to scratch tufts of the frayed shag rug over a spreading wet spot on his green, uniform pant leg.

Kicking at the retreating mutt, Tristan screamed: "WHAT THE HELL IS GOING ON HERE?"

"Don't be unpleasant, my darling. He's our family pet, Winston. Winston was a fortieth birthday present from my third husband, but he doesn't bite very often." As if to change subjects, Laura gently tried without much success to lift the elderly woman to her feet, putting a firm hand under the nearest bony elbow sticking through a sleeve hole in her baggy night dress. "Oh, and meet my mother, Mavis." All Tristan could see from his vantage point was a rigid mound of electric blue hair, a wobbling cane and a faintly gray tongue wandering randomly over her widely distributed scarlet lipstick.

Tristan was horrified! He was probably looking at a preview of his beloved Laura not so many years down the road - a long, difficult journey, littered with nasty relatives, a boring job and who knows whatever other unpleasant surprises.

"What happened to you, Laura?" he wailed. "When I dozed off, you were the lithe, young virgin I'd always wanted. Now, you're, there's this whole collection of hands out and well, 'er ah, you're, YOU'RE NOT YOUNG ANYMORE!"

"I'm not older, I'm BETTER!" Laura pouted, biting the end off a large sausage and chewing loudly. "Give us a real kiss! We're just getting to the good part," she belched. "C'mere, come to mama! You're in my dream now, and I'm hungry." Laura

exclaimed, pulling him close.

"WHADAYA MEAN? Your dream?"

"Look," she shook a nicotine-stained finger in Tristan's startled face, "you may be entitled to your fantasies. But so am I! You aren't the only one to have a dream tech on retainer, Mister Smart Guy! All that floating away on the wings of the storm stuff was pretty touching, but I need a dependable man around to take care of me and my whole family, mow the lawn and do all the other chores around here. It's my dream and you needed to have a steady job. To support me, Pixie, Slash, Mavis and Winston. Sanitary engineer is one of the few regular jobs that hasn't been shipped off to South Asia. It's not a bad job. I can get used to the smell - it actually smells like money!   Now that you finally gave up that dangerous police work and got a respectable job, you'll do nicely."

Without even being aware of it, Tristan had snatched Mavis' cane. Before he could help himself, Tristan began carving a deep line of increasingly large crosses into the surface of a smudged, maple table in front of the sofa with the sharp business end of the metal cane, his vision blurring. He looked up angrily at Laura from his work.

"GIMME BACK MY DREAM!" He dropped the cane and lunged at Laura, grabbing ferociously at her throat, squeezing the life from her as Pixie began to shriek in horror. Laura's mother,

David startled awake in his own bed, looking out the window of his bedroom at the Black Lives Matter, the LBGTQ+ and other banners David couldn't identify, snapping in the wind from flagpoles of apartment buildings across his street. He certainly understood the magic of Mordoff's invention even though it would be really important for customers to pick the right dream.

Into the Maw

Before satisfied the pleading requirements of Federal Rule of Civil Procedure Rule 8 for a valid complaint. That included a plain statement of the grounds for the court's jurisdiction (Federal courts have jurisdiction over claims related to US patents) and a description of proper venue. In MicroSquash's case, an appropriate venue was the Federal Court for the Southern District of New York because the company has a store in Manhattan which sells the infringing MicroSquash devices, "Dream Pickers." An indispensable part of the complaint was a detailed and persuasive description of Mordoff's technology and products along with demonstrating how "Dream Picker" infringes Mordoff's patents by making, selling or using products involving Mordoff's patented technology. David then needed to cite specific claims of Mordoff's patents infringed by "Dream Picker" that entitled Mordoff to relief. On Mordoff's behalf, David would be asking the court to find that MicroSquash was liable for infringement of Mordoff's patents and enjoining continued infringement. Also, Mordoff's lawyer would be seeking an award of Mordoff's damages for infringement and entering a judgement three times that amount because of specific

Federal law provisions relating to knowing infringement. Not to even mention an award of attorneys 'fees, costs and disbursements and pre-judgment interest.

In addition, David would be demanding a trial by jury. The idea of a jury trial always made the Manhattan lawyer snicker. His closely held belief was that most people serving on a jury for this difficult and time-consuming process, particularly in a patent case, would be those not clever enough to escape jury duty. One reason for David's attitude came from several complicated financial cases where he was suing bad guys for defrauding banks and the crooks 'lawyers did everything possible to keep people with even basic financial literacy off the jury.

David had also developed this uncharitable point of view when he'd been called for jury duty in a criminal case involving arson, drug running and multiple murders. That judge told the assembled pool of prospective jurors that the case would involve at least three months of their time, probably include being sequestered in some dingy motel near LaGuardia Airport in Queens. The crew at the defendants ' table looked like a really nasty bunch, perhaps likely to threaten jurors with bodily harm or worse. The criminal court judge called for anyone with a legitimate reason to not serve on this jury to put up his or her hand. When David, in his three-piece suit and flashy bow tie, put up his hand, having in mind that such a long time away from his business would likely cause him to close its doors, the judge loudly demanded that he step forward and explain. David stepped up to the judge's bench, watching the prosecution team of lawyers practically drool and said "Your Honor, I don't believe I could be unbiased in this matter." The judge spat out: "This better be good." David tartly said "well, your Honor, my son was recently arrested in Queens for painting graffiti and was viciously beaten by the arresting officers with their flashlights. I'm afraid I might be biased against the prosecution." Without even thinking about her response, the judge barked "Get out of my court." David later learned that the case ha eventually consumed nearly seven months. How could anyone with a demanding job or business put them on hold for that long, however exemplary the obligations and responsibilities of jury service might be? But, still, a biased or inept judge could be assigned if no jury were involved and, in Mordoff's case, an individual inventor was being damaged by a large, well-funded corporation which a jury might find persuasive even if jury members had no clue about the intricacies of a patent infringement case. David Garvey had already experienced judges who could not be described as honorable or independent, and money from one of the parties to litigation had been known to create bias, and a victory for the party with more money to offer. David couldn't help but imagine how his former law partner had stolen from their firm by having his clients pay him directly instead of the firm but that also brought to mind the meaty thump of the subway train's impacting that dishonest lawyer.

On the issue of the value of service on a jury, David remained amused by the political correctness of long-standing in the State New York, which demanded that those called for jury duty include lawyers. Most lawyers trying cases would not want someone on a jury who could point out their mistakes and otherwise ridicule them. One of David's former law partners, who was then a Federal judge, was called for jury duty in state court at 100 Centre Street in Manhattan. During jury selection, she was asked by defendant's lawyer what she did for a living. She answered: "I'm a judge." The lawyer interviewing potential jurors snickered and asked sarcastically "And WHERE are you a judge?" He sounded like he expected her to say something like "Justice of the Peace in the Duchy of Lower Train Switch". With her answer: "I'm a Federal district judge in the Federal courthouse, right across the street," she was immediately dismissed as a potential juror. And David remembered when "America's Mayor," Rudy Giuliani, was called for jury duty and ended up as Jury Foreman – we can only imagine how that case unfolded and how that might have felt when Rudy pointed out mistakes of the lawyers involved in that litigation.

Once Mordoff's complaint was filed in the Federal District Court for the Southern District of New York, MicroSquash would retain counsel to represent it in that court, at least initially. Even though the defendant might later attempt to have the case transferred to a jurisdiction more friendly to MicroSquash, David remained nervous about the application pending in New York's First Judicial Department in Manhattan, which controls attorney licensing in that part of the State of New York, to revoke his law license for having attended a Trump rally and having donated money to Trump's 2020 campaign. It would have sounded preposterous just a few short years ago, the idea of silencing lawyers for their beliefs. But then Rudy Giuliani's law license had been suspended, supposedly because he questioned the validity of the 2020 election although the proceeding related to Rudy's law license remained subject to continuing litigation.

Mordoff had endured the delay and expense of obtaining broad US patents while bringing a commercial product to market - that had been more than a challenge. The challenge included Mordoff's unwillingness to take in investors because potential investors expected to see numbers and rapid return on investment multiplied several fold and perhaps even replacing Mordoff with someone's cousin to run the business into the ground.

But then MicroSquash Corporation had launched a commercial version of its own, which infringed Mordoff's patents in several different but important ways. Both David and Mordoff subsequently learned that large corporations don't often bother to investigate whether their proposed products might violate existing patents before launching them. Of course, trying to wade through the huge volume of existing patents worldwide and carefully consider their elaborate and sometimes poorly written provisions, would likely retard product development and cost time and money. Or corporations might rely on being protected by the huge expense of litigating against a well-funded corporation should infringement or alleged infringement become a relevant factor. These protections were fortified by anti-individual, inventor changes under the US patent laws weaseled into the patent laws by Barry Hussein Obama; even if a plaintiff has threaded his way through a phalanx of patent examiners and received issued patents, a judge in a patent infringement case has the option of sending the patents in question to an entirely new set of patent examiners for re-evaluation, perhaps only to get the case off her calendar. That injects additional delay, expense and uncertainty into the formidable list of challenges for individual inventors, all while the infringing party's cash register keeps ringing up sales. As he carefully reread the sixth draft of Mordoff's complaint, David Garvey decided it was time to file it and get the show on the road.

MicroSquash Corporation might move to transfer the case to a less neutral court but that wouldn't be worth considering until that threat became real. David Garvey preferred to submit the complaint by physically filing it with the Southern District Clerk in the courthouse. The filed complaint would then be served on MicroSquash Corporation. That would trigger the next procedural steps and reveal which lawyer or law firm would appear in court on behalf of MicroSquash.

David's complaint included specific evidence of its infringement of Mordoff's patents by comparing Mordoff's patent claims with technical features of "Dream Picker," which would be hard to deny.

MicroSquash immediately selected an individual Westchester attorney David Garvey had never heard of to receive process. That lawyer promptly forwarded representation to the San Francisco law firm of Ducovny &

Thrush to continue with this new litigation. As soon as David learned that Ducovny & Thrush would be representing MicroSquash, he delved into that firm's list of lawyers and investigated its prior cases for MicroSquash and other high-tech companies in detail. Apparently, Ducovny & Thrush was known as the "go to" law firm for high-tech companies involved in patent litigation where the defendant judged it should hire a firm with the requisite number of "oppressed" lawyers as compared to cases involved huge amounts of potential damages – apparently MicroSquash figured Mordoff's case fell into the former category. David Garvey was determined to make good use of that apparent miscalculation.

MicroSquash's answer to Mordoff's complaint was due within 21 days after service of the filed complaint on MicroSquash, measured from date of service on MicroSquash's initial Westchester lawyer. In Mordoff's case, MicroSquash's answer had not been filed more than 30 days after service of the complaint so David Garvey moved for a default judgment, which yielded a video conference with Judge Marvin Stillwater, a George W. Bush appointee to the Federal bench, now in senior status. That video conference included David, Judge Stillwater and Petunia Thrush, presumably a member of Ducovny & Thrush. She demanded the court's indulgence, offering her personal participation in "peaceful" protests by Antifa and BLM in Minneapolis and Portland, Oregon, as her reason for missing the deadline for submitting MicroSquash's answer. She also demanded at least an additional 30 days to file the required answer. David Garvey pointed out to Judge Stillwater that there are no exceptions in the Rules of Civil Procedure or related cases for failure to timely answer a complaint because of a lawyer's busy social schedule. When David asked who was being honored by those protests, Ms. Thrush seemed perplexed. David politely wondered aloud if the honoree might be Winston Smith. Ms. Thrush thanked David for refreshing her memory and confirmed he was in fact the honoree of those "peaceful protests." David raised his voice more than a notch when pointing out that Winston Smith was the protagonist of the monumental "1984" by George Orwell, the pen name of Eric Arthur Blair, a book that catalogued and challenged the evils of socialism and other similar dictatorships. He argued forcefully that there was less than no chance that the BLM or Antifa rioters had read a word of "1984," much less honored Winston Smith, a fervent advocate of freedom and a definite enemy of dictators. David then asked Judge Stillwater to ignore Ms. Thrush's feeble excuse and enter a default judgment against MicroSquash in favor of his client.

Judge Stillwater wavered and wisely agreed to supply the parties with a written order in due course but David was not optimistic. David understood any careful judge's reluctance to issue verbal decisions, having in mind his own witnessing the murder of Judge Fischbein after an angry litigant had beaten him to death in his own courtroom. David's own research had revealed Ducovny & Thrush had done work for the Covenant as well as Antifa and BLM. Even though Judge Stillwater had been on the bench for decades and had graduated to senior status, which offered him a reduced caseload, he had undoubtedly been regularly badgered and harassed if he appeared to cling to old, "domestic terrorist" concepts such as the rules of Federal Rules of Civil Procedure or the Constitution, which specifically mentions patents itself.

If MicroSquash ever were required to answer Mordoff's complaint, its answer would supposedly be required to admit or deny Mordoff's allegations and assert any affirmative defenses. It would not have surprised David Garvey if a defendant could delay almost indefinitely responding to an important claim by simply advancing "woke" excuses for not answering a Federal complaint. Even when there was no legitimate reason why MicroSquash could be considered "woke, (lavish contributions to Antifa and BLM aside), particularly a complaint which sought an injunction against continuing patent infringement might be very difficult to predict.

MicroSquash Continues Woke

David Garvey should have been surprised and, in more rational times, would have been thrilled to receive such a meandering and sloppy answer from MicroSquash's attorney, Petunia Thrush, who included her/its pronouns throughout the document as well in its cover letter. First, Ms. Thrush identified herself as "oppressed" by virtue of her claiming Lakota Sioux ancestry as the basis for special treatment under the Federal Rules of Civil Procedure without citing any relevant authority. Second, Counselor Thrush entirely rejected the viability of any patent claim on the basis of the 1619 Project, which, according to her, demonstrated that the Constitution is invalid because of its foundation on slavery. Third, Mordoff, being white, was portrayed as a "domestic terrorist," and MicroSquash, having lavishly funded BLM and Antifa, was obviously a righteous party, which should owe nothing to the likes of Mordoff, whether or not it benefitted greatly from infringing Mordoff's patents.

Of course, a well-drawn answer to a Federal civil complaint need not cite relevant case law, but such a rambling answer without really denying Mordoff's claims or asserting any affirmative defenses gave Dave Garvey a vague sense of how MicroSquash's lawyers planned to handle its defense, a good thing for Mordoff if the court would stick to the facts and law and not necessarily buying into current "woke" objectives. In the current legal climate, that was likely to remain a chancy proposition.

Spring in the North Country

The enraged husband waved Buddy Lassiter away from the unmade bed with the long, double barrels of a shotgun the size of a compact car, his unfaithful wife s long legs calling to Buddy over the sweat-stained sheets. The lithesome wench pouted, pleading with her deep green eyes for still more of Buddy s attentions in a way that only he could understand. Fighting to keep from tipping over, Buddy tried to hurriedly pull on his Italian silk trousers, now several sizes smaller than he remembered. No time to even retrieve his butter-soft cordovan, tasseled loafers. He edged toward the spacious bedroom s partially open window and tried to slide over the low windowsill onto the black iron fire escape outside without falling down and cutting his face, hands or bare feet on its rusty slats. As the big man collapsed heavily on the fire escape s landing, two corroded carriage bolts holding it to the brick façade of the building squealed in pain then sheared off. As level after level of the fire escape under Buddy Lassiter separated from the building, the entire structure teetered slowly away from the perpendicular. Faster and faster, it rushed toward the ground, like a tall tree sawed off at its base. Timberrrrrrrr!

Buddy Lassiter awoke with a start just before hitting the ground outside his paramour's apartment building, instantly aware of the intermittently whirring hover, scurrying north through a spring snow shower four inches above the Interstate's icy surface. Buddy's neck jounced painfully as the hover clanked over a lump of frozen tarmac in the center of the otherwise deserted roadway.

Under the Cornfield

The Franklin County Courthouse is located at 355 Main Street in Malone, New York. One of the offices in that building was assigned to the Franklin County Commissioner. The current Franklin County Commissioner, tasked with managing local County services, was a "pregnant" male identifying as female. Going by the name of Wilemena Soames, using pronouns she/her/hers, that official was recently appointed by progressive NY Federal and state authorities even though Franklin County is overwhelmingly Libertarian and Republican. To most of the local population, this was the same as poking a thumb in everyones 'right eye. The County Commissioner's office is on the third floor of the Franklin County Courthouse. His/her Honda 2020 Blue Clarity Hybrid is regularly parked in a specially assigned space in the lot behind the Courthouse because of his tender medical condition as well as his/her generally demanding nature and fussiness.

Once settled in a comfortable place with beds and a kitchen, Lea and Drak let themselves into two local dry cleaners 'stores in the middle of one night by prying open weak door locks and helping themselves to several sets of nondescript clothing as well as USPS worker and police uniforms in sizes somewhat likely to fit them both. After piling that clothing into the Honda's trunk, they spent more than a couple of hours rearranging finished dry-cleaning on racks of the dry cleaners so that what was missing might not be noticed, at least for a while. Store employees 'trying to figure out the resulting tangle of clothing was further complicated by switching labels on many of the hangers.

On the way back to where Clara was probably sleeping peacefully, they stopped by Rodney Herbert's double-wide to request a meeting with local Movement leaders to discuss who should be put on their "cornfield" list. Clara was being cared for by the 17-year-old daughter of a local Movement member, who, even at her tender age, was better than proficient with her own .45 pistol and not afraid to use it if necessary. She kept it nearby, with its magazine firmly in her coat pocket, so that it would be easy to reach but not present a danger to Clara. Even though Lea was becoming more and more familiar with weapons, that had taken some time because her own childhood had nothing to do with pistols; back then, weapons centered on hunting, not personal protection as was presently the case.

Lea and Drak were directed to meet a local Movement leader in the far edge of the Walmart SuperCenter parking lot at sundown the following night. Late in that summer evening, after the sun had set, it was raining when they drove to the meeting. They had been told to park in the northeast corner of the parking lot and wait for a large black Cadillac to pull up next to the driver's side of the Honda. Lea and Drak waited with the Honda's motor running quietly. Drak was more nervous than Lea. He was wary of a trap. He kept popping the magazine out of his pistol, clicking it back into place, and fiddling with his unbuckled seat belt. Drak was in the driver's seat of the Honda and had left the window down a couple of inches. He could hear rain dripping from nearby trees and the sound of tires on the wet highway behind those trees. Lea seemed less tense.

An ebony, older four-door Cadillac with its windshield wipers clicking across its darkened windshield slowly pulled up next to the passenger side of the Honda. There were no lights inside the Cadillac. It was impossible to see who was driving that black car or if there was more than one person in it. Its driver rolled down her window enough to motion for Lea to roll down hers. Lea complied but said," What's up? We expected you on the other side of our car."

What sounded like a nicotine-stained voice of an older woman said," We know from your prior meetings with our representative that you make the decisions but that your guy drives. I'm by myself.   What are your questions?"

Lea announced," We're thinking of taking out the new County Commissioner and the judge who sent me away to Penal Colony 627. How does that strike you?"

"We know you've been through a lot, but we've made a significant investment in you, getting you back to America and all that required. The fact your minders have been eliminated since your return to our country shows your skill and temerity, a good thing. The most important thing for us is to loosen the hold of the feeble administration in DC surrounded by wire barriers and armed troops," the gravelly voice answered. She exhaled strong cigarette smoke from the Cadillac's open window into the rain.

" Killing the trans County Commissioner is approved, but it needs to be done in a way that makes a public example and demonstrates very clearly to the "woke" people that none of them are safe. We prefer that be done by someone other than yourselves.   Surely you understand if you or your companion did it, we wouldn't be able to help the two of you or your young daughter, and she might be at serious risk, particularly if either of you get scooped up by the authorities. We'll provide a volunteer, as you like to say, 'to put the County Commissioner under the cornfield.'   You'll be informed of the time and place so that you both can watch from a distance. Our 'volunteer 'is not very well balanced but is willing to 'take one for the team 'if necessary. You can think of the man who will be doing this as 'Ned; 'he doesn't know about you and won't, in case he is interrogated by the local authorities or the State Police. Rodney will stop by where you are living to tell you about the plan for the time and place of the assassination but will not be involved in the plot itself."

"As for the judge who presided over your trial and ultimately sent you away to northern Russia, we need to think about that in more detail because her husband, Dr. Kissane, who provides us clandestine medical services, is an obvious part of the equation. We wouldn't want him to become unavailable because injuries and other problems come up at the least opportune times. We'll get back to you after the County Commissioner is "under the cornfield.""

Lea signaled her assent, rolled up her window, and asked Drak to drive them back to their hideout.

Lea and Drak returned to their hideaway. Their arrival awakened Clara, so they read her a bedtime story. The babysitter rolled up the garage door and drove home in her own car. The couple sat around the kitchen table, thinking about the details of how to kill the County Commissioner even though someone else would apparently do it.

As a new day was dawning one Tuesday morning, Lea and Drak were both wearing thin plastic gloves, home-spun clothing and black "Covid" masks. After leaving Clara with the babysitter, they drove past Giuseppe's Pizzeria on the north side of Main Street and parked on the street a block north, behind Giuseppe's. The pair then crossed into the green space north of the Courthouse and hid in bushes overlooking the Courthouse parking lot where they could clearly see what was about to happen. Someone from the Movement had left a green Bobcat R-Series Skid-Steer Loader with its forklift in place beside a "Road Work" barrier and a string of yellow "Do Not Cross" plastic tape in the Giuseppe's parking lot. A Movement operative had borrowed the loader from an enthusiastic, local agricultural equipment lessor with a noticeable shortage of business for a "try-out."

As Lea and Drak watched, a gangly young man in what looked like bedraggled farm clothes struggled with a crippled gait along the sidewalk on Main Street toward Giuseppe's pizzeria and into its nearly empty parking lot. He looked around, climbed into the Bobcat's cockpit, poked under its floormat for the keys, and started its gasoline-powered engine. At first, the Bobcat's engine roared, then jerked to a stop. But the young man that Lea and Drak were thinking of as "Ned" persisted, started it again, and then easily drove the Bobcat jerkily out into Main Street toward the Courthouse parking lot. He looked nervously through the thick wire mesh surrounding the Bobcat's cab, probably hoping that no one would think the Bobcat loader was out of place on its way to the Courthouse parking lot. He used the joystick controls to move the vehicle's forklift up and down and finally positioned it slightly above the chest level of a normal person's height while sitting in a mid-sized vehicle. The young driver waited in a quiet corner of the Franklin County Courthouse parking lot with the Bobcat's engine purring quietly. He kept the Bobcat idling during what might be called the morning rush in Malone grew, and the parking lot began to slowly fill. Nearing the end of the morning rush, the parking lot was more crowded as civilians as well as uniformed workers, left their vehicles to enter the Courthouse. From a distance, Lea carefully scrutinized the eaves of the Courthouse and spied a slowly moving camera; she understood if they were closer, perhaps they could be identified at least in part by height, types of movements, and other signs people show just by being alive. She couldn't help but wonder who had access to whatever surveillance systems the bureaucracy in DC had allowed to be installed and if those same people had access to surveillance from other places she'd passed through, such as the Helsinki train station and other places around that Finnish city.

Befitting the senior position of his office, Commissioner Soames arrived in leisurely fashion. As Wilemena Soames's sparkling blue Honda Clarity Hybrid entered the lot, he spun it around to back into his assigned space, demonstrating that everyone knows that backing into parking spaces demonstrates superior IQ. Soames had been assigned a disabled space because of his delicate "pregnant" condition. That left two disabled spaces for vans empty next to his driver's side door. Wilemena Soames lingered to complete his makeup by prepping with lipstick, eye shadow, black eyeliner, and powder for his long and narrow nose. Preening in the hybrid's mirror, he combed his long and curly hair with his manicured fingers so that it would look just right.

> Waiting only a moment, but what seemed like forever to Lea and Drak, the Bobcat's driver dipped his chin and accelerated the Bobcat forward at its paltry maximum speed, its motor whining and its tires squealing, while he adjusted the front loader just enough to match the height of Wilemena's neck. Although Wilemena was intently focused on his makeup, the sound of the Bobcat attracted his attention from across the parking lot. He turned to see the vehicle coming slowly his way and tried to open his

door, then was reminded by its tug that his seatbelt was still fastened.

As the Bobcat picked up speed and raced closer, Wilemena dropped his lipstick. Looking in the direction of the oncoming Bobcat, Wilemena's eyes widened with fear as he scrambled to find the catch under his suit jacket needed to unbuckle the seatbelt that was holding him firmly in the driver's seat. He kept trying to crawl over the Clarity Hybrid's bulky center console toward the car's passenger seat and the closed door beyond. The Bobcat lunged into the freshly waxed driver's door of Wilemena's blue Clarity Hybrid, shattering its driver's side window. The raised forklift then bounced off Soames's left shoulder, digging deeply into his neck, jaw and upper back while he kept trying frantically to reach the passenger's side door. He was stymied by the confusion generated at least in part of his still-buckled seat belt, now ragged nylons, stiletto, high heels and a tight woolen skirt that was riding up around his waist. During Soames's repeated attempts to escape the humming Bobcat, the Clarity Hybrid's airbags deployed, confusing Soames even further and preventing him from getting to the passenger's door. He was weakly scratching at the car's fancy leather upholstery with his long, violet fingernails as he kept trying to reach the passenger side door. "Ned" backed up the Bobcat and slammed it again and again into the Honda Clarity Hybrid while watching with pleasure as he raised its fork-lift up and down until the blue Clarity Hybrid's driver's side was entirely ragged as bits of safety glass glittered to the pavement. Wilemena Soames's mangled and heavily bleeding body had been pushed toward the car's passenger side door with gaping wounds in both his back and butt. Ned left the Bobcat in gear. It kept trying to push further into what was left of the Clarity Hybrid. "Ned" opened the Bobcat's flimsy door and stepped out onto the pavement, looking very confused.

"Ned" turned around when a black female teenager in orange sweats with long braids clattered into the parking lot on a skateboard, rolling toward a bike stand near the back door of the Courthouse. As she rolled past the last row of parked cars, she jumped off her skateboard and threw it over her shoulder. "Dude!" she exclaimed, watching the Bobcat futilely pushing against the wrecked Clarity Honda. Dropping the skateboard back to the pavement, she rolled toward the car's smashed side and looked into the missing driver's side window of the blue Clarity Honda. "What happened here? Looks brutal! Who are you?" She blurted out. "Ned" didn't answer.

In front of the parking lot, the back door of the

Courthouse banged open, and people began to pour out, shouting and demanding to know what was going on. The young woman with the skateboard, now over her shoulder again, pointed toward Soames's crushed vehicle and began explaining what little she knew and pointing toward "Ned." From their hiding place in bushes behind the Courthouse, Lea and Drak continued to watch the unfolding events while turning toward Giuseppe's Pizzeria on the way toward their parked Honda. What looked like an oncoming Franklin County Sheriff's patrol car, with its flashers blinking brightly and its siren blaring angrily, came speeding from the east end of Main Street. Trying to turn right into the Courthouse parking lot, the patrol car skidded and bounced over the fat curb at the entrance to the parking lot and landed on its rear center panel. The patrol car's driver backed up, its rear wheels spinning, to free the vehicle from the curb and then slid around it and screeched to a stop at the edge of the growing crowd. Two patrol officers spilled onto the pavement and ran toward what was left of Wilemena's new car with guns drawn.

"What the hell happened?" the sergeant bellowed at the kid with the skateboard and the crowd generally.

An older man in work clothes with gray hair and a patch over his left eye stepped forward. "Look like that tractor hit the tranny Commissioner's brand-new car. Don't look like he gonna be driving it anywhere any time soon. He be pretty beat up."

"What you talking about? Looks like a woman in what's left of the driver's seat."

In the background, the sound of an ambulance's siren grew louder, along the honk of an accompanying fire truck. Both vehicles rolled into the parking lot and parted the growing crowd as they approached the remains of Commissioner Soames and his Clarity Honda. The ambulance crew piled out of its vehicle with their equipment and moved quickly toward the wrecked Honda to see if any medical attention was needed. The burly, red-haired woman leading the ambulance crew felt under Soames's neck for a pulse. She turned to the rest of her team and shook her head.

The older man responded to the officer's question. "That ain't no woman. He's just like that farce Barama perpetrated on the American public with that Michael Robinson he pretended was his female mate. Public sure was fooled – one survey found a large number of Americans rated "Michelle" as one of the most admired women in America. What a disgusting joke! Michael Robinson never had the clip, and the phony over in that crushed car ain't no different –

you could see his package, too whenever he wore them tight female clothes. Too many people just accepted as true whatever nonsense they saw on the Mockingbird media, like the evening news we all grew up trusting."

The second Sheriff's deputy unhooked his handcuffs and walked over to "Ned." "You're under arrest. Anything you say can be used against you in a court of law," he bellowed as he pulled "Ned's" arms behind his back and snapped on the pair of shiny handcuffs.

"Ned 'looked confused and dejected as the sheriff's deputy pushed him into the back seat of the Sheriff's patrol car and slammed the door.

The growing crowd erupted in shouting. "He lives out to Lamice Lake." "That kid ain't never been right." Probably didn't even know how to operate that tractor. When you cops gonna apologize for knocking that farmer off his tractor las ' month?"

Lea decided they had seen enough, so she motioned Drak to walk quietly with her back to their own less elegant Honda in the block behind Giuseppe's Pizzeria. In this time of near total lockdowns in the State of New York, they were dressed in a nondescript way and slowly returned to the hideout by navigating back streets in order to approach where the babysitter was caring for Clara from the home's site, on a side street well away from Finney Boulevard.

Once back in their own car, Lea racked the slide on her Beretta by habit, confirmed extra magazines were in the Honda's glove compartment, and said to Drak "Now how do we find the judge who sent me off to that seaside vacation spot on the shores of the Chukchi Sea, where even now the temperature is only a balmy 11°? For that, we need to get in touch with Rodney Herbert right now!"

Arriving promptly at Rodney Herbert's double-wide, Lea walked quickly to his front door and knocked. As before, the door swung open promptly. Lea looked Rodney in the eye and reported: "the County Commissioner is no longer with us. The Movement's man, "Ned" got her in the parking lot of the Courthouse with that front-loader one of your associates left parked nearby. When we could see what had happened a few minutes ago, the Courthouse parking lot was jammed full with all the usual vehicles, Soames's wreck, a Sheriff's patrol car, an ambulance, a fire truck, onlookers and, by now, what passes for news reporters in this area. I think we slipped away without being identified but there's no way to be sure. It's probably time to ditch our own Honda. Too many people have seen it. How can we find the judge who sent me away?" Lea underlined the successful operation by showing Herbert a short video of the wreckage of Wilemena Soames's car with the bloody body in it. Herbert swallowed and asked if he could send that photo to one of the Movement member's burner phones. Once he plugged in the number, the video swished on its way.

Lea continued," I don't see how killing the Commissioner that way will convince other officials that their lives are in danger, but that's the Movement's problem."

"Let me get you some more information about that judge from the Movement and other available resources. Getting some useful information shouldn't take long, but it won't be simple because her husband has some indirect connection with the Movement. Question is whether those connections are more valuable to the Movement than disrupting the local political court system. I know this is a really big deal for you, but the Movement may have other priorities. Whether or not going after that judge will be approved, I'll leave you the same kind of note or may have someone else deliver it so the same car won't be noticed. If it's approved, the note will include details about her appearance, maybe a picture, plus details on different places to find her."

Lea slowly walked back to their Honda and climbed into its front passenger seat. Drak looked at her and wondered why she had not put on her seat belt. Lea looked at him and said "we need to talk about what comes next. So far, we've been lucky to not be recognized, particularly me because I used to teach school around here. You're more of a cipher because your appearance is somewhat different although even the North Country is getting its share of illegal immigrants rushing through the unguarded southern border and lately even the northern border then dispersed around America by this pathetic administration in DC. I wish I could stay here with Clara and that life would be as it used to be. But that's unrealistic, just wishful thinking. I don't know where Clara and I will end up but I wonder what you prefer. Maybe you would be happier back in your frame shop in Camden, collecting all those great benefits of being an asylum seeker. Whatever we decide to do, we must get another car – too many people have seen this Honda. Once we finish with the judge or find out what I want to do, maybe you'd rather just take this Honda back to Camden. Wouldn't it be funny if you could leave the Honda in the parking lot behind your frame shop? Maybe the original owner or the police would find it and, even with so many miles on its odometer, forget about it because the authorities are spending all of their efforts and time on whether everyone is complying with the latest mask mandate, yet another variant flu strain or vaccination passports."

Drak looked away from Lea and started to sob quietly. "You know," he said with a husky voice, "I love you since I save you from Execution Box and you finish Thrasher. You a fine woman. It make me very sad if you only want to send me away, like dirty laundry."

Lea put her hand on Drak's shoulder: "it's not anything like that. I more than appreciate everything you've done for me. And Clara really likes you. But we may get caught, shot, or worse because the police may be after us after what "Ned" did to the County Commissioner or anyone who might have even been peripherally involved. Once word gets out, there will probably be a team from the corrupt FBI sent to investigate the Commissioner's unfortunate demise, not to even mention what happens after we get to the judge. You're basically clean, while I had what many would consider a criminal record even before I came ashore on the Maine seacoast with those two minders. If you went back to Camden, maybe after I could get another car, leaving the Honda for me or taking a bus, probably no one would bother you - we have many choices. I like you, Drak. I just don't love you. But I don't want any harm to come to you. And the more time you spend around me, particularly if we whack the judge who sent me away to die, the more likely you'll get hurt or worse. Let's think about how to find the best ending for you. I'll be fine. Hopefully I can connect with Clara's father. Last I checked, he was influential and rich. But who knows?"

Drak swallowed. "I was hoping for more. How do you say my early life made me reality? I really had hard times where I grew up so I know disappointments. But we can talk about what we do next. Before I fade away."

Lea pulled him close. "After everything I've been through, I may not be able to love anyone but Clara. Maybe if I can complete some of my assignments for the Movement, that might change. But I'd rather be honest with you and not let you count on something more later. If you're willing to still help me at least finish up here in the North Country, let's go back to the house and talk about it. Besides, I want to make sure Clara is all right."

Once back at the hideout, near the intersection of Woodward and Webster Streets, Lea hugged Clara, thanked the babysitter, and sent her home in her own car. She looked over the groceries and other supplies a helper from the Movement had delivered while Lea and Drak were attending to Wilemena Soames. Among other things, Lea had asked for a pound of maple bacon, eggs, white and red wine, fresh white button mushrooms, virgin olive oil, Parmesan cheese, two packages of spaghetti, a pound of unsalted butter, a gallon of whole milk, freshly baked white bread, fresh onions, several garlic cloves, parsley, spinach, and chocolate chip cookies for Clara. She checked the red wine, a 2020 Arabella Cabernet Sauvignon from the West Cape of South Africa and was amazed that whoever was buying food for the Movement was that sophisticated and that such a fine wine could be found in this part of Franklin County. She asked Drak for his Swiss Army knife, the one with a corkscrew. Deftly removing the bottle's cork and sniffing it, Lea grabbed two ordinary glasses from a nearby cupboard and poured some of the dry Cabernet into each glass. Handing one to Drak, they each raised a glass, clicked them together and said "to good times and all the special things you've done for Clara and me" before taking sips. Then, dicing an entire onion, Lea added olive oil to a pan over a burner of the gas stove, added the chopped onion and set about making her signature Spaghetti Carbonara while Drak set out knives and forks on the kitchen table and added a third chair with child seat for Clara.

Paper Avalanche

David Garvey's right ear slammed against the passenger bus's overhead chrome handrail as it hissed and knelt beside the Plexiglass-walled bus stop on the northeast corner of Madison Avenue and 96th Street in Manhattan. "Entirely consistent with the rest of my day," he grumbled to himself as he grabbed his briefcase and scrambled down the steps of the bus's rear exit door. A mangy gray and white Borzoi squatting between the bus and nearby bright yellow curb yelped in pain and bounded off toward Park Avenue as David landed on its stringy tail. As the lawyer watched the unleashed canine lope around the corner of the adjacent apartment building, he became aware of a brown, foul-smelling pool reforming itself around the soles of his freshly shined cordovan wingtips.

"Goddamn it! They ought to shoot anyone that would let a dog like that run loose!" he raged, doing his best to remove the pungent and sticky mess from his right shoe, using the luminescent curbstone as a shoe scraper. He looked up from the task at hand to see a Sanitcop opening a small notebook and beginning to write furiously, occasionally frowning at him over the dark rims of his wrap-around lenses.

"Let's see," the brown-uniformed officer mused, "one offense for criticizing the God-given right of citizens to treat their pets as family, a second offense for fouling a public conveyance stop with animal waste and..."

"What the fuck are you mumbling about?" David Garvey shrieked.

The Sanitcop ignored David's outburst, ripped the perforated ticket from its pad and handed it to David, who snatched it from the Sanitcop's hand.

David scanned the yellow cardboard ticket and noticed an additional charge for being unkind to a public official. Rather than respond in any way, he turned toward Park Avenue and put the index finger knuckle of his left hand into his mouth and bit down hard, to keep from having steam vent from his ears. This was not a good start to visiting his home-bound trusted mentor to see if he had any unusual ideas about how to prosecute Mordoff's case against MicroSquash in this strange, new legal and social environment.

David stomped angrily around the corner onto East 96th Street, breathing deeply to hopefully lower his blood pressure, heading toward the apartment of his long-time friend and advisor, Charlie Hertz, in a multiple-unit building called "The Gatsby." Although Charlie was not a lawyer, he had been in enough disputes in various creative businesses to perhaps have some helpful advice about how best to prosecute Mordoff's patent claim in light of the current topsy-turvy world of Federal court litigation practice. David's challenges were not wholly legal. So far, David Garvey's interactions with MicroSquash's lawyers had wandered all over the lot and he needed an improved and more focused strategy to get over or around what seemed to be Petunia Thrush's lackadaisical approach to Mordoff's life-or-death patent lawsuit.

David pushed open the outer door of the now mostly unattended lobby of Charlie's building and stepped in front of the facial recognition unit, the type that had replaced many doormen in Manhattan residential buildings. Since Charlie knew David was coming, the facial recognition unit instructed the lawyer to lightly push the inner door toward a bank of elevators, followed by "welcome my friend" in a cheery female voice of someone probably from the Chicago area. David bustled toward the blinking green light above one elevator, stepped into the elevator car, and waited for it to deliver him to Charlie's floor since the building's facial recognition system had programmed the elevator to only allow the lawyer to exit on Charlie's floor.

Charlie was standing in front of his open co-op door with a broad grin on his face. "Hi, David. Come here and let me give you a big hug - haven't seen you since that band practice where I resigned as President to devote more attention to my illnesses." David hurried to the bulky Charlie Hertz and gave him a warm hug.

Charlie gently guided his friend through his apartment's door into a comfortable but crowded living room, where they both sat in upholstered chairs separated only by a butler's table. David Garvey opened his briefcase, pulled out two copies of Mordoff's complaint, and passed one to his friend.

"Charlie, I'm hoping for your insight, but I'm really most interested in your health. Cases come and go, but friends are more important," he said, tossing a copy of the complaint he'd brought for his friend onto the nearby wooden table. "How about a status report?"

"You may remember my early involvement in medicine, when I organized the first real patient clinic at the University of Pennsylvania, all the way forward to my disappointment when my primary care doctor decided to change his medical practice into a concierge arrangement. That involved annual personal cash payments for things previously covered by Medicare, but many of the out-of-pocket charges for things like lab tests, rays and specialist fees would still be covered by Medicare. Seemed unprofessional to me. Even though I've never tried to have my own private practice since Medicare and Medicaid entirely invaded America's healthcare system, I could sort of sympathize with that doctor. Those government programs didn't really allow doctors to spend the necessary energy or time on the needs of the patients. In a way, it reminds me of Lucille Ball and the doughnut machine – more patients, less time, and all the paperwork to satisfy the needs of the medicrats. So, the allowable government charge for each unit of time is directly related to a doctor's income, and the bureaucrats regularly whittle away at allowable charges. And, of course, related to all of the costs associated with maintaining a professional medical office with its rent, employee expenses, utilities, equipment, etc. It was difficult for patients to connect with a new specialist or another provider because of staffing issues getting up to speed with additional doctors. When my internist changed the nature of his practice, I would have had to pay a significant quarterly fee just to continue to see him, supposedly any time I needed to, but I really can't imagine it would actually work that way. It took me a long time to find a replacement, in part because the current government system doesn't encourage people to become doctors, given the continuing high costs of medical schools, internships, and advanced degrees. In my case, there are heart problems plus non-Hodgkinson's lymphoma and other cancer issues. Any doctor who considers my current condition on the way in will know I'll need lots of attention and care."

"How are you right now?" David Garvey interjected.

"Let's leave that for another time," Charlie said sadly, turning slowly to look out his living room window toward the East River, lost in thought. "Right now, it feels like there may be a banana peel on the path in front of me. But please fill me in on what you're up against."

David Garvey reluctantly outlined the background and present status of Mordoff's case, lightly describing the complaint, what he's learned about MicroSquash's counsel, and the Zoom hearing before Judge Marvin Stillwater. He couldn't resist describing Petunia Thrush's antics during that event in more detail, if only for its humorous entertainment.

Charlie asked," Can you summarize where the case is now and what comes next?"

"We served the complaint to get the ball rolling. Petunia

Thrush, who turned out to be counsel for MicroSquash, demanded much more than the time prescribed by the Federal Rules of Civil Procedure to answer the complaint and assert any affirmative defenses. Judge Stillwater is considering Ms. Thrush's request for more than the usual time because of the time she's spent on what look like political activities, things which would not have passed the "red face" test in earlier times. We don't know when he will render his decision on whether to grant Mordoff's motion for summary judgment based on Ms. Thrush's failure to file a timely answer. Given the present state of politics, I'd be surprised if he grants my motion for summary judgment. Even judges like Judge Stillwater can be intimidated by all of the "woke" bluster and threats being thrown around today, even directed at members of the judiciary and their extended families. I'm guessing he'll give her more time to answer, but hopefully, some sort of fixed deadline; that might seem like a Solomon's choice. If that's how Judge Stillwater comes out, to avoid an appeal by Ms. Thrush, it will take longer to move forward," David Garvey responded with a scowl. "At least she hasn't moved to send the case to another jurisdiction such as California, which would be really annoying, inconvenient, and more expensive for me as Mordoff has me on a very limited budget unless we get somewhere fast."

Charlie asked: "if that's the case, what comes next?"

"There will be a pre-trial order setting out the salient facts, which witnesses will be deposed, when a pre-trial conference with a magistrate will be held, what interrogatories will be posed, etc."

"Who prepares this pre-trial order?" Charlie asked with a smirk.

"Well," the lawyer mused "I guess the parties are supposed to work on it together."

"What's the chance of Counselor Thrush's participating in this process when she's out taking part in demonstrations and riots to honor Winston Smith?" Charlie snickered. "Why don't you prepare a proposed pre-trial order that colors all of the facts in exactly the way that proves Mordoff's case, sets out discovery in a way that would suit you and your client best, and so forth and so on? And put together a long list of people to have their depositions taken, including the President of MicroSquash, its top technology officials, and store managers from several states. You get the rest."

David stopped to think a moment and said," That might work because she might not even bother to read it, much less respond. If she doesn't respond at all or if she misses the required response date, the draft pre-trial order should become the final pre-trial order unless Judge Stillwater decides otherwise. But it still might give me a leg up, and if the judge gives Ms. Thrush complete leeway, that it might be appealable. Great suggestion, Charlie. I like the concept of burying her in paper and seeing what happens. I can also do that with interrogatories, notices of depositions, witness lists, and all manner of non-essential but weighty and voluminous garbage."

Then Charlie asked," What if you sent her 'Your Dream or Mine" using Mordoff's system as discovery related to Mordoff's actual product?" Or an even more disturbing dream from his system to mess with her head?"

David Garvey leaned back in his seat and beamed at Charlie: "This is very helpful. Guess I'd gotten stuck in the details and what feels like swimming across Holly Pond during a very cold winter in a three-piece, woolen suit, towing a leather briefcase filled with muddy water. Thanks a lot, Charlie. Let me shake your hand and run back to the office to get to work on your great ideas before I forget them."

Little Drops of Paper

Energized by Charlie's suggestions, David Garvey settled into his comfortable leather office chair behind his mahogany Portuguese partners 'desk and began sifting through his electronic files of litigation form documents. Since he imagined that Petunia Thrush probably had no idea who were the important officers of MicroSquash Corporation, David quickly organized notices of deposition for its President, Treasurer, and Chief Technology Officer, attached service documents, and left them to be processed by his office manager in the morning.

Then the lawyer began working on his proposed pretrial order, laying out in detail what amounted to admissions by Microsquash that it knew its new product would infringe Mordoff's patent in several important ways (knowing that admitted infringements rate higher penalties) and even including descriptions of how MicroSquash technicians had actually researched Mordoff's patents and their claims while developing its offending product. David Garvey then began working on detailed interrogatories, in effect asking MicroSquash to answer detailed questions about the development of its offending product, how much was spent to create that product, detailed amounts of product sales since it was launched, projected sales in many relevant markets, its own plans for patent applications relating to the offending product and its various potential applications, knowing well that these documents would take time to complete. But if they could remain part of the case's pretrial order, at least MicroSquash would be boxed in and denied ordinary flexibility in presenting its defense. And, if Petunia Thrush violated the rules for responding to the submission of the pretrial order, she should be stuck with its limitations and later be required to follow its difficult script. As with other issues, in the current topsy-turvy world of Federal court litigation, perhaps she would get a pass because of her purportedly "oppressed" status. Such a result would not completely surprise David Garvey based on his careful preparation of a favorable pretrial order in another case long before the "woke" era. There, when the defendant's attorneys ignored or forgot the deadline for submission of his pretrial order response and the hearing date arrived, the judge, since deceased, treated it with a perfunctory "Oh, well. Not going to penalize defendant by using plaintiff's pretrial order just because the lawyer at the big firm missed the deadline for filing his own version of the pretrial order." That judge didn't impress David Garvey, but his favoring defendant's lawyer did not help David in that case. After that case, David Garvey wondered if judges in Federal court were more likely to favor lawyers from big firms than in state court, perhaps because more lawyers from big firms end up as Federal court judges.

As the hours ticked by, David became more and more tired. Then his phone pinged. He looked at its screen and noticed his subscription to a feed of articles related to MicroSquash had delivered an announcement that Tredyffrin Investments had launched a tender offer for the common shares of MicroSquash Corporation. David flexed his shoulders, relaxed, and thought to himself," *Maybe this offers another way to skin the proverbial cat if that offer is successful and the buyer takes Mordoff's patent litigation seriously. Time to go home and get some sleep. Tomorrow will be another day to joust for Mordoff.*"

Before the lawyer packed his green Nathan's Famous bag for the trip home, he sent the electronic documents destined for Petunia Thrush to his office manager with instructions to ready them for filing electronically with the court as well as sending them by Postal Service registered mail, return receipt requested to Counselor Thrush at one of her firm's satellite offices on the East Coast. David intended to comply with the provisions of the discovery rules but not in an especially helpful way. His theory: Counselor Thrush would be more likely to be confused by those reams of paper and perhaps bungle her response than she might otherwise do when dealing with electronic versions if she even bothered to analyze them. Fortunately, Federal rules retained some paper-version requirements, comfortable for older lawyers like David Garvey but not as appealing to younger litigants accustomed to reading everything on their phones and other varieties of electronic communications.

Petunia Thrush was so much younger than David Garvey that the situation reminded him of a recent meme someone had sent him, where a grandmother gave her grandson a paper book of children's stories. He put the book on the floor and asked his grandmother: "How do I turn the pages? No screen or mouse."

There Go the Judge

Lea, Clara, and Drak awoke the next morning to a warm, early summer day with bright sunshine and only a slight breeze from the southeast. They played soccer on the overgrown, green, backyard lawn and mostly watched Clara run around with the ball and occasionally kick it, now more forcefully and straight than ever before. Suddenly, a strange car veered into the driveway. Running toward the house, Lea immediately racked the slide of her Beretta that had been resting in her right jacket pocket, jacking a live round into its chamber, carefully leaving her right index finger outside the pistol's trigger guard. But the car's driver quickly jumped back into the driver's seat after slipping something under the mat by the front door and immediately disappeared down the road toward town. After he left, Lea would find a penny on the nearby windowsill.

They went inside and turned on a Christian cartoon channel on the Internet for Clara to watch while Lea and Drak unfolded the crumpled paper note that had been left by the Movement's messenger. Two different pictures fell out, probably taken with a cell phone, showing a short, thin woman with dark brown, curly hair, brown eyes, prim lips, and a golden pendant earring dangling from each ear. Then they sat shoulder-to-shoulder at the kitchen table to look over the Movement's note.

"Whoever wrote this note is probably the old woman who met us in the Walmart parking lot. I can smell nicotine on it," Lea said. "The good news is the Movement doesn't mind if we put the judge under the proverbial cornfield. Apparently, the judge is one Linda Beckinsale, married to an influential local surgeon who provides serious medical help to members of the Movement, not limited to just patching them up after encounters with local authorities. According to the woman in the Cadillac, Judge Beckinsale is far on the 'progressive 'side of the ledger. She became part of the Covenant 'judiciary 'as the result of substantial funding by every liberal's friend, George Soros, and another pretend election. In other words, the couple doesn't see eye-to-eye on politics, but her husband helps the Movement without her knowing about it anyway. I guess if you're a surgeon, there are many calls at odd hours. The Movement's best guess is there's a lot of marital friction on many issues, not the least of which is what to do with their son, who's at a pricey boarding school in Connecticut, beginning to identify as female and wears women's clothing and high heels, not even a little bit popular here in this conservative North Country town. The judge only works in the courtroom, which was the beginning of my journey to Penal Colony 627 on Tuesdays, Wednesdays, and Thursdays. She takes long weekends, mostly alone with her two Weimaraners, at their lavish mansion on a hill overlooking the west side of Lake Titus. I vaguely remember Lake Titus as being south out of Malone, off Route 30, the way we came in from Carthage. The Beckinsale country home apparently cannot be missed on Poplar Drive, which bends along the western shore of Lake Titus. Let's think about how best to pay Judge Beckinsale a visit after her weekend begins on a Thursday afternoon."

They talked about the best time of day to call on Judge Beckinsale, having in mind how late summer sunsets are in the North Country. Lea wondered whether home-spun clothing or postal worker uniforms might work best; she could not forget all of the home-spuns crowded around the door to the train that carried her away after her "trial." But then, if wearing the postal employee uniforms they already had folded in the Honda's trunk after burglarizing the local cleaners, they could borrow a USPS truck and pretend to deliver a package to the Beckinsale mansion overlooking Lake Titus at the end of working hours on a Thursday. Drak pointed out: "If judge can be killed on a Thursday, maybe no one notice her missing until next week, if no one check Lake

Titus house. Movement note said she and her husband don't spend weekends together." And then he said, "If we can do this, we could take one of her cars. With car keys, using her car to move on would be easier than hot-wiring one like Thrasher had to do with Honda, and we still have to do. As you've said before, this Honda has been seen here too much. Maybe you take one of the judge's cars, and I go back through the forest to Vermont, across New Hampshire, and through part of Maine to Camden."

"OK," Lea said, "let's see if the babysitter can be here on Thursday afternoon. I want to be sure Clara will be safe and far removed from this action. Hopefully, we can get into the local USPS work lists and find a worker who's on vacation for a while, given the lavish benefits employees of the Postal Service get, and most likely leaves their personal vehicle at home or use it to travel on vacation. If we're even lucky, we can convince someone from the Movement to either copy or steal keys for that truck."

On the chosen Thursday, the babysitter came to the hideout in the afternoon with a new bag of toys for Clara. Clara was so excited about the toys that she barely noticed the hugs and kisses she received from Drak and Lea. Dressed in their stolen Postal Service uniforms, they drove the Honda to the parking lot of the Malone Postal Facility (recently renamed in honor of George Floyd, as were several government buildings in conservative areas around the country). In a stroke of good fortune, the vacationing postal worker had left her truck in the parking lot and had her husband pick her up on the way to Plattsburgh to visit relatives. Obtaining the key to her truck was no more difficult than walking into the facility and taking the truck's key out of the truck's slot in the office. Drak drove the truck back to the hideout, followed by Lea in the Honda. They left the Honda for later and Drak's trip back to Camden.

Climbing into the postal truck, Drak drove it down the driveway onto Hillsdale Terrace and turned left with Lea on his left in the truck where letters and parcels were usually stacked, but today, including several packages the worker had neglected to deliver before leaving on vacation. They were both heavily armed, Lea with her Beretta and several spare magazines and Drak with at least two of the guns liberated from the good Reverend Lamb's compound on the far side of Lake Champlain, plus assorted magazines of ammo and a very sharp knife. Hillsdale Terrace became Woodward Street, which ran into Finney Boulevard, the northern end of Route 30. From his right-hand seat, Drak checked for oncoming traffic from both directions, turned left, and drove south on Route 30, just under the speed limit and stopping at mailboxes on the right side of Route 30 just to dress up the pretense.

Drak slowed the postal truck while turning left into Poplar Street, which turned out to be heavily wooded with few houses as he turned a gentle corner, a large doe ambled across Poplar Street in front of the postal truck. "Stop," Lea yelled, "There's probably more." Drak jumped on the truck's brakes. It squeaked to a halt. One, two, then three fawns followed their mother across the country road and disappeared into a swale of bushes and small trees on the other side. One of the fawns stopped to nibble fresh, green leaves but then scrambled along to follow her siblings. After waiting to make sure there would be no more animals crossing Poplar Street, Drak pushed forward, smiling at Lea for understanding more deer might be crossing the road. Even hitting a deer might have unraveled their plans. Around the next corner, the pair could see the shimmering waters of Lake Titus with two small sailboats racing across its waters and a rowboat where the single occupant sitting next to an open cooler appeared to be fishing with a plug. On the right, both Lea and Drak saw an ostentatious, wooden mailbox with large letters trumpeting the names of the two owners with a printed plate that said "9 Poplar Street" accompanied by a reflective "No Trespassing" plastic addition. Lea said," If we have to shoot her, that's OK. But I'd rather find a quieter way to put her under the cornfield so we don't alarm the neighbors and maybe generate potential witnesses. I'll think of something once we're in the house. The important thing is to keep her off balance until she's under our control."

"Game Time," Lea muttered, lifting the larger of two packages, aiming to pick the lightest. They both checked their COVID-19 masks as tightly in place, pulled down their white safari hats as low as possible, and made sure their plastic gloves were well above the cuffs of their jackets. Drak turned into the smoothly paved driveway; it wound slowly down a slight decline through blooming apple, cherry, and pear trees toward what looked like a dwelling at least as grand as Reverend Lamb's mansion, making them both wonder which was the home's real front door. The wide expanse of Lake Titus before them as well as forest and cabins on its eastern shore, framed the judge's mansion.

A nearly new black, four-door Mercedes-Benz sedan was parked in front of what looked like it was most likely the home's main entrance. Drak carefully surveyed the building's facade then slowly slid the postal truck smoothly to a halt beside the Mercedes-Benz with Lea's side next to it. After putting the truck in park and turning off its ignition,

Lea and Drak quietly slid open their doors of the truck. With a package under her left arm, Lea leaned over to put a hand on the Mercedes-Benz's hood. "It's still warm," she observed quietly, "She must have arrived not too long ago." Drak said "She leave driver door open." Lea snickered "must have had to pee."

Together, the pair walked quietly up three slate steps past two pots of brilliant marigolds on the left side to a lacquered set of double, oaken doors with a polished brass knocker in the shape of a dog at head level on the right half slightly below a tempered glass peephole. Still with the package under her left arm, Lea raised the brass door knocker and banged it hard twice. Loud barking of two dogs announced the arrival of visitors from the back of the house. She handed the package to Drak.

A woman in jeans and a sweater, smaller than they expected, opened the door slowly and moved two steps back into the mansion's entry hall.

Drak said in a muffled voice, "Package for Linda Beckinsale. Could you please sign here?" He offered the package to her and deliberately let it slip from his grasp and drop onto the waxed maple flooring just inside the open right-side door.

"You clumsy asshole," the judge spit out indignantly and bent over to pick up the package. Drak stepped off with his right foot, head down, and charged the judge like a center linebacker. She toppled backwards and landed on her butt while scrambling and trying to roll over to get away. Drak jumped on her chest with both knees. The terrified woman immediately lost her breath, gasping for air. Everyone could hear the judge's two Weimaraners barking loudly and scratching at sliding doors to a glassed-in porch overlooking Lake Titus.

Lea could not resist pulling off her mask, leaning over Judge Beckinsale's squirming body and barking "I'm back!" Momentarily gaining her senses, the judge groped in her right jean pocket and came up with what both Drak and Lea recognized as an Austrian M22 Glock pistol. As if she had been trained to win football games with field goals, Lea squarely kicked the judge's Glock in a loop against a nearby fireplace screen in the adjoining room before the judge could even get her index finger inside the pistol's trigger-guard. Drak was already applying zip ties to the wriggling jurist's wrists and ankles as she tried frantically to creep across the entryway's polished maple flooring. Lea walked around the adjoining room and paced off the dimensions of what looked like a Double Dorje Tibetan Rug in front of a slate fireplace topped by a wooden mantel and an 1830s wooden clock with a forest scene hand-painted on its glass door. She estimated the rug was about five by eight feet in size. "Perfect," she exclaimed, "just the right size for this purveyor of justice. Guess what we're going to do with her – we're going to take her for an afternoon swim in Lake Titus."

She walked slowly over to the now quiet judge and said: "How many others have you sent away to die in the frozen Artic," kicking her hard under the chin. Lea and Drak could both hear the judge's teeth crack as she bit her tongue. Through bloody lips, the judge mumbled "I only did what I was told."

Lea spat back: "That, your Honor, is the long-discredited Nuremberg defense, as anyone even trained a little bit in the law should know. German criminals were hanged and imprisoned after the 1947-49 trials in Nuremberg even after making that argument. You knew or should have known that dressing in a costume to conceal your identity while sending simple, God-fearing people to their lingering deaths in penal colonies for merely speaking the truth was wrong and worse."

"I have expensive jewelry here, and I can get you almost any amount of money," the judge blubbered, "Please don't hurt me; I've done nothing to you and certainly nothing to you, young man. What are you anyway, an Arab?"

Drak looked at Lea. "I seen much violence in what was Yugoslavia, but I do not hurt people. People are killed for no reason. But this what you call her, judge, is like those bugs come out of garbage pail when you turning on lights. Must be squashed. Taking this bug swimming may be fun."

"Drak," Lea said, putting her left hand on the shoulder of his postal service uniform, "please find a couple of long extension cords and bring them back here. They're probably orange."

After Drak returned with three very long, orange extension cords he found in a small closet on the way to the garage, they rolled screaming Judge Linda Beckinsale into the Tibetan rug and used all three extension cords to bind the antique rug firmly around her struggling body. Then they dragged the wiggling bundle along the waxed, maple floor out the backdoor toward the top of the hill overlooking Lake Titus. Along the way, they could hear and see the pair of Weimaraners jumping against glass-paned doors to the porch where the pair was passing and scratching the doors and their glass panes with their long claws. After reaching the back door, Drak kicked the squirming bundle down four wooden steps to the neatly manicured, green lawn below.

The Kissane/Beckinsale home was screened from nearby properties by a stand of second-growth, tall maple trees to the north and tangled underbrush in front of what looked like wide-ranging forest to the south. Lea and Drak were unlikely to be seen from either side and were blocked from Poplar Street by the large building. Lea and Drak could hear the judge's muffled cries as they dragged the colorful Tibetan rug down the grassy hill toward the rocky shore of Lake Titus, stopping every few minutes from making sure the heavy bundle did not get out of control. Drak lost his footing on the moist grass but recovered quickly. Lea and Drak stood on either side of the shaking roll of antique fabric, bound in three places with heavy-duty orange extension cords, looking down the hill at Lake Titus.

Halfway to the rocky shore, Drak said to Lea "You really want to do this? Maybe always on your mind for long time. Like you said before, almost like stepping on a bug!"

Lea firmly set her jaw and only nodded.

Once they reached the edge of the lake and their boots were partly in the water, Lea directed Drak: "we're going to swing this mess back and forth, first toward the other side of the lake then back toward the house up the hill behind us, three times. When it reaches the top of the swing third time, and it's hopefully pretty high, I'll say 'Go! ' and we'll both let go."

"One, two, three. Go!"

At the end of its third swing, the Tibetan rug and its passenger left their hands and landed in the cold water just a few feet away from the shore but floating freely. The old man wearing a cowboy hat who was fishing from the rowboat yelled," No garbage in the lake!" but seemed to lose interest when the tip of his fishing pole dipped. Aided by a soft breeze from the south, the tightly bound rug floated slowly toward the lake's deeper water. As Lea and Drak watched, the antique rug and the entombed Judge Beckinsale began to sink slowly out of sight as the rug became more and more waterlogged. Lea and Drak could hear faint coughing as the woolen rug and its reluctant passenger sank deeper.

Together, the pair walked slowly up the hill toward the mansion and around it toward the postal truck. Lea felt anything but happy and prayed to be forgiven for killing even someone so evil as Judge Beckinsale because she knew the Bible forbids murder.

"What other kind of cars judge have here?" Drak asked. "None here in yard. Let me check garage – there are two large garage doors. We can probably get into garages from kitchen and utility room where I found extensions wires. I'll go into house and open garage doors so we see what we got."

Shortly, the pair of garage doors opened, revealing what looked like a fully restored four-door 1929 Studebaker Erskine sporting a NY Antique Car plate parked alongside a four-door, chrome-colored Cadillac Escalade. Lea looked inside the Cadillac to find four, empty Utica Club beer cans in the passenger seat well and some rose lipstick and green eye shadow in the center console. The Cadillac had MD plates. She turned to Drak: "I'll bet this is the son's car." Since he's at prep school in New England, probably no one will notice it's missing until we're long gone. Maybe whoever comes looking for the late judge will think the kid has this car at school."

After Drak found a key-board inside the door to the garage and handed her the Cadillac's key, Lea started the Escalade and pulled it out to the paved space in front of the garage doors and used the door opener clipped to the Cadillac's visor to close both garage doors. Drak returned with the package he had thrown at Judge Beckinsale's feet and added it to the pile in the left side of the postal truck.

All the while, Judge Linda Beckinsale's Weimaraners continued to howl and scratch at the sliding doors to the glassed-in porch overlooking Lake Titus. *"Only innocent animals,"* Lea thought. Then she said to Drak "Please go around near the porch door in the back and let the dogs out so they won't starve to death before her husband or some functionary from the court system notices the judge is missing and sends someone to check. Then we'll go back to the hideout and Clara." Soon Lea could hear the Weimaraners running around the mansion's back lawn and then off into surrounding trees and bushes.

Later, Lea drove the Escalade slowly along Poplar Street, followed by Drak in the postal truck, both watching for animals 'crossing the road, until reaching Route 30, where they turned north, back to Malone. They turned off of what had by then become Finney Boulevard into the street leading to their hideout then pulled both vehicles around behind the house.

Lea met Drak between the cars. "What if you pass by Rodney's house and ask if someone could pick you up at the Postal Facility parking lot once you leave the postal truck where you found it and bring you back here? If that doesn't work, I'll come get you in the Escalade although I'd rather that vehicle not be seen before we leave the North Country. As soon as possible, Clara and I will be on our way out of here. I won't tell you where we're going so you won't be burdened with that knowledge, especially if you get stopped by police and taken into custody. I'll miss you and Clara will miss you too, for a while. We both really like you and wish only the very best for you. But tomorrow morning may be a good time to go our separate ways."

Drak left to find Rodney, and then hopefully, he would be on his way to the Postal Facility parking lot. Rodney was home. Drak continued on to the Postal Facility Parking lot, left the postal truck where its assigned driver had parked it, and took a minute to put its keys back on the USPS office keyboard. Since Drak was still wearing the USPS uniform, no one seemed even to notice. A Movement messenger arrived shortly and drove him back to the hideout. Drak didn't realize that his movements were being tracked by a satellite version of recognition software, based on intercepts from Finland, Camden, and that minimart along the way across New Hampshire and Vermont as well as surveillance records from both sides of the Lake Champlain ferry. Scanning the pair's travels across the Adirondacks as well as Carthage and Franklin County provided details about their journey and perhaps events along the way. The crown was footage from rotating cameras under the eaves of the Franklin County Courthouse, which picked up the pair even though they were some distance away from the cameras. Once, when Drak removed his plastic gloves, the equipment clearly noted Drak's missing fingertips. Although they were both masked, Lea was identified not only by her posture but the way she moved her taut body. All of this information probably became available to Tariq and the Governor as they trekked north toward Malone. Following Drak from the Postal Service Facility parking lot wasn't even much of a challenge for Tariq and the Governor. They were now enjoying their new rental car with its sophisticated electronics system, the hover having failed before the pair even reached Oswego County on the eastern shore of Lake Ontario on their way north after leaving Syracuse-Hancock airport. They had to call an Uber for a ride to a nearby car rental place and then return to the disabled hover to retrieve luggage and equipment. After that, their journey continued.

The tracking electronics even noted two people riding in the USPS truck, an unusual event that might have alerted local authorities if they were paying attention.

Relieving Some Tension

Despite some closure from disposing of Judge Beckinsale, Lea remained concerned about the explosive device embedded in her neck and the amulet between her breasts. It was supposed to fool the bomb about Lea's location, making the explosive device think she was still within the bounds of Penal Colony 627 in faraway Russian territory. Being more than pragmatic, some might say paranoid; she wasn't willing to count on the fact the amulet would protect her from the fatal consequence of an unexpected explosion, despite the fact that shards of the Execution Box were somewhere around Rochester, New Hampshire. Lea wanted to be rid of the explosive device and would need a qualified and trustworthy surgeon to remove all of it from her body.

She said to Drak: "Time for another visit with Rodney Herbert so I can arrange another meeting with that heavy smoker in the old Cadillac."

Before long, Lea was knocking at the door of the Movement contact's double-wide trailer. She could hear the single engine of a light aircraft revving up for takeoff at the nearby airport. Rodney Herbert almost immediately opened his door again and peered out.

"How can I help you?" he asked, fondling his heavier beard.

"I need to meet with the woman in the Cadillac, and I must be able to trust you and the other Movement people. Long story short, after I was sent to Penal Colony 627, a doctor there attached a bomb to my spinal cord. It was designed to monitor whether I stayed within the boundaries of that island."

She turned to show the Movement's man the ugly scar on the back of her neck, still visible even though most of her red hair had grown back. He sighed sympathetically, understanding there was very little he could do personally to help.

Then Lea continued her explanation: "The Movement provided a means for me to escape and come back here to further the Movement's agenda, things like making sure certain local officials loyal to the controlling government in DC identified by the Movement as important were eliminated. I was given an amulet to wear around my neck; it fools the explosive device into thinking that I'm still on Penal Colony 627. So far, it seems to be working, but I have no idea how long the electronics in the bomb or amulet will keep working. I need a skilled and trustworthy surgeon to remove the bomb without delay. As you can imagine, this lurking death is driving me nuts. Please arrange an appointment as soon as possible with the lady in the Cadillac, the heavy smoker, so I can get some real help."

"Let me make a call right now on one of my burner phones. Do you want to come in and wait while I do that?"

Lea nodded but motioned for just a minute's wait.

Lea hurried back to Drak in the car while checking to make sure her Beretta had a round in the chamber. She said: "he's calling the heavy smoker lady. I'll wait inside, either to talk with her or arrange to meet her as soon as possible. If I'm not out within 20 minutes or you hear shots, please come and help me."

"You can depend on me," Drak answered with a "thumbs up."

Lea rushed back to the trailer and pushed open its front door. Rodney Herbert was waiting to hand her his burner phone, saying," She's on the line."

She put the phone to her left ear and said: "I'm listening."

The smoker lady coughed, cleared her throat, and said," I understand what you need. Here, we use Dr. Kissane, but he might not be a good choice. He may not be the best surgeon, and whatever he thinks happened to his wife, Judge Beckinsale, might get in the way. What you need will undoubtedly require anesthesia, so I'll try to arrange the services of a surgeon from Massena we can count on and use. Let me check and see if removing the bomb needs to be done in a hospital – that could be complicated because it would involve putting an explosive device inside a hospital. But maybe she could do the work somewhere else. Besides, I'm not sure if even an experienced orthopedic surgeon would necessarily have the tools to remove a bomb laced into your spine. I'll try to meet you at the same place in the Walmart parking lot about 7:00 tonight."

Ending the call with a "thank you," Lea handed the phone back to the Movement's waiting man and sprinted back to Drak and the car. She explained to Drak what had happened and suggested: "Let's go back to the hideout, get something to eat, and read Clara a bedtime story before our appointment."

Lea and Drak arrived at the designated corner of the Walmart Center parking lot. The weather was clear and dry.

Before long, the black Cadillac parked beside the passenger side of the faithful Honda. The driver rolled down her window, followed by a throaty cough and spitting phlegm onto the pavement. The older woman announced: "I've contacted that surgeon in Massena, who demands to remain nameless for fear of getting in trouble with the progressive politicians, the medical licensing authorities, or worse. But I think we can trust her, if only because she knows we know about her children and where they can be found, as horrible as that concept might seem. She's assembling information about how to remove that bomb from your spine, which is not exactly a well-known or documented procedure. She's right about at least one thing – trying to get you into a real hospital with whatever cops might be around when you could be on more than one or more lists of wanted people may be a risk not worth taking; she can arrange somewhere after hours for the operation at another semi-medical place like a veterinarian's office with an operating facility, oxygen tanks, etc., another complication being you'll need a real anesthesiologist. Probably no one worried about risks or side effects when they put that bomb in your neck at the penal colony."

Lea let out a long sigh, looking to Drak for even a

small amount of comfort. "I'll do it," she said without flinching. "The risk isn't small, but what's the risk if there's an electronic problem, like the battery or whatever powers this amulet fails, and the bomb blows my head off? I really have no idea how the amulet works. Can you find out from the Movement's people who supposedly designed the amulet? Even that wouldn't be any guarantee of my permanent safety. How soon can we have my bomb removed, and where?"

"Let's plan on the late evening two days from now so you better eat very lightly until we find out something specific from the anesthesiologist she'll be using. The surgeon owes me that information." The Movement's local leader said, handing Lea a new burner phone.

"I'll call you in the morning with the details you'll need."

Lea rolled up her window and motioned for Drak to take them back to their temporary quarters so they could spend time with Clara.

Bumping along Malone's back streets, Lea thought to herself,

Someone else put me in this mess and I have no help I

can really trust in getting out of it.   So far, these Movement people have performed as promised but having what amounts to major surgery seems like a step too far yet it s probably the only decent alternative I have. I just cannot continue worrying about what s next with that heinous device. Although my mechanical skills aren t the best, I wonder if the bomb is designed to explode if whatever wire is holding it to my spine is severed. Maybe if the heavy smoker woman can get in touch with the amulet s designers, they can shed some light on that issue, assuming they don t object to disabling the device. While I m worrying about the bomb, I wonder if the Movement even knows Thrasher is no longer with us and that what s left of the Execution Box is wherever that church in Rochester dumps its trash.   If only I had someone to take care of me and Clara and be there during this procedure. I know God loves me, but I cannot expect him to manage these details. Drak should be present during the operation because I ll be out cold and if it s successful, he can put the bomb in a bucket of concrete or plaster for later disposal."

Back at the hideout, they played with Clara, and Lea warmed up some leftovers for the trio before reading Clara a bedtime story and putting her to bed in her own room.

Drak and Lea went to sleep as the sun was going down. For her, sleep was chaotic and restless as dreams of what had already happened to her and what might happen to her next ricocheted through her brain like the silver ball in a pinball machine, creating more worry than rest.

As daylight crept over the small North Country town, Lea's burner phone buzzed and rattled on the nearby night table as if trying to creep over its edge. She jumped up in bed, momentarily unaware of where she was. Drak remained beside her, peacefully sleeping and snoring lightly.

"Hello?"

The throaty voice asked "Are you awake enough to talk about your operation?"

Lea wearily cleared her own throat and reached for pen and paper on the nearby table. "Sure, go ahead."

"There's a veterinary center owned by a patriot on 10035 State Highway 56 in Massena the surgeon can use in the late evening tomorrow night. I'll text you some directions. The surgeon's bringing a dependable anesthetist; he'll bring Midazolam or something similar to knock you during the surgery, along with his gear and a monitor for your blood pressure and heart rate. In a hospital, there would be a review of your medical history and conditions in preparation for your surgery, but apparently, doing this in a hospital here isn't even an option because you haven't been vaccinated with those phony experimental vaccines. Even this far from the 'woke 'centers further south, many doctors and medical facilities are more fascinated with those useless masks and mask protocols than actually caring for patients. And, of course, hospitals enjoy huge taxpayer subsidies for every 'Covid 'test administered, each positive 'Covid 'test, each admission of a 'Covid 'patient, each administration of Remdesivir, whenever a patient is put on a ventilator as well as each death recorded as a 'Covid 'death. What started out as counting motorcycle or snowmobile deaths as caused by 'Covid, 'has grown in many different ways as the burgeoning hunger of hospitals for more and more subsidies, whether not actually caused by 'Covid.' Hopefully there will be a reckoning for all those crimes against humanity and the huge financial subsidies, but I digress. Let's focus on fixing your immediate problem. Another bit of good news: the surgeon's wife is some kind of mechanical nut – she may be helpful when the surgeon has opened up the back of your neck, to figure out the best way to disconnect the bomb."

Lea thought a moment. "I hope this can all be kept more than sanitary so I don't end up with an infection. I want

Drak to be there with me, for moral support and in case anything goes wrong. It goes without saying that we'll need someone dependable to be with Clara while we're doing this operation as well as someone to be there afterward while I'm recovering, which hopefully won't be a long process."

She looked over at Drak and noticed he was awake and listening carefully to her side of the conversation so she turned on the speaker of the burner phone, saying to the Movement leader," I hope you don't mind that Drak is listening to our conversation, to cover the fact I may not remember every detail."

"No problem," the older woman coughed. "The time for your surgery is 9:00 P.M. tomorrow evening. I won't be there but the surgeon, the anesthetist, and the surgeon's wife will, and they can let you into the Veterinary Center. Good luck"

Lea turned to Drak. "Please go to one of the local hardware stores today and pick a couple of bags of quick concrete, a metal pail and a tool to mix the concrete using some of that money we rescued from Thrasher's stash or Father Lamb's home. If tomorrow night is successful, we should seal the bomb and amulet in concrete and ditch them where they cannot harm anyone.

As evening drew near, a different woman arrived in a

modest Hyundai sedan. The new arrival announced that she was a nurse, introduced herself as "Rosalee," and said she'd been sent to take care of Clara as well as provide whatever nursing care Lea might need later. Her canvas bag included several children's books.

When it became darker still outside, Drak and Lea both hugged Clara and kissed her, then climbed into the Honda for the ride to the Veterinary Center in Massena. Along NY 95, just before the town of Bombay, they passed over the Little Salmon River. Drak pointed to it and said," if we come back this way, river be good place for bomb in bucket."

"Great idea, Drak. Keep an eye out for animals on the road."

He snickered.

Further along, they reached the Veterinary Center and pulled into its darkened parking lot. Two other cars were parked there, near a corner of the building where a soft light was visible through the gap in a pair of heavy drapes. Drak maneuvered the Honda to park right next to them. He opened Lea's door and offered her his arm as they walked together to the only nearby door, standing slightly ajar.

After walking along a narrow hall, the pair turned into a brightly lighted room with a flat table in the middle, covered by a clean white sheet. A tall, blonde woman with a stethoscope around her neck in a surgical gown and surgical mask was standing next to a shorter woman also in a surgical gown and mask. To one side of the table, a bulky man was hunched over monitoring equipment and his other equipment, also in a surgical gown and mask plus a full head covering. All were wearing plastic gloves. The trio said "Welcome" almost in unison but didn't introduce themselves.

The taller blonde woman, who was probably the surgeon, motioned Lea to the table while the other woman began helping Lea out of her outer clothes and into a surgical gown while arranging Lea on her right side on the table and strapping her comfortably down with cloth belts. The large man, the anesthetist, approached Lea with a needle attached to an IV line to a drip bag, rubbed her lower left arm with a sterile swab, and asked Lea," Are you ready for me to put this needle in your arm so we're ready to begin your sedation? I won't get started with the sedation drip until you're ready to go and these light breathing arrangements are comfortable on your face. Any questions?"

"What sedation are you planning to use?"

"We'll be using Propofol - we call it the 'milk of sedatives 'because it actually looks like thick milk but flows smoothly through the IV line into your body through that needle in your left wrist. Propofol will keep dripping into your arm as long as the procedure continues so you will remain entirely asleep until it's over. Your admitting nurse used some Lidocaine on your wrist before inserting the IV needle. When you were getting ready for this procedure, your blood pressure was almost 200; we gave you some Hydralazine through the IV to reduce your blood pressure. Couldn't give you anti-hypertensive pills because the surgeon wanted to limit your intake of water."

Lea was still more than nervous but smiled politely at the anesthetist, who patted her on the left shoulder. She was trying to be hopeful but wary because she couldn't see anyone's face except Drak's - everyone else was wearing a surgical mask.

Lea reached out to Drak, who had been sitting on a wooden chair nearby with no mask, his fully loaded pistol in his right coat pocket. "Would you please come here so we can have a brief prayer?"

Drak came to her side, softly took her left hand, careful to avoid the swath of tape holding her IV needle to her left arm and bowed his head.

Lea breathed deeply and said "Heavenly Father, thank you for our friends and helpers, particularly this wonderful man who is holding my hand and the surgical team my life depends on. Please give us all courage and wisdom. Please guide the hands of these professionals and help them do your will. In Jesus's name, Amen."

As she looked at the surgeon, Lea noticed her wiping a tear from her right eye as all three also said," Amen."

Lea looked over her shoulder at the anesthetist. "Please put on the oxygen clip under my nostrils where I hopefully won't even notice it. I'm ready. Roger, go, throttle up (the last words heard from the Space Shuttle Challenger)!"

The anesthetist checked Lea's heart rate and blood pressure, which was down as a result of the drug he added to her IV line, then opened the port on her drip line. Lea wondered if he knew where those words had come from as the room around her melted away into darkness.

She could hear the faint conversation as if far away. Her old computer keyboard clattered as she tried to finish the outline for her history class in Malone middle school, but what was on the screen kept disappearing as she tried harder and harder to finish it before the next class. Lea was beginning to sob, but she didn t know if she was crying for herself, for her deceased parents, or for Clara s father, wherever he might be. She felt a blonde woman in a

The tall, blonde woman in the white surgical gown was saying,“ How are you feeling? We removed whatever was in your neck without incident, even though it was moderately difficult to disconnect from surrounding small bones and tissues. Your male friend has the metal parts, along with what he calls the amulet; he's in the bathroom down the hall, mixing something from a cardboard box into a metal pail. Do you feel like sitting up? You'll probably feel unsteady for a bit. Can we help you swing your legs over the side of the table you're lying on?”

Drak came back into the room with a pail of nearly solid cement, beaming, making an enthusiastic “thumbs up” sign. He hurried over to Lea: “It took a while, but looks like all is fine. You have new bandage on your neck. surgeon shave your neck before going inside.”

Lea put her arm around Drak's shoulder and looked around the trio of professionals. “Thank you very much for what you've done for me, getting that horrible thing that the Covenant jailers put in my body so that it would detect if I ever left the Penal Colony. Fortunately, the Movement provided me an electronic device that fooled the bomb into believing I'm still on that disgusting island. I'll never forget what you've done for me tonight, even though I don't know your names and you may never know mine. I have some serious work ahead of me for the Movement, and I pray for strength in getting my job done. May our futures be brighter!"

Drak let Lea lean on him as they all helped her get into her clothes and put on her shoes. Then he helped her down the narrow hall and out into the back seat of the Honda, where she could relax and probably fall asleep as he drove them back to the hideout. Along the way, he pulled the car to the side of the bridge over the Little Salmon River, looked both ways in the darkness to make sure there were no cars in either direction and tossed the concrete-filled bucket with the remains of Lea's bomb and the amulet into the swirling waters below.

Once back at the hideout, Lea was already feeling better and they were delighted to see Clara and the nurse, Rosalee, reading together on the ragged living room sofa. The nurse traded places with Drak and came over to Lea to take her temperature and blood pressure while checking the condition of her new bandage. She expressed satisfaction at those conditions and then produced two pill bottles from her jacket pocket – one containing opioids for any post-operative pain, the other with post-operative antibiotics, both supplied through the Movement with handwritten labels from a pharmacy that preferred to remain unidentified. Lea scrutinized the antibiotic's label, dumped two into her left palm, and went into the cottage's kitchen for a drink of water to take those pills. She had no intention of taking any opioids but would keep them, just in case.

"Drak, please help Clara and Rosalee with some food and coffee for the nurse. I'm really worn out and am going to bed right now."

A Voice from the Past

Late the next afternoon, the Governor and Tariq were rolling up Route 30 in a newly rented, dark, gray 2019 BMW Series 5 SUV with an unusually sophisticated electronics package. Tariq was at the wheel but closely attending to the Governor's occasional instructions. Fortunately, with its separate front seats, Tariq had just the right amount of legroom while Buddy Lassiter could lounge comfortably in the passenger's seat with more than enough room for his long legs when a nap came over him. Relying upon the GPS positioning of Lea and the well-used Honda, the new arrivals slid to the side of the street leading to the hideout to await the vehicle's return. Buddy Lassiter had already dozed off by the time the Honda had turned into the driveway of the hideout. Tariq nudged the Governor as the Honda pulled up in front of the house but then watched it disappear behind what they would later learn was the hideout. Buddy tapped Tariq on the elbow, pointed toward the house, and said," pull up tight to the front door." Tariq complied even though he didn't understand the point of Buddy's order. Tariq had expected the home's occupants to have other cars but didn't see any.

Suddenly refreshed, Buddy Lassiter grabbed Tariq's

right elbow and squeezed it very hard. The young Iraqi yelped. Buddy grabbed both of Tariq's ears and looked deeply into his eyes. "I GOT YOUR ATTENTION? You brag about snorting coke on your way here from Europe and getting some pussy in the airplane bathroom but get this clear and straight right now – act like a gentleman (pretend if you have to) once we find Lea and our daughter. I have no idea who was driving that Honda. If you're on other than your very best behavior, I'll pull your balls out through your scrawny throat. I may have made some terrible choices with this woman when I was still in politics and before she got shipped off to that penal colony. But she's been through more than a lot, and I'm gonna do whatever I can to make her life better. GOT IT?"

Tariq swallowed." Got it Buddy. You can count on me. What's next?"

"I'm gonna politely go into this house and see if Lea is there and find out who is that guy driving and where are the other cars. I'll go first because she probably isn't expecting me. So, you wait here until I tell you otherwise."

Buddy Lassiter flipped down the BMW's sun visor in front of his seat, turned on its light, straightened his tie and finger-combed his thinning hair. He looked in the back seat for his hat but then decided against wearing it. Then the former Governor released his seat belt, opened the car door and stepped heavily into the hideout's driveway. Buddy looked around the yard, exhaled as much as his gut would allow and pulled his belt two notches tighter than usual. He paused and closed his eyes as if saying a prayer before striding purposefully to the home's front door. A tiny corner of one curtain slid sidewise as Buddy heard steps coming toward the green entry door; it was shortly opened just a crack by the man Buddy had seen driving the Honda sedan. As the door opened just a bit further, Buddy could see the man was holding a .45 next to his right leg. "What you want?"

"I'm Buddy Lassiter, and I'm here to see Lea Holderness," he mumbled as calmly as he could, fighting his considerable nerves and trying his best to project honest concern without much luck. His gaze kept flittering to the man's pistol.

"Let me see if there's anyone here with that name," Drak answered. "Wait here," he continued while shutting the door and pounding its locking bar into place. Buddy could hear the man's steps walking across a wooden floor to another room and soft conversation in that room, too faint to understand.

Drak returned, opened the door wider and motioned

Buddy into the house and toward that second room. "You look OK but you go ahead slowly. I'll be behind you and I have loaded .45 in case you try anything. Lea's willing to talk with you."

As they rounded a corner into the back room, Lea looked surprised. "Buddy, Buddy Lassiter? What are you doing this far from the bright lights and politics?"

"Lea, ma'am, I've been looking all over for you. Please forgive me for treating you so poorly when we were last together. My life has greatly changed and I want to make up for my mistakes and lack of gratitude for all the good things you mean to me." He turned to see a young girl dragging a blue blanket toward Lea and Drak, who was now standing beside Lea.

"Who's that man, Mommy?" Clara asked, looking at both Drak and Lea.

"Buddy Lassiter?" Drak said, seeking some insight from Lea. "That's what he told me."

Ignoring the pain in her back and neck, Lea hugged Clara and enfolded her daughter in her arms. She said brightly, "he's your father, honey."

"But Mother Ruth said I don't have a father," Clara announced.

Lea put her hand tenderly on Clara's pink cheek, turning the child's head so she could look directly into her daughter's bright, blue eyes. "We all have a father. You just didn't get to know yours yet, but he's right here now. Let me introduce you to him."

The Governor held both arms open wide with a sincere smile on his face, and Lea walked toward him with Clara in her arms.

Clara wrinkled her little nose. "He smells funny, Mommy." Everyone but Buddy Lassiter laughed weakly, but he admitted to having smoked one or two Cuban cigars in the BMW during the considerable drive from the Syracuse airport. He nervously patted his coat pocket but announced," If cigars bother anyone, even you, Clara, they won't be around often."

Loud knocking at the front door interrupted the conversation.

Drak stuck his pistol behind his belt in the middle of the back and scurried over to the front door to open it. He swung the door open to reveal a tall Franklin County sheriff's deputy in the requisite gray, felt cowboy hat, pointing to the BMW and Tariq standing dejectedly beside it: "Who owns the Beemer? Its registration's expired, and I just gave that Arab a ticket for driving with expired plates that I noticed when he drove by my patrol car. You own that car, boss?"

"No, sir," Drak responded. "I believe car belong to him," pointing to Buddy Lassiter.

The Governor stepped across the room and out into the yard beside the deputy. "The BMW was leased, kind sir, and I got no idee why its registration may not be current. Please allow me to get them there papers out of its glove compartment, and we can hava look. Doesn't that problem belong to the leasing company?"

"Maybe," the deputy said," but the driver still gets a ticket for driving an unregistered vehicle and has to pay the fine. That can be taken care of in traffic court right here in Malone, no later than a week from Tuesday. Here's the ticket."

"Thank you, officer. We'll make sure the ticket is paid and we'll notify the leasing company."

The sheriff's deputy climbed into his patrol car, called into his dispatcher to tell her he would be back on the road shortly, and rolled slowly out of the driveway.

The Governor turned to Tariq. "Not really your fault. Who checks stickers on license plates, even here in New

York, where there are plates on both the front and back ends of cars? Let's go inside. I don't much like any attention from cops, so let's see what comes next."

Back inside, Buddy Lassiter looked around the room and introduced Tariq to the others. "This here's Tariq. We been working together for some time. He's awful pompous, but don't ya'll hold that against him cuz he's real smart. I wouldn't let him hold my wallet or my gun but I'm sure he'll be helpful to us all. I'll bet ya'll know more about this area than us. I'd appreciate some suggestions about what comes next."

Back to Judge Stillwater

David Garvey was still steaming over the electronic notice from Judge Chu's chambers imposing Rule 11 sanctions and remedial training in the "fight to end oppression" in connection with *habeus corpus* action David had filed to free Lea Holderness from the penal colony. He knew the sanction was bogus because the Covenant not only kept its penal colony prisoner lists secret but may not have even known back at its headquarters that Lea had escaped before or during the litigation. How was he supposed to know that secret? The lawyer really wanted to stuff that nonsense into the shredder beside his desk but instead rolled open his "Current Matters" file drawer and calmly added the notice to Lea's file. But he did slam the rolling metal drawer shut, unable to completely contain his exasperation.

David Garvey's phone and desktop calendars dinged almost simultaneously to remind him that his remote conference with Judge Stillwater and Petunia Thrush would begin in 15 minutes. Although it was already 4:00 P.M. here in Manhattan, these conferences were usually scheduled to cater to Counselor Thrush, whose office was in the California time zone, three hours earlier than New

York City now that the East was on Daylight Savings Time. He flipped open the Mordoff file to check the various documents and noted that Microsquash's attorneys still had not filed an answer or affirmative defenses, much less responded to David's proposed pretrial order or discovery requests. David was determined to poke those bears during the coming Zoom call, even if Petunia had still more wacky excuses.

David's phone buzzed, showing the number of Judge Stillwater's chambers on its screen. He answered the call by poking the center of his phone's earpiece: "Hello, this is David Garvey."

"Mr. Garvey, this is Samantha Stebbings," the young voice ventured. "I'm Judge Stillwater's senior clerk. Judge Stillwater asked me to call and reschedule today's remote conference because MicroSquash has retained new counsel in this matter."

David was more than perplexed.

The clerk continued," MicroSquash is apparently now owned by Tredeferiss Investments or something like that. Its counsel in this matter is now Lance Bridgeford, Esq. of the Dallas, Texas law firm of Goodbody & Winesap, PLLC. Mr. Bridgeford apologizes for this unexpected last-minute change but requested your contact information so that you could communicate with each other in order to provide his firm with the relevant documents on the way to rescheduling today's hearing. He said there didn't seem to be any point in trying to get what he needs from Petunia Thrush, but I have no idea what that means. In any event, it might be simpler if you provide all pending documents to Mr. Bridgeford rather than my trying to find them in the Court's files. We already have your evidence that the last round of documents was served by certified mail, return receipt requested, on Counselor Thrush's firm. We'd appreciate your connecting with Mr. Bridgeford and providing him with whatever documents he needs, and perhaps he can provide you with whatever relevant documents you lack. We appreciate your help."

"Of course," David exhaled "consider it done." The Manhattan lawyer thought," *Damn! I lost track of that tender offer. Apparently, Tredyffrin Investments successfully completed its tender offer for MicroSquash. Maybe MicroSquash is owned enough by Tredyffrin Investments to control it, even if it hasnt already completed the corporate squeeze-out of any remaining minority shareholders. I was expecting more delay and obfuscation from Petunia Thrush and her firm, but hopefully, this guy in Texas means business.*

After I speak with Mr. Bridgeford to break the ice, I ll get my office manager right on top of connecting with Mr. Bridgeford s firm so we can agree on what he needs from me even though he could perhaps get what he needs from the Court s website. If my cooperation would move this case forward, I m delighted to do whatever I can. I ll do everything electronically if only to speed the process. Perhaps the light at the end of the tunnel isn t the subway train."

David Garvey was suddenly more hopeful but wouldn't let Mordoff know what was going on unless he had something solid to report. As hungry as he knew Mordoff to be, the lawyer also knew him to be a realist.

As soon as possible after the call with Judge Stillwater's clerk was completed, David Garvey poked the number of the Goodbody firm in Dallas, Texas on his phone, where the time was nearly 3:30 P.M., a reasonable time for both lawyers to talk.

"Goodbody & Winesap law firm, how may ah hep ya?" the male receptionist answered.

"Lance Bridgeford, please. It's David Garvey calling about the MicroSquash case."

"Ah'll connect ya right away. He's expecting y'all's call."'

During the short pause that followed, the New York lawyer could hear "The Eyes of Texas are Upon You, 'til Gabriel blows his Horn'...with marching music in the background." Even from growing up where Texans would call "Back East," David knew this to be the State Song of Texas and the fight song of the University of Texas teams.

"Howdy, this is Lance Bridgeford."

"Good afternoon, Mr. Bridgeford. It's a pleasure to be connected with you as the result of the recent call I received from Judge Stillwater's chambers. A jurist, I understand, was nominated to the Federal bench by a fellow Texan," David responded.

"You're no doubt calling about the Mordoff patent case."

"Yes, Sir! Did you receive the electronic copies of my current papers – complaint, discovery requests, etc.?"

"I surely did. Thank you for your promptness. Looks like you've been having quite a time with Petunia Thrush. I couldn't convince her to send me anything at all. My continuing impression is that she might be called where I grew up in west Texas, something you've likely heard before, "big hat, no cattle." When I finally got to talk to her, she wanted to prattle on about her own oppressed nature because of supposed Indian ancestry and the demonstrations she was attending. But said nothing about the case or what she intended to do about her overdue answer to your complaint on behalf of Mr. Mordoff as well as your motion for default judgment, penalties, *etc.* As Judge Stillwater's chambers must have informed you, Ducuvny & Thrush has been replaced by our firm now that MicroSquash has been purchased by our clont's although we're still working on squeezing out its minority shareholders who didn't respond favorably to our clont's tender offer. We've been lawyers for Tredyffrin Investments for some time and have been instructed to deal with Mr. Mordoff's patent infringement case expeditiously. As an aside, the former President of MicroSquash has been arrested for child trafficking and child abuse, things not taken lightly even in California, where he resides and, if you can believe it, held without bail. Can I call you on Monday at 10:00 A.M. next Monday, after I've had more time to review the papers in detail, to discuss what comes next?"

"Suits me fine, sir. I'll look forward to hearing from you."

David Garvey leaned back in his leather chair, relaxed and breathed a sigh of relief. "Time to stop for sushi on the way home," the lawyer said to his antique office clock before stuffing paper files into his briefcase and adding a thumb drive containing his relevant electronic documents.

Looking for Judge Beckinsale

While Lea, the Governor, Clara, Drak, and Tariq were getting better acquainted, Detective Luther Franks was taking a sip of cold and stale police department coffee. He put his scuffed engineer boots up on the scarred desk between him and the second-floor window, looking over Arsenal Green Park in front of the Malone police station, belched loudly, and started chewing a yellow antacid tablet. He turned in his seat and said to the department's only other detective: "So, according to her admin, Judge Beckinsale never showed up for work earlier this week. We went to see her husband, Dr. Kissane; he hadn't seen her since the middle of last week. He didn't seem all that interested but told us she usually spends her weekends by herself at their place, looking over Lake Titus. He told us where the weekend place was located on the west side of Lake Titus. You and I went to check out that Lake Titus house. Really an expensive weekend place. Do you remember the Judge's Mercedes was parked outside the building's front door with its driver's side door ajar? We didn't find anything unusual in the car itself. No keys so we couldn't check the trunk. Then we called in here to have someone in the office check the DMV database on cars owned by the family. Found Dr. Kissane's Lexus, parked in front of his office when we went to see him. Also, a fully restored, old Studebaker four-door with an elaborate interior, including ceramic flower holders, with antique plates, and a Cadillac Escalade with MD plates. After we searched the house for the judge, we checked the garage. No Escalade. No one in the house. We did see two large dog dishes in the kitchen with old, dried-up food but no dogs. That's when things got weird. There was a bare spot on the polished, maple floor in the den with a slate fireplace beside the front hall – looked like a large rug used to be there."

George Farney, the other detective, interrupted Luther's monologue:" We found a loaded Austrian Glock lying against a fireplace screen near where that rug might have been, but put on plastic gloves before we jacked its slide to verify it was loaded. Then there were skid marks on the floor where it looked like something with heavy backing had been dragged past an elaborate, glassed-in porch and out the double-glass doors toward Lake Titus. Bits of brightly colored threads were caught on a couple of the wooden step edges, going down to the lawn. Maybe Dr. Kissane could tell us about the bare spot on the den floor. Outside, something heavy had been dragged across the manicured, grass lawn and down the hill toward the lake."

Luther continued: "We had two patrolmen go out there and canvas the neighborhood. Mostly a waste of time because those plush houses are mainly for weekends and our canvas was during a weekday, so we really couldn't wait to get started. Luckily, one cop saw a guy sitting out in a lawn chair who'd been out fishing that really warm afternoon last week. He told the cop he remembers seeing two people at the bottom of the hill in front of the Kissane mansion swing something bulky into the lake. According to him, it made a noisy splash. Being a long-time resident of the North Country and a serious conservationist, he remembers yelling at them about throwing things in the lake but lost interest when a large rainbow trout took his bait, and he got pretty busy making sure it didn't get away. Provided him and his wife a nice dinner. Another homeowner up Poplar Street from the Kissane mansion toward Route 30, a retired Scoutmaster, interviewed by the second cop, was cutting underbrush on the side of the road and saw a postal truck coming slowly along the road like it was looking for an address that same afternoon. The guy had been the leader of that cop's son's Boy Scout troop, where the son made Eagle at age 13. He thought it was odd because there was a driver in USPS uniform at the steering wheel on the normal right side for postal delivery trucks and someone extra sitting on a pile of mail on the left, something he'd never seen before. The postal truck slowed, put on its blinker and turned into the Kissanes' driveway but he went back to his work and then quit for the day because it was so hot."

"On my own initiative," George interjected, "I talked to people at the Postal Facility about anything unusual that day. One driver remembered a civilian car came into the lot when it was getting dark and picked up a brown-skinned man wearing a postal uniform from the truck parking area and quickly drove off."

"Did he report that?" Luther asked.

"No. He'd already punched out for the day but the car that picked up the brown-skinned guy was a battered Chevy sedan with a big crack in the windshield. So, I put out a bolo on the Chevy. It was found by the side of the road in that neighborhood where the kid that drove a front-loader tractor into the tranny County Commissioner lived. Not even close to the best part of town."

"We need to push hard on this," Luther observed. "Chief Premo, the Mayor, and the poohbahs in the County government are all entirely focused on this case, particularly after the murder of that tranny County Commissioner; it's making many people, particularly "progressive" government hacks really nervous. And the fact Judge Beckinsale's missing or worse has got everyone's attention. Hopefully, we can make some headway before the Staties take over the case and we're left playing with ourselves and filling out meaningless paperwork. Before that, hopefully, we can get some help or leads. I've got a bad feeling about where this case will lead."

"What's next, Luther?" the junior detective asked.

"Take a cop with you to see if we can find out who was driving that beat-up Chevy that picked up the brown-skinned guy in the Postal Facility. Then, let's see if we can squeeze the driver to find out what was going on with that postal truck. Maybe that would give us some idea about what happened to Judge Beckinsale. In the meantime, have someone in the court system put together a list of all people that the judge sentenced to things which might make them want to do her harm."

The junior detective and a patrolman who liked to be called Skooter took a squad car to where the battered Chevy had been found. They jimmied its driver's side door with a hacksaw blade and searched inside. There was mail in the passenger's foot well inside addressed to a nearby sagging mailbox for a ramshackle cabin with a "Don't Tread on Me" flag on its outside wall at the end of a short, rutted dirt road. The two policemen trudged down the dirt road, stepping over a dead Copperhead and then up the creaky steps of the cabin. They banged on the flimsy cabin door – it swung open to reveal an old woman with stringy, gray hair and a multi-colored Afghan over her knees, under a double-barreled shotgun with its breech open. "What you want?" she croaked. "Name's Goodnough."

The patrolman, a left hand on the butt of his own pistol, replied," Who's drivin 'that Chevy at the side of the road?"

The woman said in a low voice, gesturing to the closed door of a corner door in the sparsely furnished room "Bridget, you better come out here."

A young woman peeked sheepishly out of from behind the door and came out to the old woman's side. "It's my car. I use it for errands," she declared.

Detective Farney announced," Bridget, I'm a detective with the Malone Police. You need to come downtown with us. We'll bring you back if need be after we talk with you about what you've been doing with that Chevy."

Breaking Camp

The throaty roar of a motorcycle's rolling into the overgrown lot of the derelict house next to the hideout scared a raccoon. The scrambling animal's running into the yard of Lea and Drak's redoubt was closely followed by Rodney Herbert, pushing his way through tangled branches. He sprinted to the home's front door, rapped on it with his knuckles, and then pushed it open.

"You folks need to get your shit together and be ready to get on the road. Your babysitter, Bridget, has been arrested by the cops – someone saw her car pick you up at the Postal Facility," he blurted out, pointing to Drak. He was evidently surprised to see Buddy Lassiter, Tariq and Clara.

"I'm outta here," he said, raising his voice. "If Bridget tells the cops anything about this place, I need to be somewhere else. Here's a burner you can call for possible contacts if you move west. The Movement still expects you to help eliminate 'woke 'public officials wherever you're going – your job isn't done." Good luck," he said to Lea before disappearing out the front door and through the bushes into the next yard. The sound of the motorcycle's roaring to life underlined the uncertainty of the four grownups standing in the hideout's living room. They wondered what to do next on such short notice.

Clara asked," Who's that man, Mommy? Is he my father, too?" Her question brought smiles to everyone's face as Clara looked around the group expectantly, but that reconnected the four to their current situation and reminded them there remained much to do.

Lea held the bandage on the back of her neck and walked smartly over to the Governor and got right up in his face. "Buddy," she hissed," if you're serious about making up for your past indifferences, including leaving Clara to the Lost League when Judge Beckinsale sent me off to the penal colony, and you really want to help us, let's sit down at the kitchen table right now and work out a plan as quickly as possible."

The Governor looked sheepish and croaked," Darlin, ah'll do anything ah kin. Let's go to it."

Tariq looked skeptical, wondering what Buddy had gotten them into. But he sat back from the kitchen table on the Governor's left side, across from Lea with Drak on her right with Clara bouncing on his left knee. Lea and

Drak's pistols were out of sight.

While they sat around the oak table, Lea set out glasses and passed around what was left of the red wine.

"We should go west, toward the Flyover States, as far as possible from the coastal cesspools of liberalism and submission to central control. Unfortunately, we can't stay here, particularly if the locals or Staties make progress on what happened to Judge Beckinsale, and it's probably counterproductive to go east." Lea said, focusing her attention on Buddy Lassiter. "I'm open to other suggestions, but we don't have time to dither about the alternatives or write long memos."

"What's your question, Buddy," Lea responded to the Governor's weakly raised hand."

"What's this thing about a judge?"

"Better you don't know," Lea answered dismissively. "A lot of bad things have happened here that we won't discuss in front of Clara, but we need to be far gone without a trace as soon as possible."

She looked down at Clara, who was playing "horsie" on Drak's knee with a broad smile on her face. Drak said, "Giddy up" and gradually stepped up his pace.

"Let's get started by simplifying things," she continued with her hand behind her neck. "Buddy, will you and Tariq take us west in that big BMW SUV? We've been traveling pretty light and, beyond putting Clara's car seat in your car, we don't have much to bring along except our weapons. Does the BMW have a concealed place where they can be stored while we're traveling? For starters, Tariq needs to call the local municipal court to see about to paying the ticket he got for driving the BMW with an expired registration. That might cost less if you could show that the registration has already been renewed, but that will likely take the leasing company a while. Maybe you can talk the local Malone office into taking payment of the fine by credit card rather than hanging around to actually appear at the local court to pay it. We can't just leave because if the ticket remains unpaid, it might get into some database and pop up when least expected. Around the same time, though, he needs to call the leasing company and demand they fix the problem – with what you're probably paying for the lease, neither an expired registration nor the fine should be your problem"

The Governor looked at Tariq with a grim smile. "Take care of it, Tariq. It goes along with being part of the team. You can probably do all of that from the BMW. Get rid of that small loose end without further discussion. Use this here business credit card." He fished in his wallet and handed Tariq a black Amex card.

Tariq left through the front door to take care of his ticket, glad to remove himself from the discussion. It was obvious to him that Lea would get whatever she wanted from Buddy, so why even participate? Buddy was clearly under Lea's thumb, but that might be an advantage because the Governor wasn't the sharpest knife in the drawer and she seemed really focused, like a laser. At least he, Tariq, might not be criticized later for defects in the planning.

Lea turned to Drak. "What should we do about the Escalade parked out back with the Honda?"

"I was thinking when we doing other things...what if we leave it in the parking lot of 355 W. Main Street, the same place where tranny Commissioner die? Many government offices in that building, including courts and office of probation. Many criminals come and go, even those get arrested and immediately get let out without bail because of that silly New York State law recently passed. Maybe we leave Escalade in the parking lot with door part open and keys on the driver seat?"

"Great idea, Drak?" Lea said. "At one point, I thought we might use the Escalade to drive toward flyover-country but the MD plates might be a problem unless we liberated another set. But there's no way to know if stolen plates carry their own problems with them. Maybe leaving the Escalade after dark in the high school parking lot with its key in an obvious place so some kid can steal it would be easier than going to the center of town to leave it. We'll come back to that later."

"Back to you, Buddy," she continued, pointing at the Governor. "Can we depend on you to drive us as far west as we want without any funny business, especially from your Batman, Tariq? I need to understand how the years have changed you – they have certainly changed me from the docile schoolteacher you once knew. This is your real chance to step up to the plate like a real man, treat me right, and even spend some time with your very own daughter."

"Show me what you need," Buddy said, offering with a wan smile. "I'd surely love to make you and Clara happy."

"As soon Tariq's done with paying his ticket and arranging to get the BMW's registration renewed," Lea directed, "he can drive the Escalade to the high school parking lot and leave it off on the side with driver's door ajar and keys in a cup on the car's console. School's mostly done for the day except late classes and sports. Tariq can get directions to the high school with the Escalade's installed mapping software. Drak will follow you in the Honda out back – it was hot-wired so the driver still needs to fool with that and your man, Tariq, doesn't look like he can handle anything mechanical or dirty. After a while, assuming Tariq is successful in getting the leasing company to renew the BMW registration, that should be up on the DMV computer so any cop could check it even if the sticker itself on the rear plate has expired. After the Escalade is where you want it to be and you've cleaned every possible place that could retain fingerprints with Clorox wipes from that plastic can behind the driver's seat, Drak can bring you back here. Before you leave, give me both sets of keys to the BMW."

Lea thrust an open palm under Buddy's nose.

"You don't trust me?" the Governor whined.

"Trust is built, Buddy. You left me pregnant the last time we were together, then slithered off and disappeared. I was alone for more than six years without any way to even find you, then in that disgusting prison camp for a blissfully short time before the Movement helped me escape and come back to America. That whole experience has really hardened me. Plus, I know nothing about Tariq except that his demeanor suggests he's a weasel. So no, I don't trust you again, and I have no reason in the world to trust your sidekick. And what are the two of you working on? You both must EARN my trust."

Buddy Lassiter sat back in his chair, looked at the mother of his child and nodded his head vigorously.

Before long, they turned as Tariq came back into the kitchen from the front room after they heard the front door click shut.

"I paid the ticket with Buddy's credit card after explaining to the clerk about the unfairness of giving me a ticket for something the leasing company bungled. Then I spent quite a while on the phone getting bounced around within the leasing company to convince them to renew the BMW's registration. By the way, the cell service here sucks."

The Governor cleared his throat and pointed at Tariq. "Here's the plan. I'm staying here while you and her man, Drak, take the Escalade to the high school parking lot and leave it there with the keys clearly visible. Hopefully, some kid will steal it and distract the locals from whatever the problem is with the Escalade, at least until we're gone. Not sure why that's important, but part of my job is to do whatever I can to begin convincing Lea that you're an honorable guy and can be trusted around her and Clara. We'll begin working on a plan to get us out of here as soon as possible, which way to drive in the BMW, and them such details. You come right back here as soon and as quietly as you can. In the meantime, gimme here your set of BMW keys. When you get back, we'll use the BMW's mapping software to figure out an escape route so nothing we leave behind here can help anyone find us."

Buddy Lassiter took Tariq's set of keys, fiddled in his pants pocket for the other set and dropped both into Lea's outstretched hand.

Lea said: "thanks Buddy. That's a start at building trust."

She turned to Tariq: "Remember, I used to be a teacher here. The high school is Franklin Academy, at 42 Huskie Lane. It's simpler if you get directions from the Escalade's mapping software even though Drak knows where it is. But basically, you take a left out of the driveway, turn right on Route 30. From there, you'll be better off to go cross-lots and hopefully avoid being seen on principal roads like Main Street. The high school is pretty much off by itself, south of Main Street but always stay under the speed limit. Once you dump the Escalade, Drak can bring you back here."

Off to School

Tariq and Drak went out the home's back door to get into the Escalade and the Honda after taking Clara's car seat out of the Honda. Drak stuck his pistol in his deep, right pocket while the pair cleaned everywhere possible in the Escalade that might have prints of either Drak, Lea, or even Clara. They started the cars and rolled around the hideout to the driveway. Before leaving, Tariq put in his earpiece, called up Sibelius's "Karelia Suite" from the vehicle's Sirius XM music service, and put the high school's address into maps on DuckDuckGo so that the mapping software would interrupt his music to provide specific directions to their destination as needed.

Lea picked up Clara with her left arm took the Governor by his jacket sleeve, and dragged him toward the bedroom: "You can help pack what little we have, and then we need to wipe wherever Clara, Drak or I have touched, here or in the bathroom or kitchen including doorknobs. Clara's too young to have ever been printed but let's start by being extra careful in case those witches in the Lost League did it."

Before leaving, Tariq ran a search for 42 Huskie Lane,

enlarged the map and turn on voice directions. As instructed, he drove around the hideout and turned left at the end of the driveway so the software wouldn't drag him off into what looked like marshy land around the high school property. Drak was right behind him with the Honda but Tariq rolled down his window and motioned Drak to hang back. When Tariq got to Route 30 (the street sign said "Finney Boulevard"), the English voice in his ear told him to turn right. When he could see the Price Chopper grocery store in the distance, the voice instructed Tariq to slowly take a right turn. He could see from the street sign that was Franklin Street. Through his earpiece, the mapping software directed him around the south then eastern sides of Malone Middle School to Harrison Place. It was only a short distance to a right turn. There was a street sign on the ground at the intersection that looked like it said "College" something. The voice in his ear then instructed Tariq to turn right, where he pulled over to the right side of the road to figure out what came next. Drak pulled up behind the Escalade and motioned for Tariq to take the right fork ahead. The entry to the high school complex was a one-way street which split into two directions once inside the property. Tariq took the right fork and began looking for the best place to leave the Escalade once he could see the buildings and parking areas. Drak was about 50 feet behind the Escalade. Tariq immediately saw a crowd of teenagers coming out of a side door into two parking lots, some getting into different kinds of parked cars and even a pair of motorcycles. Tariq parked the Escalade several rows back from the group of raucous students and looked around to see where Drak was parking the Honda.

A police car with flashing lights had followed Drak and the Honda into the parking lot. The crowd of students all turned toward them.

The lone patrolman squeaked to a stop directly behind the Honda and yelled through the patrol car's speaker: "Police! Turn off your car and throw the keys on the pavement. Keep your hands on the steering wheel!"

Drak opened his driver's side door and stuck out his head: "I am having no keys to put on pavement – I lost them." Tariq thought to himself: '*Absolutely fucking brilliant – the cop probably couldn't imagine how Drak got the Honda to the high school without keys.*'"

The Malone policeman stepped out of his vehicle, stood behind his car door and drew his pistol. "Get out slowly and put both hands on the roof! Get out your driver's license and put it on the car roof."

Drak did as he was told and put his license as well as

his refugee documents on the car's roof.

As the patrolman approached Drak, he said in a loud voice: "We don't see many Maine plates up here in the North Country but our office got a BOLO about a Maine warrant for stolen plates which seem to be on your Honda. Spread your legs, move your feet back and keep your hands on the car roof – I need to pat you down. How come you don't have any car keys?"

Drak again complied with the officer's instructions. "I'm oppressed person and a refugee from Kosovo."

The cop leaned over and began feeling Drak's body and legs; he immediately stiffened. "That feels like a gun. Put both hands behind your back. Here come the cuffs," he said as a jingling sound showed the patrolman was unhooking cuffs from his belt. "You're under arrest. Anything you say may be used against you in a court of law. Beside the warrant about the stolen Maine plates, you cannot have a pistol without a permit in New York. Can you show me a New York permit for your weapon?"

Drak said "no, officer."

Shortly, Drak was fully handcuffed and being stuffed into the back seat of the patrol car, with a heavy-duty screen between front and back seats. The patrolman went back to the Honda and looked inside. He returned to the patrol car and leaned in the open back window and said to Drak: "what's going on? That car's been hot-wired." Drak only looked out the other window and bit his lower lip. The cop promptly called his dispatcher, announcing "Car 5. Just arrested someone with that stolen Maine plate we've been getting notices about and found he's carrying an unregistered, loaded pistol so I'm bringing him in. And it looks like the Honda he was driving was stolen. You can get the VIN when we get back to the station and check it against the databases."

Tariq watched what was unfolding in horror. He knew Drak was important to Lea and had helped her a great deal but he was most worried how these events might spill over onto him. Certainly, there was little he or anyone else could do to help Drak at the moment, so he got back into the Escalade, closed its doors and windows and called the Governor.

"Whassup, Tariq?" the Governor asked on only the second ring.

"We got a problem, Governor. We got to the high school and were about to leave the Escalade but Drak was arrested by some local gendarme who followed us into the parking lot and, when he was patting Drak down, it looks like he found Drak's pistol. Looks like the cop saw the hot-wire job in the Honda, handcuffed him and probably took him off to the local police station."

"No shit! I'm gonna give you to Lea. She may have some creative ideas."

Lea grabbed Buddy's phone "What happened?"

Tariq repeated his account of the arrest, gritting his teeth for fear of what Lea might say.

"Was Drak hurt?"

"No, ma'am. From what I could see, the cop didn't hit Drak or anything else. Just put him in cuffs and drove off with Drak in the back seat of the patrol car. I could hear the cop calling his dispatcher and it sounded like they were on the way to the police station." Tariq could hear Lea's sobbing.

Lea took two deep breaths, paused and said in a weak voice. "probably no way to spring Drak. He's got refugee papers. Refugees are treated better than Americans, so he probably won't have such a bad time. Now we really need to be out of Malone immediately, if not sooner. Please drive the Escalade to the large Price Chopper grocery store you saw on the way to the high school. It's near the top of Finney Boulevard on the west side of the street, after where you probably took the turn toward the high school. Park in the middle of the Price Chopper parking lot and leave its doors unlocked, throw anything in the glove compartment or elsewhere in the Escalade into the store's trash and leave the keys on the console next to the driver's seat. Then you go into the Price Chopper and buy some takeout food from its deli, sandwiches and drinks for our drive somewhere else and some Mac and Cheese for Clara, if they have it. We'll throw our things and guns into the BMW, strap in Clara's car seat and pick you up near the front doors of the Price Chopper in about 20 minutes. Then we can be on our way sooner than expected. Any questions?"

"I don't have much cash but I still have the Governor's black Amex card. I'll be waiting out front in about 25 minutes or sooner if possible."

Lea ended the call and shrieked at Buddy "time to go! Help me put our things and guns into the BMW while I strap in Clara's car seat. As soon as we're done with that, we'll both check to see if there's anything here cops could use to find or track us. Any questions?"

Lea was watching Buddy carefully, trying to get a sense if his care for her remained in any real way while she wondered why he had at last tried to find her.

Together, they ripped a blanket from one of the beds, piled their clothes, toilet articles and plus guns and ammo into the blanket and dragged the bundle toward the BMW in the front yard. While they walked to the SUV with Clara toddling along behind, the Governor popped its back hatch and lifted a fabric floor panel behind the vehicle's back seats. Lea was pleasantly surprised by the large space under the panel, empty except for what looked like marijuana in a large plastic bag.

Buddy cussed and said "that there Tariq always looking for an angle but for now let's us wrap the guns and ammo in this here blanket and put them on the bottom, with clothes and toys on top in case we get stopped. Plenty of small compartments around them seats in the cockpit and back seats for smaller weapons." Clara immediately tried to play with the first plastic toy with reach until her mother put her car seat in the middle of the SUV's back seat, fastened it in with nearby seat belts and strapped her daughter comfortably into it.

Lea smiled appreciatively. "Now, we go back and quickly go wipe surfaces, door-knobs, faucet handles and even both sides of the toilet flushing lever with Wet Wipes to get rid of any possible fingerprints." Buddy's eagerness told her the pair were somewhat on the same page. She used her burner phone to call "Rodney Herbert" to let him know what was happening and to find out if the Movement had any more instructions for her as they escaped from Franklin County, hoping it might not be a long list.

When Lea finished her call, she handed Buddy Lassiter one set of the BMW keys and pointed him toward the driver's seat. She went back to close the front door of what she'd considered their safe house and climbed into the back seat of the SUV with Clara.

Westward Ho!

Buddy fastened his seatbelt before starting the BMW, drove it to the end of the driveway, and followed Lea's directions to the Price Chopper.

As the Governor smoothly drove north along Finney Boulevard, he took a slow left turn into the Price Chopper parking lot, where they could both see many people entering and leaving the large store.

Noting Clara had fallen asleep in the car seat beside her, Lea leaned over the back of the vehicle's plush leather front seat said in a low voice, "Buddy, I can sense your political juices 'flowing, seeing two signs in front of Price Chopper for a candidate for Malone Mayor in the coming election. Plus, we both see workers 'collecting signatures on nominating petitions from shoppers so their candidate can get on the primary ballot. Whatever you do, don't get out of the car and start shaking hands with YOUR public. We're not here for that! The last thing we need is for someone to remember your face from one of your major political campaigns and tell friends about it later. Something like 'you know, I saw that guy who was running

"

for governor of some Southern state, right outside our Price Chopper. 'Our objective: to slide out of Malone quietly and get on our way to somewhere much less threatening. Just so you know, Buddy (but you cannot share with anyone, even Tariq), the police may be looking for us. Drak and I put the local Covenant judge who sent me off to Penal Colony 627 under the cornfield. It may not take long for the authorities to figure out what happened there. We must be long gone by the time that happens and I pray that Drak won't tell anyone about any part of that event. I don't think he will and the fact he has this special pampered 'refugee 'status may result in the police not making any connection with more than the stolen Honda. Oh, look, there's your man, Tariq, standing near the front door of the Price Chopper. Fortunately, the windows of this SUV are moderately tinted but don't get out to try and help Tariq with the groceries. We don't want anyone to see us. Just pull over beside him and don't get out! He can open the back hatch to load his groceries."

Buddy looked surprised at the news and asked: "what's that there cornfield thanng?" Lea looked at him sideways as he maneuvered the sleek BMW toward the front doors of the Price Chopper, threading his way through families with full shopping carts, couples with empty carts on the way in, children skipping alongside, some with family dogs. Without warning, a disheveled old woman with stringy, grey hair stumbled from between a row of parked car; she began to pound on the SUV's hood with mittened hands, yelling "get outta my yard." Lea was startled and shuddered, remembering the same chants surrounding the long, diesel train as it had chugged away from the courthouse in Malone, beginning Lea's journey across many time zones to Penal Colony 627.

Buddy could see the fright in Lea's face. He put his right hand over hers. "What's wrong, honey?" He stopped the car to assess the situation.

Lea sniffed back tears and rubbed her eyes with her free hand. "People were yelling the same thing around the train when I was starting my endless trip east toward that island prison. I couldn't even see Clara because she'd been grabbed up by the Lost League once the court considered me as good as dead. It makes me cry just to think about it. Don't hit that poor woman but get to Tariq as smoothly and fast as possible."

Buddy patted her hand as they pulled alongside Tariq. He rolled down the passenger's side window from the driver's seat. "Tariq. Open the back hatch, put the groceries on the floor in back, close the back gate then come around to my side. Y'all going be drivin'"

The Governor stepped out of the SUV with his head down, let Tariq slide into the driver's seat and climbed into the back seat with Clara and her car seat between him and Lea. He smiled fondly at Clara and smoothed her tousled, blonde hair. "What do you have in mind for our route out of here, honey?"

Lea swallowed and said "if Tariq could please put LaFayette, NY into the car's navigation system. It's south of Syracuse. The system should tell us to take a right out of the Price Chopper parking lot onto Finney Boulevard which becomes US 11. That will take us to Watertown where we get on US 81 south, on the way toward Syracuse. We could take US 90 (the NY Thruway) at Syracuse but that always seemed more crowded and may have more police. If we stay on US 81, we could perhaps stay at the Syracuse Crown Plaza, just south of the NY Thruway, for a day or two in case we change our plans and want to use the Thruway to go west out of New York. If we stay on US 81, it would take us to cross-Pennsylvania routes; that might make it easier to get quickly to my next assignment in Chagrin Falls, Ohio."

"Just so's we can avoid them home-spuns at security checkpoints in busy places," the Governor grumbled. "Ain't that right, Tariq? Dealing with them probly wasn't your finest hour. Lea, honey, what's your assignment in Chagrin Falls?"

Tariq looked angrily at Buddy in the mirror and announced: "those directions are in the navigation system. A little over three hours to Syracuse with little turns along the way but not a challenge unless there are weather or police problems. By the way, esteemed Governor Lassiter, I arranged with the car rental to let us turn in this BMW at a different location than where we picked it up, in part as compensation for jamming us up because of the expired registration. Any other special arrangements, SIR?" Tariq suspected this entire exercise would be a complicated burden and had no idea how this could be related to what he and the Governor had been doing to serve the Iranians before they veered off track to find Lea Holderness.

Buddy barely looked up from enjoying Clara and her mother. "Head for Watertown and we can pick up US 81 there. Along the way, find a quiet place off the major highway where we can have some of the lunch from what y'all picked up at Price Chopper."

On the Road Again

"What kind of music ya'll like now, honey?" Buddy asked as the trip began.

"Not much different from before, Buddy, still the kind of music my parents enjoyed – Everly Brothers, Johnny Cash, Willie Nelson."

"Say, Tariq. How 'bout dialing up some Willie Nelson on our sophisticated audio system?"

"Yes, SIR, coming right up," Tariq responded, inwardly gritting his teeth. "*Looking forward to driving across America listening to cracker music when I very much prefer sophisticated classical music like Karelia Suite or even the Bach-Stokowski Passacaglia and Fugue in C minor I was enjoying on the way to where we planned to leave the Escalade, before Drak was arrested and taken off the board,*" he thought angrily, holding the steering wheel so tightly that his fingers turned almost white.

"Jesus, Tariq," Buddy Lassiter yelled from the back seat. "That there 18-wheeler is gonna hit us. Pay attention to your drivin 'or you're gonna get us all killed."

Tariq swerved the BMW back into the right lane and

slowed down a bit. "Sorry, Lea and Buddy, I'll pay better attention to my driving," he said apologetically.

As the BMW rolled along US 11 more carefully, it entered Potsdam, NY, home of Clarkson University and SUNY Potsdam. Trying to ignore the merriment in the backseat and following the voice in his ear, Tariq took a right in front of the North Country Children's Museum and followed the loop of US 11 until it crossed over the Raquette River past a sign announcing the Sandstone Bridge before continuing southwest toward Canton. Tariq scanned road signs ahead and followed directions on one sign to the Oliver Appleton Golf Course at St. Lawrence University, pulled into its parking lot and stopped near its clubhouse. He looked over the seat to his passengers and announced "Here's a good place for lunch, right near a bathroom. Let's take some time to eat and wash up before rolling down US 11 toward Watertown."

Lea looked up from the toy she was sharing with Clara. "Good idea, Tariq. Great timing!" She walked around to raise the BMW's back gate, took out the wool blanket she and the Governor had taken from the hideout and spread it on the sunny and well-manicured lawn beside the golf course clubhouse, watching golfers and their carts and caddies drift out toward the course and others back into the clubhouse. Then she hollered to Tariq: "can you please help me put out the food you got a Price Chopper? You know better than I what you got for us there."

Before long, all four were lounging on the blanket, picking through what Tariq had bought at the Price Chopper and enjoying the break from riding in the BMW. As lunch was finished, remaining food and drink loaded back into the SUV and everyone had washed up in the clubhouse, they piled back into the BMW. Tariq turned the BMW back to US 11 south and followed it through DeKalb Junction and Governeur. Bypassing the small town of Antwerp and rolling through another little town, Philadelphia, Tariq continued along US 11 into Watertown. On the far side of Watertown, US 11 became NY 232, then under US 81 until the road on the west side of the interstate looped past Tracey Road Equipment around to the ramp for southbound US 81. Tariq was focusing on his driving while Lea was playing with Clara and Buddy Lassiter had stretched out his long legs, fallen asleep yet again and was snoring lightly, drooling ever so slightly.

After a few miles, Lea reached over the sleeping Clara to poke the Governor in his right shoulder. He woke up, startled "What you want, honey?"

"We're counting on the fact that you and Tariq are willing to take Clara and me west, maybe far toward the Left Coast but I want you to understand what is involved. The fact is the authorities are likely looking for me if only because I escaped from Penal Colony 627 with the help of two of the Movement's goons. One was killed in Camden, Maine by a runaway oil truck on Memorial Day, the other from an unfortunate occurrence with a floor cleaning machine in Rochester, New Hampshire – some might think I was involved. Then there's the judge who sent me away to the Penal Colony; Drak and I put her out of her misery, which may soon be figured out by the Malone police. In any case, there are several reasons why the authorities may be looking for me, even if Drak doesn't spill the beans. Oh, and I forgot to mention the assassination of the tranny Franklin County Commissioner in the courthouse parking lot that Drak and I watched. There were several surveillance cameras on the courthouse just like many places we passed through on the way back to America from Russia. Who knows what search programs are following me and where I am on the government's priority list? Bottom line: I'm far past being the sweet young schoolteacher you first knew and left alone in Malone with newborn Clara. How does all that strike you and how will you and Tariq deal with it? Getting far out of this area without being apprehended won't be easy."

The Governor bowed his head sheepishly and professed his devotion again "Like I said when we found you in Malone, I'll do anything I can, honey, to make things right for you. Like you sure got yourself into a passel of trouble. We're probably helping a fleeing felon to escape but I'm up for that. It's not as if Tariq and me bin acting like Eagle Scouts. Ain't that right, Tariq?"

Tariq nodded his head, putting on a weak smile while thinking to himself: *This keeps getting more complicated and worse. What a long list of offenses with more to come, like whatever the assignment is in Chagrin Falls, Ohio. And who knows what is her next assignment for the Movement after whatever she must do in whatever is in that garden spot outside Cleveland? I must find a way to protect myself or get out of this mess.*"

As the group continued south on US 81, Tariq saw signs for Parish, New York, and an Exxon Mobil Station on the east side of US 81. He said to the Governor without looking away from the road ahead "I'm getting off at the next exit and taking the local road under the interstate to fill up the BMW's tank. Here's the exit but it may take me a few minutes to roll around on local roads to get into that gas station."

Since the BMW is foreign made, Tariq not only remembered that its gas cap is on the right side but noted the icon on its speedometer of a gas tank pointing to the right. He pulled up to one of the pumps next to the vehicle's right rear, stepped out to the nearest pump, inserted the Governor's black Amex card and began fueling at the highest grade available. The BMW's other passengers scurried out towards the station itself in hopes of finding clean restrooms. Shortly a dented and dirty white van with windows in its cargo sides covered with dark paper pulled into the other side of the same island, closer to the station itself.

By now, the Governor, Clara and Lea were returning to the BMW. Lea buckled Clara into her car seat and walked back behind the white van. She could smell feces and vomit and saw a yellow liquid running out under the van's back door. Lea walked toward the open driver's door of the van and peered inside. "*What a pig, she thought. The whole driver's compartment smells like the driver really needs a shower. And look at the bottles, food containers and other trash on the floor.*"

She leaned over the van's greasy steering wheel and saw that its keys were dangling from the ignition. Looking toward the Exxon station itself, Lea could see a dark-skinned, young man standing in the sun outside the station Exxon, talking on his phone as if he hadn't a care in the world, munching on what appeared to be a Moon Pie and drinking from a bottle of Dr. Pepper. He began walking in a leisurely fashion back toward the van. She pursed lips, thought for a moment then snatched the van's keys from its ignition and hurried back to the BMW. On the way, the young mother could hear young girls yelling: "Ayuda me, ayuda me (help me)!"

Lea jumped into her seat in the BMW and screamed at Tariq "out of here as fast as you can and back to southbound US 81!"

"Whassup?" the Governor burbled, turning around to see what was going on.

"That van is probably involved in child trafficking. Once we're on our way, I'll use one of the burner phones Rodney Herbert gave me to call the local police. That trafficker won't go anywhere soon – I liberated the van's keys. So, move it, Tariq!"

As the BMW bolted out of the Exxon Mobil gas station lot, Lea dialed 911 on her burner phone.

"Parish Police Department. This is Officer Kenehan.

How can I help you?"

"There's a child trafficker's beat-up white van next to the pumps at the Exxon Mobil just off State Route 104 on the east side of US 81. I could hear young girls screaming inside the van, trying to get help. Please send a patrol car" Lea demanded through a handkerchief held over the burner-phone's face and then disconnected her call.

About 50 yards along State Route 104, she asked Tariq to pull over to the highway's right side so they could see what was happening. A few minutes later, a police car with lights flashing raced into the Mobil gas station and pulled up beside the white van. One of the officers leapt out of the patrol car and drew his service pistol as he began to chase the young man who was probably the van's driver, now running into a nearby field after dropping his drink. The woman officer who was driving the patrol car appeared to hold her hard-wired radio microphone next to her mouth, apparently calling to get more help.

Lea rolled down her window and tossed the van's keys into the nearby field of new corn. She brushed her palms together, smiled with satisfaction and said "at least one good deed done today! Let's get back to US 81 south and on our way toward Syracuse and whatever comes after that."

Tariq maneuvered the BMW along State Route 104, under US 81 and onto its southbound ramp. The Governor and Clara were fast asleep while Lea carefully considered where to stop next at the same time as she kept massaging the new bandage on the back of her neck with her right hand. One of those opioid capsules might dim some of her pain but she refused to start down that road.

After a few minutes, she leaned over the front seat and spoke quietly to Tariq: "I know you and Buddy had a bad time at the Syracuse airport, but we'll be coming through North Syracuse very soon. What would you think about taking the exit for the Syracuse airport, head for the "arriving passengers" ramp and pull up next to the curb where city buses and tour buses pick up passengers? Are you armed, by the way?"

Tariq looked at her quizzically: I have a small pistol in a holster on my left ankle and, once I'm not belted into this seat, I'll have a fully loaded 9mm with a ten-round magazine full of hollow points. But what's your real question?"

"Once we're pulled up to the curb in the arrivals lane," Lea said conspiratorially, checking over her shoulder to make sure the Governor and Clara were still asleep, "I'll get out and see if I can find a bus load of foreign tourists, maybe some Japanese or Chinese, on the way to something like the Baseball Hall of Fame in Cooperstown. As you probably know from your time at Hamilton, the Hall of Fame is sort of diagonal from here toward the southbound Thruway, going into New York City. Since you're part of OUR team, what do you think about a plan for each of us to call different direct lines at the Malone Police Station until we get voice mail on two of the burner phones and talk long enough with a muffled voice about the case of the missing judge very generally so the calls will be recorded on voice mail and perhaps can later be traced. Once I find buses that are going in different direction from where we're headed, which is south on 81 and then, much later, west across northern Pennsylvania, we'll turn both phones back on, leave them on and put each of them somewhere out of sight on the two different buses. With any luck, the police will track those phones and hopefully follow them while we're speeding in another direction. If someone finds the phones on either bus, maybe they'll steal them and use them, another way for the police to waste time and effort in following the phones. How does that sound to you?"

"Sounds like the sort of deceptive plan I enjoy but what are you planning to do for muscle even if you don't need it right now?" Tariq asked.

"What do you mean?"

"Although I'm pretty good with many things, mostly figuring out clever ways to get legal and illegal projects done, but I'm not exactly a tough guy. You used to have Drak's help but he's gone and now there's just the Governor and me to keep you out of danger. Buddy has influence and money plus a great many connections but I wouldn't bet my last ruble on his ability to take down someone who's trying to hurt you or Clara, may Allah forbid the thought. You really should give that some serious thought, particularly now that we apparently have a lot of driving in front of us where I'll be here in the pilot's seat, hopefully listening to my classical selections while monitoring driving directions."

"You may be right about that," Lea pondered out loud.

"Of course, I know very little about your relationship with Clara's father. But it's really none of my business."

Before long, the BMW pulled into the arrival lane at the Syracuse-Hancock Airport, the scene of Tariq and the Governor's prior adventures and stopped behind a large, silver bus belching gray fumes.

Buddy Lassiter snorted awake and grumbled "where

the hell are we? Looks like the same place where Tariq and me had a passel of problems with them there home-spuns and that there phony beggar with the wheelchair and metal spear. The hovercraft was even more of a problem. What're we doing at this here airport?"

Lea leaned back, smiled at Clara, who was again playing with her green plastic turtle, and put her hand on Buddy Lassiter's shoulder. "We're taking a few minutes to plant running burner phones we'll use to leave messages on individual lines at the Malone police department in different buses. Perhaps the police will track those phones and help us escape undetected into Flyover Country. While we're on this subject, what different ways can you personally, Buddy, help our progress going west and protect me and Clara? You and Tariq have apparently been working together for a while. Perhaps you could fill me in on any part of that which might impact what we're doing. While you're thinking about whatever information you could help me with, I'm getting out to see if any of these buses are on their way to places east of here. For the moment, you and Tariq can wait here with Clara. Just in case, I'm taking my gun. Please lock the car doors until I return. And remember, Buddy, trust is a growth thing."

Lea stepped out of the BMW and slowly walked

toward the idling bus in front of it. The door of that bus was partly open, revealing a heavily bearded man wearing a kippah, lounging behind the bus's steering wheel with his right boot up on its door lever. "Can I help you?"

"Is this the bus into Syracuse?"

"Sorry, ma'am. I'm here to pick up a part of our travelers on the way back to Kiryas Joel in Orange County. If we were going into Syracuse, you'd be welcome to ride along but we're going directly from here to the eastbound Thruway then past Albany down to Orange County."

"Thank you," she said, thinking "Perfect." She walked back toward the BMW and stopped to leave one activated burner phone between suitcases in the Orange County-bound bus's luggage hold. Then, she walked forward past the open bus door, toward what looked like a local bus, where people were streaming into its forward entry door. Lea joined the group and filed into the rapidly filling bus, past the driver whose attention seemed riveted on several lottery tickets. She slipped the second burner phone into an overhead compartment above the fourth seat on the right side of the center aisle. Then she turned in the other direction and asked loudly "is this the bus to Buffalo?" A grossly obese woman beside her snorted "this is the bus to the downtown terminal, dumbass! Says so right on the front of the bus." Lea appeared to apologize profusely, pushed through the entering crowd, tripped lightly off that bus and quickly returned to the BMW.

Lea rapped on the BMW's door, which promptly opened. "Golden! Now let's get on our way back to US 81 and continue south." As soon as her seat belt was clicked shut, Tariq started the BMW and accelerated it toward the airport exit ramp, leading to US 81 south.

An Opening for Mordoff

Never one to tarry, David Garvey was on the phone with Lance Bridgeford, Esq., of the Dallas, Texas firm of Goodbody & Winesap, PLLC., exactly at the appointed hour.

"Good morning, Mr. Bridgeford. How are you this fine day?"

"Just fine, Mr. Garvey. It's a beautiful day here in the Great State of Texas."

"What did you glean from reviewing my papers and discovery requests from <u>Mordoff v. MicroSquash</u>, Mr. Bridgeford?" David ventured.

"Of course, I must talk it over with ma clont but ma basic take is that you've laid out a pretty detailed and persuasive case. I cannot imagine why it's taken so long to make headway with MicroSquash's prior counsel in this case. Maybe MicroSquash or its counsel didn't take your claims seriously. But I can assure you that my clont will be brought up to speed promptly and I'll keep after it. With the motions you have pending, this cannot be delayed or ignored. Judge Stillwater may have been cowed by all of this "oppressed people" nonsense but, after the tender offer, MicroSquash is again focused on making money and a profit. I'll get back to you in the next couple of days to respond to your claims and motions."

"Thank you, Mr. Bridgeford. I'll look forward to hearing from you."

David Garvey relaxed in this comfortable leather office chair and put a foot up on the edge of his antique partners 'desk and dialed the number for Lucas Mordoff on his smart phone.

"Hello, David. Anything to report on my case?"

"I don't want you to get too excited, Lucas, but we may be getting somewhere. MicroSquash was acquired in a tender offer. Long story short, it is now owned by a more serious company, MicroSquash's CEO has been arrested for child trafficking and its new counsel, unlike that nutcase, Petunia Thrush, seems to have his head screwed on the right way. He sounds normal and promises to respond to your complaint and the various discovery motions I have pending in the next couple of days. I'm thinking about not only a generous settlement but some arrangement where your business will continue, with your being a large part of the products related to your technology. Without getting into the weeds, how does that sound to you in concept? Of course, I would never agree to anything on your behalf without your complete participation."

"Give 'em hell, David, and keep me in the loop."

Looking Over Lea's Shoulder

Soon, Lea, Clara and the Governor were rolling along US 81 south of Syracuse toward its intersection with Interstate 80 with Tariq at the wheel. After their turn west, they would be traveling along the northern tier of Pennsylvania, above most of its major cities, into northern Ohio. Lea and the Governor were discussing what had happened since they left Malone and what might be coming next, hopefully including somewhere pleasant to stay and relax for a couple of days. Lea's remaining burner phone started ring.

"Hello?" Lea answered tentatively, having no idea who knew that number or who might be calling.

"You don't know me," a muscular, male voice responded, with machinery sounds in the background. "I'm your controller in the Movement. I've been keeping an eye on you since we helped you escaped from Penal Colony 627. Most people would have been demoralized by the experience you suffered, might even be in bed, drinking wine and sucking their thumb. But you bounced back in spectacular fashion. You're made of special stuff. You disposed of your second Movement minder, an amazing act

351

if self-preservation even if a little messy. You and Drakulič met the challenge of crossing Maine, New Hampshire and Vermont to find and rescue your daughter from the despicable Lost League in Carthage. You might have then disappeared into the woodwork but you had the nerve and temerity to return to your home in the North Country of New York. You were instrumental in whacking that tranny Franklin County Commissioner, an important step in weakening that part of the feeble, central government. I suspect you had an important role in the disappearance of that hateful, religious court judge who sent you away to Penal Colony 627, although the police apparently haven't solved that one yet. Our leader in Malone reported you finally got rid of the remains of the Penal Colony 627 monitoring system buried in your neck..."

Lea was fascinated with this information but reached up to gently massaged the healing scar L her neck.

The unknown voice continued "We're using our infiltration of the central government's surveillance systems to track your three burner phones. Great that someone put two of them on vehicles going far from your destination at the job in Chagrin Falls, Ohio, so potential pursuers may be confused. While you're on your way west across Pennsylvania, please stop off in Punxsutawney,

Pennsylvania, to compare notes and plans with a former Marine sniper who was booted out of the Corps when he refused to take the jab. He might be able to help you the same way Drakulič did; I'll text you the Marine's contact information. I've spoken with him and he's eager to get to work, helping to fix things in America. By the way, Drakulič is doing fine – he was able to talk his way around almost everything and is back in his Camden frame shop, living high on those lucrative benefits for illegal immigrants. Apparently, the famous Honda was "found" in the parking lot behind his store. I'll be in touch as your journey unfolds."

Lea was astounded as the call clicked away without another word from what the caller called himself, her "controller", with no indication on her phone where the call came from, no record of a calling number thus no way to return the call. At least she thought, *there s apparently no direct monitoring of us here – he s not aware of what actually goes on here. So far, for example, he doesn t know we knew our friend and helper as Drak. I have no idea whether the Movement can listen to what is going on in this BMW but I m relatively sure the electronics in that dependable Honda were so old as to preclude any hacking. All definite food for further thought."*

After a few more miles of quietly rolling south on US 81 through more rural countryside south of Syracuse and into northern Pennsylvania, she leaned over the front seat and said to Tariq: "would you mind putting on your earphones, so you could listen to your own favorite music? That would save our having to listen to what you prefer and vice versa, plus the Governor and I have some planning to do."

"Works for me," Tariq responded with a smile, pulling a set of streamlined earplugs from his suit jacket pocket and inserting them smoothly into each ear. Then he plugged them into the BMW's dashboard. Turning to Lea, he said "if you hear anything weird outside the SUV, tap me on the shoulder. My hearing may not be the best while listening to my favorite classical music on these earbuds, which can be pretty loud."

By now, Clara was again immersed in her toys in the space behind the passenger seat. Lea was careful to cinch Clara into a safety belt which she clamped to one of the fittings behind the passenger seat – not as safe as Clara's car seat but pretty good under the circumstances. She moved the empty car seat to the floor, next to the far car door, then turned toward the Governor.

"Time for us to figure out what's ahead, to the extent

we have any control over that factor," she said with a smile, looking carefully at Buddy Lassiter's face for any sign of reaction. "I know this has been complicated and hectic, getting out of Malone, hurrying down through Watertown and Syracuse and now continuing on US 81. Before long, we'll be turning west across Pennsylvania. How does this affect you and Tariq and what do you want to happen next?"

"Darlin, 'ya know I'll do anything I can to make you and Clara happy," the Governor smiled.

"I appreciate that, Buddy, but what does that mean as a practical matter? Since you and Tariq arrived at my hideout in Malone, we've been swamped with serious problems, potential involvement with law enforcement and now running away toward Flyover Country. How does that fit with what you and Tariq were doing before you came to find me?"

"Well, honey, me and Tariq are managing this network to raise money to help children, sort of like that there Lyndon Larouche used to do. You're too young to know about him but he ran as a minority candidate against Ronald Reagan for President. That didn't go really well for him because he was in prison at the time for raising money from little old ladies for charitable purposes while illegally spending the funds on his campaign. I'm not real proud of what Tariq and me are doing, raising money to supposedly help children but most of what we raise goes to them there Iranians. It's actually kinda like the politics I used to spend my time doing. Ain't really figured out if that can fit with you and my daughter and what y'all are doin – right now that seems to be mostly runnin 'and schemin."

"I value your telling me the truth but can't say I'm delighted to learn you're helping some of the same folks involved in ruining my country. That's something I'm committed to fighting, as hard as I'm able. Thing is, Buddy, I'm very different than before I was sent off to Penal Colony 627 and have had to scramble back, mostly on my own. And my life will likely never be that of a sedate schoolteacher. Look at me now, loaded with guns, on my way to eliminate an enemy of the Movement in Ohio but with a younger child to care for. How would you and Tariq fit into this evolving picture? There's no chance we'll wake up one morning and my life will be back to a normal schoolteacher's pleasant small-town life. To put it bluntly, I've got places to go and people to kill."

"Ah, ah," the Governor mumbled, first watching the increasingly dense forests the BMW was passing through then inspecting the luxurious carpet beneath his smartly shined shoes. "Guess I was hoping to find that there sweet young thing who bore my daughter. Maybe like no time had passed. When I tried to think about what might come next, there was always one crisis after another, like starting as soon as we arrived and that there cop showed up with a ticket for Tariq. And it was like a machine gun spraying problems after that. Ah don't know what to think."

They both looked at Tariq. He seemed captivated by the distant music flowing through his ears but still evidently paying close attention to the increasingly open road ahead even as his lips were moving, perhaps to the sounds of a famous pastoral chorale.

"That call I got on my remaining burner phone," Lea explained, "was a guy who calls himself my controller from the Movement. He says he's been keeping close track of me, ever since I escaped from the Penal Colony, arranged by the Movement itself. He sounds like he has a high regard for what I've accomplished so far but also has more work for me in the near future, things continuing to disrupt the feckless, central government and its local toadies. I'm guessing the Iranians have that in mind as well, now that the actor who's pretending to be President, has renegotiated that deal which was supposed to keep the Islamic Republic from getting nuclear weapons but has no prayer of doing so because its success depends on good faith of the Iranians. Even though I keep hearing what he's "negotiated" is entirely toothless. I'm having trouble seeing how you and I can have anything together in the midst of this madness. What do you think, Buddy?"

"Sounds to me, darlin', like we're on opposite sides of the field, like them there Crimson Tide teams and our Dawgs. Ah may be wrong but it don't look like there's much chance of us living happily ever after in some blissful state, particularly if you have these dangerous jobs for what you call the Movement."

"How about we stop in Scranton, Sniffy's pretend old hometown, find a nice hotel and discuss the next best steps for everyone?" Lea ventured.

The Governor looked sad but nodded.

As the ride down US 81 continued, Lea's burner phone rang again.

Figuring only one person was likely to be calling her on that phone, she answered "yes, sir?"

"Me again. Some more about the former Marine you'll find in Punxsutawney. He's a younger nephew of Chuck Mawhinney, the very famous Marine sniper from the Vietnam War – killed 16 NVA soldiers crossing a river at night in 30 seconds plus 103 confirmed kills and 216 probable kills during that war. The nephew is also named Chuck, in honor of his uncle. This Chuck rents a small place on Oakland Avenue across the street from the Punxsutawney Post Office; it's just across Mahoning Creek from 'metropolitan 'Punxsutawney. In case you never heard of it, Punxsutawney is famous for its annual festival where a groundhog, called Punxsutawney Phil, emerges from his lair and predicts when spring is supposedly coming. I'll text you the Marine's his phone number and street address."

With the Governor's looking glum, Clara's becoming increasingly cranky and the result of her bomb removal aching even more, Lea could tell it was time to stop for some serious rest and relaxation. She tapped Tariq on his right shoulder: "please crank Radisson Lackawanna Station Hotel in Scranton into your navigation system. It used to be the city's main train station but now it's a modernized, upscale hotel. See if you can book a double-queen room for you and the Governor, looking over her shoulder at Buddy Lassiter, and an adjoining queen room with a child's bed for two nights. Clara will have a great time running in the halls after being cooped up in here for so long. This Radisson has many amenities and advertises two good restaurants and excellent room service. Plus, it's right off US 81 – we'll be a little south of where we want to head west toward Ohio, but this place should give us the chance to relax and decide what should come next and how to go about it."

As if he could tell there was a parting of the group's ways in the near future, the Governor said sadly "I don't like it, but I get it. You got your own work ahead and probably me and Tariq need to get back to serving them, there Iranians."

Trying to sound like the Captain of the Starship Enterprise, Tariq commanded the BMW's navigation system: "set course for the Radisson Lackawanna Station Hotel in Scranton, Mr. Sulu, and patch me into its communications cluster at 570.342.8300 so I can make us reservations.   No   need   for   Warp   Factor   Three. Acknowledge!" Then he turned to look proudly at Lea, hoping for a favorable response. She was already absorbed in details and what would come next after a couple of days' rest and didn't respond - whatever humor Lea might have previously enjoyed had been missed.

Before long, the BMW was rolling along Moosic Street past the Krispy Kreme store, following PA 307 over a wide bridge over what appeared to be a narrow but congested river. Everyone smelled fresh doughnuts – Clara licked her lips and said "Mommy, I'm really hungry." At the end of the bridge, Tariq followed signs to the hotel and rolled the SUV down a ramp into its underground parking garage. He parked the vehicle a few spaces away from a battered brown Dodge Caravan where a young blond boy was unloading a cage from its back gate. As soon as the BMW stopped and Lea released Clara from her car seat, she opened the rear passenger door and helped Clara jump down to the concrete floor. Clara was delighted to not be in the car and ran over to the young boy just as he dropped the cage; its latch spilled open and many little rabbits went running all over the garage floor. Clara jumped up and down, yelling "bunnies, bunnies!" The Governor quickly leapt to her side, grabbed her little hand and said "it's OK, Clara. The bunnies will be fine." They watched the boy chase the young rabbits, catching them one by one and returning them to the cage as an older, gray-haired woman helped round them up. "See," Buddy Lassiter said, "they're fine. Let's get our things out of the car and take that there silver elevator to the reception desk on the main floor to get signed into our rooms," pointing to double elevator doors only a few feet away with his right hand. He looked over at Lea, who was helping Tariq unload the BMW, make sure their weapons were fully secure and the SUV locked in every way possible. She smiled at him while carrying their bags toward the nearby elevator doors.

Shortly, the three adults and Clara were second in line at the hotel's reception as Tariq played his recoding of the conversation with the hotel staff during the drive into Scranton. Without delay, the Governor produced his black Amex card and all four were soon on their way down lushly carpeted corridors to adjoining rooms on the third floor. "How about if we meet for dinner in the main dining room in an hour?" Lea watched as Tariq looked back while the Governor pushed a plastic key card into a slot in the granite wall at the entrance to their double room, noticing the Governor's sad glance in her direction. She opened her own door as Clara rushed inside and began jumping up and down on the smaller bed. Lea walked across the ruby red carpet to open window curtains and admire the view with lights of the city coming on as darkness fell. She found the hotel's dinner menu in a desk drawer, sat down in a very comfortable chair and took Clara into her lap to review dinner choices in the main dining room.

Later, as the three adults and Clara walked into the hotel's Carmen's 2.0 Restaurant with its polished, golden marble walls and period light fixtures with glowing frosted glass globes, Clara scampered ahead and had to be corralled on the way to the hostess station. They were ushered across the restaurant's plush carpet to a table on the north side with its signature black, wooden chairs, trailed by a waiter's bringing an elaborate, child seat for Clara and fastening it securely into one of the restaurant's regular, more formal chairs. Once they were seated, had unfurled napkins while Lea tied one around Clara's neck and put another in her lap, they accepted menus and drinks were ordered including orange juice for Clara.

Lea raised her glass and said "thank you for all of your good ideas, help and perseverance. I'm hoping what we've done so far will prepare us for whatever comes next. Clara and I are indebted to both of you, Buddy and Tariq." They clicked their fine, crystal glasses; Buddy chuckled as Clara reached out to also click her small glass of orange juice.

The Governor asked "what would you like Clara?" Clara ran her right index finger over an open menu page in front of her mother and pointed to the color photo of an elaborate dish and said "shicken" with a smile, "like me and Mommy saw in the menu in our room." The others each ordered their own meals, one with the tenderloin steak specialty and two with braised scallops and angel hair pasta.

The meal continued with pleasant if tentative conversation as everyone was concerned about what was coming after their brief respite in this Radisson hotel in Scranton although the Governor seemed reluctant to bring that concern out into the open. Lea felt sorry for Buddy but could not get over the fact he'd left her pregnant and disappeared from the scene for reasons never ever shared with her, before those many bad things erupted or any time later.

Lea looked over to see Clara's playing with one of her new games amid the shambles of her meal. Unable to contain herself any longer, she looked around the table and finally ventured in a conspiratorial voice: "let's meet in your room, pointing to the Governor and Tariq, at 9:00 tomorrow morning. I'll arrange for someone to stay with Clara in our room and you order room service for the three of us in your room plus something for Clara and the babysitter, for delivery to our room. Over breakfast, presumably with lots of coffee, we'll work through what comes next. Hopefully, by then, you will have considered what you and Tariq want to do after we leave Scranton. While she was saying this, Lea couldn't help marveling at how much Clara had matured even in the short time since she escaped from

Penal Colony 627 and how well she seemed to be coping with the continuing chaos of the group's escape from the North Country. Perhaps the several positive factors included how well Clara was being treated by the Governor and even Tariq, without even mentioning the games, toys and new clothing acquired for her during the trip west so far. Plus, Clara seemed to have a natural sense of good humor, a surprise to Lea after Clara's being left with the Lost League and having no idea of what had really happened to her mother for a long time. More merriment ensued when Lea asked Clara what she wanted for dessert – no one was really surprised when she picked vanilla ice cream with hot fudge sauce. Since everyone was tired after a long day on the road, they moved toward the elevators and bedtime after the Governor paid the check. After tucking Clara into her trundle bed, her mother called the front desk on her burner phone, having to identify her room number, to arrange for a babysitter to come to her room at 8:00 the following morning. With that task completed, Lea got ready for bed, wearing a warm sweatshirt, and crawled into the queen bed close to the already sleeping Clara. As she dozed off, the memory of using her burner phone to call the hotel's room service worried her but she quickly fell asleep anyway.

With the room's heavy curtains still wide open, Clara awoke with the sun, even though the day was cloudy, and she quickly shook her mother awake. Lea promptly struggled into her clothes and dressed Clara while consulting her watch to notice it was nearly time for the babysitter to arrive. She was still cleaning her teeth and brushing her hair when the room's doorbell rang. Carefully checking through the eyehole, using a mirror while standing at the edge of the doorframe, Lea saw an elderly lady with gray, curly hair, probably a wig, standing outside the door with what looked like a shopping bag in her left hand with a brown wooden cane hanging on her right forearm. She opened the door and extended a hand: "Hi, I'm Jane and this is my daughter, Clara, please come in and make yourself comfortable. I appreciate your helping me. Remind me what you charge for about two hours; my business meeting may not take that long but here is cash for you. Breakfast for you and Clara will be along soon."

The older woman smiled, put her bag on the carpet next to the room's upholstered sofa and went over to look at Clara, leaning on her cane. Clara smiled as well. Together, they sat down on the carpet and began to play with Clara's toys. On the way out the room's front door, Lea quietly cracked the connecting door to the Governor and Tariq's adjoining room.

Once outside on the plush hall carpet, she stepped quickly to the Governor's door and rapped on it gently. Tariq promptly opened it with a beaming smile on his face. "Good morning, please come right in," he said, gesturing to a large, round table in front of the plate glass windows looking out over Scranton. Lea had a feeling she could guess what Tariq and the Governor had been discussing about future plans but she took a seat at the table next to Buddy, with Tariq on Buddy's left. Before any discussion started, there was a knock at the door " –room service!" Tariq leaped up to let the waitress roll in her cart next to the round table, scrutinized the bill and handed the young woman a few bills; he moved items off the cart and guided the waitress toward the door. As the trio sat down to eat, they could hear a knock at the door of Lea and Clara's room.

"What's on your mind, Buddy? What do you and Tariq want to do after we leave this hotel?

Tariq looked at the Governor. Buddy hesitated and then said: "as much as I like spending time with you and my daughter, it's pretty clear to me that you have several other priorities, like that there job and whatever comes next, whatever it is, and like whoever's chasing you. Can't imagine you're looking forward to any kind of normal home life. We need to get back to our work for them there Iranians. I'm kinda hopin that might lead back into politics for me, at least for yours truly. Tariq here has all sorts of different skills, way beyond what them there Iranians need even though his last boss ended up at the end of a rope. So...

Lea's burner phone rang; "someone's onto where you are. I've had someone trying to watch you and he saw some old woman go into your hotel room in Scranton where you and your daughter were sleeping..." The voice continued but Lea had stuffed into her pocket and was already on her feet, jacking a round into her Beretta and pushing open the door between the two rooms. She screamed: "Buddy and Tariq! Get in here immediately!" The "babysitter" had grabbed Clara around the neck and was dragging her toward the suite's door. Clara bit deeply into her forearm and was growling fiercely. The old woman kept trying to drag Clara toward the door while the little girl refused to stop biting her. Her captor gritted her teeth and kept demanding that Clara stop. But Clara refused and soon blood was dripping from the woman's arm.

Lea ran up to the woman holding Clara and put her pistol to the woman's right temple. "Freeze or I'll blow your brains out. Release my daughter!" The Governor and Tariq ran to her side. "Here, Buddy, please take Clara, sit on that sofa, and calm her down. Tariq: Please come with me so we can help this woman find her way out of this mess."

To the woman: "I'm Jane Struthers, a personal friend of the Governor here, Tom Wolf, famous for stuffing all those old people into nursing homes where they died, so don't fuck with me anymore. He's firmly on my side and will come after you and your family if you reveal a word of this to anyone."

Clara's assailant blubbered: "I'm a good person. Didn't mean anyone any harm. Just got paid to do this and they're holding my invalid husband until I report back. Please don't hurt me." She tried unsuccessfully to push the Beretta barrel away from her temple.

Lea ordered Tariq: "take her arm and we'll find a way for her out of this floor of the hotel. I'll be right here to make sure she does the right thing."

Buddy was already holding Clara close on the sofa as Lea and Tariq maneuvered the babbling woman out into the hall. Lea looked up and down the hall and spotted a sign for a fire exit. "That looks like an easy way out of the building. Let's go over there."

As Tariq pushed open the cumbersome red fire door, the trio entered a bulky, concrete landing with sturdy stairs going both up and down, with heavy, metal railings on both sides of each set of stairs. They could see it was very far down it to the next landing. Lea turned to Tariq and said: "Please shut the door to the hallway tightly and hold my pistol." To the woman Lea was holding tightly, she advised: "let's go down this way. You may want to reach out for the metal railings on both sides."

The old woman leaned forward painfully and struggled to grasp both metal railings leading downward over the top concrete step, one of many staring up at her. Lea crept up close behind her, grabbed the sturdy metal posts on either side of the concrete steps leading down to the distant landing below then leaned back, snapped both feet into the woman's backside and pushed with all her strength. Her target screamed, flew over the first three steps, landed hard on the metal edge of the fourth step and bounced, head over heels, down the rest of the stairs. Her inert body stopped at the next landing without another sound.

Lea turned to Tariq, who looked frightened. "I won't hurt you, Tariq, but we need to move quickly now, to get our things together and be gone from this place. Please give me back my Beretta." Together, they ran out into the hallway and back into Lea and Clara's room. Lea scooped up Clara and looked into her eyes. "Are you OK, honey?" Clara grinned through bloody teeth: I bited her, Mommy. I want to brush my teeth." All three grownups smiled broadly.

To Tariq: "call the front desk on the house phone, tell them we're checking out and that we don't need any help leaving. The front desk has the credit card so they can just charge it. We can take the elevator directly to the parking garage." She then said tersely to the Governor: "Get all of your stuff together so we can leave shortly while I clean up Clara and make sure all of our things are ready to go. Use these sanitary wipes to clean everywhere we may have touched, and I'll do the same here."

Lea heard her burner phone talking in her pocket. "What the hell is going on? Did you hear anything I said before?"

"Just that someone had found us. The woman pretending to be a babysitter tried to kidnap Clara. Fortunately, I short-circuited that mess and the woman unfortunately fell down a very long set of concrete fire stairs. If you have a cleanup crew in the area, it's the set of fire stairs leading down from the third floor of the

Radisson Lackawanna Station hotel, across from room 327. Do you have any idea how they found us?"

"Did you use your burner phone in the hotel?"

"Yep. Guess that was a bad idea."

"Yes, probably traceable. You need to pick up a new burner phone at the first electronics store you see. Here's a number to call so I can get in touch with you even though it is not my direct number."

"Thanks. We're leaving here shortly and will be traveling west on I-80, heading in the direction of Punxsutawney.

Shortly, the group scrambled into the third-floor elevator and let Clara push the button for "parking garage" and, as soon as the polished metal doors open, moved quickly toward the BMW, got in and fastened seat belts. While that was being done, Tariq set the vehicle's travel electronics to direct them toward Punxsutawney: they pointed the BMW in the direction of US 11 toward Wilkes Barre then onto to I-80 west across northern Pennsylvania.

As the BMW picked up speed, Lea suggested to Tariq: "Please pull into the first large drug store or electronics place you see so I can get a new burner phone. Thankfully, we still have a good bit of cash from the guy who had the fatal encounter with the floor polisher. You didn't know him, but, even though he helped me get out of Russia on the Movement's initiative, he was very nasty, not to mention his horrible breath."

She then turned to the Governor: "let's finish our discussion of what you and Tariq want to do next. You obviously understand that I will continue to get instructions from the Movement, which has quite different objectives than your work for the Iranians. As much as I'd like to have a loving mate who could be a good father to Clara, I don't see that in the cards in front of me. Maybe in another lifetime but we seem to be stuck in this one. You may be reluctant to admit our relationship doesn't have a future but that's where we are. If you have any different thoughts, now would be a good time to tell me."

"Ya, know, honey, I looked for you, hoping for more but you're not the soft country, school marm I first loved. I do love our daughter and hope there will be times I can spend with her. But maybe Tariq and I need to get back to our work for them there Iranians. Maybe this guy in Punxsutawney can help you with what you need better than me or Tariq."

Lea sat back and thought to herself," *I heard part of that from Drak. He was a good man and maybe a bit more focused than Buddy. But maybe what I ve experienced since getting to Penal Colony 627 has hardened me, made me less able to love anyone except Clara. Plus, it s increasingly hard for me to trust anyone. It s not that I think Buddy might hurt me but that he might not protect me, might not keep others from doing me harm. Particularly when he s involved in this scam for the Iranians or thinking that he could get back into politics - I don t like either of those. So probably best if Buddy goes his own way. Of course, Tariq is part of the same package even though he s much brighter."*

The BMW was quiet after the discussion about what comes next, as the SUV sped west on I-80, sometimes just a few miles below the border between New York and Pennsylvania. As the vehicle passed through Ulysses County, Pennsylvania, Lea remembered from her geography studies in college that they would soon cross the Appalachian Divide. From that point, rivers and streams flow east into the Chesapeake Bay estuary and, a couple of miles west, on the other side of that divide, waters flow west into the Mississippi River system, ultimately emptying into the Gulf of Mexico. Tired from all of the excitement, Clara was again sleeping peacefully, the Governor staring blankly at the nondescript foliage and Lea lost in her thoughts of what had just happened and what lay ahead. While Tariq carefully guided them along this boring highway toward where the sun would set as he listened to his favorite classical music.

After what seemed like an eternity, Tariq took an exit onto PA Route 119, south toward the ultimate destination suggested by what Lea was now calling the "voice," to meet her potential helper, Chuck Mawhinney. Punxsutawney is a smaller town with a population a little over 5,000 souls in the middle of nowhere. Before the trio and Clara reached their next destination, the SUV wandered along country roads through DuBois, West Liberty, and Sykesville. Punxsutawney's name is of Indian origin, founded in 1818 according to a dingy blue and gold metal sign leaning beside the tarmac at the village's outer boundary once they reached it. Punxsutawney was brought to modern fame, in addition to the annual groundhog event, by the exceptionally creative and funny movie, "Groundhog Day," starring Bill Murray and Andie McDowell.

As if on cue, Lea's burner phone began ringing and the "voice" announced," I've asked Chuck to meet you at Punxi Phil's Family Restaurant; it's at 116 Indiana Street, a dead end. I'll text you Chuck's cell number; it's a 702 because he was living in Las Vegas when he bought the phone. I'll call you tomorrow to see how your meeting turned out." Without another word, the call ended.

"Huh," Lea said before passing the address to Tariq for insertion into his navigation system. She mulled over the many coming challenges: *"This could be awkward. I don t know enough details about the Governor to be fully informed even though I m willing to act on what little I understand. As to Mawhinney, he s a total cypher - we ll have to play it by the proverbial ear. The objective is to move toward my next job in Chagrin Falls, keeping an eye on whatever might happen after that. This requires foresight to which I m not fully accustomed. Please, God, hold my hand as I blunder along."*

With new directions in hand, Tariq piloted the BMW toward Punxy Phil's, paying careful attention to speed limits and watching for police cars. Shortly, Tariq maneuvered the SUV into the eastern side of Punxy Phil's spacious parking lot and pulled in next to a clean and sparkling Ford F-150 pick-up truck with a gangly guy standing next to it, kicking a soccer ball with a boy about Clara's age wearing a dark blue sweatshirt. The pair paid attention as Tariq pulled the BMW SUV to a stop. As Lea, Clara, Buddy Lassiter stepped out onto the pavement, Tariq shut off the powerful BMW's engine and joined them.

"Are you Chuck?" Lea asked, carefully watching the

man who was apparently Chuck Mawhinney as he stooped to pick the slightly bouncing soccer ball.

"Sure am, Ma'am," he answered tersely, "Been that since I was born. And this here's my son, Caleb. Been expecting you since hearing from the Movement guy on the phone. You guys interested in something to eat? You'll find this restaurant like a step back in time but good food – they serve breakfast all day and things like two eggs and toast for three dollars. This young lady and I need to talk but, if the rest of you want to join us, that's fine with me."

While this brief conversation continued, the Governor and Tariq leaned against the BMW, Tariq's checking his messages and the Governor's looking glum, likely thinking about getting back to the work he'd interrupted to find Lea. Both he and Tariq were only somewhat interested in what the new guy had to say. Ever curious, Clara drifted toward Chuck's son. "You want to kick the ball?" Caleb responded angrily "Don't play with no girls!"

Somewhat pleased at being called "young lady," Lea was impressed by this tall and wiry ramrod of a man, finely muscled with piercing focus but a pleasant smile; then she remembered he'd been a sniper like his famous uncle. As she noticed his wearing a holster on his left hip, she smiled while thinking to herself *"it would be interesting to know more about him."*

Chuck Mawhinney herded the group toward wide, wooden steps leading into Punxi Phil's Family Restaurant, Caleb striding close at his right side, eager to keep up with his father. Lea Holderness followed, holding Clara's right hand with her left. "Who's this man?" Clara asked. "Is he my father?" She looked up at her mother, who energetically shook her head while Tariq snickered; the Governor didn't seem to even be paying much attention.

As Chuck held open one of the restaurant's double doors. Lea could see it was clearly a family restaurant with noises of people talking loudly, ceramic plates and silverware being dumped on a metal counter in the back. Two waitresses were delivering meals to diners in different-sized groups, others seated a bar looking through a large opening into the front of the kitchen and its cooks further back – hardly the elegance of the Radisson hotel back in Scranton. But Lea surveyed the scene and thought *"this is American, no starched, white shirt manners and classical music but good, wholesome Americans, living their everyday lives."* Smells of pancakes and sausage were in the air.

They waited inside the doors to be seated. While they were standing there, the Governor eased himself over to

Lea's side. He said quietly "how about you and Chuck and the kids take one table and me and Tariq take a another one? It's pretty clear you won't need us much longer so why prolong what's making me uncomfortable and maybe you too. Ah hope we can work out a way to see my daughter every once-in-a-while but that probly depends on where you and Clara end up." He moved toward Tariq as a very large woman clumped toward the waiting group with an armful of menus. "How many? Where ya wanna sit?"

Once seated at a round wooden table with a circular Lazy Susan in the center with maple syrup, catsup (Heinz, of course), hot sauce and packets of sugar and coffee creamer and remains of what looked like maple syrup leftover from pancake breakfasts, Chuck asked Lea "what's good to know about you, Lea? The guy on the phone didn't tell me much except that you did some good work for the Movement." As he was asking that question, another waitress brought water for everyone plus crayons and colorful placements for the two children, with shapes to draw and color.

The question reminded Lea of her recent past; she lightly rubbed the disappearing scars on the back of her neck before answering. "You mean the guy I call the Voice? Do you know his name? He seems to know many details about me and my life but not everything."

"Don't know his name. He just calls every so often. Most recently to tell me to meet you here. What's with these other two guys?"

"I was once a schoolteacher in the most northern part of New York State before all this political mess sucked me in. Before Clara was born, I didn't always even vote. The bulky guy with the bad posture is Buddy Lassiter – he's Clara's father and used to be Governor of Georgia. The darker, thin guy is Tariq al-Tikriti, an Iraqi, nephew of the notorious Saddam Hussein. Maybe we can talk about other stuff another time."

The head waitress lumbered up beside Chuck. "What can I git ya, Chuck?"

"The flapjacks and sausage are really good here. They also have great eggs. I'm not much of a cook. I eat here a lot. See anything on the menus that appeals to you or Clara?"

Lea opened her menu, leaned over to Clara and ran a finger down the menu items. Clara enthusiastically exclaimed '"shicken!" "That's easy," Lea grinned and said, "That's it for her, plus a glass of your freshly squeezed orange juice. I'll have two poached eggs on well-done toast with butter and a cup of coffee."

Chuck answered with a grin without looking at the menu '"shicken-fried steak for me plus burned-to-a-crisp fries and a green salad with Thousand Island Dressing, in honor of our visitors from Northern New York, probably not far from the St. Lawrence Seaway and the Thousand Islands. Caleb here will have a bacon cheeseburger with fries and a vanilla milkshake."

"What do you think the Voice has in mind?" Lea asked, looking at Chuck intently. Out of her peripheral vision, she could see Clara dumping sugar packets into her glass of water as Caleb watched in amusement while he was already filling in shapes on his placemat with a purple crayon.

"He told me you have an assignment in Ohio outside Cleveland, not that far into Ohio. If you would like me to come with you and help, I have a 2017 Ford F-150 double cab with a turbo-charged V-6 engine and a 10-speed automatic transmission – it's comfortable and easy to drive. I had WeatherTech build me a lockable metal storage unit under the front seat for all sorts of things including my weapons. If you'd like me to come along, we can drop Caleb off at his mother's; she lives near Lordstown where her husband used to work when it was building Chevies but it was just sold to FoxConn - makes phones there. Don't know if the husband can keep his job but not my problem unless he can't feed his family, which now includes three younger kids, not counting Caleb. Fortunately, my own family is not without resources."

"This is sounding better and better," Lea was thinking about her challenges and how to deal with them, particularly transportation west and getting dependable help from a man who was not a wuss. And Chuck was seeming more attractive to her, particularly his wry sense of humor and what looked like very strong hands. However, Lea had felt more than positive about the Governor when she was still teaching school in Malone long before Clara was conceived; that seemed long ago and far, far away. She had no wish to look back or rekindle her relationship with Buddy Lassiter; their time together recently gave her no incentive to do so.

While everyone was enjoying their meals, Lea saw the ad for Cobblestone Hotel and Suites on the back of Punxi Phil's menu. On the hope that doing so would set the right result in motion, she dialed the motel's number and made a reservation for herself and Clara for the night.

Then she looked over at Chuck and smiled "I hope you'll come with me on my trip west, which may get a little messy. Can we use your Ford truck? I made a reservation for me and Clara at the Cobblestone motel for the night. Clara'll love it because that place apparently has a pool although we must find Clara a bathing suit. It's time for Buddy Lassiter and Tariq to go their separate ways; I'll firm that up after we finish our meal, including making sure we get our things and weapons out of the BMW before they leave. Count on Clara to want a hot fudge sundae for dessert."

"Sounds like a plan, Lea," the former Marine sniper grinned. "I'd enjoy spending more time with you."

As their meal wound down and Caleb was actually talking with Clara, Lea removed some of Thrasher's money from her compact purse and left it beside the check, with a generous tip, hoping no one would notice the occasional blood stains on the bills. Then she excused herself and walked over to the table where the Governor seemed deep in some sort of planning. "Can you and I talk?" she asked Buddy Lassiter." He said "of course," heaved himself out of his wooden chair and followed Lea to a quiet corner away from restaurant traffic.

"Wass up?"

"Buddy, it's time for us to part company for a while.

Clara and I are going west toward Chagrin Falls with Chuck in the morning. I would be unkind of me to continue to rely on you and Tariq, especially when my job is to put someone in Chagrin Falls under the cornfield and who knows what else down the road. Involvement in those events in any way would not look good on your resume and might even be dangerous for you or Tariq. If questioned by anyone, you could legitimately say I've committed no crimes since you and Tariq rolled into the driveway of where we were staying in Malone. I certainly appreciate everything you and Tariq have done for us and bear neither of you any sort of ill will. But we need to go our separate ways. If you want and will give me a way to find you, I'll find a way for you to occasionally visit Clara. Does that work for you? Before we leave the parking lot outside, I need to get our things and my weapons from your SUV and transfer them to Chuck's Ford truck – he's taking us to the Cobblestone motel."

"Lea, honey, you know I came for more but it's clear we can't start back up where we left off, when I left to do other things when you became pregnant with Clara. Too much water under the dam since then."

"I think you mean under the bridge but I take your point. If you want to stay in Punxsutawney tonight, I'm sure Tariq can investigate what's available here. We're staying at the Cobblestone motel, mostly because it has a pool. That could be fun for Clara."

"Honey, we'll go back up to that there DuBois and get back on I-80, probably heading east. But that's not your problem. Can I give you a hug?"

Lea didn't recoil from Buddy Lassiter's holding her close in his bear-like grip but felt not even the slightest wish for more affection from him. The fact he had disappeared to pursue his political ambitions before he even knew she was pregnant and left her to fend for herself was a bar to any of that.

"Thank you, Buddy, for all of your help in getting us this far. I hope you find what you're seeking in the future. Just to finish this off, I already paid the check at our table, over there," she said, pointing to the table where Chuck was getting the children ready for travel to the next stop.

The Governor went back to his table with Tariq and asked for the check by twirling his right index finger in the air until he got the attention of a waitress.

Lea walked back to her own table, stood behind Chuck and put hands on both of his muscular shoulders. "Would you mind taking me and Clara over to the

Cobblestone with a stop along the way so we can pick up bathing suits for both of us? We can check in, have some together time before bedtime and be ready for an early morning start toward Ohio, if that works for you and Caleb."

He looked up into her eyes and said with a smile, "that would be terrific."

They helped Caleb and Clara out of their full-sized chairs and walked slowly across the restaurant toward the parking lot and Chuck's Ford truck. Lea looked back at the Governor and Tariq and was pleased to see they were apparently having a lively discussion as the Governor was giving the waitress his black Amex card to pay their check. In a way, Lea was sorry to lose the Governor and his financial resources but was newly hopeful about what was coming next. Chuck softly took her left hand as they stepped out into the sunshine, down creaky wooden steps, and across the parking lot, with Clara skipping along, holding her mother's right hand.

Chuck and Lea followed Tariq to the SUV. He unlocked the vehicle, helped her move Clara's car seat to the back seat of Chuck's F-150 and watched her belt it into place. "You know," he said, looking over at the Governor as he was standing near the BMW, fiddling with his phone, "you're a very savvy lady. That impresses me and I'd hate to be on your wrong side. But the very best of luck to you and Clara going forward. If you give me your burner number, I'll do my best to make Buddy responsible. I'm a firm believer in family; he really should stay connected with Clara even if someone else becomes a bigger part of your life."

Then the two walked back to the BMW to move the rest of Lea's and Clara's belongings to Chuck's truck. Chuck had already unlocked the metal locker under the vehicle's front seat and made room for Lea's weapons, which she and Tariq stealthily transferred there from the Governor's SUV.

"We're ready to go," Tariq called to the Governor. Buddy Lassiter walked slowly over to Clara and bent down to give her a warm hug and a kiss on the cheek. Removing his phone from his baggy suit pocket, he said to his daughter," Honey, your papa's gonna miss you. Can I please take a picture of you on my phone, so I can have something to remember you by? As soon as you and your mother get settled, I'll find a way to come see you."

Clara looked confused but wrapped her tiny arms around Buddy's hefty left leg. "Bye, Papa."

With that done, the Governor and Tariq climbed into the BMW. It took a moment for Tariq to enter DuBois into the vehicle's navigation system and for Tariq to adjust his ear buds. He then drove the BMW out of Punxi Phil's parking lot onto the single-lane road toward town. Although it seemed a little awkward, Lea waved at the departing SUV while she guessed Tariq was already listening to his classical music and Buddy was checking his messages, his mind elsewhere.

Chuck and Caleb came over to his truck from the sidelines. "I know just the place to find bathing suits. Let's do it."

On their way to the Cobblestone Motel, Chuck Mawhinney took Lea and Clara by the Peebles store on Mahoning Street in the center of town to find them bathing suits.

Time for Mordoff

Dave Garvey deliberately waited to hear from Lance Bridgeford of the Goodbody firm in Texas about Lucas Mordoff's patent infringement claim against MicroSquash – at this point in his well-documented case, the Manhattan lawyer saw no advantage to Lucas Mordoff in appearing anxious, desperate or needy. He was well aware that MicroSquash was long past the normal deadlines for answering the complaint, asserting any affirmative defenses and responding to David's many discovery demands, not exactly a comfortable position for a defendant in a substantial case, with time continuing to drip away. And now that MicroSquash was owned by another public company, potential risks might also have to appear in the parent's public financial reports, not good for share value or related publicity.

It was only 9:00 A.M. (Texas time) the second day when David Garvey's cell phone rang and showed itself on his computer screen, perhaps showing a number of Lance Bridgeford's firm. Dave let the call go to voicemail. After a deliberate delay of at least 20 minutes while he played a couple of games of Mexican Train on his phone, David

389

returned the Zoom call on his computer, to take advantage of its better acoustics and graphics.

"Lance Bridgeford here. How are ya today?"

"Good morning, Mr. Bridgeford. Just fine. Sorry for the delay but I was in the middle of settling another case. What can I do for you?"

"I'm sitting in one of our conference rooms with MicroSquash's Assistant Games Director – she'll probably be moved up since her boss was fired, among other things, for letting your case drag on so long and not having a tighter rein on Counselor Thrush and her firm when it presented huge potential liabilities. Can we talk about how to move this case along? Is Mr. Mordoff there with you?"

"No, he's in his office, talking with several different gaming companies. But I'm fully authorized to hear what you have in mind," David answered evasively, admitting to himself that he needed to be careful to be frank with opposing counsel in order to not violate general honesty rules. But the New York lawyer was certain it was in his client's best interests that his client be absent from this conversation so that his counsel could hear what, if anything, the defendant, had in mind. Later, Lucas Mordoff could discuss whatever came out of this Zoom conference with his counsel, David Garvey. Nothing wrong with insulating the client from initial discussions, if only to protect him from being impulsive and perhaps giving things away in an first conversation. Lucas Mordoff was certainly more than frustrated at how cavalierly he'd been treated by MicroSquash even before getting indirectly jerked around by Petunia Thrush. David would surely review every point in detail and would even record this conversation if Mr. Bridgeford and his client, Merrily Hector, did not object. Apparently, they didn't mind at all and even viewed that additional process as something positive as well as a means to preclude any erroneous recollections.

"OK," Mr. Bridgeford opened. "What's your client looking for in this case?"

"That's pretty simple," David Garvey retorted. "All the normal things a patent holder wants when another company is hugely profiting from an obviously infringing product. It's pretty well laid out in the complaint, embellished by everything in the public record. Mr. Mordoff has a creative and well-designed product, strikingly similar to the device your client is using to rack up spectacular sales."

"How do you think this case will go, Mr. Bridgeford," David continued, "if we get back in front of Judge Stillwater without all the 'I was so busy demonstrating at BLM protests honoring Winston Smith (hogwash) that I didn't have time to even read the papers or I'm an oppressed person nonsense? 'Have you listened to the recordings of the "hearing" we had with Petunia Thrush? Your client apparently bought MicroSquash and is now tarred with what it did and didn't do. Judge Stillwater has had a long, distinguished career, dealing with many complex cases back when they were decided by usual things such as the Federal Rules of Civil Procedure, precedent and formerly the normal rules. Unlike many Federal judges, he doesn't avoid the complexity of patent cases and the complications of patent jury trials, where the jury might be less than adept at dealing with the usual torrent of technical issues. All the while, in his earlier trial years, without this 'I'm so special I don't need to follow the rules 'nonsense. I'm willing to bet Judge Stillwater could handle a case like mine just fine, in an efficient and honorable way, particularly when dealing with two professional attorneys." David finished, getting more than a little hot under the collar.

"You can call me Lance. Do you prefer Dave or David?" "I doubt it'd be productive to go over every detail in the complaint and discovery documents in this case during this conversation," the Texas lawyer said. "My business clont is here today to explore some binis approaches to show we can deal productively with this case."

David Garvey was tempted to "accidentally" lose the call as he thought," *Pay Dirt!*" to himself. But he said into the Zoom call as calmly as he could muster, "I'd appreciate hearing what you and your client might have in mind. David would be fine, Lance."

Lance suggested: "I'll let Ms. Hector say a few words if we can agree nothins over till it's over."

David was somewhat perplexed but answered: "whatever...go ahead."

Merrily Hector, a rather attractive young blonde with a silver nose ring and a noticeable tattoo of a bronco on her left forearm, cleared her throat and started out: "I haven't delved deeply into these legal papers, but I've looked into Mr. Mordoff's business and his personal life. From what I could tell, he seems to be a brilliant and driven man. Likely built his business mostly by himself, probably rejected taking in investors even if that made his life more difficult because he didn't want his ideas ruined when some investor brought in an idiot cousin to run his invention into the ground. We thought perhaps there could be an arrangement where Mr.

Mordoff's creative business could grow in a way that would be easier for him personally. If Lance would be comfortable with it, without creating any legal problems, I'm willing to go Back East to meet with Mr. Mordoff, to talk about business opportunity points. I don't pretend to have the skills to create computer games or anything close to dream machines but I'm pretty good at making products hum. Besides, it's my impression of most lawyers that they can miss a forest of business opportunities while focusing on the trees and twigs of the litigation, which may win the case but... I had a cousin who was working for a big firm in Manhattan; his assignment was to interpret for a banking client letter of credit language written by another junior lawyer - the language occupied an entire page with a subject and no predicate. Gobbledygook! But I digress. If you wouldn't mind my meeting with Mr. Mordoff, without lawyers, Mr. Garvey, perhaps we could explore some business opportunities you gentlemen of the Bar might not have seen."

"Works for me, if you could meet somewhere safe, outside New York City," Mr. Bridgeford responded, showing his disdain for current conditions in the Big Apple and its lawlessness.

"Fine with me," David Garvey agreed. "I'll send you Lucas Mordoff's contact information but I'd like to meet with him and share with him this conversation before you contact him. I hope this can be done expeditiously so we can move this litigation along. Thank you for your time on this call."

David waved a finger through the holographic disconnect button floating below the lower edge of his computer screen and thought to himself,' *Before I get some lunch, I ll call Lucas and see if we can meet for lunch so I can fill him in on what seems to be real progress and what he should and should not discuss with Merrily Hector."*

As soon as David had poured himself another cup of mint tea, he called Lucas Mordoff on his cell phone.

"David, how ya doin? I recognized your number. What's up?"

"You free for a sushi lunch? I'm buyin. 'I'd like to fill you in on my latest conversation with MicroSquash's Texas lawyer."

"You're in luck, my friend. I'm in midtown at the moment. What do you have in mind?"

"How about my favorite sushi place, Takezushi, on Vanderbilt, just up the street from what used to be called the PanAm Building? It's not that far from my office. You've been around long enough to be able to find that place. Remember when you and I were sitting at the sushi bar there, next to a couple of visiting firemen. One of them popped a big glob of wasabi into his mouth; I thought the top of his head would come off!"

"When?"

"How about 45 minutes? I'll call to ask Mr. Nakamura's head waiter if he can reserve us two seats in front of him at the sushi bar."

Before long, David Garvey and his client were ushered to upholstered seats at the sushi bar in front of Mr. Nakamura as the young waiter handed them each stylish bamboo trays bearing steaming towels and menus. Both could plainly see special varieties of raw fish behind the sushi bar's immaculate glass panels, waiting to be enjoyed.

Once they were seated by the waiter and had used the steaming towels to both enjoy the warmth on their faces and clean their hands, he asked "Would either of you like something to drink or perhaps some miso soup while you're thinking about your order?"

"Lucas?" David asked, looking at the older man.

"I'll have a Kirin beer from the bottle and a bowl of miso soup, please."

David Garvey merely ordered hot green tea.

"May I order for us?" the lawyer asked his client as Mr. Nakamura bowed and waited expectantly.

"Fine with me, Counselor, as long as you skip the uni (sea urchin's gonads) - that stuff reminds me of yellow wallpaper paste. But otherwise, like many other things, I trust your judgment." Lucas retorted.

"Nakamura, san," David said, looking over the sushi bar at the elderly Japanese man, immaculately clothed in traditional sushi-man dress. "Onegai shimasu, for each of us, a salmon skin handroll, three pieces of yellowtail sushi, three pieces of your best tuna sashimi, two pieces of mackerel sushi and three pieces of eel sushi. Maybe more later. Arrigato."

Turning to Lucas, after taking a sip of his hot green tea, David said "Even if preparing our food won't take long, let's talk about where your case stands after my Zoom call with the Texas lawyer and MicroSquash's Games Director. I didn't expect her to be on that call but my take is her involvement may be a positive development for you. As I blather along, please break in with any observations or questions."

"What's her name and what is she like?"

"She is Merrily Hector. She's very attractive if you don't

mind nose rings or tattoos on women and she's apparently in charge of what she calls game production."

"How does she figure into my case?"

"First of all," David responded, "we were getting nowhere with that idiot Petunia Thrush and now, with the new Texas lawyer on the case, the process seems almost normal. Plus, I looked up Merrily Hector and found her office is in California but she was actually in the room with Bridgeford – that may be a small thing but, if MicroSquash went to the trouble of having her in Dallas for our call, that may be evidence of its desire to get something done. Just sayin'"

"So, where do we stand in my case, right now?" Lucas persisted.

"I'm happy to go over every detail in the complaint, our discovery demands or anything else of interest whenever you want. But, right now, let's kick around the idea of meeting with Merrily Hector near your turf and what that could mean for you and your business. You're a great detail guy but let's look at a larger picture for a bit."

Lucas grumbled but nodded his assent.

Just then, Mr. Nakamura bowed and set a delicately arranged assortment of sashimi and sushi in front of each of his two guests with a smile. "Prease enjoy," he said.

"The thing is, Lucas, Merrily Hector volunteered this idea of exploring with you how to make your business more comfortable for you, something I've never heard in the context of any settlement discussions. Perhaps because most lawyers are focused on hammering home their particular litigation points. It's not the sort of thing I would have ever suggested. Then, after proposing this pretty vague concept, she offered to travel, as she put it 'Back East' to meet with you on MicroSquash's dime to discuss potential opportunities FOR YOU on the condition that no legal issues would be discussed. I don't see any downside for you and I have a pretty good idea how difficult and expensive your entire product development and commercialization has been for you. If there's something good there for you, what is the downside?"

Lucas Mordoff blinked slowly twice and briefly looked away from his lawyer, staring blankly into some faraway memory.

Taking the moment as a way to move on, David said "let's enjoy this terrific sushi, in my view the best outside of Japan," and handed Lucas Mordoff a pair of ivory chopsticks while keeping a pair for himself. Both men began to eat enthusiastically.

After the enjoyment that followed, David suggested "how about some consideration of possible good that might come from your meeting with Merrily Hector as long as there is no discussion at all of legal issues. And you should never come near how you came up with your technology for Dream of Choice. Maybe she has something positive to talk about and, like I said, there's no downside for you. We have a very good case; if we return to legal issues only after your meeting with her, no harm, no foul. But, basically, what's your view on meeting with her and hearing what she has in mind?"

Lucas didn't respond for a moment. Then he said "MicroSquash has been trying to ruin me, put me out of business – seems like ever since I invented Dream of Choice and made it into an appealing product all by myself. Now, you've represented me in basically saying to MicroSquash: 'STOP!' You're breaking the law and you can't do this anymore.' If I understand what you've told me about your negotiations with the Texas lawyer, whatever his name is, you may have him by the short hairs. Assuming what you've told me is true, there's no downside to a meeting with MicroSquash's Gaming Director. We might even uncover something you lawyers missed. I'm willing to meet with Merrily Hector and I'll try to think of somewhere appropriate outside this New York City mess, maybe a friend's house in northern Westchester. I'll stay clear of legal issues and will call you immediately if she tries to steer our discussions in that direction."

"How about some green tea ice cream?" David asked as a waiter refilled his own cup of tea and brought a fresh one for his guest. To himself, he thought *"Lucas seems to have taken a pragmatic outlook toward this meeting with the Games Director. I don t see any downside because MicroSquash has never responded to any of the pleadings and could always push harder if anything negative comes out of this meeting. MicroSquash is still between a rock and a hard place thanks to Petunia Thrush s lackadaisical approach."*

As Ye Sow, So Shall Ye Reap

The next morning came early in Punxsutawney at the Cobblestone Motel for Clara, which meant early also for Lea. The pair dressed and took the elevator down to the lobby for its meager buffet breakfast then returned to their room to pack the few things they had brought in from Chuck's truck the prior afternoon. Along the way, Clara chattered about her new bathing suit and her swim in the warm pool before bedtime. She teased her mother because she'd only watched her daughter swim from the pool's tiled edge while relaxing in a soft chair. Clara was too young to appreciate the emotional winds buffeting her mother, whether that involved the departure of the Governor and Tariq, meeting Chuck and finding him so attractive or the trip ahead, leading to the job ahead Chagrin Falls, Ohio.

Lea checked them out of their room, paying in cash, and ushered Clara outside the motel's front, double doors into the brisk morning sunshine. At the time previously agreed with Chuck, his black Ford truck with Caleb in a child's booster seat pulled up under the motel's front awning. Chuck turned off the truck and got out to help Clara into her safety seat in the back next to Caleb and Lea into its front seat.

Once everyone was buckled in, Chuck turned the truck toward the main road to Dubois, PA 310, where they would take I-80 west toward Ohio. As the trip began, clouds rolled in, and it began to rain softly.

Lea was losing herself in the non-descript hardwood foliage on the winding road's right side when her burner phone buzzed.

"I'll bet it's the Voice," she said to Chuck before answering the call and added "I'd really like to understand how he knows we're already up and about, and getting on the road."

"Hello?"

"You must have connected with Mawhinney – you're moving back toward DuBois, probably to get back on I-80. If you can do that, it will be the quickest way to Ohio."

"Some more details about your assignment in Chagrin Falls, Ohio - it's not that far away. There's an older guy hiding there while working as the produce manager of Heinen's of Chagrin Falls, right in the middle of that affluent little town. In his immediately prior life, he was the Medical Director of Cleveland Clinic's Children's Hospital, where a 9-year-old boy was born with a disease that necessitated a kidney transplant. Fortunately, his own father was a viable donor. The procedure was approved, but the parents delayed the process because certain types of transplants are only good for about 20 years, so they wanted to give their son as long a respite as possible. Then the plandemic was launched, but the father refused to take the jab for religious reasons. At that point, the Medical Director reversed approval of the procedure on the grounds that the father was not vaccinated, because of the 'science, 'even though the entire family had endured 'Covid 'and survived just fine on their natural immunities. The Medical Director would not back off from his ridiculous position even though the hospital often conducted surgical procedures such as abortions on people who remained unvaccinated against 'Covid, 'in part because the Government views abortions as politically correct. Besides, hospitals across America reel in as many patients as possible, give them bogus 'Covid 'tests, admit them as 'Covid 'patients, dose them with harmful Remdesivir; then they usually end up on ventilators and die, which qualifies the hospitals for huge Federal subsidies. Despite many attempts, the family could not find another hospital to complete the kidney transplant and the little boy died. The Medical Director went into hiding but we found him, not that far away from his medical digs in Cleveland. He needs to experience justice and will likely be easy to find in Chagrin Falls or its surroundings. Or maybe he sneaks back to his home in the outskirts of Cleveland but that's a ritzy neighborhood so somewhere in Chagrin Falls, perhaps whatever apartment where's he's hiding in would be a better idea. All in keeping with our objective to make sure the especially "woke" know they're not safe but are in extreme peril. There are many criminals in the medical industry who have willingly murdered patients, in no small part because of at least $30,000 in premiums paid to each facility which carries a patient from phony "Covid" test to death on a ventilator. We're still trying to verify that this young man's death was documented as due to "Covid," so that hospital could collect the large premium. In this heartless criminal's case, although somewhat different, his demise should be captured in a video so it can be widely shared online, you know, TikTok, YouTube, FakeBook, and so on. As you and I have discussed before, one of our objectives is to make "woke" officials feel in extreme danger and perhaps promote whistleblowing on topics like how hospitals received extra payments promoting the deaths of patients. If you stop at the first substantial rest stop inside Ohio, I should have more specific information on this guy. And..."

"Wait," Lea interrupted "if you know where this guy is working and probably hiding, why do you need me to put him under the cornfield? Why can't one of your local people do it? Could be as simple as running over him with a truck or a bomb in his car. You told Chuck Mawhinney that I'd already done good work for the Movement. And I have a young, little girl who might be reeled into danger by whatever I do to help the Movement to eliminate "woke" officials. I'm guessing the Movement doesn't have a retirement plan or anything like witness protection to hide me somewhere quiet with new identities for me and my daughter."

"On the most important level," the voice of a male representing the Movement pointed out loudly, "the Movement arranged for your escape from Penal Colony 627 and return to America even though using a minder, from your perspective, Thrasher, who may not have been properly vetted or indoctrinated may not have been our best idea. Even after that, the Movement arranged to have that bomb removed from your neck and provided a place for you to hide in Malone. Fortunately, your persistence helped you survive Thrasher's nastiness and make impressive progress. On another level, since our object is to make 'woke 'officials afraid, the idea of a wandering assassin fits that narrative, if we can publicize it in a way that doesn't reveal your identity. And, on another level, putting you together with Mawhinney will increase the efficiency of our operation. Then, I..."

Again, Lea interrupted "did the Movement have any role in getting me pulled into the Covenant's so-called justice system? That ended in getting me sent to Penal Colony 627 in lovely northern Russia, intended to be a life sentence?"

"There's nothing I can tell you about that. But the Movement definitely appreciates how you have triumphed over those challenges. You should not forget the help you got in traveling to America, at the Movement's expense, and traveling across the East to rescue your daughter. That was no small..."

Lea continued to interrupt: "the Movement should have kept the Lost League from basically kidnapping Clara and holding her in their abusive control. Its first intrusion was while I was being put on the train away from that kangaroo court toward the holding pens under Newark Airport's flight paths, when they grabbed Clara and kept her from even seeing me before I supposedly disappeared forever. I'm horrified to imagine what was probably done to Clara while moving her from Malone to that collection of those nasty old women in Carthage and whatever was in between. Those were the worst and ..."

The Voice broke in while Lea kept the burner phone to her ear, unwilling as she was, at this point in her relationship with Chuck Mawhinney, to burden him with many details of her history, "the Movement was instrumental in connecting you with resources in Carthage, New York, pointing you, Drakulič and your daughter toward a place to stay in Malone and arrangements that led to assassination of the tranny County Commissioner of Franklin County plus whatever happened to the judge who sent you to the penal colony. We had no control of the Governor and his sidekick's arrival in Malone or how they interacted with what came next. But, having connected you with Chuck Mawhinney, to help you with at least your next assignment, the Movement continues to provide you with direction and material support."

"What else is on the table for me and when will the Movement be satisfied with what I've done?" she asked.

The call abruptly ended - Lea found herself listening to electronic noise from the burner phone at her ear. She scanned the landscape outside the Ford truck with a number of continuing concerns. Further down the road ahead, there was a large green sign pointing toward the ramp leading to I-80, heading west. Chuck slowed the Ford's pace and turned smoothly onto the ramp. As the Ford truck accelerated onto I-80, a large truck filled with several grown horses visible through its side slats loudly beeped its horn as it passed their truck in the highway's fast lane. Clara yelled "horsees!" as the loaded truck sped by while Chuck settled their truck at the posted speed.

Is the Worm Turning?

Since eliminating the judge who had sent her to Penal Colony 627, Lea had become less and less enthusiastic about eliminating the Movement's assigned targets, in no small part because those targets had done nothing to her or Clara. In many ways, she just wanted to be left alone. But Lea leaned over to share with Chuck some of her conversation with the Voice.

Clearly somewhat rattled, Lea blurted out: "I'd really like to understand how the Voice knows what we're doing. Do you have any idea how he first contacted you? He first called me on the burner phone the Movement's local contact in Malone had given me for local communications there. The Voice's unexpected first call came while we were rolling down I-81 toward Syracuse in the Governor's leased BMW SUV."

Keeping his eyes on the empty two lanes of interstate highway ahead, Chuck explained," I guess the first time I heard from the Movement was when it was rounding up ex-military talent. I've always wondered what the Movement had in mind for ex-military people, particularly those with combat experience. They probably told you that I was a Marine sniper, forced to resign from the Corps because I refused to take the jab. I've been doing other things and living at least temporarily in Punxsutawney, partly because Caleb's mother isn't that far away plus there's good hunting nearby, both in Pennsylvania and north over the border in New York State. Then they contacted me about helping you. My lucky day!"

Lea couldn't help but smile. "This latest conversation with the Voice left me with more than a few questions," she said to Chuck. "For example, how many more assignments will the Movement expect me to complete? Besides giving me some limited details about the target in Chagrin Falls, he didn't answer some of my questions and was hazy about some others, like why the Movement let the Lost League grab Clara as if I were no longer her mother after being sent to the penal colony. And he acted as if it was only some minor administrative detail that the murderous minder, Thrasher, somehow was in charge of getting me out of Russia and back to America. I'll never forget the rabid look in his eyes as held the Execution Box over his head and held down its button until I could taste my fillings."

"Execution Box?"

After confirming that both children were asleep in

their car seats, Lea moved closer to Chuck and whispered into his right ear: "a doctor at the Penal Colony sewed what amounted to a bomb with a GPS sensor into the back of my neck. It was designed to monitor my position in relation to the colony's location, to keep me there without the need for guards. The Movement provided a necklace that fooled the bomb into thinking I was always on that island but Thrasher had a device that could turn off the necklace. He seemed to really enjoyed energizing it to demonstrate his control. Thrasher didn't survive our trip west to rescue Clara and the Movement arranged to have the bomb surgically removed while we were in Malone. The bomb ended up in a river in a concrete block where it can't hurt anyone. You can feel what's left of the scars in the back of my neck."

First checking to make sure the road ahead was empty, Lea leaned forward and gently guided Chuck's right fingers from the truck's heavy steering wheel to the back of her neck, where he tenderly touched the remains of her stitches.

"Nasty!" he moaned. But then he softly kissed her cheek. "I won't ever let anyone do anything bad to you again. We may be caught up in the Movement's program. That means we'll have to work together pretty hard to get the best result for both of us and our children."

"I'd welcome that with open arms, Chuck. I can't remember when anyone's looked out for me, taken care of me except maybe Drak."

Chuck returned his right hand to the steering wheel and asked "Who's Drak?"

"He's the Eastern European refugee who met the Liberian freighter offshore in Camden, Maine, took me and the two minders ashore. His real first name is longer. One of the minders was killed in a suspicious traffic accident during the Memorial Day parade in Camden. Thrasher, Drak and I traveled west across New Hampshire and Vermont to New York State where we rescued Clara from the Lost League. Fortunately, or unfortunately, depending on your point of view, Thrasher didn't survive beyond Rochester, New Hampshire. Now that I think about it, Drak he must have gotten his instructions from the Movement because two of its minders were bringing me back from Russia. But he never told me about his instructions from the Movement. I don't know if he was really Albanian, Croat or Serb but he was operating a frame shop in Camden as a 'refugee, 'with lots of 'Covid 'and other subsidies, more monthly money than you or I could imagine. He was faithful and helpful to me and Clara but got arrested in

Malone when a local cop noticed a stolen plate on the old Honda we'd 'borrowed 'in Camden. Unfortunately, Drak, at the time was carrying without a NY license – New York takes that somewhat seriously unless you're "oppressed." I think the Voice told me Drak avoided serious trouble later, which I would expect because 'refugees 'are treated better than American citizens. Drak got arrested soon after the Governor and Tariq showed up and you know some of the rest. I'll happily tell you anything you might want to know. In case you're interested, both Drak and the Governor wanted more from me than I was willing to give."

Lea leaned back in her seat and watched Chuck carefully navigate the heavy Ford truck west on I-80, which again seemed bleak and endless. She thought to herself *"Thank you, Lord, for connecting me with this man. Maybe I m too needy and optimistic, after so many disappointments, but he seems like a real person. If it s in your plan, help me to be closer to him and to do whatever you have in mind for us. I understand my assignment includes killing bad people and that s prohibited by the Bible but please forgive me for that. I m trying to return our homeland to your reign. In the name of Jesus, Amen."*

She looked over at Chuck. "Are you a God-fearing man? If so, how do you reconcile killing people with the

Biblical commandment to never kill?'

Chuck Mawhinney kept his eyes on the road ahead and quietly answered: "I count myself as God-fearing. But some people are like roaches in your house and need to be exterminated. I'm, in part, sort of in General Patton's frame of mind: 'The object of war is not to die for your country but to get the other poor, dumb bastard die for his 'or something like 'It's not my job to decide who's a good or bad guy, it's my duty to introduce them to God so He can decide.' So, I'll ask for God's forgiveness whenever I do something wrong."

Lea felt no need to immediately respond to Chuck's point of view but was more than pleased that his point of view sounded close to her own. Given he had been a sniper, directly involved in killing other combatants, Lea had not been surprised at his outlook. She didn't mention her connection with Thrasher's demise or what happened to the judge who sent her to Penal Colony 627 but would be fully transparent with Chuck going forward. She was feeling closer and closer to him.

Chuck handed Lea his cell phone. "Could you please press the icon for 'Caleb's mother'? It will ring in my earpiece so I can tell Jodi we're about an hour out." He listened as the dialed number rang and rang then went to voice mail. "Hi, Jodi. It's Chuck. We're about an hour away from your house. I have a job west of here and hope Caleb can stay with you and Percy for a while."

"As you can perhaps guess, Jodi is my former wife. My relations with her are moderately chilly. There is still a fair amount of animosity from the divorce, caused in part by her running off with Percy, and ultimately leaving Caleb with me. Jodi's not a bad person but is under a lot of strain, including having twins after marrying Percy and whatever may or may not happen with Percy's job at the Lordstown plant. Jodi used to sell Avon products but the combination of the lockdown nonsense and taking care of the twins, Percy's two children and sometimes Caleb make the family's economics really difficult. While that mess was unfolding, Caleb went through a lot. Turns out, I like having Caleb with me. I missed him when I was deployed with the Corps and later, after my refusal to take the jab pushed me unexpectedly into civilian life around my last base before I moved into my rental in Punxsutawney."

Although the two children were awake and talking with each other, the boring landscape fluttering by the truck's windows and the hissing of its large tires put Lea to sleep. Although she was increasingly relaxed since getting to know Chuck Mawhinney and after the Governor and

Tariq's departure, Lea slipped into a dream about the judge who'd sent her off to the penal colony, mixed with what might have happened to Drak and what could be ahead in Chagrin Falls, Ohio and who knows what was after that as she tossed and turned, half asleep, against her seatbelt.

Before long, Chuck guided his truck into Jodi's driveway and touched Lea's arm to awaken her. They both unfastened their seat belts and stepped out of the truck to help both children to the driveway's pitted, gravel surface. A short and skinny woman walked up to them and said "Hi, I'm Caleb's mother. Chuck, you got yourself a real looker, like me before these kids and all the anguish that went with our divorce."

To Lea, Jodi said "what's your name and what you got going with Chuck?"

Chuck intervened "me and her have work together. Can I leave Caleb with you and Percy for a while? Where's Percy?"

"He's down signing up for unemployment. His job at the Lordstown plant went away. He's looking for something else but this isn't exactly a booming economy. Although he's been a good mechanical worker, there aren't a lot of opportunities for someone with his limited electronic experience and skills. Maybe time to visit Percy's in-laws in Arizona. See what that economy is like."

"You know I don't want to be far from Caleb," Chuck observed.

"Well, it's not like you're gonna keep us fed, Chuck," Jodi answered dismissively. "And what do you do, sweet thing," Jodi glared at Lea.

"Used to teach school in northern New York but some other things have come up. It's not like I'm sitting home and eating bon-bons."

"Come on, ladies, you barely met. Lea, this is Jodi, Caleb's mother, and the woman I enthusiastically married. Jodi, I've been asked to help Lea, related to some of the things she's suffered, like being incarcerated abroad for nothing substantial. I'm not suggesting the two of you take long, warm showers together, just hoping for basic cordiality. I doubt you'll be spending much time together in the same place."

"I do the best I can without many resources," Jodi said.

"You OK staying with your mom for a while?" Chuck asked Caleb.

"I like to be with you, Dad, but there are kids here to play with. Clara's OK but I'd rather play with boys and the school here is better than in Punxsutawney even though I didn't spend very long there."

"Let's get your stuff out of the truck. Lea and I have to move further west in Ohio. I hope to be back for you before too long," he said, walking over to his truck. "Jodi, you have my number so you can keep me posted on how Caleb is doing and maybe what's going on with Percy. Please at least keep me in Caleb's loop."

After delivering Caleb's things to Jodi, Chuck hugged him and motioned Lea toward the Ford truck and opened the passenger door for her.

Moving Toward a New Home

Chuck maneuvered the truck from the suburb of Lordstown where Jodi and Percy lived back to I-80 West with Clara buckled into her safety seat. He explained to Lea that he thought it would be a good idea to pick up an RV rather than look for commercial places to stay in or around Chagrin Falls. "With an RV, we can park it somewhere legitimate without being cornered in a motel and maybe get a junker to go about our assignment, something we can ditch if things go wrong."

"How can we do that?" Lea asked. "I don't know anything about RVs."

"First of all, the lease or purchase price of an RV is not a financial challenge for me. And they probably have a discount for veterans. We can easily get a two-bedroom RV at a dealer in Mantua, just north of Shalersville. It's just north of I-80, not very far from here or from Chagrin Falls. Our destination is only about an hour from Jodi and Percy's so we're already well on our way. You probably noticed there's a trailer hitch on this truck so hooking up an RV is no big deal."

Lea looked into the back seat to see Clara quietly

playing with her plastic toys. "Sounds like a good plan to me. What do we do about beds and other furniture? However this works, I'll need to be in touch with someone local with the Movement for help with things like someone to take care of Clara while we're attending to the assignment. I don't want Clara anywhere near that."

As if on cue, Lea's burner phone buzzed. Before she answered the call, fully expecting the caller to be the Voice, she leaned closer to Chuck and asked him if his truck might be bugged or if there might be some sort of tracking device attached to it."

"I looked the truck over very carefully before we met at Punxi Phil's and found nothing, but anything is possible. Whatever the case, I don't really trust these Movement folks."

Lea pushed the "answer" button on her burner phone. "Hello?"

"Where are you now?" the Voice inquired.

"Why do you ask? I thought you had tracking equipment installed in Chuck's truck."

"We don't have the time or people to monitor such a thing. Where are you in relation to Chagrin Falls?"

"Actually, not that far away, probably less than an hour although we have some things to take care of before getting close enough to Chagrin Falls. I need the local equivalent of that guy Herbert, the contact you assigned to me in Malone. We'll take care of our own place to stay but I'll surely need someone to look after Clara while we're attending to our assignment. Please send me contact information to my phone." Without saying anything else or waiting for any response from the voice, she punched the button to terminate the call.

"Past time to try to take more control," she declared to Chuck.

"That's my girl," he smiled, patting her shoulder.

"As this process grinds along, the more I wonder what was the Movement's role in my life, starting back when I was scooped up by the Covenant and subjected to that ridiculous religious trial? Did the Movement get that started to co-opt someone in great physical shape who could do its bidding once I escaped from Penal Colony 627? Maybe Thrasher was too erratic and the Movement wanted to get rid of him anyway. And once I was sort of involved in assassinating that tranny Franklin County Commissioner, was I supposed to worry more about getting arrested, so I'd be willing to keep doing the Movement's bidding? The almost constant checking in by the Voice underlines my worries. Do you think I'm being too paranoid?"

"Some of that may be a little extreme but I've had similar thoughts since being forced to resign from the Corps because of my refusal to take the jab. For example, right now I don't remember how the Movement found me and got me interested in helping you. I'm glad it did because I like everything I've learned about you and your daughter," the former jarhead admitted. "And I want to know you better."

Ahead, they could both see a sign for Exit 193. Chuck slowed his truck. They followed the looping Exit 193 onto a local road toward nearby Mantua. Chuck had previously checked for RV dealers in Mantua and decided to try one on Mennonite Road. On their way into the village of Mantua, they stopped at McDonald's for coffee and Clara's favorite "shicken," some fries for everyone plus a Coke and later vanilla ice cream with chocolate sauce for Lea's bubbly daughter. As always, Clara was fascinated with the plastic toys which came with the meals from the friendly clerk with the shiny nose ring.

Chuck explained some of the RV options he'd explored while doing research at the Punxsutawney library.

At the moment, his suggestions included a used 2015 Forest River RV Wildwood 26TBSS that was being offered for about $20,000 with one bedroom, a complete kitchen and dining area and a separate compartment with two bunk beds – not elaborate but would not only fit their needs but could be towed by Chuck's truck. "How's that sound to you?" he asked Lea.

She'd been intrigued by the chance to sleep in the same bed with this former Marine and was more than willing to see how that felt. Since high school and gropings in the back seats of ratty cars of two male friends and an on-and-off relationship with a nerdy chemistry major in teachers' college, Lea's social life had been tame. Since Penal Colony 627, her life had been entirely focused on survival and whatever dangerous steps came next. And, with what sounded like a comfortable place to stay, where they would not be stuck in a specific place, that might be a good option. "Let's give it a try," Lea smiled, understanding that her options would narrow once Chuck bought or leased an RV even though her limited experience with him had been very positive. She thought Clara might like an RV with her own room plus a television and a regular kitchen.

As the truck continued through Mantua and turned right onto to Mennonite Road, Clara was paying close attention. "What's that red thing going up and down by all those trucks?"

"That's a moving sign with a smiley face to coax people to stop in and look at RVs. There's a gadget at the bottom of that red tube that blows air in to inflate it, lets some out and blows it up again," Chuck pointed out. "That's actually where we're going to stop. You'll be able to look at RVs with your mother and me."

"What's an RV?"

"An RV is a home on wheels which can be pulled by a truck like mine – you'll see."

He slowed the truck, put on the truck's left blinker and waited until the westbound lane was clear before pulling into the RV sales lot and parking beside a tiny sales shed. "Let's see what they got," as he opened Lea's door and helped Clara down from her car seat. "Please hold my hand – there's traffic here." Chuck walked with Lea and Clara toward the sales office but were met by a portly, old man with a white beard."

"Hi, neighbor, my name's Jason Hochleitner. What can I show you? Figured you weren't selling anything 'cause you got nothin 'attached to your truck's hitch."

"My name's Chuck Mawhinney. Just discharged from the Marine Corps," he said, introducing himself but seeing no reason to complicate Lea's life by introducing her or Clara. "This is my family," he continued, winking at Lea. We'd like to see the 2015 Forest River Wildwood prominently featured on your website. How many miles on it?"

"Why, let's take a look. It's right over there, in fine shape," the salesman said, pointing to the black and white RV on the side of the lot. "It's almost like buying a TV from a little, old lady with weak eyes. The prior owners bought it to go camping and fishing, didn't get to it and then the wife took her show on the road and left the guy with it – very low mileage and clean as a whistle."

The salesman guided them toward the RV Chuck had in mind, opened its door and helped Clara up the RV's pair of steps. Clara turned left and stopped to look at the kitchen installation and immediately started to turn knobs on the gas range.

"Here, Clara, please take my hand so we can look around and check out this unit's features," Lea said, winking at Chuck as she patted the queen bed just inside the RV's door. Chuck walked ahead of them, opening a closet and then looked into three tiers of smaller beds inside a closet door just past the refrigerator and cooktop. This RV included both a bathtub and a separate shower. There was also what looked like a plastic-covered sofa-like unit around a dining table pointed toward a wall-mounted television. Almost everywhere were rollout storage drawers plus a large wardrobe to the right of the kitchen unit. Lea checked the refrigerator and bathrooms and was surprised to find them very clean even though the RV itself was pretty stuffy.

Chuck said to the salesman "Mind if we talk separately outside? You probably know who makes these decisions."

"No problemo."

The trio stepped out into the sunlight. "What do you think, Lea?"

"In the abstract, I might not have picked having the main bed in front of the only door but that may not be a disadvantage. I've never even stayed in an RV so I'll defer to you on what living in one is like and whether this would meet our needs. It looks like there's plenty of storage for things we may want to be near us like weapons. I like the fact Clara will have some of her own space even if the three of us may have different times to go to sleep and get up but we can keep control of the TV to ourselves. Assuming you're also good with this, you might want to consider leasing for a couple of years rather than a purchase. Who knows where we'll be after our travels and assignments?"

"Living in an RV is different than living in a house –

every time the RV is moved, you need to find a suitable place to park it, where you can hook up electricity, sewer and water and perhaps cable for the TV. It's not like you can just park it anywhere, which usually means an RV park with all the necessary connections. But I've done that before and it's not a huge inconvenience. I'll go with Mr. Hochleitner and work out a deal. Hopefully he will offer a veteran's discount. I didn't get around to getting a driver's license that proves I'm a veteran but I always keep a copy of my DD-214, the document the Corps gave me when I mustered out. It shows my honorable discharge."

While waiting for Chuck to complete the transaction, Lea twisted away red and white cellophane on one of the hard candies the salesman had given her and offered it to Clara. Without hesitation, the little girl popped the sour candy into her mouth and said: "Thank you, Mommy."

Taking a bit of a chance, Lea asked her daughter: "how has Chuck treated you since we met him?"

"Is he my father, Mommy?"

Lea chuckled: "Your father is Buddy Lassiter, who came to see us with Tariq in Malone. The big man with the fancy car. We rode with them all the way to Punxsutawney where we met Chuck. Once we get settled, we'll find a way for your father to see us. But he's your only father so you don't ever need to ask again about who's your father. Any questions?"

"No, Mommy."

"Has Chuck been nice to you since we met him and Caleb and ate at that restaurant with them?"

"He's funny, Mommy."

"What do you mean, honey?"

"He laughs, makes jokes and smiles. He likes you, Mommy?"

"How can you tell, honey?"

"He's really nice to you, Mommy."

Lea turned aside, beaming. *If my own young daughter can see something I already felt, what a miracle. Thank you, Lord. It s been so long since I ve felt cared for. I just wish we didn t have this nasty job in front of us and who knows what after that?"*

Chuck walked over from the sales shack with a smile on his face and a folder full of papers under his arm. "All done. I've got all the keys we for need the RV and Mr. Hochleitner even gave us a temporary Ohio license card for the RV. That's a really big help because apparently the DMV is closed today, it's being Saturday. Clara, would you like to help me move my truck to the RV so we can hook it up to my trailer hitch?"

Chuck and Clara walked toward his parked truck as Clara looked over her shoulder at Lea with a knowing smile. Lea thought to herself *I shouldn t be surprised that Clara picks up on so many important things. Probably shouldn t be – I m no dummy and the Governor may seem a little slow now but he s pretty bright even if he probably has too much going on right now."*

By the time Lea followed Chuck's truck to their new RV, Chuck was already showing Clara how to connect the RV hitch to his own vehicle and the brake light connectors so that the RV would show when Chuck hit the brakes or used turn indicators on his truck as their trip continued toward their assignment in Chagrin Falls, not very far down the road from Mantua.

While in the sales shack signing papers and paying Mr. Hochleitner, Chuck had looked into places to park the RV somewhere nice but not far from Chagrin Falls. One was Punderson State Park with many facilities including a swimming beach and only about 10 minutes from Chagrin Falls. Having in mind the recent purchase of swimsuits for both Clara and Lea, Chuck made a week's reservation for the new RV at Punderson State Park.

Once Chuck and Clara had finished connecting the RV with Chuck's truck and its brake lights and turn signals, Chuck wiped his brow and cleaned his hands with a wet rag. He turned to Lea: "I made us a reservation for a few nights at a nearby state park with a swimming beach, not far from here. It's called Punderson State Park and is only about 10 minutes from Chagrin Falls. We can stop for groceries on the way and have some rest and relaxation before work."

Before long, Chuck pulled his Ford truck with the new RV trailing behind it to the side of the road just past a drab brown, white-framed cabin. It appeared to be the reception station for Punderson State Park. Before stepping down from the truck's cab, he gave Lea a kiss behind her left ear and said "I'll take care of our reservation, find out where our assigned lot is and arrange to get our services hooked up. I know you'll entertain Clara, but I'll try to be right back."

An Ugly Head

As his left foot hit the cracked pavement, his cellphone rang.

"Hello," he said, putting the phone to his left ear.

"You better be closer to finishing your job," the Voice snarled, in the middle of a sneeze. "It's a simple assignment – dusting that medical bureaucrat who let the child die of kidney failure even though his own father was a qualified match for kidney replacement, all because the father wouldn't take that phony jab. On camera. As you probably heard from Lea, that event must be creatively recorded on a video so we can spread the word: 'medical people who follow instructions from their overlords rather than care for their patients are worse than not safe.'"

Chuck looked through green leaves of fully grown maple and oak trees in front of him, toward the shimmering blue lake beyond. He couldn't ignore increasingly strident tones of their minder, thinking about how that might affect what might come next. Chuck was particularly concerned about how Clara might be protected while completing the assignment and whether he and Lea could count on Clara's safety with anyone the Movement provided as a caregiver. On

432

one hand, Lea had faithfully completed her assignments for the Movement, but he was new to this program and had no reason to trust the Movement or its minders.

"Our plan is to rent a couple of motel rooms for cash near Chagrin Falls so it would be hard for anyone to trace us," Chuck lied, already thinking ahead to getting the RV hooked up to water and power. Once that was completed, his Ford truck could be disconnected from the RV and available for independent use even though Chuck had more involved plans.

He continued: "neither of us is a videographer. We don't have any video equipment, or the training needed to create an effective video of what you want us to do. There's no possibility Lea and I could, as you say, 'dust 'the target, while tending to audio and lighting issues pertinent to achieving your desired result of a convincing and persuasive presentation. To eliminate him effectively would demand attention to that detail, not worrying about video production issues. You need to provide an experienced videographer who can film the event and provide it to your organization. I'll suggest a time and place for your videographer to meet me or Lea; we'll go from there to wherever your target is, so your guy can film what comes next. We also need several packages of the J&J vaccine, the same amount of the Moderna vaccine, similar amounts of the ChinoVac, just to avoid any charge of discrimination, and several syringes. My plan involves giving the target several shots of the 'vaccines 'at the same time until he can't take any more."

"I don't much like your tone, Mawhinney. You were a Jarhead and should understand about following instructions," the Voice barked. "We have plans and expect you and Lea to follow them and figure out how to get the job done most efficiently."

Chuck smiled to himself and thought *"Like I ll meekly salute and enthusiastically do whatever stupid thing you demand."* But he replied "Of course, Sir, we're doing our very best to successfully implement your instructions." At the same time, he noted that his phone was connected to an actual number, unlike calls to Lea's burner phone, where the caller's number was blocked. Chuck wondered about the effectiveness of the Movement's tracking them and whether it could tell where he planned to set up the RV. He made a note for his 'gee whiz 'file to remind Lea to leave her burner phone off."

"Call me near the end of the day tomorrow and I'll have a location for your videographer to meet us, with the medical supplies we need and get going," Chuck said while pushing the "off" command on his phone and pushed open the front door of the Punderson State Park reception center. As the call faded away, he could hear an angry voice yelling "what's this about vaccines...?"

On Toward the Jab

Once the new RV was fully connected in the afternoon sunshine to utilities at their rented lot at Punderson State Park and groceries were put away, Lea and Clara put on their bathing suits and gathered up some clean towels. Lea could not resist giving Chuck a hug before they walked away toward the swimming area while Clara clutched her sandals and looked up at her mother with a smile. Chuck Mawhinney made his rounds to the neighbors, introducing himself as a recently discharged U.S. Marine. Besides making new friends, Chuck was looking for a passenger vehicle he could rent for the mission to Chagrin Falls; he planned to find transportation that wouldn't require taking his Ford truck into Chagrin Falls. He met one older couple where the guy was a Korean War vet; they had two cars and were willing to loan one to Chuck, insisting on no exchange of money because of their veteran connection but Chuck would not avoid paying them, in part because there was no way to predict how the assignment would work out. Soon he walked back to where his RV was parked with keys to the neighbor's Jeep Wrangler. On the way back, he stopped to check his weapons in the safety locker under his truck's front seat and was happy to slide a hand over his trusty well-oiled and polished Springfield '03, a memento from his first arms training, a cleaned and ready .45 automatic pistol with two full magazines and his more sophisticated sniper rifle. He thought to himself *"I hope using these isn t necessary to get this job done."* Chuck noticed that Lea's Beretta was not there, probably with her.

Chuck was already working on a pasta dinner with fresh salad when the ladies returned from swimming. Lea and Clara set the table while Chuck finished meal preparations and opened a bottle of red wine and poured some orange juice for Clara. They sat together around the table, said" Grace" and began eating, bantering happily about the day's events, telling Chuck about the beach, what Caleb might be doing at the moment and the bright sunny day predicted for tomorrow. Together, Lea and Chuck washed the dinner dishes, made up Clara's bed and then their own while Clara was watching a Christian channel cartoon show. Before long, Clara dozed off in the middle of one of her shows and Lea carefully tucked her into her new bed in the far corner of the RV.

Chuck walked up behind Lea and hugged her from behind "You smell like lake water, clean and fresh" he said. "I want to take you in my arms and kiss you to sleep," turning her to face him. Her eyes were bright; and he began to unbutton her blouse and slide it down over her slightly tanned shoulders. She unbuckled his belt, helped him out of his pants. Together, they moved slowly toward their new bed, turning off lights as they went. Lea and Chuck embraced, kissed deeply and slowly relaxed onto the open sheets as he slid a soft pillow under her naked hips, his hands trembling with desire. She eagerly pulled him to her.

"Mommy, Mommy! I see a bluebird out the window," Clara brought the new day just after sunrise. Chuck was holding Lea in his naked arms but pulled on his pants to see what Clara was talking about. He kissed Lea on the cheek and said "Sweetness, it's time to get up. We have a lot to do today and I'm guessing Clara is up for the day."

After coffee and breakfast, Chuck explained his plan. "Please just listen until I cover everything. I've borrowed a Jeep from a neighbor who's another vet of the Corps, in his case Korea and 'Nam. Hopefully I can find a novelty store nearby to get a couple of serious Halloween masks. Once the Voice tells me where our target is hiding, I'll drive into Chagrin Falls to wake him up about 3:00 A.M. I know from my time in the Corps and experience with police work that's likely to be the time of his lowest functionality. I plan to strap him to a chair and give him endless jabs with different types of what they call vaccines while the videographer provided by the Movement films it. If that doesn't put him under the cornfield in a reasonable amount of time, I'm taking my silenced pistol. I know this may be different than what you had in mind but I'd rather leave you here with Clara than expect a babysitter supplied by the Movement to keep her happy and safe while we both do it. Plus, I've unhooked my truck from the RV so it's easy to use if things go south – I'll leave you the keys."

Lea looked over her coffee cup at Clara's playing with her toys in a far corner of the RV, her eyes rapidly blinking. "I always thought I'd have to do this all by myself and tough out details like how to make sure Clara stays safe. I was planning for both of us to put this guy under the cornfield. I'm more than grateful you care so much for Clara's safety and mine. But what about you?"

"According to the Voice, this guy's in his late 60s, has spent his entire career behind desks in Cleveland medical facilities and isn't exactly Arnold Schwarzenegger. I'll hopefully wake him from a deep sleep, I will be fully armed and will be sure to take the necessary tools. Unless I run into unexpected problems with him or the videographer the Voice sends, I should be able to take care of it by myself and be back in time for breakfast. Can we spend the day enjoying this park even though I'll be surprised if I don't hear from the Voice."

"I'm still very concerned about your safety," Lea said, putting her around Chuck's shoulders and pulling him close.

Lea, Chuck and Clara spent most of the early part of the day at the beach and eating the egg salad sandwiches Lea had prepared. As they were walking back to the RV, Chuck's phone rang, his screen showing the Voice's number.

"What have you got for me?" Chuck answered. "You told me our target is hiding in a one bedroom rental at 151 Carriage Drive in Chagrin Falls. What apartment number? Are there any access controls to the building where his apartment is located? I'm going there at night so there's almost no chance someone would be entering or leaving his building when I try to get in. And how do I contact the videographer?"

The Voice sounded harried as he answered. "The complex has electronically controlled entry with a touch screen at all points of ingress – it has the stupid code of 115511 (a variant of the street address). If you have any trouble getting in, your target has an apartment on the first floor with a sliding glass door out to the lawn. Your videographer is John Chen; I'll text you his cell number.

When do you plan on getting together with your target?"

"3 A.M. tomorrow morning. Have the videographer meet me with his equipment on Carriage Drive at the entrance to 151 Carriage Drive not later than 2:30 tomorrow morning. You know my description. If he's not there on time, I'll complete the assignment whether or not you end up with a video to terrorize the 'wokes.'"

"The sooner the better," the Voice barked. "Where are you right now?"

"Prepared and ready," Chuck replied as he turned off his phone.

Lea, Chuck and Clara had an early supper and Chuck laid down on their bed, trying for at least a short nap while Lea and Clara walked around the RV park, meeting people, making friends and generally enjoying being in one place for more than a day or two. Chuck actually dozed off, putting what was coming aside for a while.

On to Chagrin Falls

After removing its license plates and putting them behind the vehicle's back seat, Chuck Mawhinney drove the red Jeep Wrangler along wet local streets toward Chagrin Falls, windshield wipers clicking occasionally until he reached Carriage Drive and parked one-half block from the apartment where the target was supposed to be hiding, where he could see the entrance to the complex. It was 1:50 A.M. He settled down to wait to see when and if the videographer arrived and whether he was alone. Would the videographer be careful enough to arrive early to check the site and whether anyone else was there? Chuck checked his .45, removed its magazine, emptied and reloaded its bullets, clicked the magazine into place and jacked in what he hoped would be an unnecessary first shot. The street ahead was quiet with only a few parked cars. He remembered the Voice had told him the target's complex had large off-street parking facilities.

What looked like a dark-colored Chevy Camaro pulled up close to the complex's driveway entrance. In the darkness and light rain, Chuck couldn't see who was inside. Someone careful would have looked for Chuck before the meeting time, particularly given the gruesome nature of the assignment. As a door of the Camaro opened, its roof light showed two people climbing out onto the damp pavement, the sagging long coat of the burly, taller man suggesting a side arm in the coat pocket. The smaller, thin man went to the Camaro's trunk and took out a wheeled equipment carrier. *"Huh," thought Chuck to himself. Maybe I should have brought along some help. But I'd most rather that Lea and Clara be safe."* He opened the locker under the truck's front seat to take out the fully loaded Springfield '03 and set it on the black, vinyl seat beside him.

Chuck had already disabled the Wrangler's overhead light. That enabled him to quietly step out onto the damp pavement with his Springfield '03 in his right hand without warning anyone outside his vehicle. He watched the two men walking carefully around the back of the apartment complex. After putting on his Biden Halloween mask and thin plastic medical gloves, Chuck crept toward the complex's main door and punched in the code provided by the Voice; to his surprise, the door swung open. *"At least the Voice didn't screw me up on that part,"* Chuck thought as he softly walked down the padded carpet toward the target's door. He took a wad of chewing gum out of his mouth and stuck it in the apartment door's eyehole than banged hard on the door.

"MAINTENANCE, MAINTENANCE! There's a water leak in the apartment above yours!"

Chuck could hear small steps behind the apartment door, it opened slightly and an older man, in tee shirt and ragged underpants, rubbing his eyes looked up at him.

"What's going on?"

Suppressing a faint twinge of sympathy, the former Marine stomped hard with his right combat boot on the target's bare left foot and barreled into him, jamming his left shoulder into the small man's chest. The target ended up on his back on the frayed carpet, gasping for breath. Chuck immediately turned him over and secured his hands behind his back with silver duct tape. He dragged the target to the nearest wooden chair beside what looked like a rented dining table, slipped the target's taped hands behind the back of the chair and taped his legs to the chair's white, metal legs, with more silver duct tape.

Chuck slapped the target sharply twice across his worried face. "Do you remember the little boy who died of kidney failure in your hospital because his family couldn't find a donor after you wouldn't let his father donate a kidney? Because of your stupid 'he can't donate because he hasn't been vaccinated 'rule?"

The target looked up at Chuck Mawhinney, very frightened and surprised. "What you talking about? I'm a refugee from Guatemala. I work in vegetable section of a store downtown for minimum wage, live in this dump because I got no money. I don't know nothing about medical stuff. You crazy!"

While Chuck was digesting this brown man's upsetting answer and trying to figure out if it might be true, the two glass doors in the back of the apartment partly burst open, scattering broken glass over the frayed, gray carpet. A tall man wearing a helmet and facemask stooped under the remaining top part of the right glass door, catching the sleeve of his coat on a pointed piece of glass jutting out of the door's bottom frame. He caught his balance with a hefty baseball bat in his left hand while pointing the pistol in his right hand at Chuck, who yelled "put down your gun!" The first man through the broken glass door was elbowed aside by a shorter man in black clothing and a cloth mask pointing a video camera with a bright light on its top at Chuck. The man with the lighted camera grumbled "let me in, asshole. We have to get pictures of this." And he stepped into the room.

The taller man shrugged and dropped the baseball bat among the shards of glass on the apartment's carpet and completed his pistol grip by wrapping his left hand around the stock of the pistol pointing at Chuck. Chuck had already laid his Springfield '03 on the carpet and removed his silenced .45 from the pit of his back, instantly brought it up and fired two rounds into the taller man's chest, whose knees buckled. Two large pops. Chuck quickly crunched through the remains of the back door and delivered a third shot between the tall man's fluttering eyelids. Chuck immediately turned toward the videographer, sticking his .45 almost into his mouth. He still had five rounds left in the pistol's magazine.

"Give me a reason to not put you down while I count to five and tell me what's really going on. You were supposed to make a video of my delivering justice to this doctor. Turns out he probably isn't even the real target."

"I was just paid to come here to take a video," the shorter man blubbered. "I had no idea what was going to happen."

Chuck Mawhinney glared down at the diminutive videographer. "You have only a few seconds to come clean!" Pointing to the convulsing body on the glass strewn rug, he continued. "What's he doing here if you were only here to complete a video? You supposedly had my cell number and didn't need muscle to run that camera. What's really going on?"

Keeping both eyes glued to Chuck's pistol barrel just below his nose, the short man whined "they told me I might need some help if things got out of hand."

Chuck grabbed him by the throat, pushed the whirring camera to the floor and pulled the frightened man to a nearby dining room chair, where he used several lengths of silver duct tape to secure both of his ankles to the chair's legs and zip tied his hands behind the chair's metal back. He lavishly taped each man's mouth shut and stomped on both of their cell phones. All the while, Chuck kept scanning the lawn outside the apartment's broken door as well the apartment's entrance door, which Chuck had previously bolted shut. So far, no additional challenges.

Chuck broke open the dead man's pistol, stuffed its bullets into his own right pocket and check the man's pockets for identification. He wasn't surprised to find nothing except a large handful of twenties, which Chuck stuffed into his pockets with the bullets.

As an added caution, remembering he'd been in the camera's spotlight, Chuck opened the camera and popped out its memory chip and slipped it into his pants pocket, then he repeatedly slammed the camera into the apartment's kitchen sink until its internal components began to fall out.

"Time to go, he thought to himself" as he poked the .45 behind his belt in back, picked up the Springfield '03 and eased himself out the apartment door, down the hall and warily out into a light rain on his way to the borrowed Jeep. He brought with him what was left of the videographer's camera. Chuck continued to survey vehicles parked on Carriage Drive, glad he's disabled the overhead light in the Jeep. Once in the driver's seat, Chuck thought *"I should call Lea but the Voice may have a trace on her burner phone so I'll just get back to her and Clara as quickly as possible without attracting any attention."*

Without much delay, he was on the road toward Punderson State Park, already looking forward to hugging Lea and Clara if she hadn't been asleep at this early morning hour. Passing through sleepy Punderson State Park, Chuck slowly wound through quiet streets, to finally park the Jeep Wrangler beside his Ford truck, its windshield and hood covered by evening dew. He immediately stepped out onto the gravel driveway. Lights immediately came on inside the RV.

Almost immediately, the RV's lights went off and its only door slid open quietly. In weak light from nearby RVs, Chuck could see Lea crouching in the doorway with her Beretta by her right thigh.

"It's me," he said softly.

"Come right in," Lea whispered. "Why didn't you call me? How did it go?"

Chuck moved toward the RV and hugged Lea's legs. She pulled him close and held him tightly. Together, they slipped into the RV where Lea turned on a small light near their bed before they sat down on the soft bed's nearest edge.

Chuck looked off into the distance. "I'm not really sure how it worked except the videographer showed up with armed muscle and the target probably wasn't even a doctor. He told me that he's an illegal immigrant from Guatemala; I'm inclined to believe that he had nothing to do with the young boy's death. In either case, something about the Voice or the Movement is not working in our best interests. The armed muscle pulled a gun on me after they broke through the apartment's glass doors so I had to put him down. I left the videographer and the immigrant duct-taped to metal dining room chairs after smashing their cell phones. Finally, I didn't call you because it seemed to me the Voice might be using your burner phone to track us. Once we get going, we'll get you a new phone and throw that burner phone in the first dumpster we pass after removing its sim card before we turn it on. But we should move out of here as soon as Clara wakes up and I've returned the borrowed Jeep."

Lea's naked left arm had been resting on Chuck's shoulders. She reached over with her right hand to turn his face closer to her own and kissed him enthusiastically on the lips. "Are you OK? You seem more than a little stressed. You did a great job and Clara and I were safe here. You got the assignment off our list even if it turned out differently than we'd been told. Lie back, let me take off your clothes and rub your back. You need some rest. I'll stay half-awake while you sleep in case someone followed you home."

Chuck Mawhinney rolled over and let Lea cover him with soft sheets and a blanket. As she rubbed his neck and back, he was snoring before long. But then, he awoke with a snort, sat up and mumbled "Gotta get out of here when the sun comes up," before falling back to sleep.

Starting West

Morning came earlier for Lea than Chuck, in part because Clara almost always awoke at the crack of dawn but Chuck was accustomed to sleeping anywhere at any time. Lea had already started coffee when Chuck rolled over and sat up.

"We need to get going," he mumbled. "I'll return the borrowed car to the vet down the road and then let Clara help me disconnect the RV's electric, plumbing and sewer connections. What do you think about trashing all connections with the Movement and heading west, far west, maybe Arizona?"

"Never been in the Grand Canyon State except for tourist adventures, but I'm game for almost anything. I'm really tired of some of the Eastern nonsense such as the NY law requiring some bureaucrat's approval to get a gun permit for self-protection – just read the Supreme Court threw out that law as an infringement on the Second Amendment. Besides, don't you have a relative in northern Arizona?" Lea continued brightly with a smile and a warm caress on Chuck's shoulder.

After they shared some hot coffee, Chuck went outside

the re-install the borrowed car's license plates and slowly drove it to the owner's RV. He couldn't help but admire the vet's Korean and Vietnam service ribbons on his Marine Corps baseball cap. Even though he knew it was time to head west, he couldn't miss the chance to talk about his uncle, Chuck Mawhinney, and his exploits in 'Nam. The vet wouldn't take the money Chuck offered for using the Jeep Wrangler and for gas used but Chuck surreptitiously slipped three $20 bills into the old man's back jean pocket when he was going on about Choisin Reservoir and his many friends who didn't survive the horrible cold and Chinese attacks there. Chuck thanked him again profusely and walked quickly back to his own RV.

Once there, he opened the RV's door, leaned in and said "Say, Clara, would you help me disconnect services from our RV, the ones you helped me connect when we first arrived?" Lea looked out the RV's door while folding bedding and towels; she smiled approvingly as Chuck and Clara busied themselves with completing departure arrangements, her showing surprising aptitude and interest in the RV's connections. Lea said "On our way, let's stop at a reputable electronics store so we can both get new phones and leave the old phones under the rear wheels of a nearby truck, so we can sever as many ties with the Movement as possible –

we've now both had experiences which suggest the Movement may not have our best interests at heart. And maybe we can even find an entertaining toy for Clara. It's apparently going to be a long trip west."

Lea and Chuck carefully checked the RV and Chuck's truck before belting Clara into her car seat then stopping at the park's office to check out early, offering some imaginary excuse about a family emergency and the need to return to Pennsylvania. Chuck looked around to check everything and then powered his truck west on Kinsman Road toward Russell Center. He took a right at the only intersection and drove into a Circle K, where he topped off the truck's gas tank and suggested that Lea pay for the gas with cash in the station. While there, Lea bought two prepaid cell phones and a puzzle game for Clara with her Circle K card. After that, both she and Chuck fastened their seat belts, Chuck took a left out of the Circle K lot. Then, he followed Chillicothe Road until it ran into Ohio 422 west and on toward I-480 west. They both knew it would be a long drive to the sparsely inhabited part of north central Arizona where Chuck Mawhinney had relatives he could count on. He remained worried about the Movement and how it might affect him, Lea and Clara.

It may have escaped Lea's notice that using her Circle

K credit card might allow the Movement to pinpoint her location and perhaps even track her travels with Clara and Chuck Mawhinney. Even the new phones might not protect them from the Movement's attention.

Just before turning onto ramp 26A of, I-480 West in Bedford Heights, Chuck Mawhinney pulled into an empty parking lot, put his truck in "park" and called a 928 number on his new burner phone. When a male voice answered, Chuck said "I hope you recognize my voice. We shouldn't use names because we're having trouble with bad people trying to track us. I've got a new RV behind this truck so I'm hoping you can find us a place near you where we can find suitable RV hookups while we're thinking about where to live permanently and safely. Since we're coming west on I-480, I guess we should be thinking about it as "the 480" now that we won't be "Back East" any more. Along the way, please call our Jarhead buddy in Tucumcari; we'd like to stop and see him on the way to you, if he can point us to a convenient place with RV hookups. RVs are nice but you need hookups for sewer, electric and internet to be comfortable. You can give him this number. Please suggest that he get a new burner phone to decrease the chance the bad people can find any of us. "Semper Fi!" Chuck smiled, turned off his phone and turned his truck toward the on-ramp for the 480, heading west.

Chuck beamed at Lea and Clara, delighted that the young girl was quickly learning the details of RV hookups, something beyond even many grownups, and was visibly happy to be part of helping her family.

As the 480 unfolded before them, the skies opened and it began to pour. The truck's heavy-duty windshield wipers created a steady rhythm as the trio slowly but purposely motored west through the storm. Clara predictably fell asleep.

Lea's new phone buzzed.

"Hello" she answered tentatively.

The raspy and vaguely familiar voice of an older woman responded "You may not remember me but I helped you find the talent to remove the bomb implanted in your neck."

"Why, yes, the lady we first met in the Walmart parking lot in the rain in Malone," Lea answered after taking a split-second to think. "Thank you for that but how did you find me after all this time and distance?"

"Can we leave that aside for a bit?" as the caller cleared her throat and spit into something nearby her vehicle. "I'm calling to thank you for all that you've done for us and to apologize for the bad guys who infiltrated our operation in Chagrin Falls and tried to take down your sniper as he worked on your assignment. I'm sorry to hear your prior helper was scooped up by the police but he'll be fine as an 'oppressed person. 'I'm hoping we can get back on the same page – we're still in a bitter struggle to defeat the feeble central government and win back our freedoms. The bad guys are also trying to ooze Commiefornia into Arizona so you may be able to help where you're going. We want to take advantage of your talents. That's why you can see my phone number. Please think about whether you and Chuck might be willing to help at the end of your travels and call me. But make that no later than tomorrow, midnight – there's much to be done. You won't be hearing from the guy you call "the Voice" again; he's experienced what law enforcement calls 'end of watch 'since we figured out he was actually helping the bad guys."

Lea had put the call on her phone's speaker so Chuck Mawhinney had heard the entire conversation. As she clicked off the call, she looked over at him expectantly. He was paying close attention to the rainy interstate and traffic ahead.

An Unexpected Diversion

The 480 blended into the 80, the Ohio Turnpike, the beginning of an assortment of Midwestern toll-roads. As Lea, Clara and Chuck rolled west, Clara started to moan and cried "Mommy, my tummy hurts!" As Lea unhooked her seatbelt and turned toward the truck's backseat, Clara threw up down Chuck's back. Lea said soothingly "You'll be fine Clara. We've done this before. Chuck, could you please pull over as soon as possible so I can take Clara to the RV and clean her up and bring you some clean clothes and a wet, washcloth and a towel?"

Already slowing down and turning on his Ford truck's blinkers, Chuck snickered," Don't worry. It's not like this is my first rodeo. Caleb used to get sick real often on pizza cheese. I see the ramp for a rest stop just ahead. If it's OK, I'll park us off to the side where there's room for both our truck and the RV."

In less than ten minutes, Chuck had maneuvered their vehicles into a spacious parking slot on the far edge of the facility's sparsely occupied lot. After locking the truck's cab, he helped Lea carry Clara and her soggy clothes into their RV to wash Clara in the shower and help everyone into fresh clothing. Then back to the Ford's cab to clean up that mess. Lea couldn't help but smile at Chuck's calm and helpful demeanor.

In the midst of mopping up the back of the front seat of his truck, Chuck heard a soft buzzing behind its dashboard even though the ignition was off, gradually growing louder. Chuck wondered about that but thought it might be an unknown tracking device. He heard a loud DJ from an approaching car yelling "...and now we'll enjoy Cyndi Lauper's Grammy Award winning "True Colors," a show of appreciation and respect to our LBTQ+ friends." The yellow Prius squeaked to a stop near the driver's side door of Sergeant Mawhinney's Ford truck.

Chuck saw a slovenly guy with long, disheveled hair, who looked like the guy named Levine who used to be the Health Secretary in Pennsylvania, lean clumsily out of the Prius and stumble onto the tarmac. The heavy man, wearing nylons and stilettos reminded Chuck of Rachel Levine. In his official "healthcare duties," Levine had been in charge of imprisoning the elderly in Pennsylvania nursing homes to fit the government "lockdown" during the plandemic while quickly sneaking his own mother into a safer place. If Chuck's limited awareness served him correctly, Levine pretended to be a woman and was now some sort of senior health official in the Federal government, apparently an Admiral even. The angry man ignored Chuck, stomped around the rear of their RV and loudly banged on its only door.

The banging and continuing loud strains of "True Colors" quickly captured Chuck's attention from inside his truck. But he quietly dropped to the pavement from the driver's side of the Ford truck's cab, sliding his .45 behind his belt. Walking around the back side of the RV quietly, he scrutinized the Levine look-alike carefully.

The fat guy, who was wearing lipstick and rouge, noticed Chuck and yelled angrily "you must be the guy who killed my brother back in Chagrin Falls. After I learned from my brother's boss how to find you, I've been following you."

"Was just cleaning up a mess in my truck," Chuck responded, adjusting his Marine ball cap with his left hand while removing his .45 from behind his belt with his right and jacking a round into its chamber. "Now," he said, "here's apparently another mess to clean up."

Then to the large guy, apparently without a weapon: "Down on your knees facing that row of dumpsters opposite the RV, carefully if you want to avoid scratching those lovely stilettos and expensive nylons. Well, maybe the nylons will soon be shredded no matter what."

Without advance warning, a younger man wearing an Afghanistan Marine Vet tee shirt peered around the back of the RV. "I couldn't help but hear the banging and the loud music. Need any help, brother?"

"Maybe, if you could wait just a second. Semper Fi!"

"Susan," Chuck shouted toward the RV, "Please put Debbie in her room for a nap and come out here.

After just a few moments, Lea appeared in the RV's doorway, her loaded Beretta against her bare right leg.

"What's your name and where'd you serve?" Chuck asked the recently arrived Marine veteran.

"John McMasters," the curly-haired, blonde replied, adjusting his hearing aid while keeping an eye on the kneeling tranny. "Most recently served at LeJeune before I got booted out for refusing the jab. How about you?"

"Chuck Mawhinney. I was a sniper in Afghanistan before I got sent home and also discharged for refusing the jab."

"Any relation to that hero sniper in 'Nam? Heard he got over 15 VCs crossing a river in just a few minutes, at least confirmed 100 kills during the whole war. Wow!"

"My uncle," Chuck admitted. "But can you help me get this guy into some traveling clothes and stomp on his phone? Shame on me; I didn't even ask its pronouns. But he does have nice, lavender nail polish." He handed Sergeant McMasters a roll of heavy-duty tape. "Please tape its hands together behind its back and tape them together with both feet after you toss those lovely stilettos into one of those dumpsters. I'll make sure it doesn't sneak away. Let's put it in the trunk of that swell Prius right over there. We're leaving here as soon possible and hope leaving it in the Prius's trunk with that loud music on will help someone to find it. I'll tape that exquisite ruby mouth."

Lea broke in to introduce herself, basking in how easily Chuck seemed to connect with new faces.

The two former Marines dragged the restrained porky guy, trussed like a Thanksgiving turkey, into the trunk of the nearby yellow Prius, covered by a wet canvas tarp they borrowed from the back of another pick-up truck parked a few yards away. The pair had carefully searched its body to make sure it had no way to identify Chuck or his vehicles, not even his fancy watch, which could probably take pictures. Chuck took smashed leftovers of the guy's watch with him, to be dribbled along the Ohio Turnpike as the trio continued west. Chuck slammed the trunk of the yellow Prius, ignoring the guy's groans.

Chuck said to the other Marine "this tranny wasn't the sharpest knife in the drawer, maybe doesn't even belong in the drawer if it was dumb enough to chase someone for killing its brother without any sort of weapon. What do you think?"

"Pathetic!"

Chuck extended his right hand. "Thanks for your help, Brother. Wanna come in for a beer while we figure out the rest of our trip and learn more about you and your service?"

"Thanks, Brother, but my wife and kids are waiting for me in our car. We have some miles to go before we reach our in-laws."

Chuck pulled a card from his back pocket and handed it to his fellow Marine. "Send me an email if you want to stay connected. I don't have any permanent phone right now because bad guys are chasing us right now. Semper Fi!."

As an aside to Lea, Chuck said, "would you mind staying here with Clara just a bit while I walk into the snack bar to see if I can find a way to make us a reservation at an RV park near Toledo up ahead? We need a couple of days to relax after all this.

When Chuck returned to the RV shortly, he hugged Lea, folding her into his arms.

"I'm more than ready for a beer. How about you? I'd like to relax a bit then call that lady with the smoking habit, to see if we can establish a credible working relationship with the Movement without always having to watch our six. She's the only one who helped us without creating new problems. It's obvious from our recent adventures that there's much to be done but if we can't count on a more-or-less dependable arrangement, I'm in favor of just disappearing. What do you think?"

"I'll pass on the beer. Given the RV's been unplugged for a while, don't know if the beer is even cold. I'd prefer tea but have no idea how we could get boiling water."

"Actually, I have a battery pack in the truck we could use to boil some of our bottled water with that old-fashioned, electrical pot here in the kitchen cupboard. And make some tea here. Would you like some?"

"Thanks, but I'd rather call the coughing lady and see if we can learn anything useful. Then leave here, buy a completely new set of burner phones, dump all of the others and get tucked into the RV park where you just made our reservation. Plus, we must find whatever is behind the dashboard of your truck, which is apparently still tracking us: maybe whatever is in the Prius would give us a clue. There's an ocean of free space in Flyover Country ahead of us, not to even mention your friend in Tucumcari, relatives in Arizona and people we don't even know yet.

More Challenges

"Do you mind if we call her now?" Lea asked.

"Let's do it," Chuck agreed.

Lea dialed the coughing woman's number with the call on "speaker."

The woman answered almost immediately," What did you decide?"

"We need to know more about your objectives in Arizona," Lea answered carefully.

"That's fair," the older woman responded. "let me give you an overview because I have no idea how familiar you are with Arizona's mess, which first became noticeable outside the state when Fox called the 2020 election for Biden before all the votes had even arrived. Kari Lake, a popular and articulate Republican former newscaster, ran for Governor in 2022 against Katie Hobbs, then Democratic Arizona Secretary of State, a mess from the beginning because Kari Lake was running against the officer in charge of Arizona elections. How could that conceivably be a problem?"

"Excuse me," Lea interjected "but how could that be

allowed? It's like hiring a fox to run a hen house."

"Don't know," the woman they now considered their controller in the Movement responded, "but Kari Lake's efforts to fix that were unsuccessful. Kari's campaign barreled along, Katie Hobbs refused to debate Kari Lake, refused to answer questions (of course shielded by the Mocking Bird media) and generally sounded like a 12-year-old whenever she did open her mouth. And later hid in a bathroom to avoid a reporter's questions. After the election, loaded with a huge number of 'mail-in 'ballots and many endless lines of voters in person who were discouraged from actually voting, Katie Hobbs was declared the winner by about 17,000 ballots. That was greatly at odds with public opinion and the polls. Kari Lake brought a lawsuit challenging various aspects of the election. That litigation ended up before Judge Thompson in Mesa; despite much credible and detailed testimony, Judge Thompson dismissed Kari Lake's case."

"Do you know what that was about?" Chuck asked

"Maricopa County, where Phoenix is located, is very large, has an oversized impact on Arizona elections, and is run by Democrats and RINOs. More than a few think Judge Thompson was compromised from the beginning, either financially or by fear for his family's safety. Several people noted, during the most important parts of Kari Lake's case and testimony of her voting experts, that Judge Thompson seemed to be writing his Christmas cards," their Controller coughed after drawing deeply on her cigarette.

She continued "Judge Thompson denied Kari Lake's claims even with solid facts and expert testimony. She appealed that decision; her appeal was denied at the first appellate level but the Arizona Supreme Court sent the case back to Judge Thompson on the issue of signature verification. That's whether signatures of voters on mail-in envelopes matched actual voter record signatures. The number of signatures at issue grossly exceeded the difference of votes counted for Katie Hobbs and Kari Lake. Huge numbers of 'verifications 'were approved in 2 seconds or less even though it takes at least one second for envelope images to load onto computer screens and more time for the official signature image to load onto them, where they could be considered by 'evaluators. 'Kari Lake's voting expert testified that it is impossible for images to be properly compared in that short a time but the Maricopa County witness testified 'no problem 'even though a large number of 'validators 'were working from home without supervision. Judge Thompson confirmed Katie Hobbs's election as Arizona Governor. With what seems like unshakable evidence in hand about the absence of signature verification, not to even mention faulty chain of ballot custody evidence, Kari Lake will be pursuing further appeals in hopes of finding a judge or court which isn't compromised."

"Wow," Lea exclaimed "I can't imagine why aren't people out with pitchforks."

"Unfortunately, the Arizona public includes a collection of Normies who believe whatever the captured media blathers, hard-core Democrats who will do everything possible to keep perverting elections and conservatives who are unwilling to take decisive action like they did in Prescott when BLM first came to visit – a large number of patriots met the BLM bus with guns and convinced them to go bother someone else," the controller continued.

Lea and Chuck looked at each other and said in unison "Count on us for help once we finally get to Arizona!"

ABOUT THE AUTHOR

Doug McPheters lives in Arizona and plays tuba in the Central Arizona Concert Band.

Doug is a licensed New York attorney, patented touchless, holographic, human-machine interface technology and served as a commissioned officer in the U.S. Navy Submarine Force. In his last seagoing billet, he served as Chief Engineer in USS Tigrone, where he was qualified as Officer of the Deck, both Surfaced and Submerged.